THE
LAST
WILD
RHINO

AN AFRICAN ADVENTURE STORY

TONY MAXWELL

Maxwell, Tony, 1943-
The Last Wild Rhino
Print Book – ISBN:978-0-9938127-4-3
E Book – ISBN:978-0-9938127-5-0

Published in 2017 by
Tony Maxwell
PO Box 146, Red Deer
Alberta, Canada T4N 5E7

'It's just possible the last wild rhino
in Africa has already been born!'

— *Jacob Riley, Languleni Game Reserve*

PART ONE

CHAPTER – 1 –

ALARMED BY THE SCENT THE light breeze carried to her sensitive nostrils, the white rhino cow nudged her six-month-old calf on ahead of her. Although the pair had grown accustomed to the unsettling scent of humans during the six weeks they spent confined in the Kruger Park's rhino *boma* at Matetsi; the female still harboured a wary attitude towards anyone who approached her and her calf too closely.

The cow's acute hearing had picked up the sounds the two men made earlier as they cut a hole in the *boma* fence. Once they were in the enclosure, she became frightened by their furtive attempts to approach her and her calf, as most humans who entered the *boma* did so quite openly. But not these two men. Her immediate instinct was to start running but, knowing her small calf could not keep up, she jabbed his rump with her horn to get him moving a little faster, her senses warning her the two men were close.

The sting of the dart in her left flank galvanised her into a gallop, but her instinctive reaction to protect her calf prompted her to turn and deal with the source of her fear. She could hear them scrambling up trees but, hampered by her poor eyesight, she was unable to find them. Feeling weak and struggling to stay on her feet, she tried to get away but, as the etorphine injected by the dart took effect, she stumbled and collapsed to her knees in an upright position. Heavily sedated by the drug, she was acutely aware of the plaintive puling noises her calf made as it butted its head against her flank but, even the terror brought on by the approach of the two men, was not enough to get her to her feet.

Phinius Mulema leant his Pax 22 tranquilliser gun against a tree while he watched his partner, Hamba Ndio, approach the downed rhino cow, his

AK47 rifle at the ready. Hamba kicked the animal on the rump and, getting no response, he called to Mulema, 'It is dead!' Leaning his rifle against the body of the rhino, Ndio pulled out an axe from his backpack and began chopping at the grey hide surrounding the front horn. Dropping his pack, Mulema took out his axe and set to work on the smaller horn, all the while keeping an eye on the calf as it cautiously approached its mother from the opposite side. Waiting until it was only feet away, he leapt out bringing his axe down hard on the head of the calf. Crying piteously, the young rhino tried to run but collapsed as Ndio, joining in the brutal attack, hacked at the animal's neck, severing the spinal cord. 'Its horn may be small, but it will repay us for our troubles,' he laughed as he expertly set about chopping out the nub of horn.

'Xana u endla yini? – What are you doing?' An African ranger carrying a .303 rifle shouted as he emerged from the tree line.

'Ku njhani? – How are you?' Mulema replied, waving his arm to distract the man while Hamba, grabbing his AK47, shot the ranger in his chest. Mulema ran to the wounded man and, wielding his axe, split his skull in two. 'We must hurry; someone may have heard the shot. Leave the small one; we must get the horns off the big mkhumbi and get away from here.'

Now desperate in their haste to get away, the two men hacked into the bone and cartilage surrounding the female rhino's horns, eventually chopping them free. 'It is not dead,' Ndio said pointing to the small puffs of dust disturbed on the ground as the stricken animal struggled to breathe.

'Leave it; this mkhumbi will soon die,' Mulema ordered.

'But it can see me – its spirit will come and find us!' Ndio replied pointing to the animal's eyes, 'I must stop it looking at us.' Hefting his axe; he hacked away at the rhino's eye sockets.

'Enough of this nonsense! We must get away from this place.' Shouldering their weapons and stuffing their grisly trophies into a sack, the two men set off at a steady trot towards the hole in the fence separating the boma from the rest of the game reserve.

It took thirty minutes for the effects of the etorphine to wear off and for the rhino cow to struggle to her feet, leaving behind a large pool of blood now covered with flies. Blinded and in extreme pain, she staggered around, blundering into trees and bushes as she instinctively searched for her calf. A hundred yards from where this brutal attack took place, a borehole fed dam provided water for rhinos released into this square mile, temporary holding area. Smelling as much as sensing the water, the rhino cow stumbled down the gently shelving bank of the dam and collapsed at the water's edge. She was still in this position when Languleni Game Reserve safari guide, Dennis Middlebrook, responding to a game scout's report of a shot fired in the holding area, discovered her. The white rhino cow had drowned, unable to lift her shattered head from beneath the shallow waters of the dam.

CHAPTER – 2 –

DEREK HAMILTON WALKED INTO THE guest lounge at the Rhenoster's Kop Safari Lodge in the Kruger National Park looking for his father, James Hamilton. Gazing around, he spotted him sitting at a table near the bar, talking to an elderly man and a young woman. 'This is my son, Derek,' his father said by way of introduction to his guests, 'he only recently returned from Mozambique. Son,' he continued, 'I'd like you to meet an old friend of mine, Jacob Riley. Jacob owns and operates Riley's Camp and Archer's Post Game Lodge in the Languleni Game Reserve. Forgive me, but I don't know your name,' he said looking at the young woman.

'This is Sylvia Kingston,' Jacob Riley said turning towards the attractive young woman sitting alongside him, 'Sylvia's the Africa correspondent from one of those London newspapers. She's out here doing a story on the white rhinos we are relocating from the Matetsi capture area in Kruger Park to our *boma* in Languleni.'

Derek reached out and shook Riley's hand, 'Pleased to meet you, sir. My father has often spoken of you. However, I must ask you all to please excuse me,' Derek said. 'I'm in the middle of replacing the drive shaft on my Land Rover *bakkie*, and I'm holding up the servicing of our game drive vehicles which, as my father frequently reminds me,' he said smiling at his father, 'are far more important.'

'And so, they are,' Jacob Riley laughed, siding with Derek's father.

'I'd better go along and make sure he gets on with it,' Sylvia said getting up and following Derek out to the vehicle workshop. 'If I remember correctly, you once worked as a close protection officer in Somalia guarding some British government official,' she said watching him as he sorted through some tools. 'Is that true?'

'You tell me,' he replied hoping to discourage her from asking any further questions.

'And, while you were there,' she continued, 'you were unfortunate enough to be kidnapped and held for ransom by some Somali group whose name escapes me for now.'

'I've never heard anyone call al-Shabab some Somali group before!' he snorted. 'Is that how you think of those bastards? From personal experience, I can tell you they are nothing more than a gang of bloodthirsty terrorists and murderers.'

'So, it is true; you did work as a close protection officer in Somalia?' she said ignoring his outburst.

'Your sources managed to get that much right.'

She continued, 'For a British intelligence officer; a woman called Rachel Cavendish, I believe?'

'How the hell do you know that?'

'Seriously? You got quite a write-up in the Nairobi Times. As it happens, I was in Nairobi at the time of your rescue by the Americans.' Derek didn't reply, all the while wondering just what this bloody woman wanted.

'Tell me, off the record,' she said smiling, 'what is your opinion of the Cavendish woman?'

'I make a point of never discussing a client.'

'Funny, no one else will talk about her either; especially now she's been appointed Deputy Director of MI5.'

Startled, he looked up at her, 'When the hell did this happen?'

'She accepted the appointment two days ago; as soon as she returned from leave.' Seeing the confused expression on her face, she continued with a knowing smile, 'You didn't know about that, did you?'

'No, I didn't.'

'I take it you were close to her?'

'Not really. She was just a client to me,' he lied.

'Well, that's not quite how I saw it. A few weeks ago, I flew from the UK to Johannesburg on the same British Airways flight which carried our Ms Cavendish to your waiting arms in the arrivals lounge at OR Tambo Airport.' Seeing the expression on his face, she continued in a conciliatory tone, 'I'm sorry Derek, I'm not trying to be smart; I only want you to understand I know a whole lot more than you think.'

Wandering around the vehicle workshop, Sylvia stopped and stared at the Land Rover *bakkie* he was working on. 'While I'm no expert,' she said, 'it looks to me as though you have a bullet hole in your windscreen and, from what else I can see, there appear to be at least two more in the bodywork? What on earth were you doing in Mozambique?'

'Fishing trip.'

'You honestly expect me to believe that? Did you have any luck with the fishing, as you call it?'

'Not really; it was more of a holiday – I just felt I needed a break.'

'Look here Derek; I won't beat around the bush with you. Are you interested in making some serious money?'

'It depends. But I have no intention of revealing any information about my clients.'

'Oh, no! I'm not asking for anything like that; I was thinking more about the time you spent in captivity with al-Shabab. I believe it would make a damn good story for my paper. What do you say?'

'Give me some time to think about it. But, as you can see, I'm rather busy now.'

'Fair enough! Jacob and I will likely be back through here in a week or so; you can give me your answer then. Also, you might want to think carefully about your experiences in Mozambique; I keep hearing all sorts of interesting rumours. If it turns out to be another good story, it could put quite a bit of money your way.'

Not wanting to answer any more questions posed by Sylvia Kingston, Derek made clear his lack of interest in continuing their conversation by crawling into the service pit underneath his Land Rover.

Later, troubled and upset by Sylvia Kingston's revelation, he left the workshop and walked over to the camp office. While there was no one around, he used one of the office computers to bring up the MI5 website. A brief search confirmed that Sir Anthony Williams still held the post of Director-General and that a Rachel Cavendish had recently been appointed to the position of Deputy Director. Feeling as though his world had been turned upside down and, wanting to confide in someone, he went over to the guest lounge hoping to have a quiet word with his father. He arrived just as Jacob Riley and Sylvia Kingston were about to leave.

'Are you sure you won't stay for dinner?' James Hamilton asked his guests.

'Thanks for the kind offer old man, but I'm anxious to get back to see how mother and calf are doing. From what Sylvia and I saw at Matetsi this morning, it should only be a week or so before the bull joins them. As you can imagine, he's not very happy being confined in a holding pen; nor, I expect, will he take too kindly to the long drive ahead of him once the veterinarians finally give him a clean bill of health.'

'It doesn't make any sense,' James Hamilton remarked, 'having to transport rhinos to your boma at Languleni all the way through Phalaborwa and Skoonspruit; given that it's only fifty miles from here as the crow flies.'

'Only trouble is I'm not a bloody crow!'

'Tell you what Jacob, I'll have a word with the Director of SAN Parks. Perhaps there's some way we can utilise fire breaks and patrol roads to shave a few hours off your drive; especially in light of the number of white rhinos you will be relocating over the next few months.'

'James, I'd be eternally grateful if you could swing that. Nice to have met you, young man,' Jacob said shaking Derek's hand, 'you and I should have a talk about Mozambique some time.'

Father and son stood watching as Jacob Riley and Sylvia Kingston climbed into their Toyota Land Cruiser and headed out to join the road to Phalaborwa. 'You don't look too good son; is there anything troubling you?'

'No dad, it's nothing; I'm just a little tired that's all. I'd better get on and finish the work on my *bakkie*.'

'Beats me Derek why you don't use some of your money to buy yourself a more reliable vehicle.'

An hour later, as Derek completed the repairs on his Land Rover, his mother, Edith, rushed into the workshop, 'Any idea where your father is – I've just received an email from a Dennis Middlebrook chappie at Languleni. He says poachers have shot dead a ranger and killed the female white rhino and her calf. To make matters worse, he can't get through to Jacob Riley on his mobile phone.'

'Oh, my God! This news will break the old man's heart. By now,' he said looking at his watch, 'they'll be coming within range of the phone tower in Phalaborwa; send this Middlebrook fellow a reply, suggest he try calling them every five minutes. Poor bugger. I wouldn't like to be the one breaking this news to Jacob Riley!'

'I'll give Jacob a call at Languleni tomorrow,' James Hamilton said, 'right now the poor man's up to his arse in crocodiles and won't be in any mood for platitudes expressing our concerns.'

'When you do call,' Derek said, 'let him know I'd be only too happy to drive to Languleni and do what I can to help him get through this awful business.'

'That's very decent of you son; I know Jacob's always short of staff and he'll be at his wits end over this setback. By the way, you've done such a good job repairing your old Series Two, that I'm willing to let you take one of our Defender 110's; should Jacob decide to take you up on your offer.'

CHAPTER – 3 –

'I told Jacob you'd give him a call at Riley's Camp when you reach Skoonspruit. He said he'd be grateful for your help safeguarding their relocated rhinos and, if you wouldn't mind, stepping in whenever one of his safari guides goes on leave. I know it's not the sort of position you were hoping for, but it's a foot in the door. Jacob's a bit of a rough diamond as you may have gathered, but I think you'll get along with him just fine.'

The sun had just cleared the horizon when Derek drove out of Rhenoster's Kop in his newly acquired Land Rover Defender 110 pickup, headed for Phalaborwa and Skoonspruit. The night before he left, he gave in to his better judgement and sent an email to Rachel Cavendish in London, congratulating her on her appointment and briefly mentioning his plans to take up a position protecting relocated rhinos from poachers in a nearby game reserve.

Exiting the Kruger Park, he stopped for lunch at Lozi's Diner on the outskirts of Phalaborwa, ordering a meat pie and coffee. As he sat at one of the outdoor tables waiting for his order, he noticed a small terrier limping around the patio, looking for something to eat. 'Do you know whose dog that is?' he asked the waitress who brought his order.

'He doesn't belong to anyone now,' the young woman replied. 'Some visitors from Jo'burg dumped him off a few days ago once they found out they couldn't take a dog into the Kruger Park. The cruel bastards never came back; probably didn't want to pay for a kennel to look after their pet while they enjoyed themselves. I would take him myself, but we are not allowed to have animals in the block of flats where I'm living.'

'Please bring him a bowl of water and a hamburger; I'll be happy to pay.' The waitress did as he asked and, calling the dog over, Derek scratched him behind his ear as the dog wolfed down the burger and lapped at the water.

'He's a Jack Russell terrier you know,' a woman sitting at another table remarked as he paid his bill and prepared to leave. 'Jack Russell's are a wonderful breed; very loyal and super intelligent. I do hope you're going to give him a good home?'

'Before I do that, I'd like to take him somewhere to get his leg checked by a veterinarian. Do you know if there is one in town?'

'There are a few, but most specialise in large animals – horses, cattle, that sort of thing. Brian Hanson, he's a vet in Skoonspruit, is probably your best bet for a patient of this guy's size. Hanson's clinic is just off the main road on your right. Watch for it as you drive into Skoonspruit.'

'Brian Hanson – Veterinary Services,' read the sign above the clinic in a small shopping area on the outskirts of Skoonspruit. Parking out front, Derek picked up the terrier and walked into the office. Responding to his tap on the counter bell, a woman appeared from a back room. A good-looking blonde, she had her long hair tied in a ponytail and wore an open white lab coat over a tight-fitting tee shirt and faded blue jeans. 'Good afternoon, how can I help you?' she smiled, her face lighting up in genuine pleasure.

'Good afternoon ma'am. I picked up this little guy from outside a roadhouse in Phalaborwa; seems some visitors from Jo'burg abandoned him,' Derek said, inadvertently blushing as her blue eyes settled on his face. 'I'd appreciate you taking a look at his leg. The waitress there said a customer who didn't like dogs kicked him when he begged for food.'

'There's no accounting for some people. My husband, Brian Hanson, is the vet. He'll be back within the hour; he's finishing up a job on a farm outside of town. I'm Debra Hanson by the way; I'm Brian's wife.'

'I'm pleased to meet you, Mrs Hanson. I'm Derek Hamilton; I hope to be working with Jacob Riley at Languleni.'

They shook hands, 'Would you like a coffee?' she asked, 'I brewed it not ten minutes ago.'

'Thanks for the kind offer. Regretfully, I have a few things I've still got to do in town.'

'I tell you what; why don't you leave this little fellow here with me until my husband gets back. If you give me your mobile phone number, I'll give you a call and let you know what my husband thinks is wrong with his leg. Does he have a name?'

'Yes, it's Jack, Jack Russell.'

'I like that name; it's so original,' she laughed.

Derek's efforts to find a motel willing to allow a dog in the room were not going well when he got the call from Debra Hanson. 'My husband says it's a simple fracture; he's set it as best he can but suggests you keep Jack from running around for a few days. You can pick him up anytime you like.'

Debra Hanson was standing outside waiting for him. She had changed out of her jeans and lab coat and now wore a daringly short, dark blue floral dress which showed off her svelte figure to her best advantage. 'Brian had to go out on another call,' she volunteered as he followed her into the clinic, 'he was keen to meet you since he does a lot of veterinary work for Jacob Riley and his rhinos.'

'Not to worry, I'm sure we'll soon run into each other – Skoonspruit isn't exactly a large town. Talking of the town, I'm having a bit of a problem finding accommodation for tonight; can you suggest anywhere that won't have a problem with Jack staying in the room with me?'

'Mrs Preller has five or six *rondavels* of varying sizes on her property which she rents out from time to time. She's got a few dogs of her own, so you won't have any problems there. I'll give you directions on how to get there,' she said jotting a few lines on the back of a business card. 'Would you join me in a sundowner before you go?'

'Thanks very much, I'd like that. If your husband returns early, I may yet get the chance to meet him.'

'Oh! I don't think that's likely to happen. Once he's finished work, Brian likes to stay out late with his friends at the Bosvelder pub in town.'

'Can't be too much fun for you?'

'No, it's not; but there isn't much I can do about it; other than staying out of his way when he's had too much to drink.'

Although flattered by Debra Hanson's obvious interest in him, Derek quickly finished his drink as even he realised it would not be a good move to encourage a liaison with a married woman on his first day in Skoonspruit, especially since her husband was involved in the veterinary care of Languleni's rhinos. Pleading he'd had a long day and was anxious to get settled in before nightfall, he paid his bill and left to look for Mrs Preller's *rondavels*. As he drove away with Jack sitting on the seat beside him, he speculated on the relationship between the vet and his long-suffering wife, particularly in light of the two bruises on the side of her face that weren't there earlier in the day.

Esme Preller, a pleasantly plump, elderly woman, greeted him with a smile and a hug, 'Mrs Hanson called to let me know you'd be along shortly looking for somewhere to stay for yourself and your dog Jack. Well, young man, you're in luck. It so happens a very nice *rondavel* has just become available. I'm sure it'll suit you and Jack. It's fully furnished and has a lounge, small patio, bedroom and a small kitchen.'

'Thank you; it sounds ideal.'

'During the day, I'd be only too happy to put Jack in the enclosed yard with my two dogs,' she added.

Derek paid her a month's rent in advance with the agreement that, if things worked out for him in his new job, he could stay on longer.

CHAPTER − 4 −

'DEREK HAMILTON? YES, OF COURSE I remember you; your father said you'd be calling. Why don't you drive out tomorrow afternoon for a look around?'

'Thank you, sir, I'll see you then.'

It had been nearly ten years since Derek, together with his father, last visited the Languleni Game Reserve. On that occasion, they were searching for the location of the old Main Camp and the burial site of his great, great, grandfather, Robert Hamilton, who established the Languleni Game Reserve shortly after the end of the Anglo-Boer War. The 250-square mile Languleni Game Reserve, privately owned by the Hamilton family until the advent of the Great Depression in the 1930's, was sold to a group of wealthy businessmen who used it as their private shooting box. Then, in the mid-1950's, the idea of restoring the area to its original purpose as a wildlife reserve was again considered. Now owned by a group of private investors, select areas within Languleni were leased out to tourism operators for the development of wilderness facilities catering to visitors seeking to experience the Africa of old.

Two of these areas, Riley's Camp and Archer's Post Game Lodge were leased and operated by Jacob Riley. Named after his father, Cullum Riley, Riley's Camp consisted of six thatched *rondavels* located in a half moon shape around a central lodge, dining area, bar-lounge and splash-pool, all overlooking a permanent waterhole. Archer's Post, in contrast, offered an upmarket experience with a spectacularly sited lodge and eight luxury bungalows on the upper reaches of the Languleni River. Ably managed by Greta and Hans Richter, experienced hoteliers and restaurateurs from Switzerland, Archer's Post was popular with well-heeled overseas visitors and, consequently, was often fully booked for up to two years in advance.

Both Riley's and Archer's Post, staffed by experienced safari guides and game scouts, offered visitors outstanding wildlife viewing opportunities. Also, both provided morning and evening game drives in open Land Rover safari cars; though Riley's Camp was the only location offering walking safaris.

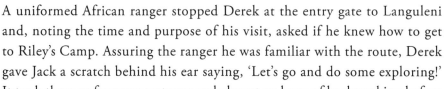

A uniformed African ranger stopped Derek at the entry gate to Languleni and, noting the time and purpose of his visit, asked if he knew how to get to Riley's Camp. Assuring the ranger he was familiar with the route, Derek gave Jack a scratch behind his ear saying, 'Let's go and do some exploring!' It took three or four wrong turns and almost an hour of backtracking before he finally drove his Land Rover *bakkie* up on the ridge overlooking the Languleni River. Using the vegetation-covered, stone foundations of the original lodge as a guide, it did not take him long to find the graves.

Remarkably, the five headstones were still intact, though the one marking the grave of Sir Reginald Lolandish had tilted forward. Using the sand shovel from his *bakkie*, he cleared the long grass, tidied up the graves and set Sir Reginald's headstone upright. He stood for a few moments before the grave of his great, great, grandfather, Robert Hamilton and the memorial to his first wife Claire, who lost her life in the Titanic disaster. Derek's memory of Robert's second wife, Alice, was clearer having seen a faded photo in the family album showing his great-grandfather, William Hamilton, standing with his arm around an elderly woman his father identified as his great, great grandmother, Alice Hamilton.

Responding to Jack's protests at being confined to the *bakkie's* cab, Derek clipped on his leash and, towed along by his dog, walked over to the enormous jackalberry tree that still dominated the view over the river. Finding the ring of boulders his father had pointed out as the lodge's outdoor fireplace, he stood for a while enjoying the view, his thoughts with the people who now rested in this truly wild place.

It took over half an hour of driving around in circles before Derek would finally admit he was lost. While trying to decide whether he was headed in an easterly or northerly direction, he encountered a South African Police Service Land Rover parked at the side of the track. Getting out, he walked up to the black police officer sitting in the cab watching his approach with interest. 'Good afternoon Sergeant, am I on the right track for Riley's Camp?'

'Who are you and what are you doing here?' Somewhat taken aback by the rude response, Derek explained who he was and what he was doing in the area. 'In answer to your question, you're on the wrong road,' the police sergeant snapped, 'go back the way you came, drive for about a mile then take the first turning on your right. It's an overgrown firebreak, stay on it for another mile until you come out on a good road. Turn left, and you are about five miles from the camp.'

Derek thanked him for his help and was returning to his *bakkie* when the police officer called him back. 'You have not explained to my satisfaction what you were doing in this part of the reserve,' the sergeant said getting out of his Land Rover.

'I was visiting the graves of long-dead relatives buried on the ridge that overlooks the river.'

'This part of the reserve is closed to tourists due to the number of armed poachers operating in the area; next time I will not be so lenient if I catch you in here again.' Derek thought to protest at being labelled a 'tourist,' but the implied threat in the policeman's demeanour caused him to favour discretion over valour.

'Didn't have any trouble finding us I hope,' Jacob Riley said as he emerged from the camp reception office; 'everyone is either sleeping off lunch or relaxing around the splash pool. Let's go over to my office; we can have a coffee and a chat.' A balding, short, thick-set man with a ruddy complexion, Jacob Riley walked with a noticeable limp; a consequence, so Derek learned later, of an encounter with a wounded buffalo, a notoriously aggressive animal. Pouring two coffees, Riley opened the conversation; 'Your father mentioned that before your unfortunate experience in Somalia, you were with the South African Police Service for a few years. Where were you posted?'

'Mostly in and around Jo'burg. I have my references and SAPS service record with me if you would like to see them.'

'Won't be necessary. Your father's reference is good enough for me. Finish your coffee, and I'll take you through to meet my wife June, she'll get all your particulars and fit you out with two uniforms which you will wear all the time you are on duty here. I run a tight ship; all my employees, black and white, must be smartly turned out. You will soon find out this is not one of those bloody white hunter cowboy outfits!' Somewhat surprised that Riley had made no mention of the African ranger and the rhino cow and calf killed by poachers, Derek thought it wise not to raise the matter until he was used to Riley's abrupt manner.

'His bark is worse than his bite,' June Riley said with a smile as Derek entered her office, 'don't worry young man, you'll do just fine; he's a softy at heart. I take it we will see you here tomorrow morning?'

On the drive back to Skoonspruit, Derek, for the first time since talking to Sylvia Kingston, allowed his thoughts to dwell on his painful rejection by the woman he was still in love with, Rachel Cavendish. His emotions in turmoil, he stopped at a Pick n Pay store where he bought groceries and enough dog food to keep Jack well fed for the next week or so. Dropping Jack and the groceries off at the *rondavel*, he returned to town and, stopping at a camping supply store, picked up a few things he thought he might need to survive a week in the bush with Jacob Riley. Throwing a light backpack, water bottle, a half-dozen pairs of thick hiking socks and a pair of *veldskoens* on the counter, he gave way to temptation and asked the clerk where he might find the nearest liquor store.

'*Ja Meneer*, just down the road to the left – Brink's *Drankwinkel*, you can't miss it.' Paying for his purchases, he drove down the road and parked in front of the liquor store. Convincing himself that he was entitled to at least a drink or two and, buoyed by the certain knowledge that he could stop whenever he wanted, he walked into the store and bought a bottle of Klipdrift brandy. The familiar feel of the bottle in his hand was so tempting that, once back in his *bakkie*, he broke open the sealed cap on the bottle and took his first drink.

It was close to midnight and the bottle almost empty, when he climbed from the cab of his *bakkie* and staggered into his *rondavel*. Feeling quite sick and ashamed of himself, even a boisterous greeting from Jack could not relieve his depressed state of mind. His attempts to sleep on the couch were interrupted by frequent trips to the toilet where, kneeling and clasping the toilet bowl, he spent much of the night vomiting until he had nothing left in his stomach.

Jacob Riley was in his office when Derek, suffering from a monumental hangover, drove into Riley's Camp. 'Grab yourself a cup of coffee while I get this week's roster sorted out. I thought we might spend an hour or so bringing you up to speed with the .458 rifle; I don't imagine you had much call in the police service to use one.' Hoping his head wouldn't fall off in front of everyone, Derek stood outside, black coffee in hand, watching half a dozen visitors climb into a game-viewing Land Rover, preparing to go out on their morning game drive.

'You must be Derek Hamilton,' a tanned young man dressed in the Riley's Camp uniform said, holding out his hand as he was about to walk to the vehicle. 'Dennis Middlebrook, I understand you'll be replacing me for the two weeks I go on leave. I'll be back in camp in a few hours; perhaps we can grab a beer and bring each other up to speed.'

'I look forward to that.'

'On your way Dennis, don't keep those good people sitting in the car getting bored while you two chit-chat.'

Middlebrook gave Riley a wave, 'On my way Boss.'

'Good, so you two have met. The other two guides, Etienne Roux and Enoch Shabangu, are out on walking tours; you'll get a chance to meet them later. Right, let's go and draw a rifle for you.' Derek followed Riley through the reception office to a locked storeroom which he opened with a key from his pocket. 'All firearms not in use we store in this safe along with all the rhino horns recovered by our rangers,' he said swinging open the heavy steel doors of a large Liberty gun safe. 'We don't have any fancy, high-priced rifles, just six Brno .458's, a working man's gun if ever there was one. We also have four R5 rifles, though our game guards usually carry Enfield .303's and R1's. We also managed to get hold of two R5 assault rifles, which are much easier to use from the close confines of a vehicle. It troubles me to have to say this, but being a game ranger nowadays is not much different to fighting in a war zone.' He heaved a sigh of resignation before continuing, 'Each safari guide and game scout is assigned a rifle and is responsible for its cleaning and maintenance. Any questions?'

'No, sir, I used an old BSA .458 many years ago; I've no doubt the Brno is an improvement.'

'Good, grab your rifle, a dozen rounds of ammunition and let's make our way out back. I've alerted everyone that we will be test firing a rifle so that we won't cause an alarm over poachers.'

'I understand you've had a lot of trouble with poaching?' Derek asked raising the subject as they walked out of the camp towards the deep *donga* used for firearms practise.

'Is the Pope Catholic?' Riley replied. 'There's the odd local out after a bit of venison, but nothing we need worry about. Our immediate problems lie with thugs like the pair who murdered one of my game scouts while they slaughtered our recently acquired white rhino and her calf. These are the bastards I'd like to get my hands on. But we will never solve this problem at a local level; at least not until someone does something about these international criminals and the government lackeys who support and protect them.'

'It's safe to say there's no one involved in wildlife conservation wouldn't back you on that score,' Derek replied. 'On the local level Boss, if you don't mind me asking, how is the police investigation into the shooting death of the game scout going?'

'As it's a murder investigation, it's being handled by a SAPS commissioned officer, a Captain Nkolosi, from Phalaborwa. However, I have to say I'm disappointed by his singular lack of results.'

'If it's any help, I might be able to get hold of someone who could light a fire under this Nkolosi.'

'Give him another day or two, and I might take you up on that.'

'Boss, when I came by the other day to meet with you, I encountered a police sergeant sitting in his Land Rover not far from the old Main Camp.'

'Dlamini; I wonder what he was doing here in Languleni? I don't trust that man.'

'I knew a Colonel Vusi Dlamini; he was with the Hawks in Jo'burg. He mentioned he had a brother serving in the SAPS. Apparently, this brother was involved in some disciplinary problem and, instead of being charged, he was transferred to Nelspruit. An out of sight, out of mind situation.'

'Anyway, here we are,' Riley said stopping beneath a rudimentary thatched shed supported by roughly hewn, wooden poles. Pulling an eight-inch square paper target from a pile on a rickety camp table, he walked down range and pinned it to a bullet-ridden sheet of plywood. 'That's about twenty-five paces, the maximum range for dangerous game. You should always keep in mind the old Voortrekker adage; get as close as you can sonny, then get five paces closer.'

Derek opened the bolt on the Brno .458 rifle and checked the barrel and breech for obstructions. Satisfied both were clear, he loaded three rounds into the magazine, cycled the bolt and, setting the safety, looked to Riley for permission to fire. 'Go ahead, fire three rounds; I'm looking for a good grouping.' Derek pulled the rifle into his shoulder, aligned the open sights on the centre ring of the paper target and fired three rounds in rapid succession. Opening the bolt, he laid the rifle down on the table and joined Riley at the target. 'Very nice; I'd say you've got a one-and-a-half-inch group. Your dad was right; he said you were a good shot. Take a break, then let me see you do it again and we're done here.'

Despite his pounding headache, Derek's next group was even better. 'Bloody hell, if I don't stop you now you will place the next three all through the same hole. Come-along, it's time you met your partner and game scout, Blessing Mananza.'

'Mananza,' Derek said thoughtfully, 'that doesn't sound like a local African name.'

'No, it isn't; Blessing came to us a few years ago from Pomfret, a small settlement just south of the Botswana border. He worked for many years for a good friend of mine in the Kalahari as a tracker. Then, when my friend's hunting business closed, I was lucky enough to persuade Blessing to join us.'

'Pomfret; isn't that the area where many retired members of 32 Battalion settled?'

'I see you know your history! Yes, Blessing was a former member of 32 Battalion; though he prefers to refer to them as the Buffalo Battalion or, by their Portuguese name, *Os Terriveis* – The Terrible Ones. He's an incredible tracker, easily one of the best I've ever seen.'

'I'm looking forward to meeting him.'

'He'll be at the vehicle park, let's go over there now and pick him up; I'm anxious to check up on Dengezi and her calf.' On their way to the vehicle park, Riley asked if Derek had managed to find suitable accommodation in Skoonspruit.

'I've rented a comfortable *rondavel* in a small park run by a Mrs Preller.'

'You're fortunate; old Mrs Preller runs one of the best establishments in Skoonspruit. The Preller family have lived in this area for more years than I care to remember. Whenever Sylvia Kingston visits us, she usually stays at Mrs Preller's. In case you don't remember her, Sylvia's the reporter from London you met at Rhenoster's Kop. I wouldn't be surprised if you've rented her *rondavel*. Serves her right for giving up her lease!' Changing the conversation, Riley asked, 'So you visited the old Main Camp? What do you think of the location?'

'Easily the finest location for a game lodge that I've ever seen. But please don't tell my father that.'

Riley laughed. 'You might be interested to know I've submitted an application to our investors for permission to build another lodge in that same location. If they agree, I intend to retain the original name, Main Camp, given to that spot by Robert Hamilton, your great, great grandfather, shortly after the Anglo-Boer War.'

'My father would be delighted! It's been almost ten years since he and I last visited the old Main Campsite – even then, we bemoaned the fact that no effort had been made to reopen the area to visitors.' Derek turned and looked directly at Jacob Riley, 'If at all possible Boss, I would like to be a part of that project.'

'Glad to hear you say that Derek; it's about time the Hamilton's were involved in Languleni again.'

CHAPTER - 5 -

RILEY LEFT IT TO DEREK to introduce himself to Blessing Mananza while he went and started up one of the spare game-viewing Land Rovers. '*Sawubona* Blessing, I'm Derek Hamilton. I understand you and I will be working together,' he said shaking the game scout's hand. 'I'm looking forward to that; I'm sure we will learn a lot from each other.'

'I too look forward to working with you *Numzaan*,' Blessing replied.

The three men drove out of the camp following one of the many tracks radiating from the entrance gate. 'We don't usually take guests out this way,' Riley said, 'we want to give Dengezi a chance to raise her new calf without any of the stresses brought on by too many visitors.'

'I assume Dengezi is a white rhino?'

'Heavens no! Dengezi is one of the few black rhinos to take up residence in Languleni. We first came across her a year ago, briefly accompanied by a male black rhino. You can imagine our delight when, about two months ago, we saw her with a young male calf. Since then, we've kept a close eye on her and her offspring. Blessing here has probably spent more time with Dengezi than anyone else I know.'

'That's true *Numzaan*, but most of that time I spent up in a tree,' Blessing replied.

'Like most black rhinos, I take it Dengezi aggressively defends her territory and her young calf?'

'Understatement of the year Derek; just you watch what happens when we find her.' Riley stopped the Land Rover at a small mud wallow, giving Blessing the opportunity to climb out of the vehicle and inspect the dozens of tracks in the churned-up mud around the wallow.

'Dengezi was here no more than an hour ago,' Blessing whispered as he climbed into the game scout's seat perched out over the left, front bumper.

Motioning to Riley to drive slowly forward, he kept the tracks in sight, waving Riley first to the left then to the right as he followed the path taken by the rhino and her calf as they moved between the patches of knob thorn, stunted marula and the occasional Delagoa thorn thicket.

'She's particularly fond of thorn thickets; mainly because they provide excellent protection for her calf from any lions that might be foolish enough to take on a female black rhino,' Riley remarked. Blessing signalled to Riley to stop and switch off. Alighting from his perch, the game scout was walking around to the passenger's side of the vehicle when Dengezi and her calf emerged from the shelter of a dense stand of marula, forty yards away. The rhino held her head up high trying to catch the scent of the strange creature intruding on her afternoon siesta. The three men held their breath while Dengezi decided whether fight or flight would be her best response. They relaxed as she turned and walked away then, without warning, she spun around and, puffing and snorting like a steam engine, charged straight at the Land Rover.

Riley started the engine, slapped the vehicle into reverse and accelerated backwards steering with one hand as he struggled to avoid large trees. 'It's okay Boss,' Derek laughed, 'she's given up. Just like a woman, always changing her mind.' Laughing with relief, they watched her swaggering rump, closely followed by the baby rhino, disappear into a concealing Delagoa thorn thicket.

<hr>

Arriving back at camp, Riley suggested Derek introduce himself to the five clients who were about to go out on their sundowner drive with Dennis Middlebrook, the safari guide he would replacing when he went on leave. Derek realized Jacob and his wife June would be carefully evaluating his rapport with the clients as he made his way around the lounge introducing himself to them individually. Fortunately, they were a friendly crowd and, in no time at all; they were responding to his questions about their experiences in Languleni. 'Well done Derek, your father was right, you're just the sort of fellow we're looking for.'

Later that evening, after the sundowner drive had arrived back in camp, Derek took the opportunity to have that beer with Dennis Middlebrook.

'I'm anxious to find out more about the murder of the African game scout and the killing of the white rhino and her calf in the *boma*.'

'Well, from what little I know, the murder of the scout is in the hands of the police at Phalaborwa; as for the rhino cow, we suspect she was immobilised by M99 before the poachers hacked her and her calf to death with axes and *pangas*.'

'Any idea how they administered the drug?'

'Dart gun I would imagine; though we couldn't find the dart. We assumed the poachers were warned not to leave any clues behind. Hanson, he's the local vet, took blood samples from the cow so we should be able to find out exactly what type of drug or drugs they used.'

It was growing dark when Derek arrived back at Mrs Preller's *rondavels*. His landlady was outside watering her garden, 'How are you feeling now young man? Though I must say, you're looking a lot better than you did when you left early this morning.'

'Thank you for asking *Mevrou*. Yes, I'm feeling a lot better. My apologies if I caused you some concern.'

———◄◄►———

To pass the long evening hours, Derek regularly took Jack for runs around the town and, on occasion, out as far as the airport. Coming back from their run one night, he was surprised to find Mrs Preller standing at the gate waiting for him, 'I've an urgent message for you to call Mr Riley as soon as possible.' Using his mobile phone, he called Riley's Camp right away.

June Riley answered the call, 'Derek, thanks for calling back; hold on, I'll put you through to the boss.'

Jacob Riley came on the line, 'Derek we have a problem, actually two problems. A white rhino was poached earlier today not two miles from Archer's Post Lodge, near our western boundary with the Kruger Park. I drove up there first thing this morning but, I'd no sooner arrived when I received a call on the radio from Blessing. While checking out a flock of vultures he had spotted a hundred yards or so off the road from Riley's Camp to the entrance gate, he came across the carcases of another white rhino and her young calf. Again, their horns had been hacked off. By his estimate, they were killed about two days ago.'

'What can I do to help Boss?'

'First thing tomorrow morning, I want you to pick up Brian Hanson at his veterinary clinic in town and drive him out there. Apparently, his Land Cruiser is in the shop for repairs. I've already phoned the police, and they promised me they would get someone out there as soon as possible. Blessing will be watching for you and the vet at the side of the road. He said there are a lot of tracks around, so he wants you to bring your camera and asks that you pick up a large bag of plaster of paris at the hardware store in town. I assume you have some idea as to what he has in mind?'

Debra Hanson greeted him as he walked into the veterinary clinic. 'Good morning Derek; my husband's out at the moment, but he should be back shortly. Can I offer you a coffee?' As he watched her walk over to a coffee machine at the far end of the reception area, he was again reminded of the fact that Debra Hanson was an attractive woman. Despite her efforts to cover up the bruises on her arms and face with makeup, it was evident the couple's marital problems were still ongoing. 'Is it true you served for a few years with the police force in Jo'burg?' she asked as she handed him a cup of coffee.

'Quite correct, though it's called the police service now – not the police force,' he replied with a smile.

'Of course; I still have trouble catching up with all the changes taking place. If you don't mind me asking, why did you resign?'

'A drinking problem largely brought on by stress and compounded by my girlfriend's fears for my safety on the job.'

'But I understood you live on your own at Mrs Preller's place?'

'Not entirely alone; you've met my dog, Jack, he's the only one keeping me company these days. My girlfriend and I parted ways over a year ago,' he added.

She looked out the window. 'My husband has just driven up; I'd better get back to work. It was nice seeing you again Derek; I hope we meet again soon.' Blushing, she hastily added, 'under more pleasant circumstances of course.'

Brian Hanson strode into the reception area, 'You must be Hamilton,' he said ignoring Derek's outstretched hand. 'Two white rhinos poached, so Riley tells me. Why the hell you people keep them around and not in a zoo is beyond me. Let me grab a few things, and I will follow you in the Jeep I've rented.'

On the face of it, Hanson was a good-looking man, probably in his mid-forties Derek estimated. Tall, well built with a shock of blonde hair which he constantly pushed away from his eyes, he did not look like the typical wife-beater; though Derek had to admit he had no idea what that sort of man looked like. On the drive to Languleni, Derek's thoughts were more about Debra Hanson and the bruises on her face than Hanson's odd remarks. But there was no denying it; he did not particularly like her husband.

Three miles after passing through the entrance gate to the Languleni Game Reserve, Blessing Mananza appeared in the middle of the road waving his R1 rifle above his head. He directed Derek to park under a knob-thorn tree close to the road, '*Sawubona Numzaan*; this way when Boss Riley comes past he will know where to find us,' Blessing said as Derek got out of his *bakkie*.

Brian Hanson pulled off the road and parked close behind. 'So, Mr ex-policeman, apart from chatting up my wife, what makes you think you are qualified to do the work of a game ranger?' he said as Derek approached his Jeep.

'For your information Mr Hanson, I did not chat up your wife as you put it, nor do I claim to be a qualified game ranger. I'm only a safari guide whose most valuable skill is my ability to put up with all kinds of ill-mannered, obnoxious people, even under the most trying of circumstances.'

Hanson laughed as he climbed out of his Jeep, 'Well said Hamilton; clearly, you don't take shit from anyone. Now, tell me what you know about this poaching incident. Though I must say, I'm surprised the animals were poached so close to a busy road and only a few miles from the entrance gate. You'd think someone would have heard the shots. While I get my bag of tricks together, ask the *kaffir* if the horns have been removed?'

Aware Blessing would have heard the racial insult; he turned to Hanson, 'There is no need to use language like that. Mr Mananza is both a friend and valued colleague; I'd like you to apologise.'

'You can forget it; I am not apologising to anyone, let alone a bloody *kaffir*! Come-on, let's get this job done so I can get out of here,' Hanson replied testily.

The hulking carcases of the white rhino cow and her small calf lay close to one another in an open area surrounded by knob-thorn trees, and the ubiquitous Delagoa thorn thickets favoured by rhinos. A dozen vultures took flight to the top branches of nearby trees and a lone hyena slouched off into the bush as the three men approached the dead animals, doing their best to ignore the appalling stench.

The full-grown female lay crouched in an upright position, her grey bulk distended by decomposition and streaked with the vulture's white excrement. Both her horns had been hacked off, leaving the area between her nose and her ears an oozing bloody mess with patches of white bone exposed where the vultures and the hyena had been feeding. The young male calf lay ten feet away from its mother, its tiny nub of horn also hacked off. 'The bastards; they even chopped the eyes out on the female and the calf,' Derek remarked in disgust.

'That's because these stupid *kaffirs* believe the rhino's spirit would come after them,' Hanson sneered. 'Don't worry Hamilton, they wouldn't have got much horn off the calf; it's far too young. I'd say they hacked the calf to death with their axes for the perverse pleasure of physically killing something.'

'I can't see any bullet wounds on the female; do you think she was darted?'

'Most likely,' Hanson replied, examining the carcase, 'but without finding the dart, it's only an educated guess. I'll draw some samples of blood to take back to the clinic. If I can't find anything myself, I know a lab in Pretoria that can.'

While Hanson returned to his Jeep to fetch his bag, Blessing took Derek aside, 'Thank you *Numzaan*; I don't like that man Hanson; did you bring the plaster of paris?'

'Yes, and a gallon of water as well. I take it you have found some tracks worth preserving.' While the veterinarian got busy drawing samples of blood from both carcases, Derek and Blessing mixed and poured plaster of paris into the boot prints and the single bare footprint Blessing had marked with sticks planted in the ground.

'I'm done here,' Hanson said, 'when Riley shows up, tell him he can contact me at the clinic. Hope you two have fun playing in the mud hey!'

Jacob Riley parked his Land Rover behind Derek's vehicle. 'Bloody awful business,' he remarked as he joined Derek and Blessing at the two rhino carcasses, 'five rhinos poached in just over a week. Did Hanson find anything?'

'Nothing specific; though he agrees the cow was probably darted. He took some blood samples for testing and wants you to phone him later to get the results.'

'I believe you've found some tracks; anything we can go on?'

'All the credit must go to Blessing; he found the boot prints and suggested the plaster of paris. Has he shown you the other marks yet? Blessing, why don't you show the Boss what else you found.'

Blessing led them to a large area, almost entirely devoid of trees and shrubs, about 100 yards away from the dead rhinos. 'You can see Boss,' Blessing began, 'how some of the trees have been chopped down and dragged to one side and the grass flattened by a great wind; in Angola, this is what we did to allow a *tjopper* to land. If you look here in the sand, you can see the marks made by the landing skids.'

'A bloody helicopter, the bastards. I never believed the rhinos poached around here and up at Archer's Post are the work of local people out to make a few rands. Take as many photos as you can of the impressions made by the landing skids, and don't forget to lay the R1 on the ground next to them; it will help the police judge the dimensions of the helicopter. Derek, I want you and Blessing to get to work on nipping this poaching spree in the bud. Are you able to drop everything and get on it right away?'

'Not a problem Boss. I can keep an eye on my dog as long as I am working from Skoonspruit.'

'Good. I suggest we leave Blessing here to finish gathering whatever evidence he can, while you follow me back to camp to pick up a radio set for your vehicle, so we can keep in touch. I also suggest you draw one of the R1's for your own protection.'

'Blessing has his R1, and I have my old service pistol; between the two of us, I think we're packing enough firepower,' Derek replied.

When Derek arrived back at the place where the two rhinos were killed, he found Blessing busy lifting the dry plaster casts of the two sets of boot prints and the single footprint. Together they carried the casts out to the road where they laid them side by side on the tailgate of his Land Rover.

'This is interesting *Numzaan*. Some of these boot prints were made by army issue boots, while the others are made by civilian boots or what some people call hiking shoes. It's an unusual pattern and shouldn't be too hard to identify. On the left civilian boot print, you can see where two of the patterned treads have broken off, probably on a sharp stone or thorn; this would make it easy to pick this boot out from amongst others, even of the same make.'

'All very well, but what about the footprint – I can't see that being much use.'

Blessing laughed. '*Numzaan*, you'd never have been any good as a tracker with the Buffalo Battalion. This footprint tells me a great deal about the man who made it, more than all the boot prints in the world put together. I know that this man once broke his ankle and, because it did not heal well, he now walks with his foot turned in.'

'Well done Blessing; we'd call that walk, pigeon-toed. What else can you tell me about him?'

'He's an old man who doesn't wear shoes. Also, he has very little money and works for the poachers only to cut down the bush and chop out the horns. I have an hour before the sun goes to rest. If I follow his *spoor* before the wind or rain wipes them away, I can find out where this man lives. I will not go too far and will stay tonight with the guard at the entrance gate; I will see you there tomorrow.'

As soon as Derek arrived back at Mrs Preller's, he changed into his running clothes, put on his *tackies* and, with the ever-eager Jack towing him along, headed out in the direction of the airport. He was thinking through the events of the day when the lights of a car coming from the airport pulled up next to him. 'It's not hard to see who's leading who,' Debra Hanson joked as she got out of the car and, crouching next to Jack, scratched him behind his ears. 'So, this is what you get up to when you are not annoying my husband,' she said as she got to her feet taking hold of his arm for support.

She was wearing a skimpy blouse and tight pair of shorts that did little or nothing to hide her pleasing feminine attributes. Likely aware of the effect she was having, she stepped closer and, playing with her blonde ponytail, stood looking up at his face, a faint smile playing about her lips. 'I didn't annoy him on purpose,' Derek stammered, 'he just made a few remarks that I felt were uncalled for.' Recovering his composure, he asked, 'What on earth are you doing out at the airport this late at night?'

'Sending off some of the blood samples from your rhinos to Pretoria for further testing; my husband wanted independent confirmation of his findings before he passed on the results of his tests to Jacob Riley.'

'I notice you said you sent off some of the samples; does that mean your husband has other samples back at the clinic?'

'Yes. Why?'

'If it's at all possible, I wouldn't mind sending off a separate set of samples to a pathologist I got to know while I was in the police service.'

'If it's important to you, I'd be more than happy to help. Of course, then you'd owe me a favour,' Debra replied smiling.

'I appreciate that; one good turn always deserves another. While we're discussing helping one another, I need to use my laptop to access the internet; any idea where I can get good wi-fi reception in Skoonspruit? Perhaps there's an internet café in town?'

'Our clinic has wi-fi, but I don't think Brian would be too pleased if you dropped by to use it; he's quite convinced you and I are planning to have an affair. It might be safer for both of us if you took your laptop to the Bosbok Bar and Grill; a bit noisy, but good wi-fi reception.' The headlights of a car approaching from the direction of the town suddenly reminded her of the risk she was taking being seen talking to a man other than her husband on a darkening road. 'We've got to be careful. Skoonspruit is a small town in every sense of the word,' she said quickly kissing him on his cheek before jumping into her car.

As he watched the red tail lights of her car disappear towards the town, he considered the risks an affair with a married woman would pose to his prospects working for Jacob Riley. 'I'd better steer clear of her until she finds someone else to lure into a relationship. Come on Jack let's get going, I've got work to do.'

The Bosbok Bar and Grill was even noisier than Debra had predicted. Securing a corner booth and, placing an order for a medium steak with all the trimmings along with a Castle beer, Derek got to work. He downloaded the photos he had taken of the helicopter skid marks and, together with an email detailing the rhino poaching incident, he sent them off to Colonel Dlamini asking for his departments help in interpreting the marks left by the helicopter's landing skids.

⋖◆⋗

The sun was rising as Derek drove up to the guard hut at the entrance gate to Languleni. When Blessing emerged from the hut, he was not wearing his usually smart uniform; instead he was dressed in old, shabby clothes. 'Don't tell me you've decided to resign from your position as a game scout,' Derek said with a degree of uncertainty in his voice.

'No *Numzaan*, today I have to work undercover. Yesterday, I tracked pigeon foot to where he crawled out under the fence. I hid my rifle and most of my uniform in a tree and, even though it was getting dark, I managed to track him to a small village nearby. Today, I would like to visit this village and see what I can find out about him.'

'You've done a good nights work my friend, but this plan of yours may be dangerous. As you know, there's a lot of money to be made from the killing of rhinos for their horns. The criminals who employ people like pigeon foot will not think twice before murdering anyone who asks too many questions. I think I should come with you.'

'*Aieee Numzaan*, then we will be discovered,' he said laughing. 'It will be much safer if I go alone. A poor old black man looking for food; who would wish to harm him?'

'Then I want you to take this with you,' Derek said taking his Z88 pistol out of the glove box and handing it to Blessing. 'Keep it well hidden and use it only if your life is threatened. I take it you know how to use a pistol?'

'For many years, I used a Tokarev pistol I took from a Cuban officer in Angola when he had no further use for it. I once offered to trade it for one of these Z88's, as I much prefer the stopping power of a 9mm over a 7.62mm round, but no one would trade. Thank you *Numzaan*, I will take good care of it. Please keep my R1 with you; Boss Riley will not be happy if I left my rifle with the gate guard. I will be back here at this gate by tomorrow morning.'

'You'd better be. If you're not back by then, I'm coming to look for you.' Wrapping the R1 in an old blanket, Derek stashed it behind the seat of his *bakkie* and drove back to Mrs Preller's.

As he pulled up in front of his rondavel, Mrs Preller came over to the *bakkie*. 'Debra Hanson was here earlier hoping to see you. She waited for a while then, saying she had better get home before her husband returned, she left this package for you. Debra said it was a medical sample and I should keep it in my fridge until you get back. *Jirre* Derek, I hope you are not sick or something?'

'No no, it's nothing like that! Debra was just dropping off a blood sample I wanted from a rhino poached a few days ago.' Picking up Jack, he drove out to the airport and Air Expressed the blood sample to Colonel Dlamini in Jo'burg before returning to town to call on the three camping supply stores listed in the local phone directory.

'This pattern reminds me of the Haucks brand of hiking boot,' the clerk in the first store said examining the plaster cast. 'The only place in town you may find them is at Betts. They're down on 5th Street...'

'Thanks, I know where they are.'

The salesman at Betts confirmed that his store had previously carried that particular hiking boot, '*Ja*, they weren't all that popular. If I remember rightly, we had a special about a month ago and sold the last of them. Hang on a bit, let me check with Leslie.' He was back in a few minutes, 'You're in luck *Meneer*, we do have a pair left; the only problem is they're size 14's.'

'May I see them?' The salesman returned carrying a Hauck's shoe box. 'These will do nicely for a friend of mine. Would you mind if I took a few photos of them to make sure he likes the style?'

'Help yourself *Meneer*; I don't imagine we're going to sell them otherwise.'

⬦

Much to Derek's relief, Blessing was waiting for him the following morning outside the gate guard's hut dressed in his uniform. As he climbed into the front seat, he handed back the Z88 pistol. 'I'm very pleased you're back in one piece; tell me, did you find pigeon foot?'

'*Yebo Numzaan*. Just as we thought, he was only hired to cut down trees for the *tjopper* and to chop out the horns of any rhinos they killed.'

'Yes, but he must have some idea who's behind it all. Keep talking while I drive; I'm sure the Boss will be very interested in what we've learned so far.'

'From what pigeon foot told me, he was part of a three-man group that works in Languleni and other neighbouring game reserves. The *Induna* of this group is given a handheld radio and a GPS device; when they find a rhino with a good pair of horns, they follow it at a safe distance while the *induna* radios in their GPS position. Usually, preferably just before sunset, a *tjopper* arrives, a shooter darts the rhino and the *tjopper* lands in the clearing the two workers have prepared. Even before the rhino is dead, the horns are chopped out, and the *tjopper* flies away with the horns.'

'Could he tell you anything about the helicopter itself and the men who arrived it?'

'He said there were two white men in the *tjopper*; the one who did the flying wore army boots, and the one who did the darting wore the civilian shoes or hiking boots, as you called them. He said he had no idea what sort of *tjopper* it was, but he did tell me it was white with blue on the bottom and the top.'

'Bloody hell!' Derek swore. Grim faced he stared fixedly at the road ahead and, for a few moments, said nothing. 'I'm surprised pigeon foot was willing to tell you all of this given the risk he was taking. I can't imagine these people would look too kindly on him if they caught him talking to you?'

'You are right, Numzaan. Pigeon foot took some persuading; but eventually, he saw things my way. He has now decided to find another, much safer, place to live.' Derek raised a quizzical eyebrow as he turned and looked at Blessing. But the game scout did not reply. Instead, he stared fixedly at the road ahead.

Chapter – 6 –

'WELL DONE BOTH OF YOU,' Jacob Riley said as they met later in his office, 'but we're still no closer to putting a stop to this awful business. If we keep losing rhinos at this rate, soon there won't be any left. One could even say it's just possible the last wild rhino in Africa has already been born.'

'That's a bit strong Boss,' Derek said, 'surely, the police can do something?'

'I have my doubts; even if we go to the police with what little we have and, given that we suspect the poachers may using a police helicopter, I don't think we could reasonably expect any positive results.'

'Boss, we still have a few irons in the fire. Yesterday, I Air Expressed the photos of the helicopter landing skids to Colonel Dlamini in Jo'burg. I also included a set of the blood samples taken by Brian Hanson from the most recent rhinos poached together with the description of the helicopter provided by pigeon foot. With any luck, the colonel might be able to help us.'

Derek spent the rest of the day familiarising himself with the camp routine and checking over the list of visitors he would be picking up the following morning at the airport. 'I see you've got five on your guest list,' Dennis Middlebrook said looking over Derek's shoulder, 'a good number for starters. A British couple, an American woman and two Spanish men; nothing out of the ordinary; you'll do just fine. Though, before you leave for the airport, I suggest you give your Land Rover safari car a thorough going over; breakdowns are a sure way to bugger up your tips!'

'Derek,' Jacob Riley said joining the two men, 'go and see June, she will give you the flight numbers and the arrival times for all your guests. Providing their flights are on time, you should be back here before lunch.'

The South African Airways flight from Johannesburg carrying the two Spanish men and the British couple arrived on time. Holding up a Riley's Camp sign, the two Spanish men, festooned with camera equipment, identified themselves first. 'If you gentlemen wouldn't mind making yourselves comfortable in the coffee shop, I will be along as soon as I meet up with the other two guests also travelling on your flight.' Nearly ten minutes had passed before the British couple finally made themselves known, 'I was beginning to get a little worried,' Derek remarked.

'Oh! I'm sorry, I had a bit of trouble finding one of my suitcases,' the middle-aged woman replied with a smile, 'but it eventually turned up.' He ushered them through to the coffee shop where they joined the two Spanish visitors.

'Please make yourselves comfortable; I've one more guest to pick up from the Air Zimbabwe flight from Victoria Falls which, according to the arrivals board, is about land. As soon as I've got your luggage loaded up and our fifth guest has joined us, we'll be on our way.' To his surprise, the American guest, a Mrs Miriam Hyde-Eshar, turned out to be a handsome, middle-aged woman who strode briskly towards him across the arrivals floor.

'You look a little surprised young man; but please don't concern yourself, I might not be a spring chicken but, I assure you, I'll probably out-walk most of your guests.'

'I'm quite sure you will Ma'am; from your itinerary, I see you've just come from the Victoria Falls...'

'And, before that, I visited the pyramids in Egypt, the Masai Mara in Kenya and finally got to spend some time with the gorillas in Rwanda; most of these attractions involved a great deal of walking.'

'I never doubted your ability to keep up with the group,' he replied.

'Liar; and for goodness sake call me Miriam!' Derek knew at once he was going to enjoy spending the next five days with Miriam Hyde-Eshar.

Once he had the luggage loaded in the back of the safari car, Derek returned to the coffee lounge and his guests. 'Good afternoon to you all and welcome to the province of Limpopo. My name is Derek Hamilton, and I am a safari guide at Riley's Camp, your wilderness home for the next five days. We will be leaving shortly for the hour-long drive to the camp. Once we arrive at the reception area, you will be shown to your *rondavels* and will have thirty minutes or so to freshen up before an orientation briefing by our senior game ranger and manager, Jacob Riley. Afterwards, we will have afternoon tea and an opportunity to get to know one another.'

Miriam held up her hand, 'Derek, I was told winter was the best time to visit the game reserve; is that true?'

'Absolutely; by June most of the smaller rivers have dried up forcing the game to congregate around permanent waterholes. Also, the vegetation is sparser making it a lot easier to spot animals, especially the large predators. Although this is our winter, you will find the weather warm during the day, but it can get quite chilly at night and in the early mornings. So, if you're going out on one of our early morning game walks, be sure to take a sweater or jersey as we call them here. Does anyone have any further questions? No? Then let's get our adventure underway.'

Derek did not allocate seats in the safari car, but rather let his guests sit wherever they wished. He was pleased when Miriam chose to sit up front with him, 'So, Derek,' she began as they drove out of the airport area, 'do you live at Riley's Camp?'

'Only when I'm working; the rest of the time I live here in Skoonspruit. We will pass through the town shortly before we reach the entrance gate to the Languleni Game Reserve.' Concerned that her next question may be about his years of experience as a safari guide, he turned the tables and asked Miriam where she lived when she was not travelling.

'I'm an Israeli-born American citizen and, since my husband's death a few years ago, I've been living in New York. When I turned fifty last month, I decided the time had come to do some travelling outside of the United States and Israel. While my husband was alive, we were too busy to find the time then, suddenly, it was too late. Let this be a lesson to you Derek, never put off until tomorrow what you can do today. Is that the entrance gate we're coming up to?'

'Yes; from now on we are in the game reserve. Everyone should keep a good look out for giraffe; they are often the first game animals to welcome visitors to Languleni.' When he glanced back, the four passengers in the back were fast asleep, the result of the long flight from Europe to Johannesburg and the short-haul flight to Skoonspruit.

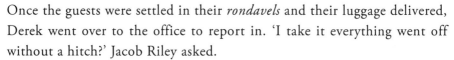

Once the guests were settled in their *rondavels* and their luggage delivered, Derek went over to the office to report in. 'I take it everything went off without a hitch?' Jacob Riley asked.

'No problems Boss. Before you start their orientation briefing, I was wondering if you had heard anything further regarding the poaching incidents.'

'Early this morning, the police finally arrived in response to my calls regarding the rhinos poached near the entrance gate. Both Blessing and I got the impression from the officer in charge of the investigation, a Lieutenant Themba, that he might have a lead on the local black poachers. Of course,' Riley added, 'it's the bastards in the helicopter I'm after. Any luck your end?'

'Nothing so far, but I'm hopeful I'll hear something from Colonel Dlamini before too long.'

The next five days passed quickly, and in no time Derek was driving his five guests back to the airport to catch their flights home. 'Are you on your way back to the United States?' he asked Miriam Hyde-Eshar as he helped wheel her suitcases into the airport terminal.

'You'll not be getting rid of me that easily,' she joked. 'I've arranged with your boss for another five days stay in Riley's Camp starting four weeks on Monday. He's promised to arrange for you and Blessing to take me to see Dengezi and her calf; something I'm looking forward to with a great deal of pleasure. In the meanwhile, I'm off Tel Aviv to look in on an old friend of mine, Shimon Peres. I hope to get his opinion on the upcoming Middle East peace conference scheduled to take place in Geneva in a month's time. Unfortunately, I hear from members of my late husband's foundation that Shimon is not very well now; so, I do hope I will be able to meet up with him.'

'I spent a month in Israel a while back as a participant in a Close Protection Officer's course. I enjoyed my time there and wouldn't mind going back for a visit one day.'

'I do hope you'll do that; it's a wonderful country. Unfortunately, here's where we part company. Take care Derek, I look forward to seeing again you in four weeks time,' she called out to him as she wheeled her suitcases through to airport security.

Mrs Preller was waiting with an overexcited Jack at the gate to welcome him home. 'Derek, would you mind coming inside for a moment, I've got a favour to ask of you.' He knew it was a big favour when Mrs Preller brought out two cold Carling Black Labels from her fridge and set them down on the table on her *stoep*. 'A young lady who used to rent the *rondavel* you're in, called this morning to confirm her booking for a two-week stay which, apparently, she says she paid for over a month ago. You might know her, Sylvia Kingston; I believe Sylvia does some work for Jacob Riley. Anyway, to make a long story short, I checked my records, and it seems she is correct. This mix-up is my fault, and I was wondering if together we might be able to come up with a solution?'

'Is Ms Kingston here now?'

'No, you've only just missed her. She arrived about an hour ago, having driven up from Nelspruit. I believe she's already dropped her luggage off in the *rondavel* and is on her way out to Riley's Camp.'

'I didn't know she had a car?'

'Apparently, she has. Sylvia said she bought it a few days ago from a friend of hers in Nelspruit. Nice little silver Mazda; quite old though. Anyway, what do you suggest we do about her accommodation?'

'Leave it with me Mrs Preller; I'm on my way to Riley's Camp now. Between Ms Kingston and myself, I'm sure we can come up with some alternative arrangements for the next two weeks.'

Sylvia Kingston was having a beer with Dennis Middlebrook in the guest lounge. 'How did it go Derek?' Dennis asked as he joined them, adding for Sylvia's benefit, 'Derek's just completed his first group tour with us."

'They were very nice people,' Derek replied, 'interested in seeing every animal, bird and even snake the bushveld has to offer.'

'Snake?' Sylvia said, 'Oh my God! I hate snakes.'

'What sort of snake and where did you see it,' Dennis asked.

'Mamba; pretty big, close to six foot I'd say. Seems to live around the balancing rock at the Nyama waterhole.'

Changing the subject, Dennis continued, 'The boss tells me on your first early morning walk you had a close encounter with Old One Tusk.'

'Close doesn't adequately describe it! At one stage, I thought I was going to have to fire a shot over the old dear's head; but she backed off in time.'

'She didn't get to be as old as she is without knowing how far she can push us,' Dennis added with a grin. 'Still, your guests must have enjoyed the encounter.'

'Not really, the Spanish guys who, between the two of them, carried more photographic equipment than you would find in the average camera store, stood there transfixed, forgetting completely to take any photos. To add insult to injury, a few moments later one of them took me aside and asked if I could arrange to do that again!'

Laughing, Dennis continued, 'So, did you manage to show them the big five?'

'It was touch and go; by the morning of their last day, we still hadn't seen a leopard and, although they all said it didn't matter, I knew they wanted to add that elusive beast to their bucket list. However, our luck was in; as we left on the drive to the airport, what should be standing in the middle of the road but a truly magnificent tom. Where he came from, I'll never know; even Blessing confessed he'd never seen that leopard before. It made my day I can tell you.'

'Well, I'd better be off,' Dennis said finishing his beer, 'I've a night drive later this evening; I'll see you both later.'

Waiting until they were alone, Sylvia turned to Derek, 'I'd like to apologise for my aggressive questioning when we first met at Rhenoster's Kop and my poorly timed revelation regarding Rachel Cavendish's appointment as Deputy Director with MI5. I'm also sorry about the mix up with your accommodation; Mrs Preller completely forgot to write it in her bookings register.'

'Not to worry, these things happen; I'm sure I can find a vacant bed in the game scouts dormitory for two weeks. The only problem is I can't bring my dog Jack into Languleni. As you may know, dogs are not allowed into the reserve.'

'Look, I feel awful about this,' Sylvia said, 'it isn't your fault and, as you say, it's only for two weeks. If you have no objections, I'd be quite happy to bed down on the foldout bed in the lounge in your *rondavel*.'

'Being old school, do you think Mrs Preller will go for that? Seeing as we are…'

'Unmarried?'

'You get the picture.'

'I don't think that's any of her business! But would you be okay with that?'

'Provided I'm the one who gets to sleep on the foldout in the lounge,' Derek said, 'then we have a deal.'

Derek was awakened by the smell of coffee brewing in the little kitchen and Jack's enthusiastic greeting as he jumped up on the foldout bed. 'Good morning,' Sylvia said as she emerged from the kitchen wearing his dressing gown and carrying two cups of coffee. 'Sorry, I had to make use of your gown; I must have left mine in the motel in Nelspruit.' Sitting on the edge of his bed, she could not help remarking, 'Hell, this foldout is uncomfortable; how on earth did you manage to get any sleep?'

'To be honest, not much. If you look at the label, I think you will find this foldout was designed and manufactured by the very same company that supplied the rack used by Henry the Eighth in the Tower of London.'

'Oh! go on; I'm sure it's not that bad!'

'You think so! Put your coffee down and climb in here next to me; then tell me what you think?'

'I think that's the slickest move I've ever come across, clearly designed to get me into your bed. Without a doubt, you get full marks for originality,' she said as she placed her coffee on the table, took off his dressing gown and, completely naked, pulled back the covers and climbed into his bed. 'I see you also sleep *au naturel* and, judging by your physical reaction, you're thinking the same thoughts I'm thinking. All of which leads me to believe we're both going to be a little late for work today!'

CHAPTER − 7 −

BASED ON HER EXPERIENCE AS an investigating reporter, Jacob invited Sylvia to sit in on their meeting to discuss the worrying increase in rhino poaching. 'What makes it especially important we get a handle on this problem as quickly as we can,' he said, 'is the call I received this morning from the capture team at Matetsi in the Kruger Park. Apparently, they have a young female, white rhino ready to be shipped to us together with the male rhino they've been holding for us for nearly two weeks.'

'That's good news boss. Any idea when they want us to pick them up?' Derek asked.

'So far they haven't given me a firm date. I'm still hopeful your father will be able to get permission for us to bring them into Languleni using fire trails and backroads, saving us the long drive via Phalaborwa and Skoonspruit. The less time these animals spend cooped up in crates, the better. Derek, as you're free for the next two days, I'd like you and Blessing to work out a possible route we could use should we receive permission.'

'While Derek's away for the next two days, and providing no one has any objections,' Sylvia said, 'I'd like to see if I can come up with anything on the people who may be behind this poaching epidemic. If you don't mind sharing your suspicions as to who these people might be, it's just possible I may be able to develop a few leads.'

'Excuse me for interrupting,' June Riley said entering the room and handing a fax to Derek, 'but I think you'll all be interested in hearing this.'

'It's from Colonel Dlamini in Jo'burg,' Derek said looking at the fax. 'Forensic experts in his department confirm the drugs used to dart both rhinos are unusual derivatives of etorphine not commonly available on the South African market. And, listen to this, based on the rough description we provided, together with the dimensions of the marks left by the helicopter's landing skids, our helicopter closely matches the profile of a Creusot R44, a two-seater machine currently in use by the police! The colonel goes on to add that there are only two such helicopters operating in this area; one is stationed at Phalaborwa in Limpopo Province and the other at Malelane in Mpumalanga Province.'

'That certainly gives me something to work with; can anyone think of anything else?' Sylvia asked looking around the table.

'What about the plaster casts of the two boot prints we found close to the rhinos poached near the entrance gate?' Blessing asked.

'Good point; based on information Blessing obtained, we know one of the prints was made by a white man, possibly the pilot, wearing police or military issue boots,' Derek said. 'The other print came from a second white man wearing civilian hiking boots. With some help from Betts Outdoor Supplies in town, I managed to confirm the second boot print is from a pair of Hauck's hiking boots; very likely sold locally.'

'So, to sum up; we could be looking for a local man with access to a dart gun, etorphine drugs, or something similar, and who knows someone who can fly a police helicopter. Sort of challenge I can get my teeth into,' Sylvia said.

'I can't stress enough just how dangerous these people are,' Jacob said looking directly at Sylvia, 'don't forget, there's an awful lot of money involved.'

'I haven't spent the last seven years working as an investigative reporter all over Africa south of the Sahara for nothing; I'm well aware of the risks. I'll make a start first thing tomorrow morning.'

CHAPTER − 8 −

ALWAYS A LIGHT SLEEPER, THE odd sound was more than enough to wake Derek. He lay without moving, listening intently for any clue that might explain what woke him. After a few minutes, the only sound came from the old grandfather clock in the lounge chiming two fifteen in the morning. Sylvia's regular breathing confirmed she was asleep, and he knew his dog Jack was safely confined in the kitchen. Concluding it was nothing he need worry about, he was about to drift off to sleep when he sensed rather than heard something moving in the room. It was a soft, almost inaudible, sighing sort of sound; much like someone pulling a small carpet across the slate tiled floor of the bedroom.

'Something must have got into the room,' he thought as he reached over and turned on the small, bedside reading lamp. Sitting up, he stared into the dark shadows beneath the window in the far wall; to his sleep-befuddled brain, it appeared as though part of the floor was moving. Reaching for his Maglite torch on the bedside table, he switched it on.

Disturbed by his sudden movement, the bright torch beam revealed the olive-grey body of a large snake as it coiled itself into a defensive position. As its head rose three feet above the floor, the gaping black mouth confirmed it was a black mamba, one of the deadliest snakes in Africa.

Freezing in position, Derek dared not reach for his service pistol on the bedside table for fear of further provoking the snake. He kept the torch beam fixed on the reptile's head as he warily considered his next move. The fact that the mamba was probably just as frightened as he was, did little or nothing to help. Of immediate concern was his fear that it might decide to hide under the wardrobe, or worse, seek shelter under their bed.

As though in response to his indecision, the snake lowered its head and began to move slowly across the floor. 'Bloody thing must be at least nine-foot-long,' he thought to himself as the mamba did what he feared most; it disappeared into the shadows at the foot of their bed. Carefully, he shone his torch around the room, but there was no sign of it anywhere; the snake had almost certainly taken shelter under their bed. 'Thank God Sylvia is fast asleep,' he thought to himself, 'she'd probably freak out at the idea of a nine-foot black mamba hiding under our bed.'

Struggling to control his fear, he thought through his limited options. Right away, he dismissed the idea of making a grab for his pistol and shooting the snake. While he considered himself a reasonably good shot, he was under no illusion he could hit a fast-moving snake in a poorly lit room; not to mention the grave danger of a bullet ricocheting off the hard, tile floor. 'So, I can forget about trying to shoot it,' he concluded, 'instead, I've got to find something I can use to pin it down while I figure out how to capture it or kill it. I've got to get hold of a broom from the kitchen.'

Unfortunately, he had no clear idea how he might climb out of bed and get through to the kitchen without further alarming the snake. Adding to his worries was the fact that his dog Jack slept on an old blanket next to the coal stove in the kitchen. The last thing he wanted was for Jack to attack the snake; a move which could only result in the death of his dog. Realising he couldn't just lie there endlessly considering his next move, he resolved to take matters into his own hands before the snake decided to explore the rest of the *rondavel*. The thought of a black mamba loose somewhere inside the house was simply too terrible to contemplate.

Moving as slowly as he could, he pulled the bed covers off his legs, all the while being careful not to wake Sylvia or provoke the snake into further action. Gripping his torch in his left hand, he gathered his legs up beneath him and, resting his right hand on the bedside table for support, he jumped off the bed and dashed towards the partially open bedroom door. Bursting through, he ran headlong into the dark lounge, where he tripped over a chair and fell heavily to the floor.

Scrambling to his feet, he heard Sylvia call out his name. 'Stay where you are,' he yelled, 'don't get off the bed, there's a snake in the room! What ever you do, don't get off the bed!' he shouted again as he stumbled into the kitchen, slamming the door closed behind him. As he switched on the light, Jack jumped up from his blanket next to the stove, his tail wagging expectantly as he looked up at Derek.

'You stay!' he shouted angrily at his dog, 'Jack, you stay!' Derek grabbed a kitchen broom and, in an inspired move, pulled the steel poker from the coal scuttle next to the stove. Again, ordering Jack to stay, he carefully opened the kitchen door and felt around the door jamb for the light switch in the lounge.

As he turned on the light, the mamba appeared right in front of him, its gaping black mouth waist high. Using the head of the broom, he managed to force it back into the lounge and away from the kitchen. Angrily, the snake struck repeatedly at the broom as he pushed it towards the front door, an idea forming in his mind to give it some avenue of escape.

Forced halfway across the room, the snake suddenly turned and, with terrifying speed, seemed to launch itself at him. Desperately fending off its attack with the broom, he stumbled backwards and, tripping over a footstool, fell to the floor. As the mamba renewed its aggressive attack on the broom, Jack suddenly charged out of the kitchen and, launching himself at the snake, clamped his jaws a foot below the mamba's head. '*Here God* Jack! No Jack, leave it alone!'

It was too late; the deadly head repeatedly struck at the dog clinging to its slender body. Scrambling to his feet, Derek pinned the snakes head to the floor with the broom, its long body wrapping and coiling itself around his legs. Driven by fear and rage, he used the poker in his left hand to beat the coffin-shaped head to a bloody pulp.

'Is it dead Derek, is it dead?' Sylvia stood naked in the doorway of the bedroom, his Z88 pistol clasped in her hands.

'Yes, it's dead,' he said picking up Jack as the nerves in the snake's body caused it to twitch and writhe on the floor. 'It's dead, it can't hurt us now, but it has bitten Jack. I've got to get him to the vet right away.' Tears in his eyes, he turned towards the front door cradling his dog in his arms.

'Derek put on your pants first.' Sylvia said as she ran to the bedroom and returned with his pyjama shorts. Pulling them on, he picked up Jack and ran out to his *bakkie*. Fortunately, the roads were deserted as he broke every rule of the road in his desperate attempt to get to the veterinarian's house in time.

As he skidded to a stop in their drive way, Brian Hanson emerged from the house. 'Your girlfriend phoned, she told me what happened. Quickly, bring him inside.' Derek carried Jack's now limp body into the surgery and laid him on the examination table as Hanson, using a stethoscope, listened for a heartbeat. After a long, agonising minute he stood and put his hand on Derek's shoulder. 'I'm very sorry; your dog is dead. Black mamba venom is neurotoxic; all it takes is two drops to kill a grown man. I'm afraid there was nothing I could have done.'

Tears welled in Derek's eyes as he shook the vet's hand and thanked him for trying. Cradling Jack in his arms, he followed Debra Hanson out to his *bakkie*. She opened the passenger side door and stepped back as he laid Jack on the seat. Weeping softly, she put her arms around him and kissed him. 'I'm so terribly sorry; I know you were very fond of him.'

He drove back to Mrs Preller's in a daze. Sylvia burst into tears as he carried Jack inside and laid him on the lounge. 'I'm sorry my darling,' he said taking her in his arms, 'there was nothing anyone could do, the venom from that bloody snake is deadly. Were it not for Jack; it could well have been one of us lying here dead.'

<hr />

'Please throw that thing outside,' Sylvia said, 'I can't bear the thought of it still in the house.' As he gathered up the remains of the mamba and took it outside, she went into the kitchen and made tea. Later, as they sat together on the sofa, Sylvia cradling Jack's head on her lap, she asked, 'How the hell did it get inside, I'm sure we closed all the doors? What was it that woke you?'

'Thinking back on it now,' he replied, 'I believe it was the sound of something falling over in the room. After listening for a while, I thought I heard what sounded like something being dragged across the floor. Even when I turned on the bedside lamp, I couldn't see anything; but as soon as I switched on my torch, there it was, a bloody great snake lying against the wall below the window sill. Then, when its head rose three feet off the floor; I knew at once we were dealing with a big mamba.'

'But how the hell did it get inside?' Sylvia asked.

'*Jirre God*!' Derek swore as he jumped to his feet and dashed into their bedroom, Sylvia close behind. Pulling aside the curtains, they stared at the ragged hole cut in the bottom of the fly screen covering their bedroom window.

'Surely it couldn't get in through that hole by itself?' Sylvia asked, 'isn't it too high off the ground?' Her question prompted him to grab his torch and rush outside. He was gone for a good five minutes before he returned holding a white linen bag.

'This is the sort of bag a snake handler uses to carry a snake. Look at the draw strings around the top of the bag; they're there to keep the reptile safely inside.'

'Where did you find it?'

'Hidden amongst the bushes near the front gate; where our would-be killers stashed it as they made their getaway.'

'What makes you say, killers?'

'The footprints outside our window. There's no doubt there were two of them. Obviously, their plan was for the snake to kill one of us or, at the very least, put the fear of God into us.'

'And they succeeded there; do you believe this is because of your efforts to track down the poachers who killed these rhinos?' Sylvia asked.

'I've no doubt this has everything to do with it. My inquiries around town must have struck a raw nerve.'

CHAPTER – 9 –

'I would like both of you to leave Skoonspruit at once,' Jacob Riley advised, 'I believe your lives are in great danger. You'd be much safer here in Riley's Camp; at least until things settle down. Derek, as you only have four guests to look after next week, the two of you are welcome to use one of the empty guest *rondavels*.'

'Thanks, Boss, but I'm planning on staying in Skoonspruit until Sunday when I'm due to pick up those guests at the airport.'

'And I for one do not intend being chased out of town by cowardly thugs who think that an encounter with a little snake is enough to frighten me off,' Sylvia retorted.

'My dear,' Jacob said taking her hand, 'this is the first time I've ever heard someone describe a nine-foot black mamba as a 'little snake!' Seriously though, I don't think either of you fully appreciate just how dangerous things have become. As I've warned before, there's an enormous amount of money at stake when it comes to the trafficking of rhino horn in South Africa; made even more dangerous by the powerful politicians and criminals pulling strings in the background.'

'Despite having been threatened by some of Africa's most brutal regimes, I've never allowed them to warn me off a good story. As a heads-up to you both, I'm off to Phalaborwa tomorrow to interview a Captain Nkolosi who, my sources tell me, may be more than just a captain in the police service.'

Shaking his head in resignation, Jacob continued, 'As we're all aware, poaching in this country is bad and growing worse every day. According to reports coming out of Kruger and, despite the best efforts of their rangers and game scouts, dozens of rhino and elephant are poached every week in the Park. As we've come to expect, the powers that be in government are doing little more than appointing utterly useless people to important positions where they gladly accept bribes to look the other way.' Glancing over towards the reception office, he said, 'I see June signalling for me to climb down off my soapbox; so, let me finish by repeating my warning to you both; these are dangerous times peopled by equally dangerous people.'

Mrs Preller, equally heartbroken over the death of Jack, readily gave permission for them to bury him under the acacia tree in the front garden. That sad duty completed, their landlady told them she had agreed to Jacob Riley's request to hire a night watchman to keep an eye on the comings and goings on her property after dark. 'That's very decent of him,' Sylvia said punching Derek lightly on his arm, 'at least I'll know you're safe while I'm taking all the risks in Phalaborwa!'

Three days went by with no further occurrences other than Sylvia's return from Phalaborwa. 'So, what did you find out from Nkolosi?' Derek asked as he carried her suitcase into their *rondavel*.

'Not a thing; he clammed up as soon as I sat down in his office. It was evident from the start he was frightened of something or someone. When I pressed him about the Creusot helicopter, he assured me it had been out of service for months waiting for spare parts from Pretoria. I asked around town and got the same story everywhere. That is until I stopped one morning for a coffee at Lozi's Diner on the outskirts of town. When the young waiter brought my coffee, I asked him if he had ever seen the police helicopter fly overhead.'

'Oh yes, Madam, many times,' he told me. 'When I came to work early this morning I saw it fly by; I think it was going to Kgopa Kopje where these *rhiyani* sleep.'

'When I asked him if he had seen more than one, he replied that there were two, possibly even three, helicopters or *rhiyani* as he calls them, that regularly flew to and from Kgopa.'

'Bloody hell; you may be onto something. I think we need to take a closer look at this Kgopa Kopje.'

'Been there, done that.'

'And?'

'Secure area, surrounded by high fences topped with razor wire and a road block which prevented me from getting closer than a half a mile of the place.'

'Were you stopped at the roadblock?'

'Not only did they stop me, but they questioned me for over half an hour as to what I was doing in the area.'

'Oh shit! That's probably not very good.'

'I don't think there's any reason to be concerned. I did my fluttering eyelashes and the silly little white girl who's always getting lost act. I'm sure they bought it. Now, enough of this interrogation, I drove the last fifty miles looking forward to a few stiff whiskies and lots of sex, and not necessarily in that order!'

Derek was shaving in the bathroom when Sylvia popped her head around the door. 'I'm going to the store to pick up a loaf of bread and a dozen eggs. Do you need anything?'

'No thanks, I'm fine.'

'While I like the idea of a night-watchman keeping an eye on things, I wasn't too pleased when I saw him getting out of my car earlier this morning. I hope he didn't sleep in it overnight,' she said as she got ready to leave, 'I'm off now, but I'd appreciate it if you'd have a word with him later.' Derek wiped the last traces of shaving cream from his chin as he washed his razor in the sink. As he stared at his reflection in the mirror, Sylvia's words came back to him.

'*Jirre!*' he screamed as he dashed to the front door yelling at the top of his voice, 'get away from the car, don't touch it!' But he was too late. As Sylvia opened the driver's side door, a short length of cord tied to the inside door handle pulled the safety pin out of one of the three fragmentation grenades taped around the gear shift lever. Startled by the hand grenade's safety lever as it sprang free and struck the dashboard, Sylvia turned and, looking towards Derek, followed his screamed instructions to shut the door and drop to the ground. Less than two and a half seconds later, the seven and a half ounces of trinitrotoluene contained in the three grenades, exploded.

Peppered with shrapnel in her back and legs, Sylvia avoided the worst of the blast which blew out the doors and windows of her car and peeled back most of its roof. Partially sheltered by the solid wooden door frame of the *rondavel*, Derek avoided the main force of the explosion as it shattered the windows in the *rondavels* facing the parking area and removed most of the thatch from the roofs of nearby buildings. Without thinking, Derek raced over and pulled Sylvia to safety seconds before the fuel tank of the car caught fire and exploded in a ball of flame.

'That bloody does it!' Jacob Riley yelled as he stood at Derek's hospital bedside, 'and I'll not take no for an answer. You're moving out to Riley's Camp the moment you're fit enough to travel. How many times have I got to warn you, these are dangerous people we're dealing with.'

'I take full blame for not taking your warnings more seriously.' Derek said looking across at June and Jacob. 'Please tell me, how is Sylvia doing?'

'She's lucky to be alive,' Jacob replied. 'Three hours ago, Nelspruit Clinic medivacked her to Jo'burg General and, once she's deemed fit enough to travel, her newspaper is flying her back to the UK.' The sound of a cough from the doorway of the hospital room caught Jacob's attention, 'Oh! I nearly forgot; there's a Lieutenant Themba from the police service here in Skoonspruit. He wants to talk to you about the attempt on Sylvia's life. Okay, we'll leave you to it then. I'll be back to see you later this evening.'

As June and Jacob left, the policeman came into the room and stood at his bedside. 'Mr Hamilton, I'm Lieutenant Themba. Please accept my sympathy for the terrible attack on you and Ms Kingston. I understand from Mrs Preller you and Ms Kingston were close; have you any idea who may have wished either of you any harm?'

'I would like to tell you all I know Lieutenant but, to be frank, I would rather talk to Colonel Dlamini. The colonel is with the Directorate for Priority Crime Investigations, sometimes referred to as the Hawks. I've had the opportunity to work with the colonel on other matters in the past and, please understand, this is no reflection on you. You should know I've already asked Mr Riley to contact him on my behalf.'

'It's clear to me, Mr Hamilton, the colonel holds you in high regard; he has already contacted me and asked that I pick him up at the airport in three days' time.'

'Lieutenant, I'm curious. Why did you ask if someone wanted to harm both Ms Kingston and myself?'

'I apologise, I assumed you already knew.'

'Knew what Lieutenant?'

'That we discovered a similar device rigged to detonate when you opened the driver's side door of your Land Rover. Fortunately, one of my detectives spotted it in time, and we were able to disarm the device. Once our forensics team has finished examining your vehicle and the bomb, we hope to have some idea who may be behind this outrage.'

'Lieutenant, what about our so-called night watchman? Are you aware that Ms Kingston saw him getting out of her car shortly before the bomb went off?'

'We discovered the body of the night watchman soon after arriving on the scene. He had been stabbed to death and his body concealed in bushes near the gate to the Preller *rondavels*. It appears he had been dead for some hours before the bomb went off; so, it's highly unlikely Ms Kingston saw him at her car. During our investigations, we also discovered the khaki greatcoat belonging to the night watchman is missing. We believe the bomber used it to disguise his appearance and was probably wearing it when he set the devices.'

'Lieutenant, I must ask you to excuse me. I need to contact Sylvia Kingston's family in England. She worked for a newspaper in London, and I'm sure they would know how to get in touch with her relatives.'

'I believe Mr Riley has already taken care of that. And, as you may already know, arrangements are underway to medivac Ms Kingston to Britain as soon as she is well enough to make the journey.' Lieutenant Themba rose to his feet, 'Thank you for your time Mr Hamilton, I'll see you in a few days' time together with Colonel Dlamini. Hopefully, between the three of us, we can make some sense of this attack.'

'So, what did you tell Themba?' Jacob Riley asked as he drove Derek to Riley's Camp.

'Nothing; other than I wanted to speak to Colonel Dlamini first before I made a statement.'

'I'll bet he didn't take that very well? What did you tell him about the secret camp Sylvia tried to visit near Kgopa Kopje?'

'Absolutely nothing.'

'Why on earth not?'

'Because we believe this place is connected in some way to the police in Phalaborwa, I thought it best not involve Themba; at least not until I've had time to check it out personally.'

'*Jirre* Derek, surely you realise Sylvia's attempt to visit this place may well be the reason they tried to kill both of you'.

'More reason why we need to find out exactly what's going on in that area and whether it's connected in any way to our rhino poaching problems. If it's okay with you Boss, I'd like to visit Kgopa Kopje and take a look around. I believe we owe Sylvia that courtesy.'

'You've barely been out of the hospital for a day, and you can't wait to get yourself into more trouble. If you ask me, you're a glutton for punishment.' Derek did not reply. 'Okay, we'll do what we can at this end to help you, but on one condition, you take Blessing with you. His operational experiences in the bush with 32 Battalion on the Angola border will, hopefully, keep you out of trouble.

CHAPTER – 10 –

K GOPA KOPJE LAY FIFTEEN MILES west of Phalaborwa and five miles north of Hwy 8 on a dirt road that branched off next to a sign that read, 'Kgopa Research Station – Entry strictly forbidden. Trespassers will be prosecuted to the fullest extent of the law.' Using his night vision binoculars, Derek spotted the roadblock from almost a mile away. 'That's probably where they detained and questioned Sylvia,' Derek said to fellow ranger Etienne Roux as he pulled his Land Rover off into the bush. 'This is where Blessing and I get out. Thanks again for the ride Etienne; we'd be most grateful if you would pick us up when I give you a call.'

'Good luck to you both and for God's sake don't get caught,' Etienne said as he turned his vehicle around and, continuing without lights, headed back towards the highway. Derek and Blessing, wearing camouflage outfits, hid in the bush close to the side of the road for a good fifteen minutes watching and listening for any sign they might have been seen. Satisfied their arrival had gone undetected, Derek used his ground sheet to hide the light from his torch as he checked their location on his GPS device and marked it on his map. Tapping Blessing on the shoulder, they picked up their packs and set out for Kgopa Kopje.

Keeping to a low, scrub-covered ridge, they skirted the roadblock unseen and, shortly before dawn, scaled the steep side of the kopje. Using the night vision binoculars, Derek led the way over the crest and down into a brush-choked gully that provided a safe vantage point and a good view of the activities in the valley below. As the first pale fingers of dawn crept across the landscape below, dawn revealed what looked like a small light industrial facility. 'What is it, *Numzaan*, a military base?' They stared at the three corrugated iron sheds clustered around what appeared to be an incline shaft mine and a large, truck-borne rock crushing machine.

'It looks like a small mine; though I can't see any logos or company names on any of the lorries. Most likely it's an illegal mining operation.'

'I can see two armed guards patrolling around that double perimeter fence,' Blessing pointed out. 'Do you think they are mining for gold or diamonds?'

'To the best of my knowledge there's no gold or diamond mining in this area and, if that's what they're really after, why the need for secrecy?' Derek said as he took a few photographs with his digital camera. 'What I don't understand is why they would they be so concerned if a young woman travelling on her own, took the wrong road and ended up at their roadblock.'

'*Numzaan*, look over there,' Blessing said pointing to a hangar like building facing onto a large open field at the far end of the compound. Using his binoculars, Derek watched two men with automatic weapons slung over their shoulders, roll open a pair of hangar doors to allow four others to push a twin-engine aircraft out onto the field. 'I know that *vliegtuig*,' Blessing said, 'I saw it used to carry supplies to our *troepe* in Caprivi; we knew it as a Skyvan. That *vliegtuig* can take off and land almost anywhere with over two tonnes of cargo.'

'I'm guessing, but I think they're using it to fly out crushed rock or something similar, for further processing somewhere else. I'd give anything to know where that somewhere is,' Derek said, 'and if they've got an aircraft like that, I don't see why they couldn't have a helicopter or two stashed away in a shed. When it gets dark, I suggest we take a look in that hangar and see if we can pick up a sample or two of whatever it is they're so intent on digging up.'

They waited until two in the morning before making their way down to the valley below. Frequent use of the binoculars during the day had exposed a security flaw in the double perimeter fence. A recent downpour had scoured a shallow gully under both fences and, despite a half-hearted attempt to pile rocks in the washout, it provided easy access into the compound. The predictable path and timing of the two-man perimeter patrols enabled Blessing and Derek to crawl, undetected, up to the doors of the aircraft hangar. As they expected, the rolling doors were locked but, luckily, a single side door opened without too much trouble.

The unfamiliar smell of aviation fuel greeted their nostrils as they entered the hangar pulling the door closed behind them. Using a carefully shaded torch, they made their way to the front of the Skyvan where, with Blessing's help, he opened the aircraft's small emergency hatch immediately behind the cockpit. Leaving Blessing to keep watch, Derek climbed inside and squeezed into the narrow space behind the two pilots' seats. Feeling with his hands between the two seats, he soon found what he was looking for.

Switching on his torch, he carefully sorted through the handful of navigation charts. 'This could be the one I need,' he said to himself as he came across a well-thumbed map fastened to a clipboard with elastic bands. Pencil lines on the map clearly marked the various approaches to a landing field at the Hartebeestfontein Mine near Pietersburg.

The sound of voices from outside the aircraft caused him to quickly switch off his torch. '*Jirre!*' he swore, 'I hope they haven't caught Blessing.' Squeezing his body against the bulkhead alongside one of the pilot's seats he froze, praying they wouldn't notice the open emergency hatch.

'*Ja*, the *fokker* said he hid it inside the cargo space, behind the fire extinguisher,' a deep man's voice cut through the darkness, the aircraft rocking as someone climbed in through the main hatch. Derek watched in fear as a powerful torch beam illuminated the interior of the cargo compartment, 'Don't shine that *fokken* light around,' the voice outside warned, 'the extinguisher's halfway down on your left side.'

'Okay, I've got it. Shit! There's not a lot here; I thought you said there would be at least five pounds. Feels more like three to me.'

'If you've got it, come on. Let's get the hell out of here!' the voice outside said. Derek felt the aircraft lurch again as someone made their way to the hatch and climbed out.

'Should I close this fucking thing?' a voice asked.

'Christ no! Leave everything exactly as it is; we don't want anyone to know we were here.'

For five agonising minutes, Derek sat without moving, listening intently for any sign the intruders were still in the hangar. '*Numzaan*,' he heard Blessing whisper from the emergency hatch, 'are you okay?'

'I'll be good to go once I get my heart started. I take it those men have gone?'

'*Yebo*, they've gone. Fortunately, I heard them talking seconds before they came in through the side door; it seems they were looking for a bag of *dagga* someone had hidden in the *vliegtuig* when it delivered the barrels of crushed rock.'

'That was too close for comfort. Give me a few minutes to grab a few samples of that crushed rock, and we'll get the hell out of here.'

'*Numzaan*, before we go you should see this,' Blessing said leading the way to another section of the hangar. 'I found this while I was looking for a place to hide when those two men came.'

Parked at the rear of the hangar were two shrouded helicopters, their landing skids attached to ground-handling wheels and their rotor blades folded for easy storage. Pulling aside the bottom flap on one of the canvas covers, Derek used his shaded torch to get a look at the helicopter. It was a five-seater, painted a dark green with a white stripe running the length of the fuselage. There was no company name on the fuselage, so Derek made a note of the registration number.

The second helicopter proved far more interesting. It was a Creusot R44, crudely painted to mimic the colours of a police service helicopter. This time, even the registration number was missing. 'I believe we've discovered the helicopter used by the poachers; I can tell you I'm looking forward to handing all of this over to Dlamini and his team as soon as we get back.'

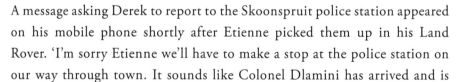

A message asking Derek to report to the Skoonspruit police station appeared on his mobile phone shortly after Etienne picked them up in his Land Rover. 'I'm sorry Etienne we'll have to make a stop at the police station on our way through town. It sounds like Colonel Dlamini has arrived and is anxious to talk.'

'Well, don't keep us in suspense,' Jacob said greeting Derek and Blessing as they arrived back at Riley's Camp, 'what did your colonel have to say for himself? More importantly, has he made any arrests?'

'None to date and, frankly, from what he told me, he's not likely to be making any soon. At least not until he can come up with irrefutable evidence that will stand up in even the most biased courts in the land.'

'So, he's telling us,' Jacob suggested, 'that the criminal organisations behind the poaching of wildlife in this country are supported at the highest levels of government, making successful prosecutions all but impossible.'

'That's it in a nutshell. Take this business at Kgopa Kopje; it seems Dlamini has known about it for months. So far, the Hawks have been unable to get the state prosecutor's office to even look at their evidence of illegal mining for monazite and other rare earth elements. At least not while some fat cat with the right family connections is running the show.'

'So, what about the companies and the people behind them, has he any idea who they are?'

'Off the record, the colonel made mention of a conglomerate based in Europe and the Far East with offices worldwide, including a connection in Johannesburg.'

'Did he name names?'

'Yes, he did, and my blood ran cold when he named Schoveldt International as the conglomerate's Johannesburg connection.'

'Oh my God!' Jacob said with a sharp intake of breath, 'surely not that bloody group involved with the Chinese surface-to-air missiles your father told me about!'

'Sounds like the same lot to me. Don't forget we never got that bastard Dieter Schoveldt or, for that matter, his old man Barendt. The last thing I heard he was keeping a low profile somewhere in Europe. Whether MI5, MI6 or the CIA for that matter, ever followed up on the case, I've no idea. As I'm sure you'll understand, I'm no longer on their mailing lists.'

'Then perhaps it's time you renewed your subscriptions,' Jacob suggested as he rose to his feet. 'Looks to me as though the sun is well over the yard arm; whisky?'

'Best idea you've had all day Boss.'

CHAPTER – 11 –

MIRIAM HYDE-ESHAR WAS THE FIRST of his guests to meet him in the airport arrivals hall. Taking Derek's arm, she said, 'My dear boy, I've only just heard about the terrible things that happened to you and that poor girl from that English newspaper; I do hope someone will soon face justice.'

'Unfortunately, it's not very likely. While the attempts on our lives are almost certainly the result of our investigations into rhino poaching, it's a regrettable fact that many of those in authority in this country are either corrupt or easily bribed. Nevertheless; thank you for your kind words.'

Walking with him over to the waiting area, she continued, 'You should know I have the greatest admiration for the excellent work you and your colleagues are doing to protect wildlife in this unique corner of Africa. And, while on the subject of wildlife,' she continued, 'I do hope you've not forgotten that Jacob Riley promised to take me on a private tour to see your resident black rhino and her calf?'

'Of course, we've not forgotten; it will be our pleasure; just don't let on to the other guests; Jacob doesn't want Dengezi to be the centre of attraction just yet.'

Following the orientation briefing for new guests, Derek took Jacob aside, 'Miriam reminded me of your promise to take her to see Dengezi and her calf, she was wondering when we might be able to do that.

'Tell you what, let's do it tomorrow. As soon as your guests are back from their early morning game walk, you and Blessing take her out in one of the game-viewing Land Rovers to look for Dengezi. With any luck, you'll be back in a few hours, and none of the other guests will be any the wiser.'

The rest of the guests were sitting down to a late breakfast when Miriam, Derek and Blessing drove out of the camp taking one of the lesser travelled back roads. 'Okay Blessing, where do you think we should start looking for Dengezi and her calf?'

'Inyoka waterhole *Numzaan*, that would be a good place to start; Etienne saw them there yesterday. If nothing else, we should be able to pick up her *spoor* in the mud.'

'Is it always this difficult to find this rhino and the little calf?' Miriam asked as they bounced over a rough stretch of the track.

'Finding her often depends on luck,' he replied, 'even though Dengezi tends to remain in the same area where she and the calf feel safe from predators and human intrusion, we sometimes draw a blank – but, who knows, today might be our lucky day.'

'Stop *Numzaan*, I see some *spoor*,' Blessing said jumping from the vehicle. He scouted on ahead and, waving Derek to follow him, set off at a blistering pace. Derek drove slowly, weaving around dense clumps of Delagoa thorn thickets and stunted marula.

'Typical habitat for a black rhino,' Derek said to Miriam, 'though not the sort of place you would want to travel through on foot.'

'Is Blessing taking a big risk just because I want to see this black rhino?' she asked.

'No, not really. Blessing has a sixth sense when it comes to dangerous game; look, he's running back to us now! I'll bet you he's seen something.'

'It's bad *Numzaan*, it's bad,' Blessing said as he jumped into the passenger seat next to Miriam, 'drive through there,' he said pointing towards a break in an almost impenetrable barrier of thorn thickets. As their Land Rover lurched over the rough ground between thickets, they entered a small clearing where, partially hidden by waist-high, dry grass, the hulking grey back of a rhino became visible.

'Oh, look!' Miriam whispered, 'Blessing has found her!'

'Oh, Christ!' Derek swore as he reached for his rifle clipped beneath the folded down windscreen, 'not again, dear God, not again! Miriam, please stay in the car.' Blessing retrieved his R1, and together the two men approached the rhino. It was Dengezi; though it was not easy to recognise her because of the gaping bloody wound that completely covered her head where she once carried her magnificent set of horns.

Alert to their approach, Dengezi made a soft, high pitched mewling sound as she struggled to raise her head. The savage attempts to chop out her horns and eyes had exposed the white bone of her upper jaw and nostrils, causing her laboured breath to froth in bloody bubbles. Choking back tears, Derek raised his rifle and fired two solid rounds into the massive head just above where her eyes once were. The huge bulk of the rhino trembled briefly as the massive head sank to the ground, wheezing out her last breath into the dust.

'The little one is dead too,' Blessing said pointing to the body of the calf lying close by, partially concealed in the grass. 'They were here perhaps only an hour ago; three, maybe four men. I can't see any bullet wounds on her body; so, I don't think they were shot.'

'Most likely they used a dart gun.'

'*Numzaan*, they cannot have gone far. We should get after them before they get out of the reserve.'

'First, I must take Miriam back to camp; it's not safe for her to be out here.'

'Go *Numzaan*; I will stay and look for their *spoor*.'

'Be careful Blessing, do not try to follow them, I will be back with help as fast as I can. I promise you; we will get these bastards. Stay safe my friend.' He ran back to the Land Rover, started it up and drove away rapidly saying to Miriam, 'We must hurry; I will explain as I drive.'

'My God Derek! I can't tell you how sorry I am. This must be awful for you. The baby calf too?' He could only nod in reply, his pain too deep for words as he struggled to think clearly. He had to contact Riley; he would know what to do. Riley would know how to organise a quick reaction force to cut off the poacher's retreat should they cross into the Kruger Park. Jamming on the brakes, he switched on the radio. 'Please God let the reception be good enough to get through to Riley's Camp,' he said aloud.

'Riley's Camp, Riley's Camp, come in please.' There was only static. Switching channels, he tried again, 'Riley's Camp, Riley's Camp, come in please.'

The radio crackled into life, 'Riley's Camp, who is this please?'

'Thank God June, is the boss there?'

'Derek is that you? Jacob's right here.'

'Boss, the bastards killed Dengezi and her calf not an hour ago. Blessing is still there; I'm bringing Miriam back to camp, we'll be there in less than fifteen minutes, we've got to get back to help Blessing. He thinks there are three or four of them and that they couldn't have gone far.'

'Drive as fast as you can, but be careful; we can't afford to have an accident. I will get things organised this end. Riley over and out.'

<hr/>

Jacob Riley, Etienne and his game scout Magezi were checking and loading their rifles as they pulled up. 'Have you got enough petrol?' Riley barked.

'Three-quarters of a tank Boss,' Derek replied as the men climbed into his vehicle while June helped Miriam over to the reception area.

'Drive as fast as you can, but try not to kill us. So, you are aware, I contacted Marius Steiner at Skukuza to ask for his help. Steiner heads up the Kruger Park's anti-poaching authority and has several four-man tactical response teams based at the larger camps. The team closest to us is at Satara, but unless they can get hold a helicopter, it will take them two to three hours to reach us.'

'They have access to a helicopter?'

'Yes, one of the last of the Agusta AW 109's that's still flying. This machine is currently in operation with South African Defence Force units posted along the Mozambique border; Steiner has promised to radio me if it is available. Failing the helicopter, I'm afraid we're on our own for the next little while.'

'I'm sorry to have brought such bad news Boss.'

'Nonsense! It's not your fault Derek. I imagine Blessing is pretty upset; he always had a soft spot for that cantankerous old cow. The calf as well you say?' Jacob Riley was silent for a few moments. 'Do you have any idea when they killed her?'

'I had to shoot her Boss,' Derek replied choking on his words. 'She was barely alive when we found her and suffering terribly. They probably darted her with a massive dose of M99 or something like it, before chopping off her horns. Come to think of it; the bastards probably ran off when they heard our Land Rover coming.'

'*Jirre*! I hope Blessing is being careful.'

'We're there Boss,' Etienne shouted, 'there she is, I can see her.' The three men jumped from the Land Rover even before Derek came to a stop.

'Where the hell is Blessing?' Riley muttered as he approached the grey bulk of the rhino. 'Scout around Magezi, see if you can find his *spoor*,' he said walking over to examine the dead calf. 'Christ! They even chopped out his tiny stub of a horn; I swear I will kill these bastards if we catch them.'

'Boss! Boss!' Magezi called from the edge of the clearing, '*Hau* Boss, it is Blessing. They have killed him!' Blessing Mananza, hung, unconscious on the ropes tying his body to the trunk of a thorn tree, blood dripping from numerous stabs and cuts to his torso, arms and face.

'He's been beaten and stabbed,' Jacob said checking Blessing's neck for a pulse, 'but he's still alive. Help me cut his down; Etienne, bring your first aid kit over here; we've got to stabilise him sufficiently for an EMS helicopter to fly him to Nelspruit. Derek, get on the radio and ask June to make the call. Tell her Etienne is on his way with Blessing to Riley's Camp; he should be there in fifteen.'

Together they watched as Etienne drove off with Blessing stretched out on a bench seat wrapped in blankets, 'Don't worry, he'll drive carefully,' Derek said to no one in particular.

'Tracks Magezi, get onto their tracks,' Jacob ordered, 'let's make sure these fucking bastards pay for what they did to Blessing!' The game scout set a blistering pace, heading east towards the Kruger Park boundary. 'Magezi are you sure these are their tracks?'

'*Yebo* Boss, there are three of them, they are running fast; now look they are bomb shelling!'

'What the hell does that mean Magezi?'

'It means they are splitting up Boss – they all run in different directions; it's an old terrorist trick used to confuse the police or security forces chasing them.'

'So, what should we do?'

'We split up as well Boss. I'll follow this one; he's continuing towards the Kruger Park boundary. If their quick reaction force shows up in time, they will help me cut him off. Boss, you and Derek should follow the other two who are heading west.'

'Right, let's get going,' Riley said, 'I don't want these murdering bastards to get away.'

'Shoot to kill Boss?' Derek asked grimly.

'Damn right; if they're carrying weapons, don't give them a chance to shoot you. Remember what they did to Blessing.' Derek followed Riley, matching pace with his steady loping run. Suddenly the two men they were following changed direction and turned north. 'Now where the hell are they going?'

'If they keep going in this direction Boss, they'll run straight into the Languleni River. With the river in full flood, I can't think why they would want to go that way, unless...'

'Unless what?'

'Unless they don't intend crossing the river and, instead, plan to follow the river all the way to the old Main Camp. The road to the old camp is partially overgrown, but is easily negotiated by a *bakkie* with four-wheel drive; I used it myself some time ago. My guess is they've arranged to meet up with someone with a vehicle at the old camp.'

'If that's the case, they'll get clean away.'

'Not if we can get back to our Land Rover; the policeman I met that day showed me an old, overgrown firebreak which, with a bit of luck, could put us in a good position to cut them off.' Retrieving their vehicle, it took Derek five long minutes of driving backwards and forwards to find the fire break, 'I'm fairly sure this is it,' he said, 'but I'm not certain.'

'We've nothing to lose,' Riley said, 'give it a try!'

After driving for ten minutes wondering whether they had made the right decision, they eventually came across the road that led up to the ridge and the old camp. Breathing a sigh of relief, Derek parked the Land Rover deep in the bush, where it couldn't be seen by anyone driving up or down the road. Carrying their rifles, the two men made their way through the old camp and, descending the slope towards the Languleni River, concealed themselves on a rocky outcrop overlooking the river bank. Fifteen long minutes ticked by without any sign of the poachers. 'I'm sorry Derek; it looks like we've drawn a blank. We'd better head back to camp and hope that Magezi has better luck.'

'Let's give it another five minutes Boss; it could be they think they've given us the slip and can see no reason to... Wait, can you hear voices?'

'Yes, by God I can. It sounds as though they're just waltzing along following the river. Careless bastards; hold your fire until they are right out in the open.' As they watched, three men emerged from the shelter of the riverine vegetation lining the river bank. A black man led the way, carrying an AK47 rifle and a bulky hessian sack; he was closely followed by a white man carrying a long wooden case and a bolt-action rifle, which he had slung over his shoulder. Bringing up the rear was another black man wearing the uniform of a South African Police sergeant, 'Where the hell did the policeman come from?' Riley whispered.

'I'll bet he's the driver of their getaway vehicle come out to meet them!'

'Shit! I know him. Unless I'm mistaken, it's that fucking policeman Dlamini.'

'He's the man I encountered the time I visited Main Camp. I thought it was suspicious, him sitting in his police Land Rover and doing nothing miles from anywhere. What should we do Boss?'

'I'm going to try and arrest the bastards! But watch them, if they make any attempt to escape, shoot them; the cop too if he tries to make a run for it.' Riley stood up and stepped out into the open, 'You're all under arrest,' he shouted, 'stay where you are, or we will shoot.'

The three men stopped where they were. 'I'm a policeman; you have no right to arrest me. Do you know who I am?' Dlamini spat.

'I know who you are and what you are. A poacher and a collaborator with murderers, not to mention a bloody disgrace to the police service.' The white man shouted something to his two companions as he dived for the shelter of a shallow donga. Drawing his pistol, Dlamini turned to follow firing a poorly aimed shot in the direction of Jacob Riley, narrowly missing him. In response, Derek fired two rounds from his R5 into the policeman's chest. The other poacher, who appeared to be having a problem with his weapon, dropped his AK47 and raised his hands in surrender. The white man, having gained the safety of the donga, fired three shots in rapid succession towards Jacob and Derek forcing them to retreat to the protection of the rocky outcrop.

'Sounds like he's using a bloody pistol,' Derek commented as the sounds of the shots died away, 'perhaps that hunting rifle he's carrying isn't loaded.'

'Put a few shots into the bank behind him; if nothing else, we can encourage him to keep his head down while we try to work our way around him.'

'No need,' Derek whispered, 'get ready for him when he jumps up.'

'How on earth…' Jacob muttered as Derek fired a round into the heel of the boot he could see sticking out in the open. Screaming in pain, the man turned to tend to his wounded foot exposing himself to Jacob's R5 rifle. Two shots, fired in quick succession, ended the standoff.

Jacob Riley and Derek Hamilton were detained and questioned in the Skoonspruit police station for three hours having to recount every detail of the day's events over and over again. 'I need to understand what led to the fatal shootings of Dawid Grossendahl, a farmer from the Northern Province and Josiah Dlamini, a sergeant in the South African Police Service,' Lieutenant Themba asked for the third time.

'They resisted my orders to lay down their weapons and surrender peacefully,' Jacob replied frustration evident in his voice. 'They knew they were guilty of the attempted murder of Blessing Mananza, a game scout in my employ and the poaching of two valuable rhinos.'

Their principal interrogator, Lieutenant Themba, while sympathetic to their predicament, made it quite clear that the shooting death of a SAPS sergeant would not be taken lightly by his superiors.

'I think we've told you everything a dozen times over,' Riley complained. 'You've got a captured poacher, Phineas Malema, a self-styled business man from Skoonspruit, who had the good sense to surrender. You have all their weapons, which, I've no doubt Dlamini supplied from police sources, including the Pax 22 tranquiliser gun and the CZ550 rifle carried by Grossendahl, together with the sack containing three sets of rhino horns. Whether he surrendered or not, I fully expect you to charge Malema to the fullest extent of the law. And the same goes to the other poacher, who is temporarily still alive.'

'Why do you say temporarily still alive, Mr Riley?' Themba asked.

'Because Lieutenant, one of my best men and four members of the Kruger Park's tactical response team are hot on his trail. Frankly, he hasn't a snowball's hope in hell of getting away. In the meantime, while my safari guides and I start looking for the carcases of the other two rhinos slaughtered by these murdering bastards, may I suggest you keep the three sets of horns safe in your evidence locker; I would hate for them to mysteriously disappear. However, before we go, I would like to have a chat with Malema before a lawyer appears to bail him out.'

'Only if I can be present and there's no physical violence.'

'I wouldn't dream of laying a finger on him; I just want to know what that bastard Grossendahl wanted from Blessing that they would be prepared to torture him to death.'

'I'd like to know the answer to that question myself,' Themba added as he escorted Jacob and Derek to Malema's cell.

Phineas Malema lay sprawled on the narrow bunk in the holding cell, an arrogant smile playing about his face. 'Oh! It's you people; I thought you were my lawyer coming to get me out of here. But that's not why you're here, is it? I thought not; so, let me save you the trouble, I do not intend answering any of your questions without my lawyer being present.'

'Don't worry,' Jacob said smiling, 'I only want to take your photo. I'm sure Blessing; he's the ranger you almost beat to death, would like to have something to remind him of you. Also, you might be interested to know Blessing once served with 32 Battalion in Angola, sometimes known as *Os Terriveis* or The Terrible Ones. I may be wrong, but I don't believe his many comrades will take too kindly to your treatment of him.'

'I was only doing what Grossendahl ordered me to do,' Malema said, his arrogant façade of self-assurance fading rapidly.

'I can't see them accepting that as much of an excuse. Thank you, Lieutenant, I've got all I need. Between you and I, this man is going to need more than a lawyer to save his bacon. If it's okay with you, I'd like to leave now and go and see how Blessing is doing.'

The last three days of Miriam's visit passed mostly without incident; though there was quiet rejoicing amongst the staffs at Riley's and Archer's Post Lodge when they received news of the death of the last poacher at the hands of the Kruger Park's tactical response team. Despite Jacob Riley's advice to the contrary, Derek insisted in driving his guests to the airport to catch their flights home or, as in Miriam's case, her flight to Johannesburg and on to Israel.

'What's next after Israel?' he asked.

'At this stage, I really can't say. A lot will depend on the outcome of a series of meetings and negotiations that will occupy my time for the next few weeks. With the recent passing of Shimon Peres, the prospects for peace between Israel and the Palestinian Territories appears to be even further out of reach. When I last spoke to Shimon, I promised him our foundation would do everything it could to further his dream of peace in the Holy Land. Sorry, I can't tell you much more than that until I've got all my ducks in a row. Anyway, this is where I get off,' she said walking towards the doorway marked security. 'Thank you, Derek, for being a good friend. You've made my visits to Languleni, despite the terrible tragedies you've suffered, one of the most memorable times of my life.'

CHAPTER – 12 –

THREE PEOPLE WERE LINED UP ahead of him at the only teller open that afternoon at his bank in town. Derek stared at the back of the white woman in the front of the line as she stepped up to the counter. His gaze took in her short, blond hair and shapely figure as she leaned forward to speak to the bank teller. He could not help noticing the dark bruises on her arms and on the back of her neck or how dirty her clothes were. Because there was something familiar about her, Derek watched as she spoke to the teller. Responding to something the teller said, the woman turned her head slightly and, opening her shoulder bag, reached in as if looking for something. He recognised her immediately; it was Debra Hanson.

'Oh My God!' Derek said to himself as he turned and walked quickly out of the bank. Not quite sure why he wanted to avoid her, he went to the parking lot where he had left his Land Rover and, getting in behind the wheel, watched and waited for her to leave the bank. A moment or two later, she emerged from the bank and walked briskly across the parking lot. They made eye contact simultaneously.

'Derek,' she said as she ran to his passenger side door, opening it and jumping in. Crouching low on the seat, she pleaded with him, 'Drive man, drive; please get me out of here before the cops come.'

Reacting instinctively, he started the Land Rover and pulled out into the sparse traffic. '*Jirre* Debra! Did you just rob that fucking bank?' he asked in disbelief, the enormity of the situation he had unwittingly placed himself in only now beginning to dawn on him.

'I had no choice. I've got no money; I can't even afford to buy food. That bastard Brian has taken everything; he screwed me over finished and *klaar*!'

'*Here God*, Debra, Jesus! What are we going to do now? The cops will be out looking for you at any minute; where are you staying?'

'Nowhere,' she replied looking straight ahead, 'I've been sleeping in the bush for three days now. Only last night two men tried to rape me but, thank God, I had my gun to scare them off. I just couldn't go on living like this any longer, so I decided to do something about it,' she said opening her handbag and producing a handful of rands. 'I had no idea tellers carried such a small amount of cash in their tills. I doubt I got enough for more than a few meals and maybe a night in a cheap motel; certainly not enough to start a new life somewhere far away from him. So much for the wages of crime,' she laughed and then began to cry.

'I'll try to take you somewhere where you'll be safe for the time being. Unfortunately, I've no idea where that might be.'

'Look, you don't need to get yourself involved in my troubles,' she said. 'I appreciate your help; but if they catch us, I'll tell them I forced you at gunpoint to help me escape.'

He smiled at her, 'Thanks, but I'm involved now anyway. If it's any consolation to you, I never liked that husband of yours; I've always suspected he was mixed up in this poaching business.'

'You don't know the half of it,' she said pointing to her shoulder bag, 'before I left, I helped myself to all of the papers he kept in the safe in his office. I think you'll find they make interesting reading.'

'That husband of yours has a lot to answer for, but first I think you should get yourself cleaned up.'

'I'm sorry,' she apologised, 'I must look a real mess.'

'Don't worry about that; Mrs Preller is out of town today, so it'll be quite safe for me to drop you off at my *rondavel*. You'll be okay there while I go into town and pick up a few things you're going to need.'

◄—◆—►

'I'd like to draw a thousand dollars from my foreign currency account,' Derek said to the assistant manager now manning the teller counter at his bank.

'It may take a few moments for me to make the necessary arrangements, Mr Hamilton. You see, we're in a bit of a muddle at the moment, we were robbed this morning, and the police haven't arrived as yet.'

'With so much crime around these days, they must be rushed off their feet. But I'm sure they'll be along soon.' Stopping at the Skoonspruit Mall, Derek used some of the money to buy a small suitcase, a lightweight jacket, two pairs of slacks and blouses, panties, socks, *takkies* that he hoped would fit her, and a pair of large sunglasses along with a red baseball cap. Then he made a quick phone call. Returning to his rondavel, Derek handed the clothing over to Debra. 'Please change into these things,' he said, 'I hope I've got your sizes more or less correct. Be as quick as you can; we've got at least a two-hour drive to Nelspruit ahead of us.'

'Nelspruit!' she protested, 'why can't I just stay here for a few days and wait for the hue and cry to die down?'

'Because sooner or later Mrs Preller or someone else is bound to notice you are living here; then we may find ourselves facing questions we would rather not have to answer.'

'Derek, please don't think I don't appreciate all you're doing, but I don't believe I've enough money to manage in Nelspruit on my own. Also, it's just the sort of town where my husband is bound to start looking for me. Honestly, I'd rather take my chances and stay here until I can make better arrangements.'

'No,' he replied, 'I've got it all worked out. I'm going to give you enough money for a motel tonight in Nelspruit and your bus fare to some good friends of my parents in Lydenburg. Jack and Lydia run the Armstrong's Rest bungalows just outside the town, I've already spoken to them, and you are good for a month's accommodation. I've told them you are an old friend who is experiencing some marital difficulties; they are a discrete couple and won't ask too many questions. This will give you plenty of time to decide what you're going to do next.'

As they headed out of Skoonspruit to join the R40 highway, he had no option but to pull up behind the two other cars already stopped at a police roadblock. '*Jirre!* They've caught us,' Debra said, fear evident in her voice.

'Pull your cap down and keep your sunglasses on. Stay calm and leave the talking to me.' He watched as two policemen approached the car in front of them, the constable talking to the passenger and the police sergeant to the driver. 'When the policeman comes up to your side, roll down your window, take off your sunglasses and smile at him.' As the police sergeant came up to his window, Derek looked up and smiled, 'Is there anything wrong Sergeant?'

'No, Sir, just a routine traffic stop,' he replied and waved them on.

Once on the open road, Derek breathed a sigh of relief. 'If you don't mind me saying so, I'll never understand why on earth you put up with that husband of yours for so long?'

Debra did not answer right away. Instead, she stared out of her side window for the longest time then, as if reaching a decision, she turned and faced him. 'I come from a poor family in Johannesburg. My father once had a good job on the railways, but when de Klerk handed the country over to Mandela and the ANC, he lost his job. No matter how hard he tried, he never managed to find work again as all the jobs, skilled and unskilled, were reserved for blacks. Black economic empowerment, I think they called it. Anyway, ashamed he could no longer support his family, my father killed himself. I had just started high school at the time, but, to help my ailing mother and two younger siblings, I had to leave. The only work I could find was as a barmaid in a fancy nightclub. That was where I met Brian Hanson; he was studying veterinary sciences at the university. I moved in with him and, despite taking precautions, I became pregnant. Six months before my baby was due, Brian reluctantly agreed to marry me.'

'What happened to your child?'

'At first, Brian wanted me to keep the child, but five months into my pregnancy, he accused me of being unfaithful and denied the child was his. Then one night, he beat me so severely I lost the baby and my ability to have any more children. I tried to leave him, but I was penniless, and my mother was in no position to help me. So, I stayed and endured the beatings and abuse. Four days ago, while in a drunken rage, he beat me so severely, I thought he was going to kill me. I ran away that night and hid in the bush so he couldn't find me. You know the rest of the story.'

He reached out and took her hand. 'You're safe now. You have my word you will never have to go back to him again. Please do as I ask and go to my friends in Lydenburg; stay with them as long as you like and get your life back in order.'

As the miles slipped by, fatigue overwhelmed Debra who slept most of the way, resting her head on his shoulder. She awoke with a start as he slowed down, 'Just going through White River,' he replied to her anxious question, 'we'll be in Nelspruit shortly. If it's okay with you, I'll book you into the Starlight Motel; it's only a short taxi ride to the bus depot. Once you're settled in, we'll go out and get something to eat – I imagine you must be hungry?'

'After a hot shower, I could eat a horse.'

'If it's all the same to you, I was thinking more along the lines of a good sirloin steak, a mixed greens salad and a bottle of a good red wine. I'm fond of horses, but not in that way!'

The restaurant recommended by the motel proprietor was every bit as good as he promised. Their steaks were done to perfection, and the wine Debra selected, outstanding. Relaxing after the meal, they sat silently, sipping on their wine, each lost in their thoughts. 'May I interest you in the dessert menu?' their waiter asked.

Both smiled and shook their heads. 'But I will have another glass of that most excellent wine,' Derek said, 'truly Debra I never took you to be a connoisseur of fine wines.'

'Thank you for saying that. I'm glad to hear my misspent youth dispensing wines in a nightclub was not entirely wasted. While on the subject of fine wines, I hope you will not be offended if I said you've had a bit too much to drink to even think of driving back to Skoonspruit tonight.'

'You're quite right; I do feel a little light-headed; anyway, I'm sure the proprietor at the Starlight can find another room for me.'

'I don't think you need waste your money on another room. I noticed the couch in my room also serves as a foldout bed; I won't mind if you'd like to make use of it. I'm sure we can find enough blankets and pillows to go around.'

It was close to midnight when they left the restaurant to walk the short distance back to the Starlight; Debra having persuaded him to leave his Land Rover in the restaurant parking lot. Their arms linked around each other, Derek fumbled with the key card to open their door, inserting it in upside down before finally getting it right. Pushing the door open, they stumbled into the room and, embracing in a passionate kiss, tugged urgently at each others' clothes.

Taking the initiative, Derek picked her up and carried her into the bedroom. Seating her on the edge of the bed, he managed to undo the belt on her slacks and was attempting to undo her zipper, when she pushed him away, 'Let me do it for you,' she said huskily, 'you've no idea how long I've waited for this moment.' Raising her bottom up off the bed, she slipped out of her slacks and pulled off her panties. 'Now it's my turn,' she said as she loosened his belt and pulled his trousers down around his knees. Sitting up, she reached out and, pulling his shorts aside, allowed his erection to spring free. 'Oh my God!' she breathed, 'you have the most beautiful cock I've ever seen; can I taste him first before we make love?'

'It will be my pleasure,' he said holding her head as she attempted to take all of him into her mouth.

'Come on, I can't wait any longer,' she said laying back on the bed and pulling him down on top of her, 'make love to me now.' He did as she asked. 'Oh my God! That feels so good, Derek, I'm coming, I'm coming.' She gave a convulsive moan and, throwing her arms around his neck, she held him tightly and kissed him, 'Oh wow!' she exclaimed laughing, 'that was so good, but much too quick; probably because we're both a little drunk. Darling Derek, it's your turn next, so let's get undressed and do it again.'

Derek awoke with the sunlight streaming into the room. He reached over to Debra's side of the bed intending to pull her closer, but she wasn't there. Alarmed, he sat up and looked anxiously around the room before noticing the closed bathroom door. 'I know exactly how she's feeling,' he thought to himself as he collapsed back on the bed, his head on her pillow enjoying the faint traces of her perfume.

'How are you doing in there darling? Are you coming back to bed,' he called out, 'it's lonely out here.' There was no reply, so he kicked off the covers and, padding over to the bathroom door, pushed it open. The bathroom was cold and in darkness; there was no sign of Debra anywhere. Assuming she must have gone for a walk, he pulled on his clothes and was about to grab his keys off the dresser when he saw the note.

'Darling Derek, please find it in your heart to forgive me for running out on you like this. I'm doing it because I don't want to cause you any more trouble than I already have. It would be best for both of us if you forgot all about me, though I know I will never forget you and the wonderful night we spent

together. I put all the papers I took from Brian's safe on the dresser for you to use as you see fit. Once you have looked through them you will better understand why I need to get as far away as I possibly can; the people he's involved with are extremely dangerous. Please be careful. I will never forget you, love Debra.

Derek sat on the edge of the bed re-reading her note. Then he paged through the papers she had removed from Hanson's safe. For the first time, he began to understand the full extent of Hanson's involvement with Schoveldt International and the now deceased game rancher, Grossendahl. The hollow sinking feeling in his stomach convinced him that Debra's fears for their safety were well founded.

Determined not to lose her, he went at once to the motel office and asked the manager for the name of the taxi company that picked her up. Retrieving his Land Rover from the restaurant's parking lot, he drove around to Bharat Taxi's where he got to speak to the driver who collected her up from the motel. 'I took her out to the airport, sir,' he said waggling his head from side to side, 'the Memsahib was most pleasant, sir, she told me you might be asking me about her and begged me not to tell you where she was going.'

'Here's fifty rands, will it loosen your tongue?'

'Oh, indeed, sir, it will. The Memsahib said you are a most kind and generous gentleman, but unfortunately, other than telling me she was travelling on the early morning flight to Johannesburg, she did not tell me anything more.'

Returning to the Starlight and settling the bill, Derek headed over to the Nelspruit Hospital to see how Blessing was doing. 'You'll find him out on the *stoep* and, in answer to your question, he's making excellent progress. For a man of his age, he's as strong as the proverbial ox. Have a word with Doctor Fuchs; I wouldn't be at all surprised if he'd allow you to take him home.'

Blessing rose to his feet as soon as he saw Derek approaching, '*Hau Numzaan*, I hope you have come to take me back to Riley's Camp, I've been in this hospital for too long.'

'I had a word with Doctor Fuchs on my way here. He is satisfied with your progress and said he'll be glad to see the back of you; you're too much of a distraction for the young nurses.' On the drive back to Skoonspruit,

Derek handed him some of the papers Debra had taken from Hanson's safe. 'I think you'll find these interesting reading. It seems our veterinarian was mixed up in a lot of crooked enterprises including the supply of Pax 22 tranquiliser guns to people like Dlamini, Grossendahl and Malema just to mention a few.'

'*Numzaan*, if you take these to the police, do you think they will do anything?'

'I believe Lieutenant Themba and Colonel Dlamini will do the best they can; unfortunately, the people mentioned in Hanson's files are small fry; it's the bigger fish we need to be concentrating on.'

Colonel Vusi Dlamini was nevertheless delighted to take delivery the papers Debra had removed from Brian Hanson's safe. Riffling through them he smiled up at Derek, 'There's more than enough here to put Hanson away for a very long time and to initiate investigations into some local politicians and game ranchers, not to mention our old friends, Schoveldt International. Though, as I'm sure you realise, a lot of this is probably not going to stick; particularly as it appears his wife, I think her name is Debra, may have been the woman who forged her husband's signature on a series of cheques, cleaning out his bank accounts. Fortunately for the perpetrator, whoever she is, the bank's surveillance cameras were down that week.'

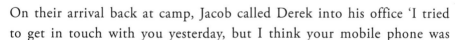

On their arrival back at camp, Jacob called Derek into his office 'I tried to get in touch with you yesterday, but I think your mobile phone was switched off?'

'It was Boss; I was down in Nelspruit to see how Blessing was doing. As you may already know, he's well on the mend and is already back here in camp.'

'Glad to hear that; in a few weeks' time, and if all goes to plan, we're going to need all hands-on deck.'

'I take it something has come up?'

'You can say that again. After lights out tonight, I want you, Dennis and Etienne to meet me in my office and I will bring you all up to speed. With that out of the way,' Jacob smiled, 'I'd now like you to tell me all about the papers Debra pinched from Brian Hanson's safe; you know, the ones she passed on to you in Nelspruit.'

PART TWO

Chapter - 13 -

'WHAT I WANT TO TALK to you all about this evening is highly confidential, and I must ask you not to discuss it with anyone other than the five of us present,' Jacob said including his wife June as she joined them. 'Miriam Hyde-Eshar, as you all know, is a frequent visitor and supporter of us here in Languleni. What you may not know is that Miriam is also involved in a peace foundation set up many years ago by her late husband for the advancement of peace in the Middle East, specifically between Israel and the Palestinian Territories.'

'I remember her saying something about that when I took her to the airport the last time,' Derek interjected. 'Knowing Miriam, she's probably got them around a table and is making them sign a peace treaty as we speak!'

'You're closer to the truth than you realise,' Jacob continued, 'actually, she's planning to invite the Israeli and Palestinian prime ministers to an informal round table conference here in Languleni in ten days' time.'

There was a stunned silence. 'Are you serious?' Dennis asked, 'they're coming here to Languleni? Where on earth are they going to stay and why here; surely they'd be going to Johannesburg or somewhere like that?'

'Now it's not definite yet,' Jacob continued, 'but, from what Miriam told me before she returned to Israel, she hopes to persuade both prime ministers to spend a few days in seclusion before the start of a major peace conference scheduled to take place in Geneva in two weeks' time. And what could be more secluded than a few days in the middle of our winter season right here in Languleni.'

'You've got that right,' Etienne chimed in, 'I was speaking to Greta Richter at Archer's Post yesterday, and she told me that it was so quiet she and Hans were considering taking a few weeks off to visit family in Europe. Archer's Post is that where they'd be staying if all of this happens?' he asked.

'That's what Miriam and I have in mind. The accommodation is first class and, if Greta and Hans are on board, the food and service could not be faulted.'

'What about their entourage; these people never go anywhere without a host of bodyguards and all manner of support personnel,' Derek said.

'Miriam plans to ask both prime ministers to limit their staff to the bare minimum to avoid attracting the attention of the world press. Of course, she hopes they will both bring along their wives to add a softer touch to the serious side of their deliberations.'

'What do we have to do now Boss?' Derek asked.

'Nothing. It's all up to Miriam and her negotiators. If her idea gets the go ahead, I imagine we can expect visits from embassy and security personnel from both sides to check us out; in the meantime, it's business as usual.'

Jacob's prediction was correct. A week later, two security teams arrived, hours apart, at Skoonspruit Airport to inspect the facilities at Archer's Post and to interview the staff who would be looking after the guests. 'They were laughing and talking together,' Derek observed. 'I never thought Israelis and Palestinians could get along so well in such a short time!'

'Bodes well for Miriam's initiative,' Jacob said adding pensively, 'it would have a nice ring to it though, don't you think, *The Languleni Accord*. No doubt about it, it would put us on the world map! Now to business. From what I understand, both delegations will be travelling, together with Miriam, on a specially chartered Swiss Air flight to Johannesburg. On their arrival, both delegations will spend two nights at their respective embassies in Pretoria while Miriam will continue on, joining us here Languleni. Two days later, both delegations will fly to Skoonspruit Airport on two chartered Gulfstream aircraft.'

'Will we be there to meet them when they arrive?' Derek asked.

'Absolutely. The delegation will disembark in a secluded area of the airport, where we will pick them up in four Land Rovers for the drive to Archer's Post. Both prime ministers will be accompanied by their wives, personal advisers and close protection officers and will be driven directly to Archer's Post. Lesser functionaries will be accommodated here in Riley's Camp.'

'What about game viewing,' Dennis asked, 'will they going out on game drives the same as regular visitors?'

'While they'll probably get see a lot of game around the waterhole from the observation deck at Archer's Post, Miriam has asked us to arrange a few early morning and afternoon game drives for the duration of their visit. Etienne will take the prime ministers and their wives out on their morning drive on the first day; Dennis will do the afternoon drive and Derek the following morning. After that, we should have a good idea what other outings they would like us to arrange. Miriam may or may not wish to join her guests on these outings, but you can expect their security personnel will be accompanying their charges every step of the way. Well, it's getting late, so I suggest we leave it at that. Now I'm sure you all have questions, but let's keep them for another meeting tomorrow.'

Derek and his fellow safari guides were sitting patiently in their Land Rovers alongside four South African Police cars at the designated area waiting for the aircraft carrying the Israeli and Palestinian delegations to land. He glanced up as two Gulfstream G550's circled low over the town before touching down and taxiing up to the four Land Rovers waiting to pick up the VIP guests. Fifteen minutes later, led by the police cars with sirens blaring and blue lights flashing, the small convoy drove through the main entrance gate of the Languleni Game Reserve.

Their task complete, the police escort fell back and busied themselves closing off all roads leading in and out of the game reserve for the next three days, effectively sealing off the VIP guests from the outside world. Derek's task, as explained to him in the final briefing, was to make sure the guests arrived safely at Archer's Post, their journey through Languleni unchallenged by elephants or large herds of buffalo.

'Miriam has asked me to pass on her thanks to you all for a job well done,' Jacob said addressing the safari guides gathered in his office. She tells me the prime ministers and their wives are delighted with the facilities at Archer's Post and the visit, late yesterday afternoon, by a pride of seven lions to the waterhole in front of the lodge. Apparently, it took her quite some time to convince her guests that these were indeed wild lions and not a gaggle of tame lions brought here for their entertainment!'

'How on earth did she manage to convince them?' Etienne asked.

'When the pride pulled down on old buffalo bull that ill-advisedly arrived at the waterhole, they needed no further convincing,' Jacob smiled. 'All we have to do now is get through the next few days without any problems, and we are home and dry.'

'How did your game drive go this morning,' Dennis asked Etienne, 'did the bodyguards invite themselves along?'

'You're going to encounter them wherever our VIP guests go; they're only doing their job,' Derek interjected.

'If I may answer your question Dennis,' Jacob said, 'everything went off without a hitch on the game drive this morning. Now don't forget you're up next with their outing later this afternoon and Derek, you're on for tomorrow morning.'

'Anything further on the online threats made to Miriam or her foundation for organising this peace initiative before the Geneva conference?' Derek asked.

'I'm not aware of any specific threats made here in South Africa, but that's not to say no one is planning anything. As Miriam has often said, terrorist groups such as Hezbollah and Hamas abound in the Middle East, and the prospect of a peace deal between the Israelis and the Palestinians flies against their most dearly held beliefs. The security of our guests must always be uppermost in our minds.'

Dennis Middlebrook parked the game viewing Land Rover at the rear entrance to the Archer's Post lodge. 'I'm here to take the prime ministers and their wives on their afternoon game drive,' he announced to the Israeli bodyguard who stopped him from going up the steps and into the lodge itself.

'It's okay Dennis,' Miriam said appearing at the top of the steps, 'the prime ministers will be with you shortly; their wives, however, have decided not to go on the game drive this afternoon.'

'What about them,' Dennis asked, gesturing towards the Israeli and Palestinian bodyguards now standing together at the top of the steps, 'are they coming on the drive as well?'

'They go everywhere the two prime ministers go; I thought you knew that,' Miriam replied.

'Of course. I'm sorry, I shouldn't have asked.'

'No need to apologise, son; just make sure you show our guests lots of wildlife.'

'Ma'am, before you go, I want you to know how much I appreciate all you have done for me personally and for everyone else here in Languleni. However, you of all people must realise we can't always control everything that happens in our lives.'

Ignoring his odd remark, Miriam turned and greeted the Israeli and Palestinian prime ministers as they emerged from the lodge, 'Good afternoon gentlemen, your safari guide Dennis is ready and waiting. I hope you enjoy your drive.'

CHAPTER − 14 −

ELPING THE ISRAELI AND PALESTINIAN prime ministers take their seats in the front row directly behind Dennis, the two bodyguards walked around to climb into their seats in the tiered back row of the game viewing Land Rover. Convinced the situation presented his best, and possibly only opportunity to save the lives of his parents and his fiancé, Dennis reached under his seat and pulled out a loaded and cocked automatic pistol. Moving swiftly before the bodyguards could react, he shot the Israeli prime minister in the centre of his chest then, shifting his aim, he fired his second shot at the Palestinian prime minister, only grazing his arm as the man turned away trying to avoid his attacker.

As if shocked by the enormity of his actions, Dennis placed the barrel of the pistol against his right temple and pulled the trigger. He died instantly, his brains splattered over the front seat of the Land Rover as the pistol slipped from his hand and fell to the floor.

The sound of the shots and Miriam's screams brought the other security officers rushing out of the lodge, weapons drawn. 'All clear,' the Israeli security officer shouted as he examined Dennis's lifeless body slumped over in the front seat, 'the shooter is down. See to the prime minister,' he added as the Israeli prime minister struggled to sit up in his seat.

'I'm all right,' the prime minister shouted to his bodyguard, 'I'm not hurt, my vest stopped the bullet; please attend to the Palestinian prime minister, he's been injured.'

'It's only a flesh wound to his arm,' the Palestinian security officer said as he placed a compression bandage on the prime minister's arm. 'Who the hell is that man,' the security officer asked pointing to Dennis's body in the driver's seat, 'how is it he got so close to the prime ministers. Was he not checked out?'

'He's one of the Languleni safari guides; your people checked them all out last week,' Miriam said shaking with emotion as tears streamed down her face. 'I can't believe he did this; I was speaking to him just a moment ago. Perhaps he is ill; I don't know what to say or think. I'm so sorry, I'm so sorry.'

'My dear lady,' the Israeli prime minister comforted her as one of his security officers helped him inside the lodge, 'there's no way any blame for this unfortunate incident could be attributed to your foundation or to the people who run this amazing place. I can assure you my Palestinian counterpart and I are, unfortunately, quite used to being the target of extremists of one stripe or another. I'm just grateful our security people insisted we wear bulletproof vests whenever we left the lodge.'

The sight of a Land Rover driving fast up the track from the direction of Riley's Camp, causing the security officers gathered around a few anxious moments. 'Don't be alarmed, it's Jacob Riley,' Miriam assured them, even though she couldn't think of a single reason why they should accept her assurances. 'Jacob, thank God you're here,' she called out to him, 'something terrible has happened …'

'I know, I just got off the radio with Hans Richter on my way up here. He told me what happened. I find it almost impossible to believe Dennis was responsible for this terrible business. He's been with us here in Languleni for over five years; I would have trusted him with my life. I can only think someone must have got to him; but how, when or where I can't imagine.'

'Mr Prime Minister,' Miriam said addressing the Israeli leader, 'I expect you and the Palestinian prime minister will now want to bring an end to your deliberations?'

'Absolutely not. That's precisely what the people behind this atrocity are hoping for; preferably with one or both of us leaving in body bags. But that's not going to happen. I'm sure my friend the Palestinian prime minister will agree with me on this, our meeting here in the wilds of Africa is too important to allow the terrorists to succeed. No, I believe we will stay and continue as though nothing has happened. However, my dear lady, not a word of this unfortunate incident must reach the media; it is most important our discussions here are not compromised in any way by this event.'

'Unfortunately,' Jacob said, 'because a man is dead, this matter must be reported to the police.'

'Of course,' Miriam said, regaining her composure, 'bearing in mind his death was the result of suicide while of unsound mind.'

'Let me get Derek up here,' Jacob replied, 'he was with the police service for many years and should be able to give us some unofficial advice on our best course of action.'

'I have no idea what might have motivated Dennis to do this. God only knows who or what put him up to it. He was a level-headed, reliable safari guide and, I believed, a personal friend. And where the hell did he get hold of that gun?' Derek wondered.

'Unfortunately, not a very difficult thing to do these days,' Jacob said. 'I recognised the pistol he used as an old Astra .38, most commonly employed in hold-ups; I expect we will find all its serial numbers have been filed off.' Taking Derek to one side, Jacob continued, 'Based on your advice, I phoned Lieutenant Themba at Skoonspruit to report that a staff member had apparently committed suicide. Barring any problems or delays on the road, he should be here within the hour; so, may I suggest we use whatever time we have left to get our stories straight.'

As the police service Land Rover pulled up at the rear entrance of the Archer's Post Lodge, Lieutenant Themba emerged closely followed by Colonel Vusi Dlamini of the Hawks. 'Wherever you go Derek,' Dlamini said with a smile, 'you seem to have a knack for attracting trouble.'

'Not guilty on this occasion Colonel,' Derek replied, 'I was miles away when this unfortunate incident occurred.'

'Suicide you say?' Lieutenant Themba asked trying to assert his authority over what he believed to be a local case well within his jurisdiction. 'I'll need to interview anyone who may be able to come up with any ideas why this young man would want to take his own life.'

'Of course, Lieutenant,' Jacob said, 'Derek, Miriam Hyde-Eshar and I are the people you will need to interview. The lounge in the lodge is at your disposal as our overseas guests are still out on their evening game drive.'

'Ah yes! Your foreign guests; I assume the two Gulfstream aircraft parked at the airport belong to them. Were any of these guests present when this incident occurred?'

'No, fortunately, they weren't. Etienne had already left with them on their evening game drive when I heard the sound of the shot and discovered this poor man lying on the ground.'

'And the weapon, where was that found?'

'Beside his body, of course!'

'Any idea why this young man might have committed suicide?'

'I'm sorry Lieutenant, I can't help you there. No one here can think of any reason why he would wish to take his own life. To all intents and purposes, he was a well-adjusted young man, recently engaged, I believe, to a young lady in Johannesburg.'

'I will require all the information you can give me on the deceased; the name and address of his parents and his fiancé will do for starters.'

'Just so you are aware Lieutenant,' Jacob said, 'I intend sending a telegram to Mr Middlebrook's parent's address in Johannesburg as soon as I return to my office at Riley's Camp.'

⊰◈⊱

'Derek,' Vusi Dlamini said taking him aside, 'I trust this unfortunate incident will not unduly upset your overseas VIP visitors?'

'We sincerely hope not. It's most important these deliberations continue without outside distractions.'

'You have no need to worry; I'm not likely to reveal their identities or their countries of origin.'

'I'm not in the least bit worried Vusi. I know you'll keep this information confidential, given the international ramifications such a leak would cause. Though I must say, I'm a little surprised an apparent suicide should attract the attentions of a colonel in the Hawks?'

Vusi laughed. 'No, my friend, it doesn't; I just saw the opportunity to hitch a ride with Themba to warn you about a possible threat to your well-being.'

'Another threat? Truly Vusi, what is it now? Another snake, or a bunch of hand grenades tied to my car door; I'm almost getting used to this.'

'I'm sure you remember your veterinary friend, Brian Hanson?'

'The one whose wife emptied his safe and then his bank account,' Derek asked with a smile.

'The same. Early yesterday morning, we pulled Hanson's badly beaten body out of the Ga-Selati River. It would appear his bosses, whoever they might be, did not take too kindly to the fact that he allowed documents of a confidential nature to be so easily removed from his care.'

'Quite understandable, I would think.'

Vusi frowned, 'I don't believe you are taking this business seriously enough,' he said. 'Now that we've started making arrests based on much of the information gleaned from Hanson's files, there are a lot of unhappy people in high places and, as you may realise, unhappy people in high places can be very dangerous.'

'I've spoken with our all guests,' Miriam said, 'regarding the terrible incident which occurred this morning. They have confirmed their intention to extend their itinerary by a further two days.'

'That's good news,' Jacob said to the small group meeting in his office late that night, 'so, it's business as usual; well, almost as usual. Derek, you and Etienne will now handle all the game drives until all our VIP guests leave and I will arrange with the police to provide an escort for them on their journey to the airport on the morning of their departure. Miriam, is there anything else we need to cover?'

'Yes, there is. Both prime ministers, realising the South African Police will not be investigating this matter beyond Dennis's suicide, have informed me that their external security services are duty bound to mount their own independent investigations.'

'And what are the implications for us?' Jacob asked.

'Both prime ministers have assured me their investigators will only be interested in finding out who was behind this attempt and how they, whoever they are, recruited Dennis Middlebrook. From what both men tell me, such information may be useful in preventing similar attempts in the future.'

'So, what are we looking at here? Squads of secret service agents poking around Languleni, asking questions to which we can't provide the answers?'

'The prime ministers assure me these would be low key investigations;

no more than one or two agents, primarily focussing on the crime itself. And, before you ask, I inquired as to who would bear the costs of these investigations and was assured that each respective government would cover all expenses incurred by their agents. You should also know that I'm providing a very generous allowance to assist the Israeli investigators should their assignment take them further afield,' she added.

'In that case, please assure them of our fullest cooperation.'

'One last thing though; when the Israeli prime minister heard of Derek's experience as a former member of the South African Police Service, together with the fact that he briefly trained in Israel, he asked if Derek might be permitted to assist their investigators while they're in the country.'

'I don't see why not,' Jacob said, 'it's our quiet season, so, providing Derek is willing, their request has my approval.'

Chapter – 15 –

A FAX CONFIRMING THE ESTIMATED ARRIVAL time of the Israeli investigators at Skoonspruit Airport landed on Jacob Riley's desk. 'It looks like they'll be here around midday tomorrow,' he said calling Derek through to his office, 'you'd better make arrangements to drive to the airport to pick them up.'

'Any idea who they are and how many?'

'If I can take the Israeli prime minister at his word, there shouldn't be more than two. Most likely hard-boiled secret service agents twice your age, I wouldn't wonder. You'd better make sure there are a lot of beers in the fridge.'

South African Airways flight SA1227 arrived on time from Johannesburg. Derek stood near the luggage carousel holding up the usual Riley's Camp sign. He studied the mixed group of passengers as they selected their bags from the pile circling on the carousel, trying to see if he could spot the investigators before they found him. As the stream of passengers dwindled, then stopped altogether, Derek began to believe they had either missed their flight, or the investigation had been cancelled. He was about to leave when he saw a female passenger, emerge from the arrivals door and head towards the carousel where she picked up the last bag.

She wore her ash blonde hair shoulder length with a huge pair of sunglasses, of a style usually seen on the French Rivera, covering her eyes. She had on a smart pair of khaki slacks, a black loose-fitting blouse and carried a khaki jacket over her arm. Looking around, she saw his sign and walked briskly towards him. 'Derek Hamilton! I can't believe it's you. When I saw your name in the report I thought it too much of a coincidence to be true; so, I didn't get my hopes up that you were the same Derek Hamilton

I once trained in Israel.' She dropped her bag and, removing her sunglasses, put her arms around his neck and kissed him.

'Hello, Avital. Wasn't your hair dark when we said goodbye that day at Ben Gurion Airport?'

'That was a lifetime ago,' she replied, 'and, for your information, it's a blond wig; all part of my plan to arrive incognito.'

'And you're still wearing my favourite perfume, Desert Citron; I like that.'

'Is there somewhere we can go and talk? So much has happened since we last saw each other.'

'Isn't anyone else joining you?'

'No, it's just me.'

'Come on then; we can talk while I drive; it's a good hour to Riley's Camp where you'll be staying.' He took her bag and led her out of arrivals and across the parking lot to his Land Rover.

'Have my counterparts from the Palestinian Security Services arrived yet?' she asked.

'Not to my knowledge; yours is the only organisation that has contacted us so far.'

As Derek opened the passenger side door for her, she said to him, 'You know I followed your adventures in Somalia and died a thousand deaths when I heard on the grapevine of your kidnapping by al-Shabab. If the stories I heard were true, you were fortunate to escape. Rumours at the time credited the CIA for getting you out while your MI5 girlfriend sat on her hands.'

He smiled. 'You should know better than to listen to rumours and gossip.'

'Then,' ignoring his comment, she continued, 'you dropped off the radar screen after your escape, and no one I contacted had the faintest idea where you were or what you were doing. So, you can imagine how surprised I was to see your name mentioned in the report on the attempted assassination of the two prime ministers.'

'That's enough about me,' he said, 'let's talk about you instead. If you don't mind me asking, did you eventually marry the guy you were engaged to when we spent the night at Shah-lome after visiting the Roman ruins in the Negev desert?'

'I'm surprised you remember all of that. Especially as we never made love as I think we both hoped we would.' She was silent for a moment. 'A month after I dropped you off at Ben Gurion, my fiancé achieved his lifelong dream of serving with Sayaret Matkal, then, two months later, he was killed engaging Hamas terrorists crossing into Israel from Gaza.'

'I'm sorry Avi, I truly am.'

'Sorry we didn't make love that night or sorry my fiancé was killed?'

'That's not fair,' he replied, 'you know very well what I mean.' She did not speak again until they pulled up at the entrance gate to Languleni.

'I had no idea,' Avi began, 'this Languleni of yours was so well protected by armed guards and high fences; surely that would have provided a high degree of security for the prime ministerial meetings?'

'Probably one of the features Miriam Hyde-Eshar used to convince both parties it was safe for them to meet here; that combined with the mistaken belief that no one could have had any advance knowledge of the meeting.'

'And that's the crux of the whole matter; someone obviously had sufficient advance knowledge to enable them to recruit that man Middlebrook to assassinate both prime ministers.'

'That's what I'm hoping we're going to find out,' Derek added. 'By the way,' he asked, 'have you ever seen an elephant close up?'

'Oh, my God! An elephant, where?'

'On your side, as we come around this bend.' Derek was just showing off; he knew where he had earlier seen Old One Tusk picking up the fruit under a marula tree, so he stopped within twenty feet of her so Avi could get a good look. As he hoped, she was terrified.

'Is it safe to be so close?' she asked nervously.

'Oh! This is nothing, wait until we encounter her on a walk; only then will you be able to appreciate her power and size.' Avi did not reply.

Derek took his time on the drive to Riley's Camp, frequently stopping to allow Avi the opportunity to enjoy the wildlife that, because it was so much of an everyday occurrence to him, he hardly seemed to notice anymore. Her squeals of delight at every new sighting pleased him so much that he was sorry when the *rondavels* of the camp were finally in sight. 'This is so much nicer than I could ever have imagined,' she said as he parked the Land

Rover outside the camp office. 'I hope you realise how fortunate you are to live and work in this Garden of Eden.'

'If you carry on like that, my boss will come to believe all his employees would be only too pleased to work for nothing. Talking about my boss, let's go through to his office so you can meet him.' Jacob Riley stood as Derek ushered Avi through into his office. 'Boss, I'd like you to meet Avital Blum, she's the investigator sent by the Israeli Government to inquire into the attempt on the lives of the Israeli and Palestinian prime ministers.'

'Please call me Avi,' she said stepping forward and shaking Jacob's hand. 'I should correct something Derek just said; I'm not here on behalf of the Israeli Government; rather, I'm a private investigator contracted to Miriam's foundation to look into this matter and to determine how this unfortunate incident occurred. You have my assurances I will not disrupt your operations in this beautiful place without clearing it with you first.'

'My dear young lady, you are most welcome. You have my assurance we will all do all we can to assist you in your investigations and to make sure your stay here in Languleni is as pleasant as possible. Derek will look after you during your visit, and he will begin by showing you to your quarters where you may rest up before dinner. He will also brief you on the few basic rules necessary for your safety while you're in camp. I look forward to seeing you for sundowners in the *boma* before dinner.'

'Now Avi,' Jacob began as they sat around a blazing log fire in the *boma* enjoying their drinks, 'where would you like to start tomorrow?'

'With your permission, I would like to begin by looking through Dennis Middlebrook's *rondavel;* I believe that's what you call his quarters.'

'No need to ask permission; you can go anywhere you like, whenever you like; though I must insist you are always accompanied by either Derek or one of the other safari guides; this is for your own safety of course.' Pausing, he held up his hand. 'Listen, Avi, can you hear that?' In the distance, the deep roars of a lion were unmistakable. 'I think we might be treated to a lion sing-song tonight, a truly South African welcome to our guest from Israel.'

CHAPTER – 16 –

'AND I THOUGHT YOU WERE a senior agent from Mossad dispatched to eliminate the enemies of democracy before they take root in Languleni Game Reserve,' Derek teased as he walked Avi to the *rondavel* once occupied by Dennis Middlebrook.

'You have an overactive imagination, Derek Hamilton! Mossad agent indeed!'

'Well, the last thing I remember you saying before we said our goodbyes at Ben Gurion airport, was that you were waiting to hear whether your application to join that august body was successful. I take it they never called?'

'No, they didn't,' she replied tersely, 'now let's get on with the job in hand.' Derek pushed open the door and led the way inside. 'I'm looking for any letters or personal documents,' she said opening the drawers in a writing desk, 'would you mind checking the wardrobe and the suitcase on top.' After a few moments, she stepped back and pushed the drawers closed. 'That's odd, no letters, accounts, no nothing. Didn't he have any family?'

'Parents living in Johannesburg and, I believe, a fiancé there as well; June Riley would have that information.'

'Then let's go and talk to her.' As they walked over to the camp office, Avi asked, 'Surely someone has contacted his parents, girl friend or next of kin? Here's Jacob, let's ask him.'

'I sent a telegram to his parents, and tried on three occasions to reach them by phone,' he replied to her questions. 'Each time, I got a recorded message from the phone company saying the phone was either out of order or disconnected. When I mentioned this to Lieutenant Themba, he said he would ask the metro police in Jo'burg to go around to the address to see if everything was okay. I haven't heard anything from him since though.'

'What about Middlebrook's fiancé?'

'June tells me she was staying with his parents until Dennis was due to go home on leave.'

'Avi and I are on our way into town to find out how Themba's side of the investigation is going,' Derek said, 'we'll also ask him if he's heard anything from the metro police.'

Lieutenant Themba waved them to two chairs facing his desk. 'Before you start asking questions I can't answer, I should tell you that this case has been taken out of my hands by Priority Crimes in Phalaborwa. The officer now in charge of this investigation is a Captain Nkolosi. I believe you've met him before Derek,' he said smiling.

'I know him alright; he's as crooked as the day is long,' Derek muttered.

'Crooked or not, he's the go-to man as far as this investigation into Middlebrook's suicide is concerned.'

'What can you tell us about the weapon, which presumably you have in your possession, and can you tell me whether your officers collected any letters, photos or personal papers from Mr Middleton's *rondavel*?' Avi asked.

'Forgive me, Ma'am, may I ask what is your interest in this matter?'

'My apologies Captain,' Derek jumped in, 'I should have introduced Ms Blum at the beginning of our meeting. Avital Blum is an Israeli investigator hired by Miriam Hyde-Eshar to inquire into this matter on behalf of her foundation.'

'I'm pleased to meet you, Ms Blum, though I'm puzzled as to why an Israeli private investigator would be engaged by Mrs Hyde-Eshar's foundation to look into an apparent suicide?'

'Mrs Hyde-Eshar was particularly fond of Mr Middlebrook,' Avi said, 'he was like a son to her.'

'Of course,' Themba smiled, 'now, as I mentioned earlier, everything connected with this case is in the hands of Captain Nkolosi.' Standing up to indicate their meeting was at an end, he concluded, 'Please be so good as to direct any further questions you may have to the captain in Phalaborwa.'

'One thing before we go we Captain, may I ask where Mr Middleton's body is at present and when is it likely to be released to his family?' Avi asked.

'As soon as the medical examiner has concluded his examination and the family has contacted us.'

'Have you heard anything from the metro police in Jo'burg?' Derek asked, 'and have they been able to contact his parents or his fiancé?'

'I've heard nothing from them so far,' Themba replied, 'I'll be sure to let you know should I hear anything.'

'This whole business sounds bloody fishy to me,' Derek commented as they returned to his Land Rover. 'I believe someone is pulling strings to get this investigation out of the hands of an honest policeman like Themba and into the grasp of a man like Nkolosi, who can be relied upon to do as he's told.'

'So, what do you suggest we do now, Detective Hamilton?' Avi asked.

'We go to Jo'burg of course; we've got to find out why no one has been able to contact Dennis's parents or his girlfriend.'

'What sort of area is Yeoville?' Avi asked as they boarded their SAA flight to Johannesburg's OR Tambo Airport.

'Many years ago, it was a relatively upscale residential area much favoured by the Jewish community. Unfortunately, due to the increase in inner city crime following the collapse of apartheid, most of the residents moved away, and the area fell on hard times. Now it's not the sort of place you would want to wander around after dark. As soon as we arrive in Jo'burg, I suggest we hire a car and drive to the Yeoville address and see if anyone's home.'

'No need, I've got a car, an old Vauxhall Astra, in long-term parking at the airport.'

'How and when did you get that relic?'

'It was arranged by the people assisting Miriam. It's an older model, looks terrible, but underneath its shabby appearance, it's an excellent car. Just the sort of vehicle Johannesburg's car thieves couldn't be bothered stealing.'

'These people assisting Miriam sound a lot like the CIA, MI6 or,' he said with a wink, 'Mossad.' Avi put her finger on her lips before she turned away to watch their aircraft's approach to OR Tambo Airport.

Derek was right when he described Yeoville as having fallen on hard times. Litter covered the streets and the shops, those not tightly shuttered, were run down, 'Not exactly a tourist area,' Avi commented. 'We're coming into Lomax Street,' she said consulting the map on her smart phone, 'number 23, that's it there, the red brick cottage next to the three-storey block of flats.'

'Doesn't look as though anyone's home; I see the gate in the security fence is chained and padlocked. I don't see how we are going get in unless someone inside can open the gate.'

'Pull over here,' she said, 'let me take a look at that padlock, I've developed something of a knack for opening things like that.' He parked on the opposite side of the street and sat watching as Avi, opening her shoulder bag, took out what looked like a short screwdriver. Seconds later she opened the padlock, set the chain aside and opened the gate. 'I'm hoping anyone watching will think I have a key,' she said as he followed her through the gate, pulling it closed behind them.

The front door yielded to his push. 'The lock's been bashed in, it looks like whoever did this used a sledgehammer to get in. That's Jo'burg for you. *Jirre*! I hope to hell his parents weren't home at the time.' To their relief, the rest of the small, two-bedroom home showed no signs of a struggle, though the table in the little kitchen was set for a meal.

'There's food still on the stove,' Avi said, 'though, judging from the mould growing on the stew, I'd say it has been there for well over a week. Check out back, see what you can find outside while I try the bedrooms.' Five minutes later, they met again in the kitchen. 'I hate having to say this,' she said, 'but, in my opinion, his parents, and likely the girlfriend, were taken against their will. Look at it this way; the front doors smashed in, the phone line's cut, and there's a newspaper lying on a table in the lounge with a pair of eye glasses sitting on top. Surely, anyone going away would have taken their glasses? Also, the rest house appears to have been 'cleaned,' in the sense that all letters, documents, photos and so on are gone. I can't find anything to prove his parents or his fiancé ever lived here.'

'Hello in the house,' a woman's voice called from outside the gate, 'are you from the police?' Derek went outside to speak to the old lady rattling the gate. '*Meneer*, are you with the police?' she asked again.

'No, we're not; we're private investigators looking for Mr and Mrs Middleton and the young lady staying with them; would you happen to know them?'

'Of course, I know them, but I've not seen them since they all left late one night a few weeks ago, with two men and a woman.'

'And you've not heard from them or seen them since? If you don't mind me asking, how is it that you saw them leaving with these people?'

'A loud bang awakened me, that's my flat up there,' she said pointing up to a window on the third floor of the block of flats next door. 'When I looked out, I saw two men and a woman helping Rose, Angus and Dennis's girlfriend, Julia, into the back of a white Ford Transit van parked in front of their house. She's going to have a baby you know.'

'Dennis's girlfriend, Julia? She's pregnant?'

'Yes; didn't you know that?'

'No, we didn't. Tell me, have you ever seen any of these people before or since?'

'Yes; the day after the metro police were here, the two men returned driving the same white van and stayed inside the house for an hour before leaving with two suitcases. I assumed the Middleton's and Julia had gone on holiday and these two men were looking after their house. I've met their son Dennis before, so I know he wasn't one of the two men.'

'What did the metro police do when they were here?'

'They rang the buzzer at the gate and, when no one answered, they left. Never came back again as far as I know.'

'What can you tell me about the two men and the woman who took the Middletons and the girl away?'

'The woman and one of the men were Asian; the other man was black.'

'Forgive me for asking, but why didn't you call the police?'

'Nobody around here ever calls the police; it is too dangerous.'

'Thank you, Mrs...'

'Goosen, Marie Goosen.'

'Thank you, Mrs Goosen, you've been a great help. Here is my mobile phone number, should you see any of these men again, I would be grateful if you would give me a call. My partner and I are going to make a thorough search of the house to see if we can find any clues as to where they might have gone.'

'You were a long time talking to her,' Avi said as she joined him standing on the front *stoep*, 'was she any help?'

'Yes, she was,' he replied as he relayed everything Marie Goosen had told him.

'It seems to me there's a definite link between the disappearance of the Middletons and the girlfriend and Dennis's attempted assassination of the two prime ministers. It's worth bearing in mind the two main terrorist groups in the Middle East, Hezbollah and Hamas, are violently opposed to any peace agreement between Israel and Palestine and would do anything to put a stop to any negotiations.' Pausing in thought, Avi continued, 'I wouldn't be surprised if some organisation, possibly connected in some way to these groups, had arranged the kidnapping of the parents and the girlfriend to force Dennis Middlebrook to carry out their instructions. Tell me, as someone who has had training in this sort of thing, if you were ordered to kill the Israeli and the Palestinian prime ministers sitting in a row of seats right behind you, where would you shoot them?'

'I see where you're going with this. Obviously, if you wanted the men dead, you'd go for a head shot; it stands to reason they'd probably be wearing bulletproof vests.'

They were about to go back inside the house when the sound of a vehicle driving at high speed down the road caused Derek to look up. 'Oh shit!' he swore as he saw what he thought was the barrel of a gun emerge from the side window of a speeding white van. 'Get down!' he yelled, pushing Avi flat on the floor of the *stoep* as the staccato rattle of an automatic weapon sprayed the front of the house with bullets, shattering the silence of the street.

Covered in broken glass and chips of plaster, they lay close to one another, slowly getting up the nerve to raise their heads above the low brick parapet of the *stoep*. 'Clearly, someone doesn't like us poking about in the Middleton's house,' Avi observed, 'do you think they'll come back?'

'Having created more than enough noise to wake the dead, I wouldn't think so. Now, unless we want to spend the next few hours answering questions in a local police station, I suggest we lock up and leave right away.'

As they were getting into their car, Mrs Goosen came running up, '*Meneer, Meneer,* are you both okay? I saw the whole thing you know. Do you want the license number of that van?'

Chapter − 17 −

'I suggest we take this car back to the airport and exchange it for another,' Avi said, 'just in case the drive-by shooting this afternoon was the result of us being followed from the airport and not because they, whoever they are, have the Middleton's house under surveillance.'

'I suspect it was the latter, but you're quite right, we can't take that chance. I once had the unpleasant experience of being followed by a hired gunman around this city, which is why I wish I'd taken the risk and smuggled my old Z99 pistol onto the flight from Skoonspruit to Jo'burg. After that little incident on Lomax Street, I feel positively naked without it.'

'Well, I can help you there. Reach under your seat, and you'll feel a metal handle on a car safe, twist it to your right while I activate the unlocking mechanism.' Derek did as Avi requested and, with a solid clunk, the car safe sprung open. 'Reach inside, you will find, wrapped in a cloth bag, two Jericho 9mm pistols with four 15 round magazines and two TiRant sound suppressors. I'll take one, and you take the other; hopefully, you're now feeling a little less naked.'

'Positively fully dressed! Sometime soon, I hope you'll sit down and tell me how it is you're able to access this particular type of pistol commonly associated with the Israeli Security Service.'

'It's all a matter of having friends in the right places. Now let's discuss how we are going to resolve the problem of the missing Middletons.'

'Well for starters, I'll send a text message to a police colonel I know with the Hawks; if anyone can tell us who owns that white Ford Transit van without asking too many questions, he can. Once I hear from him, we might get some idea who's behind it all.'

'Okay, having taken care of that, we need to think about a safe place to stay tonight,' Avi added, 'any suggestions?'

'Once we change cars at the airport, we should look for a place way out of town; somewhere we can make sure no one is following us.'

'Good idea; have you anywhere in mind?'

'Etienne Roux, he's one of the safari guides at Languleni, spoke highly of a new lodge he stayed at a few months back. If I remember correctly, it's called Leopard's Rock Lodge and is about thirty miles out of Jo'burg in the Magaliesberg mountains. I'll look it up on your phone and see if we can get reservations.' As they were leaving the airport environs, the reservations desk at the Leopard's Rock Lodge called back offering two rooms, one overlooking the pool and another the valley below. 'The rates are a bit steep; though it does include a dinner and a breakfast.'

'Go for it,' Avi said, 'Miriam has authorised a very generous budget.'

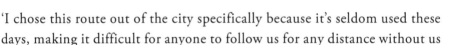

'I chose this route out of the city specifically because it's seldom used these days, making it difficult for anyone to follow us for any distance without us being aware of them,' Derek said having taken over the driving.

'You have a thing about being tailed?' Avi said smiling at him.

'Once, Rachel Cavendish, she's the MI5 agent I was hired to protect in Somalia, and I barely escaped with our lives when we were tailed to a bed and breakfast here in Jo'burg. Not an experience I'd like to repeat.'

'As I'm sure you know,' Avi began, 'that MI5 agent of yours is now the Deputy Director at Thames House. If you have no objections, I'd like to hear the full story from you, starting from the time you returned to South Africa after that business in Somalia.'

Derek began by telling her about the 'Flying Spear' missiles recovered by al-Shabab from the wreck of a coastal freighter run aground in the delta of the Rio das Mortes in Mozambique. He explained how these weapons were shipped through the agencies of Schoveldt International, a company with offices in Europe and South Africa, to terrorist groups in the UK and the United States to shoot down passenger aircraft. 'Fortunately,' he added, 'a Special Forces team flown in by helicopter from an American warship eliminated this threat.'

'I remember an Israeli covert operation which sank a ship called the

Al Rawiah after it sailed from Beira with a cargo of missiles and launchers bound for our friends in Hamas and Hezbollah.'

'Again, another little enterprise organised by Schoveldt International. Now that I've brought you up to date on my exploits,' he said smiling, 'how about being honest with me. Are you working for the Mossad?'

'Look! Those lights I can see high-up on the side of that mountain, is that where we're going?' she asked, neatly turning aside his question.

'Yes, I'd say that's Leopard's Rock Lodge.' He turned off the tarred road and onto a narrow gravel road which wound its way up the steep flank of the mountain. Ten minutes later, the gravel road ended in front of a long, single-story, stone and thatch building perched on a ledge just below a massive rock face. As he parked in front of the reception area, a uniformed doorman helped Avi out of the car and, picking up their bags, conveyed them through to the reception desk.

'Good evening Ms Blum, Mr Hamilton, I'm pleased to tell you both your rooms are ready.'

'Rooms?' Avi questioned, 'we don't need two rooms. Please put us together in the best garden suite you have.'

'Of course, Madam. I do apologise; it was probably a reservation error on our part.'

'As long as you can assure me it's your most luxurious suite, then all is forgiven,' she said smiling sweetly and taking Derek's arm.

'Now this is what it's about,' Avi said as they perused the dinner menus the maître d'hôtel handed to them. 'While we try to decide how best to spend Miriam's money, why don't you order a bottle of wine. I'd prefer a bold red if you don't mind.'

He didn't mind at all, asking the sommelier to bring a bottle of Neederberg Cabernet Sauvignon, 'I think you'll enjoy this one; it goes well with the Chateaubriand, which is what I'm planning on having.

'Who am I to argue with my favourite safari guide; please order the same for me.'

Concurring with the sommelier that the bottle of wine was as he had ordered and, nodding his approval after tasting the small amount decanted in his glass, he watched as their glasses were filled. 'Avi,' he began, 'now that we are sharing the same room, and, by the way, I wholeheartedly approve of the idea, perhaps now is the time to tell me all about your connection to the Mossad.'

'I take it you refer to the *HaMossad le Modi in ule Tafkidim Meyuhadim*,' Avi replied, 'giving the Institute for Intelligence and Special Operations its full Hebrew name. Mossad, if you prefer, has over twelve hundred employees in various operational departments. My involvement is best described as being on the periphery of the operational side of the organisation; hence my assignment to investigate the attempted assassination of the two prime ministers. You could say I'm here to decide what further action, if any, should be taken. But that's enough shop talk for today. *L' Chaim*,' she said raising her glass of wine.'

'To my comrade in arms, Avital Blum,' he replied, 'may we confound our enemies and delight our friends. Also,' he continued, 'may I say how beautiful you look this evening; I must admit I had no idea Mossad agents packed such delightful form-fitting little black dresses along with their 9mm Jericho pistols.'

As they walked arm in arm along the illuminated stone path to their garden suite, Avi turned to Derek, 'Tell me,' she asked, 'what were your thoughts that day I dropped you off at Ben Gurion Airport?'

'After we kissed and said goodbye, I walked into the airport terminal with the awful feeling that I was about to do something I would live to regret the rest of my life. I turned around and rushed back outside, but I was too late, you had already gone.' Hoping to lighten the moment, he asked, 'Do you still have that old Norton motorbike?'

Blinking back tears, she whispered, 'I could never part with that old Norton, it was the only reminder I had left of you. Derek,' she said to him, 'I've been in love with you ever since we met on that Quirinus security course in Israel.'

'Let's go inside,' he said as they arrived on the verandah of their suite, 'I would like to make love to you.'

'That's the best suggestion I've heard in years.'

CHAPTER – 18 –

THE RAYS OF THE RISING sun turned the cliffs above Leopards Rock Lodge a golden amber as Avi and Derek, sated from their early morning lovemaking, made their way out onto their terrace in their fluffy white dressing gowns, carrying cups of coffee. 'This is the most wonderful start to a new day ever,' she said nestling close to him on the cushioned bamboo chaise lounge.

'My sentiments exactly,' he replied kissing her. Their mutual feelings of idyllic bliss were interrupted by the insistent chirping of Derek's mobile phone. 'There's a text message coming through,' he said staring at the small screen, 'it's probably Colonel Dlamini, responding to my request for information on that van that tried to take us out.' Reading the reply, Derek lowered his phone and swore softly.

'Don't keep me in suspense; what did he have to say?'

'The Ford Transit van in question is registered to Schoveldt International in Pretoria; a fact that doesn't bode well for the Middletons and Julia.'

'What else did he tell you?'

'He wants us to meet him for lunch at Charlie's roadside diner on the old road to the Baragwanath Hospital.'

'Sounds like an out of the way place to have lunch?'

'He must have something he wishes to discuss with us in the strictest confidence. With Schoveldt International involved, I can understand why.'

To say that Charlie's roadside diner was off the beaten track would be an understatement Derek thought as they pulled into the gravel parking lot. 'No sign of Dlamini yet,' he said glancing around the empty lot, 'lets go inside and get two coffees while we wait.' As they walked into the diner,

Vusi Dlamini, sitting in a booth at the rear, stood and called them over. 'I didn't see your car in the lot,' Derek began.

'That's because I'm not here and this meeting never happened,' Vusi replied, waving them to the two seats opposite him. Derek quickly introduced Avi as the Israeli investigator looking into the attempted assassination of the two prime ministers. Smiling, he shook her hand, 'Welcome to South Africa my dear,' he began, 'I assume you've brought Avi up to date on our friends at Schoveldt?' he asked.

'Absolutely; she knows everything I know,' Derek replied.

'Good, then what you're both about to hear will make sense. As I said in my text, the Transit van's registered to Schoveldt International in Pretoria. Now here is where it gets interesting. Two weeks ago, this particular van was involved in a gangland shooting in Polokwane which resulted in the laying of charges against a Sakchai Sakmokon, a Thai national and his girlfriend Kamlai. Apparently, she's an exotic dancer at a local bar.'

'I remember this man Sakmokon; he's one of the partners in Schoveldt International; did the charges in the shooting stick?'

'No, they didn't; they were thrown out of court by the Minister of Law and Order, ably supported by the new Minister in charge of the Department of State Security. In other words, Schoveldt International and its hangers on are above the law. That's what I wanted to warn you about.'

'So, I take it your investigation into the illegal mining at Kgopa Kopje is also not going any further?' Derek asked.

Dlamini laughed, 'Once I discovered Schoveldt International was involved, I decided there and then, there was no point in wasting my time or my departments time investigating a case that's likely to be blocked from the start, so I let the matter drop.'

'Is there no higher authority in government that can put an end to this blatant corruption?' Avi asked.

'Not for the time being; not as long as the big man himself is unwilling to stop his family and close friends from robbing this country blind. Well, unless there's anything else you're willing to share with me,' Vusi said, 'I'd best be getting back.' As he shook their hands, he again cautioned them to be careful in their investigations. 'By the way, and it's only my opinion, I believe your friend Middleton was blackmailed into carrying out the assassination attempt on the two prime ministers. What else could he possibly do? His parents and girlfriend kidnapped and faced with certain death unless he follows the kidnapper's demands to the letter.'

As they walked to their cars, Avi remarked to Derek, 'So, Colonel Dlamini has come to the same conclusion we did. Obviously, your friend knows a lot more about our investigation than he is letting on.'

'Wouldn't surprise me; he has his finger on the pulse of everything that's going on in this country.'

'So, what do you suggest we do now?' Avi asked as they sat in their car trying to decide on their next move.

'Well, it stands to reason this Sakchai Sakmokon and his girlfriend Kamlai are most likely the Asian couple Mrs Goosen saw forcing the Hamilton's and Julia into the back of that white Transit van. The identity of the black man is a question we can worry about later. I suggest we drive to Polokwane and see if we can track down this Sakmokon and his girlfriend. If we can have a quiet chat with either of them, I believe we'd be a lot closer to discovering who's behind all of this and, if we're lucky, we might even find the Middletons and the girl.'

'Polokwane's about a three-and-a-half-hour trip north of here; while I drive, see if you can find anything on your phone that might help us in our search for this exotic dancer girlfriend of his.'

'It says here that Polokwane,' Avi replied scrolling through her phone, 'with a population of well over half a million, boasts some twenty-three nightclubs and bars that have dancers, strippers and, in some cases, bar girls, on hand to entertain patrons. I've a feeling we're going to have our work cut out trying to find a Vietnamese bar girl named Kamlai. Though, based on a map showing the locations of these clubs and bars, it looks as though most of these establishments are in the less salubrious end of town. I suggest we handle this separately; you take all the facilities north of the railway line, and I'll take those on the south. What do you think?'

'Sounds good to me, but what will we do if we find her? We don't want to spook her into running, nor can we very well stick a gun in her ribs and ask her to come with us; at least not in broad daylight.'

'Let's cross that bridge if and when we find her.'

'Any luck?' Avi asked as Derek trudged back to the car.

'Not really, but at the last bar on my list, the hostess suggested I try a place called Thai Son Greet, or something like that; the problem is it's a nightclub, and it doesn't open until ten tonight.'

'The name sounds promising; why don't we find a place to stay, get something to eat, then go nightclubbing later tonight.'

Three hours later, after checking into a motel and grabbing hamburgers in a greasy spoon diner, they left the car in a parking lot across the street from the Thai Son Greet. After paying a nominal cover charge and tipping one of the bouncers, they were shown to a table in the last row back from the small stage. 'Apart from the view,' Avi joked, 'any particular reason why you wanted to be so far away from the stage?'

'Best place to keep an eye on the patrons and watch the door at the same time.' Their tete-a-tete was interrupted by a scantily clad waitress who presented them with a grubby wine list before asking what they'd like to drink. 'A brandy and water and a glass of white wine for the lady.'

'Why didn't you ask her if she knew a girl called Kamlai?'

'Because I've a feeling we've come to the right place,' he said as the house lights dimmed, and a spotlight illuminated a pole in the centre of the stage, 'and I want to soften up our waitress with a good tip before we start questioning her.' When the waitress returned with their drinks, he tipped her with an American five-dollar bill. Her beaming smile confirmed that was the right move.

'This wine is awful; it's at least fifty percent water,' Avi complained.

'And my brandy is mostly river water. Anyway, it's dark enough back here so we can tip them out on the floor; besides, I want our waitress to come back to take another drinks order.' When an overly loud announcement informed the gathering of mostly men that Miss Venus was about to take the stage, the floor erupted with cheers, ribald comments and wolf whistles.

'I can't wait,' Avi commented through clenched teeth, 'and here comes your waitress.'

'Same again, love' he ordered, 'but a little less water in the drinks.' She smiled at him before sashaying away.

'I think she'd go home with you if you asked nicely. When are you going to ask her about Kamlai?'

'Right now,' he said as their waitress returned with their drinks. 'Tell me, love,' he said holding two five-dollar bills between his fingers, 'what time does Kamlai start work tonight?'

'She not dance tonight; she in much trouble with boss. He make her do lap dance instead.'

'We'd like to talk to Kamlai; can you ask her to have a drink with us?'

'She didn't look too pleased about that, I think she was hoping we'd ask her to join us. That gives you some idea how this place works.'

'You look for Kamlai?' a middle-aged Asian woman asked as she pulled up a chair and sat down at their table, 'why do you want her?'

Leaning closer to the woman Avi said, 'My friend here wants to fuck two women; we hear Kamlai is very good. Can you help us?'

The woman leaned back and laughed, then turning to Derek she said, 'You greedy man; this woman not enough for you?'

'Perhaps,' Avi said smiling, 'he is not enough for me.'

Still laughing, the woman held out her hand, 'One hundred dollar for one hour.'

'How about five hundred for the night?' Derek added, 'and Kamlai comes to our motel.'

'You pay now; I send her to your motel.'

'No,' Avi said, 'six hundred and she comes with us now.'

Still laughing, the woman agreed; 'You wait I bring her, but before you leave you pay me, yes?'

'Yes,' Avi agreed.

The attractive, young Thai woman who approached their table took them somewhat by surprise, 'Kamlai?' Avi asked.

'Yes, me Kamlai, we go now?'

'Of course,' Avi said standing up and, taking Kamlai's hand, led her outside to their car while Derek paid the Asian woman her money.

———— ❖ ————

As Derek closed and locked the door of their motel room behind them,

Kamlai started undoing the belt on her daringly short denim skirt. 'No, no,' Avi said stopping her, 'we want to talk to you first. Please sit down,' she said pointing to one of the chairs around a small table.

'We will pay you in American dollars for any information you can give us about a man called Sakchai Sakmokon,' Derek said sitting across the table from her.

A look of fear swept across Kamlai's face, 'No, I cannot. He very bad man, he will kill me if I talk to you. Please, I go back to club?'

'Not before you tell me where he took the old man and woman and the young girl you helped him kidnap in Johannesburg.'

'I cannot, he says he kill me if I talk about those people,' she said as she began to cry.

'It's no good crying Kamlai,' he continued, 'we know you were there; a great many people saw you. If you don't talk to us now, you will surely go to prison for kidnapping and, if anything has happened to those three people, you will be charged with murder and sentenced to death by hanging.' This threat engendered another tearful outburst. 'Of course, if you tell us what we want to know, we will pay you well, and we will give you our word this man Sakmokon will never know you talked to us.'

She was silent for a moment. 'How much will you pay me?'

'I will pay you five hundred American dollars.'

'You pay old woman six hundred for me to make fuck with you. No, I must have more money to go to Bangkok where this man cannot find me.'

'First, you must prove to me the information you have is worth a lot of money. Who was the black man with you and Sakmokon?'

'He is Phineas, he not nice man. He want to make fuck with me all the time.'

'Do you know his family name?' Derek asked.

'Sakchai call him Malema, I show you picture,' she said reaching for her handbag. She took out a crumpled and much-folded colour photo showing her holding a hunting rifle and standing next to an apparently dead, white rhino. 'I no shoot, he shoot,' she said pointing to a white man standing in the background. This man is Malema,' she said jabbing her finger at a black man standing next to her in the photo.

'Jissus, I know these bastards,' Derek said taking the photo from Kamlai. 'The black man is Phineas Malema, and the white man in the background

112

is Dawid Grossendahl. Jacob and I caught these two, in company with a crooked policeman, poaching rhino in Languleni. We arrested Malema but shot dead Grossendahl and the policeman when they resisted arrest. Kamlai,' he asked, 'can you remember when this picture was taken?'

'Two years, when I came to South Africa to shoot rhino for Sakchai.'

'Why on earth would a young Thai girl come all the way out to South Africa to kill a rhino?' Avi asked in astonishment.

'It's an old racket,' Derek replied, 'crooked private game ranchers hire Thai bar girls and supply them with legitimate hunting licenses allowing these girls to shoot rhinos on their game ranches. Of course, most of these girls couldn't handle a heavy calibre rifle, so it's usually the rancher or his sidekick who does the actual shooting. Later, the head and horns are shipped off to Thailand as legally obtained trophies. Once out of the country, these so-called trophies are broken down and the horns sold for a fortune. It's nothing more than a criminal scheme to circumvent laws against the sale and shipment of rhino horn to the Asian market.'

'Surely the authorities have put a stop to this racket?' Avi asked.

'Unfortunately, it's still going on. Everyone, from the game ranchers to the crooked officials in local government who issue the hunting licenses, all make substantial amounts of money.'

'I didn't know there were that many rhinos left in the wild in this part of the country.'

'There aren't. Most of the rhinos shot on these so-called game ranches are purchased legally from game reserves, including the Kruger Park, ostensibly for breeding purposes. But, in reality, they often end up being shot by these so called 'sportsmen'.'

'Surely a true sportsman wouldn't want to shoot a virtually tame rhino?'

'It's hard to imagine, isn't it? Regrettably, it goes on all the time; not only with rhinos but also with elephants and lions purchased from game reserves. This so-called sport, which is about as challenging and dangerous as shooting the neighbour's cat or a caged rabbit, allows some deformed twit to hang a trophy on his wall to prove to the other morons of the world just how brave he is. Makes me bloody sick I can tell you.'

'Turning to the matter in hand,' Avi said, 'if this Grossendahl is dead as you say, then who is the mastermind who sent Sakmokon and Malema to kidnap the Middletons and their future daughter-in-law?'

'That's a question we are going to have to put to this young lady here,' Derek said turning to look at Kamlai, 'but first, I've a feeling she wants to reopen financial negotiations.'

'I tell you too much already. I want two thousand dollar before I say more,' Kamlai said defiantly, 'I must have money to go back to Bangkok.'

'You're asking for a lot of money Kamlai,' Avi said, 'how do we know your information is any good?'

'I know where Sakchai take the old peoples and the girl; is good information yes?'

'If you can tell us that, we'll pay you two thousand American dollars, but I warn you, if you are lying to us we will find you and hand you over to Sakchai and his friends.'

'I no lie to you; I like young girl; she is having baby; you can help her please.'

'Okay Kamlai here's your money,' Avi said counting out two thousand dollars in hundred-dollar bills. 'Start by telling us where they took these people.'

'Here,' Kamlai replied picking up the photo of her and the dead rhino, 'they take them here to very big boss.'

'Yes Kamlai,' Derek said taking the photograph from her, 'but I don't know this place; do you know where it is?' Turning the photo over, he noticed a barely legible stamp on the back. 'It looks like Pikkie Swartz *Fotoagentskap*, but I can't be sure. Unfortunately, it doesn't give an address or a telephone number.'

'Let's hope he's still in business around here,' Avi said as she picked up the local telephone book and searched through the handful of photographers listed. 'Nothing,' she reported, 'no Swartz or anything even close.'

'Well, let's worry about that later,' he suggested turning back to Kamlai, 'the very big boss at this place, what can you tell us about him?'

'Sakchai call him Aboojemil,' she said laboriously trying to spell the name out.

'Sounds like Abu-Jamal to me,' Avi said, 'fairly common Arab name, though I can't say it rings a bell as far as South Africa is concerned. I'll send a text to Tel Aviv and see if they can come up with anything. In the meantime, I'll get on the internet and see if I can find Pikkie Swartz, photographer, while you decide what we're going to do with Kamlai. We can't keep her here all night you know.'

Derek turned to Kamlai, 'Well young lady, what are we going to do with you?'

'I must go back, or I get trouble with woman boss. First, I must look like we make much fuck.'

'I'm looking forward to seeing how you're going to handle that Derek,' Avi giggled.

'What do you mean Kamlai?' he asked ignoring Avi's giggles.

'Must tie me to bed; many peoples like to fuck me like that. Must make marks on arms and legs.'

'Oh, I understand,' Avi said, 'she wants you to tie her arms and legs forcing her to lie spread-eagled on the bed. Have we got any cord or rope?'

'Perhaps in the boot of the car,' he suggested, 'I'll go and look.'

As he left their room, Kamlai pulled off her shirt exposing her breasts and was about to undo her skirt when Avi stopped her. 'No need to undress my dear; let's not give Derek too many ideas. Put your top back on and come over to the window; I know exactly how we can make the marks your employer wants to see; though I would have thought the money we paid her would be proof enough.'

━━━━◈━━━━

'Of course,' Derek said as they dropped Kamlai outside the entrance to the Thai Son Greet, 'you used one of the sash cords from the window blinds to make the bondage marks on her wrists and ankles; why didn't I think of that?'

'Perhaps, because the thought of forcing me to lie naked, spread-eagled on our bed, with my arms and legs tied up with sash cords, would never occur to you?'

'Oh! I wouldn't say that,' he joked as she punched him on his arm.

CHAPTER – 19 –

I T TOOK OVER A DOZEN phone calls to photographers as far afield as Potgietersrus and Musina before Derek finally got to talk to someone who knew Pikkie Swartz. '*Ja*, good old Pikkie, I remember him. I used to buy his wildlife photos for this newspaper, that was before he was caught taking pictures of little girls with no clothes on for the overseas market. Last I heard he was taking photos for Grossendahl at his hunting camp near the Waterberg; that must be all of a year ago.'

'Do you know where this hunting camp is?'

'*Ja*, if you've got a good map handy, I could tell you over the phone how to find it; however, if you're planning to visit, I'd be careful if I were you. Aapie Grossendahl has grown publicity shy ever since his brother Dawid was shot dead by game rangers in the Kruger Park. Look, if you're interested in Grossendahl and his hunting camp, I'm the editor and proprietor of the Potgietersrus Evening Star, so, if you find yourself in the area, why don't you drop in and we'll have a chat.'

Ending the call, Derek turned to Avi, 'We've nothing on the go until you hear from your people in Tel Aviv about this Abu-Jamal character. In the meantime, I suggest we meet with this editor fellow at the Evening Star and get some idea of what's going on at this so-called hunting camp.'

◆

'Come on in, please make yourselves comfortable,' he said waving them towards two chairs that stood facing his small office desk. 'I'm Johann Steyn, editor and chief cook and bottle washer; can I get you any refreshments?' Declining his offer, Avi and Derek introduced themselves and, sitting down, looked expectantly at the editor of the Potgietersrus Evening Star.

'As you can see, we are not exactly a big newspaper; we've only four people on staff, but we do pride ourselves on being *au fait* with everything that's happening in Limpopo Province, particularly as it applies to Aapie Grossendahl and his hunting camp. May I begin by asking why you're interested in this man?'

'Unfortunately, at this stage, we cannot tell you anything other than to assure you that once our inquiries are complete, you will get an exclusive on the story.'

'I'll accept that. What would you like to know?'

'What does Grossendahl do for a living?'

'Where would I start?' Steyn said with a laugh. 'Grossendahl's involved in every illegal activity connected with big game hunting in South Africa and Zimbabwe. He and his brother Dawid got their start poaching rhinos in the Nuanetsi area of Zimbabwe. When things got too hot for them there, they changed tactics and switched to buying rhinos from game reserves. To make this work, the brothers arranged for tourists, often bar girls from Thailand and Vietnam, to shoot these animals legally. They then ship these so-called trophies to dealers in the Far East. Despite assurances, you may hear from local authorities to the contrary, these questionable practices continue.'

Steyn got to his feet and walked over to a filing cabinet. Pulling out a drawer, he removed a file and extracted a newspaper clipping. 'I thought so! I know who you are,' he said smiling at Derek, 'took me a while to put two and two together; you're Derek Hamilton, you're one of the game rangers who put an end to the career of Dawid Grossendahl. Sir, I'm pleased to shake your hand; you did an outstanding service to wildlife conservation in South Africa that day.'

'Avi,' Derek asked, 'please show Mr Steyn the copy you took of Kamlai's photograph.'

'Please, call me Johann,' the editor said as he studied the photo on her phone. 'Ah yes, it's that man Malema together with the late, but unlamented, Dawid Grossendal. Who's the young lady? One of those big game hunting Thai bar girls, I'll bet. I don't suppose she'd be interested in testifying against these people?'

'Not very likely,' Avi said, 'she's terrified of them.'

'Bloody miracle she was willing to share the photo with us,' Derek added.

'I'm not surprised; quite a few of these girls who couldn't keep their mouths shut ended up having unfortunate accidents or worse.'

'So, what does this Malema do for Grossendahl?'

'As far as I know,' Johann replied, 'he heads up the security detail around the Grossendahl ranch.'

'Sounds like they're running quite an operation; have you ever visited this so-called ranch?'

'About a year ago, they caught me sneaking in to have a look around. Had the living daylights beaten out of me; hell, I was afraid they were going to kill me. I've not made the same mistake again.'

'So, any suggestions on how we might be able to get inside this ranch of his?'

'Before I answer that, you're going to have to give me some idea of the reason behind your interest in these men. If I better understand your motives, I'm sure I could be more help.'

'We suspect these men may be involved in the kidnapping of an elderly couple and a young, pregnant woman,' Avi said, 'and, from what we've been told, it's possible they are holding them prisoner somewhere on this ranch. More than that, we cannot say, at least not for now.'

'Okay, I think I can give you a bird's eye view of what you're up against. A young nephew of mine, Rob Haydock, who lives in Jo'burg, has more than a passing interest in flying model aeroplanes. He occasionally provides government departments and private land developers with aerial photos taken by some of his model aircraft or drones as he prefers to call them. So, when he visited me a few months ago, I persuaded him to help me out with a few photos of Grossendahl's compound on the ranch. I imagine you'd like to take a look at them?'

Johann Steyn cleared a space on his desk and, removing a large manila envelope from a filing cabinet, spread out a series of 16x20 colour photos. 'Bigger than I expected,' Derek commented as he used the magnifying glass Steyn handed him to look more closely at the various buildings and sheds.

'Lots of places where they could hold people against their will,' Avi added. 'Johann, these holding pens; any idea of their purpose?'

'Well done, my dear; you've spotted something that is of grave concern to many of us in this area.'

'They look something like the *bomas* at Matetsi in the Kruger Park for holding captured wildlife,' Derek said peering through the magnifying glass.

'And that's exactly their purpose; we've seen up to a dozen rhinos held in them, along with buffalo and a variety of antelope including sable and kudu amongst others. But,' he said pointing to a smaller boma, 'this one over here with the higher fences is sometimes used to house lions; up to six at a time by our last count.'

'*Jissus!*' Derek said disgustedly, 'waiting to be shot by cowardly visitors; probably through the fence, I wouldn't wonder.'

'Worse than that I'm afraid,' Steyn replied, 'we have reason to believe they euthanise these lions in gas chambers and harvest the bodily organs, skins and bones for sale to medicine shops in the Far East. And it gets worse; two days ago, I received a report of two tigers, a male and a female, *en route* from a private zoo in Mozambique to Grossendahl's so-called game ranch.'

'If we're going to take a closer look at this compound,' Derek said to Avi as they returned to Polokwane, 'I want to add a friend of mine, Blessing Mananza, to our team. He's one of the finest trackers I know, and his expertise in the bush will give us an enormous advantage if we are to take on Grossendahl in his lair. Of course, to guarantee our success, we will need a few items of specialised equipment such as sound suppressed weapons, night vision equipment, communications...'

'Give me a list,' Avi said, 'I'm sure Miriam knows people who can lay their hands on this sort of hardware at short notice.'

'Just people she happens to know?' he said smiling, 'I'm glad I'm on your side.'

'Of course, we'll have to drive down to Jo'burg to pick it all up. At the same time, you can meet your friend Blessing at the airport while I make Johann Steyn's nephew Rob, an offer he couldn't possibly refuse.'

An email to Jacob Riley arranged for a temporary suspension from duty for Blessing and secured him an airline ticket to OR Tambo Airport in Johannesburg. 'I'm giving you the opportunity for another crack at your old enemy, Phineas Malema,' Derek said as he met up with Blessing in the arrivals area. 'He's up to his usual tricks again working for the brother of the Grossendahl we shot dead in Languleni.'

'*Numzaan*, I'm looking forward to it; when do we start?'

'My friend,' Derek continued, 'I remember you telling me about some fellow soldiers who served with you in 32 Battalion in Angola. Do you think you might be able to persuade a few of them to help us deal with any problems we might run into while we check out Grossendahl's game ranch?'

'Not a problem *Numzaan*. I'm sure I can persuade a few to join us here within a day or two; my only concern is these men no longer have their R1 rifles. Our government made sure of that.'

'Don't worry about that; we will soon have access to weapons they could only dream about.'

'I've arranged with Blessing to recruit a few of his fellow soldiers who served with him in Angola,' Derek told Avi, 'not surprisingly, they no longer have any weapons. The thing is, are Miriam's friends in any position to help us arm them?'

'As we speak, arrangements are in place to stash six of the latest Galil assault rifles, along with six camouflage outfits and two thousand rounds of 5.56mm ammunition, in a safe house in Germiston, a town just east of Jo'burg. I've also been in contact with Rob Haydock, Johann Steyn's nephew, and have asked him to purchase a pair of advanced drones capable of providing us with day and night infrared and visual aerial surveillance. These machines are able to give us real-time video of the situation on the ground on small, handheld monitors. Beats the hell out of trying to read a map wouldn't you agree?'

'Anyone planning to start a war would be well advised to speak to you first,' Derek said, 'by the way, any word from Tel Aviv on the possible identity of this Abu-Jamal that Kamlai mentioned?'

'Now, this is where things get a little sticky. Based on the limited information I was able to provide, the department reluctantly reached the conclusion that this Abu-Jamal may be someone directly related to the Palestinian prime minister.'

'Well, doesn't that make our case a lot easier to prove?'

'It does; too much so,' Avi said.

'What do you mean?'

'It means my original investigation is at an end. The powers that be have made it clear I'm to discontinue all further inquiries. From now on, this matter will be handled diplomatically by the Ministry of Foreign affairs, and you know what that will mean.'

'*Jissus*! Whitewash, right across the board and to hell with Dennis, his parents and his girlfriend Julia. So, where does this leave us now?'

'As far as I'm concerned its business as usual until I've spoken to Miriam. In the meantime, I want you and Blessing to drive to OR Tambo airport, drop this car off in long-term parking, hire a mid-size panel van, and then go to this address in Germiston. If any of the equipment we were expecting has arrived, load it up right away. Finally, on your way back north, stop at the Pretoria Central Railway Station and pick up the two men Blessing has persuaded to join us.'

'Do I bring everyone back here?'

'No; once you've picked up the equipment and the two extra men, carry on to Johann Steyn's office in Potgietersrus; I've arranged with him to take you to an abandoned farmhouse he knows of where he assures me we can set up base out of the public eye. While you're busy with all that, I'll get in touch with Miriam and find out just how far out on a limb she's willing to go.'

❦

The address in Piercy Street, in Germiston, was an older house set well back from the road and screened from its neighbours by rows of mature deodar trees. 'The gate code is six seven one,' Derek said to Blessing, 'key it in and hold the gate open while I drive around the back; I'd prefer to be out of sight of the street while we load up.' Following Avi's instructions, he found the back-door key taped under the sill of the nearby bathroom window. To his surprise, the back door was not locked, 'This is not good,' he said to Blessing, 'why didn't the sloppy buggers lock the door behind them?'

A quick search of the house answered his question. 'There's nothing here *Numzaan*,' Blessing said confirming Derek's worst fears. 'From the scuff marks on the floor, there were boxes stored here at one time but, from the other tire marks outside, I would say they were taken away not very long ago.'

'Damn and blast,' Derek cursed.

'*Numzaan*, if we cannot get the weapons Memsahib Avi wanted, what

121

will we do?' Blessing asked, then pausing in thought, he continued, 'the two men who have agreed to join us, Antonio and Dimas, were both good soldiers in Angola, but it has been many years since they handled rifles; will we get an opportunity to train them?'

'As someone who has had experience in these matters, I will insist on it. Don't worry; I'm sure the Memsahib will have thought of it.'

It took them the best part of two hours to find their way out of Germiston and onto the N1 to Pretoria and the railway station where they met up with Antonio and Dimas, the two ex-32 Battalion soldiers. Settling their two recruits in the back of the van, Derek drove directly to Potgietersrus and Johann Steyn's newspaper office. 'Glad you made it back safely; if you would follow me,' Johann said walking to his little Datsun *bakkie*, 'the farm is about twenty miles out of town, and only four miles as the crow flies from the security fence surrounding Grossendahl's ranch. You'll find the dirt roads a little rough and roadside fencing non-existent, so keep an eye out for stray cattle and potholes deep enough to break an axel!'

Pulling into the yard of an obviously abandoned farmhouse, Derek parked the panel van behind Johann's Datsun. 'Doesn't look like anyone has lived here for years,' he commented as Johann approached them.

'No one has since the elderly couple who lived here were murdered by a gang of farm invaders,' Johann told him. 'As you can see, the farm is isolated, it has no permanent water, and many of the local blacks believe it haunted; all of which goes to make it the ideal place to prepare for your little foray into Grossendal country. However, before we continue, there has been an unfortunate incident I which I wish I didn't have to tell you about.'

'It's been a day of unfortunate incidents. Surely one more can't hurt.'

'The young lady from the Thai Son Greet, I believe her name was Kamlai, was found dead this morning hanging from a tree on the outskirts of Polokwane. Suicide, so the local police claim.'

'*Here God*! Hanging you say? Do you believe she committed suicide?'

'No way; the poor girl was severely beaten before she was hanged. There could be no doubt she was murdered.'

When Avi arrived later that evening, Derek was of two minds whether to tell her about Kamlai's murder. Especially after having to report the removal of the weapons and equipment they were hoping to get from the safe house in Germiston. 'Those fucking people! That poor girl, we should never have allowed her to go back to that nightclub. I blame myself for that.'

'That's nonsense Avi; we're both to blame for not expecting the worst. Do you want to go after the old bitch at the nightclub?'

'And what would we do to her?' We have no idea whether she's to blame or not for Kamlai's murder; no, I think we need to base our plans on what we know and on our current resources.'

'You're right, without the weapons and equipment, we can hardly go in with guns blazing. So, where does this leave us?'

'Well, we still have a few good options available. Sometime tomorrow, Johann Steyn's nephew Rob will be joining us here. He had to wait for the delivery of some electronic equipment which, given our change in circumstances, we are now definitely going to need.'

'Did you manage to get in touch with Miriam?' he asked.

'I was wondering when you'd get around to asking?' Avi smiled, 'actually I was saving this one bit of good news for last. After I had explained our current situation to her, she assured me of her unconditional support, including financial, logistical and, whenever possible, political backing.'

'In the meantime, what are we going to do about weapons for our guys?'

'When I mentioned that to her, she said she would do her best to get hold of a few rifles. More than that, she wouldn't say.'

Chapter - 20 -

ROB HAYDOCK ARRIVED THE NEXT morning having driven up from Johannesburg in a hired panel van. 'I hope your promise of financial compensation will cover hiring this van,' he said to Avi, 'I couldn't fit both drones and all their ancillary equipment into my little car.'

'Not a problem Rob, come in the house and meet the rest of the team; it's a bit of a dump I know, but your uncle chose wisely. It's far from prying eyes and, more importantly, lies well within your stipulated maximum range of five miles to the target.'

Introductions out of the way, there was no shortage of helpers to help Rob unload the van, set up his equipment in one of the rooms and get the two portable generators he brought with him, up and running. The two, six-rotor, German built UAVs were unquestionably the centre of attraction. 'Given the relatively brief flying time to our target,' Rob told Derek, 'we should have a loitering time of around thirty minutes, given favourable winds, of course. With two units, we should be able to keep one UAV in the air while the other changes batteries.'

'Can they be seen from the ground,' Derek asked.

'Almost impossible during the day. These machines operate at around a thousand feet unless, of course, we need to get lower for an extreme close-up. And before you ask, the sound of the rotors is inaudible above a couple of hundred feet, even to the most sensitive listening devices. The cameras each UAV carries average around three pounds in weight and use the finest Zeiss lenses.'

'Sounds like the sort of device we could use spotting poachers at Languleni,' Derek said in an aside to Blessing.

Overhearing his remark, Rob chimed in, 'That's exactly the sort of job I'd like to take on when we've dealt with the matter in hand.'

The first photos to appear on the screen of Rob's laptop far exceeded Derek and Avi's expectations. 'Unbelievable,' Avi breathed, 'the image is sharp and clear. I swear if the angle of view were better I would have no trouble reading the license plate on that white van.'

'Give me a minute to change the camera angle,' Rob said as he fiddled with the controls. 'There, how does that look?'

'Bloody hell,' Derek exclaimed, 'that's the van used in our drive by shooting in Jo'burg. No two ways about it, we've got to get into this compound. And the sooner, the better.'

'Let's not go rushing in like bulls in a china shop,' Avi said, 'with these incredible machines we can find out a lot more by simply observing what's going on.'

'You're right, of course,' Derek agreed. 'Let's draw up a map of the entire compound, including the house on the hill and the surrounding *bomas* or pens. We can use it to highlight the areas Rob needs to concentrate on in our search for the Middletons and Julia. Also, if we make a list of all vehicles entering and leaving the ranch, we'll get an idea of who is going in and out and, if we're lucky, find out if anyone else is involved.'

Their efforts to identify locations within the compound where the Middletons could be held made quick progress. 'I'm curious about these two small buildings way over here,' Avi said drawing Derek's attention to a corner of the laptop screen, 'why are they located so far away from everything?'

'Could be storage rooms; though I agree their location is odd. Rob, could you keep an eye on these two over the next twelve hours; we're looking for anything out of the ordinary, such as shift changes, food delivery, that sort of thing. If they're holding anyone in there, we need to find that out as soon as possible.'

'Tell you what, at night I can use the infrared cameras to scan for heat sources; that would give us an idea if anyone is pulling guard duty near those buildings.'

'You might like to look at these images,' Rob called out to Derek later that evening. 'I've got someone entering one of the rooms around supper time, then returning a short time later. If I were to venture an opinion, I'd say they were delivering food to that room.'

'We've got to find a way to get in there. Rob, would you take a close look their security fence, concentrating on the stretch closest to where we are now. I'm looking for some way we can get in without doing anything so obvious as cutting a hole in the wire.'

Five minutes later, Rob called Derek over. 'How about this,' Rob said bringing up an infrared close-up of a small *donga* crossing under the fence. 'Apart from the odd pool of water, the washout appears to be mostly dry. I can't be sure without actually going there, but I would say the fence probably ends a foot or so above the bed of the *donga* or else it would be choked with vegetation carried there by floods.'

'It's perfect! Later tonight, Blessing and I will use this *donga* to get under the fence and, with the aid of our night vision binoculars, take a good look at those two buildings.'

A waxing crescent moon hung low in the sky as they parked their van in dense bush a half mile from the boundary of the ranch. Using a handheld GPS device, the pair made their way through the darkness to the waypoint marking the place where the fence crossed the *donga*. 'As far as we can tell from Rob's spy in the sky,' he said quietly to Blessing, 'there usually aren't any guards posted around the perimeter fence, but we should be careful just in case.'

Derek got down on his hands and knees and, crawling along the bed of the *donga*, emerged from under the fence on the other side. As he climbed up through the long grass on the opposite bank, a violent blow to his left shoulder caused him to scream out in pain. '*Jissus!* Blessing help me!' Frantically, his groping right hand encountered the thick, muscular body of a huge python as it quickly wrapped its coils around his body. He tried desperately to free himself from the jaws locked onto his left shoulder, but the snake's grip was relentless.

On the verge of panic, he felt the reptile tighten its grip around his chest, making it almost impossible to draw a breath into his lungs. Struggling to breathe, he was only dimly aware of Blessing trying to free his shoulder from the snake's jaws, but without success. As he began to lose consciousness, he felt a warm gush of blood on his face as Blessing severed the python's head from its body. To his relief, he felt the enormous pressure on his body suddenly slacken as the powerful snake, coiling and uncoiling, writhed in its death throes.

'I'm sorry I had to kill *inhlwathi*,' Blessing said as he helped Derek to his feet, 'but I could not make him let go of your shoulder. Are you able to walk back to the van?'

'Yes, I think so. *Ngiyabongo* my friend, if you had not been right there, that python would have killed me.'

Despite the lateness of the hour, the medical staff at the Potgietersrus clinic's prompt attention to the severe bite on Derek's shoulder did much to relieve Avi's anxiety. 'It's just as well we were less than an hour away from proper medical attention,' Johann Steyn remarked as he and Avi returned to the farmhouse in the van. 'The African rock python is an immensely powerful creature and, if Blessing had not been able to cut its head off, I've no doubt Derek would have been dead within minutes of the attack.'

'Why on earth did it attack him?' she asked, 'he wasn't doing it any harm.'

'Reflex action on the part of the snake I'd say; any warm-blooded creature crawling up to it is bound to provoke a strike. Luckily, much of the bite was deflected by the leather shoulder strap of the knapsack Derek was wearing; nevertheless, the fangs of a python, while not poisonous, are laden with germs and always requires immediate medical attention to prevent infection. Anyway, the doctor appears confident he will be up and about and raring to go when we pick him up tomorrow.'

'Looks like quite a fire burning over there,' Avi remarked as a red glow tinged the base of a few low-lying clouds. 'Hell, I hope it's not our place burning down,' she said jokingly.

'Whatever's burning, it's very close to the farm. Can't be our place though, Rob and Blessing are there keeping an eye on it as well as the two 32 Battalion guys Blessing brought in. If there's a problem, I'm sure one of them would have called us by now. However, if you don't mind, I'm going to step on the petrol, I'm always a little worried where bush fires are concerned.'

'I'll give Rob a call on his mobile phone,' Avi suggested, 'I think we'd both be a lot happier if we knew for certain there was nothing to be worried about.'

'Any luck?'

'No; just a message saying his phone is out of service; now I am beginning to get worried.'

'We'll get a clear view of the farm house as soon as we get over the next rise, only then will we know for sure if we need to worry or not.'

'Oh, my God!' Avi said as the flames from the burning farmhouse bathed the surrounding area in a flickering red glow. 'I can't see any sign of Rob or Blessing or any of the others. Christ! I hope they're alright.' As Johann stopped the panel van fifty yards back from the burning house, a figure detached itself from the surrounding darkness and banged on the driver's side door. 'It's Blessing,' Avi shouted, 'unlock the doors, let him in.'

Pulling open the side door, Blessing shouted out, 'Give me a hand, Rob's wounded, we've got to get him to a hospital.' He led them to a figure lying propped up against the base of a small tree, 'We tried to fight them off,' Blessing explained, 'but with only a pistol between us, it was useless. They fully intended to kill us all but, luckily for us, Rob managed to get pick up the rifle dropped by the man I shot. Together, we held them off for a while until Rob was wounded. I would say they weren't expecting us to fight back, so after setting the house on fire, they stole your Datsun and drove off.'

'How many of them were there?' Avi asked Blessing as they gently lifted Rob into the back of the van.

'I'd say at least five, but I can't be certain. But did I recognise Phineas Malema as one of the attackers; he's the poacher who once tried to kill me in Languleni.'

'What happened to your friends, Dimas and Antonio?'

'Antonio was shot dead when he challenged the first of the attackers as they approached the house. That's his body lying over there,' Blessing said pointing to a figure lying in the centre of the farmyard. 'I don't know what happened to Dimas; he either ran away or they captured him. When Rob got hit, I dragged him into the bush and hid with him there until I saw your headlights and recognised the van.'

'He's lost a lot of blood,' Avi said checking on Rob, 'we've got to get him to the hospital right away. Get in Blessing; there's no point in you staying here, those bastards might come back.'

'The police require the attending physician to report all gunshot wounds treated at this facility,' the doctor at the Potgietersrus clinic said as Rob was carried in on a stretcher by two male orderlies.

'Of course; we will report it first thing in the morning; but for now, this man is losing blood, and I will hold you responsible if he does not receive proper treatment,' Johann said looming over the little Indian doctor.

'I don't think there's any point in having any of the staff wake Derek,' Avi said to Johann, 'he might as well have a good night's sleep before we burden him with more bad news.'

'I agree; besides, from what Doctor Agrawal tells me, he doesn't consider Rob's injury to be serious and, following a few stitches and a good night's rest, he'll probably discharge him in the morning.'

'What about having to report his gunshot injury to the police?'

'I've taken care of everything. The good doctor, for a small consideration, agreed it would cause an unnecessary complication. Now I'll drop you and Blessing off at my house where I suggest you both get a few hours sleep before morning. I'm off to my office to satisfy myself that all is well on the news front.'

It was shortly after seven in the morning when Johann drove up to his house, 'I've got what I hope is good news,' he announced to Avi and Blessing as they got into the van to return to the hospital. 'I believe the wooden crate I've just loaded into the back contains the weapons you've been expecting.'

'Derek will be pleased; now, at long last, we'll be able to take on Grossendahl's thugs on a more level playing field,' Avi said as they parked in front of the hospital. 'While you two go in and check on our patients, I've got a few phone calls to make.'

When Avi walked into the hospital waiting area, Derek and Rob were in the process of being discharged. 'As soon as you're ready, let's go somewhere for breakfast; I don't know about you guys, but I'm starving. Also, I've just got off the phone with Miriam in Tel Aviv; she has agreed to some of the proposals I put forward; proposals I would like to tell you all about over breakfast.'

Finding a restaurant that offered a full English breakfast, the five of them seated themselves at a table with a good view of the van in the parking lot and placed their orders. 'Okay, now that our coffees have arrived,' Derek said, 'there's no need to keep us in suspense any longer.'

Avi smiled, 'Miriam confirmed the crate Johann loaded into the back of the panel van contains four Heckler & Koch 416 assault rifles and enough ammunition to conduct a small war. Her words, not mine. Rob, Miriam wants you to return to Jo'burg in your hired van and, as soon as possible, replace all the equipment you lost when the house burned down. Once done, you are to report to Jacob Riley at the Languleni Game Reserve; she says he's expecting you.' Taking a sip from her coffee, Avi continued. 'Blessing, she told me she would like to provide compensation to Antonio's family and, should anything untoward have happened to him, the same for your friend Dimas.'

'Which leaves the three of us ready to get on with the job we were supposed to do,' Derek said. 'Did our employer have any suggestions for us?'

'When I put that to her, she replied that all future decisions are entirely up to us. However, she did say once our objectives have been met, we were to leave the cleaning up to Vusi and his Hawks and to get back to Languleni as quickly as possible.'

Following Rob's departure for Johannesburg, Johann took it upon himself to keep the three of them supplied with coffee and rusks while they unpacked and cleaned the four HK416 assault rifles, using Avi's suggestion of mineral spirits to remove the cosmoline packing grease. 'I can't imagine how Miriam was able to lay her hands on four brand-new assault rifles, complete with night vision scopes, at such short notice,' Derek remarked.

'Just be grateful she managed to do it; it'll prevent us being caught flat footed again by Malema and his thugs,' Avi said as she applied a thin film of gun oil to the weapon's working parts. 'Now, what's our next move?' she asked.

'Now that the *Numzaan* has taken care of the *inhlwathi* that guarded the *donga* that *Baas* Rob's flying birds found,' Blessing suggested, 'it would be foolish if we did not use it to get into Grossendahl's ranch.'

'Blessing is right,' Derek said as he oiled and reassembled his rifle, 'we know it's the shortest route to the compound and, apart from marauding reptiles, it offers the densest cover. Johann, if we may impose on you further, would you mind dropping us off at our departure point and then remaining on call should we need to make a rapid withdrawal?'

'Not a problem; I only wish I was going with you.'

Avi leaned forward and kissed Johann on his cheek, 'Believe me, I'm much happier knowing someone like you is watching our backs.'

CHAPTER – 21 –

THE DIM LIGHT PROVIDED BY the moon now in its first quarter, was partially offset by low scudding clouds, while capricious breezes rustling the dry leaves of the Mopani bushes, set everyone's nerves on edge. Blessing led the way, crawling along the shallow *donga* and under the fence where he disturbed a pair of jackals feeding noisily on the dead python. Derek made frequent use of his night vision binoculars surveying the way ahead while Avi kept them on course with her handheld GPS device.

Almost an hour into their journey, Avi tapped Derek on his shoulder and whispered in his ear, 'We're about a hundred yards from the buildings where they could be holding the Middletons, Julia and, possibly, Dimas.'

Derek and Avi held back while Blessing scouted ahead. He was back in fifteen minutes, 'There's one man keeping watch not far from the two *piccanin kia's*; he's very careless, I saw him strike a match under his coat and light a cigarette. Should I kill him?'

'No; it would be better if we can take him alive. We need to know how many men Malema has working for him and whether they have anyone locked up in those buildings. While I draw his attention, you hold your knife under his chin and persuade him to keep quiet or run the risk of having his throat cut.' Their plan of action in place, Derek got to his feet and sauntered over towards the man on watch. 'You're not smoking while you're on duty, are you?' he asked in a loud voice.

'Oh! No *Baas*,' the man stammered as he stubbed out his cigarette only to feel the blade of Blessing's knife press against his throat as he tried to get to his feet.

'Who's in that *kia*?' Derek demanded.

'Only one man. *Baas* Malema catch him and bring him here.'

'Are there any other people in the *kia*?'

'No peoples, just one man.'

'Are you sure? No *umndeni*, no *intokazi*?'

'*Ikona, fileyo!*'

'He says the young woman and the old people are all dead,' Blessing said.

'Ask him how and when were they killed,' Derek said to Blessing as he walked over and put his arm around Avi who was keeping watch a few yards away.

'I heard you question him,' she said, 'what did he say? Are they alive?'

'Bad news, I'm afraid; according to him, the Middletons and Julia are all dead. I've asked Blessing to question him further.'

Blessing came over to where they were standing, pulling his prisoner along with his knife still firmly pressed against the man's neck. '*Numzaan*, this man says Malema was ordered by Sakmokon to shoot all these people some time ago. He's not exactly sure when they were killed.'

'What did they do with the bodies? Did you ask him?'

'*Yebo Numzaan*, I asked him.'

'And?'

'Sakmokon ordered them thrown into the lion enclosure.'

'The bloody bastard. Ask him if Sakmokon is still here on the ranch.'

Blessing questioned the man at length in Zulu. 'He says Sakmokon and Grossendahl left yesterday with the lion bones and rhino horns.'

'How does he know this?'

'He says Grossendahl and Sakmokon had all the lions killed, forcing the skinners to work all day and through the night skinning and deboning the carcases. The two men then shot the five rhinos still in the enclosure and ordered him to chop out all the horns. He told me he and another man then loaded all the bones, skins and horns into boxes and put them in a big lorry. He says they were in a great hurry to leave because they feared soldiers were coming.'

'Well, if nothing else, we can at least lay our hands on our old friend Malema,' Derek said.

'What do you propose we do with this one,' Avi asked nodding towards their prisoner, 'we can't very well let him go?'

'In my pack, I've got a roll of canvas tape and a handful of plastic ties. We'll gag him, then tie him up and hide him in the bush until we've dealt with the others in the compound. But first, let's find out if Dimas is the man being held prisoner in the other building.'

It took two solid kicks to break open the flimsy lock, allowing Blessing to push open the door. The room was in complete darkness, so he called out softly, 'Dimas, are you in here?'

'*Hau* Blessing, what took you so long?' came the reply.

'I thought being in jail would do you some good; perhaps make you less cheeky, but I see it did not work.'

'What about that *kaffir* Malema? I hope you haven't killed him yet; I'm looking forward to doing that myself. Come on man, get these *blerrie* handcuffs off me and let's get on with killing these people. You know they killed Antonio? Without guns to fight back, we were fucked.'

'Watch your language,' Blessing warned, 'I'm going to bring a lady in here to open your handcuffs. If I hear you *vloek* just once, I'll tell her to leave you chained up in here until your manners improve.'

'Do I not get a gun?' Dimas complained.

'All in good time,' Derek said, 'but first you're going to help us clean out this rat's nest. Are you up to it?'

'*Yebo Baas*, tell me how I can help.'

'You can start by telling me how many people work on this ranch?'

'Apart from the Chinese man, the Boer and Malema, I think there are nine men. Six who kill and skin lions and three who work with Malema. The man making sure I did not escape told me the Chinese man and the Boer left in their big lorry yesterday. He said they were taking the lion skins, bones and rhino horns to *eGoli*.'

'Johannesburg! Are you sure?' Derek asked.

'I am sure *Baas*. I heard them telling Malema to meet them in *eGoli* once he cleans up everything at this place.'

'What did you think they meant by that?'

'That Malema must kill me. But when he told them there were no lions left to eat me, they said he should bury me in the ground.'

'I've heard enough! Come on Dimas, show us where we can find this Malema.'

The night watchman was asleep in his chair outside the gated entrance to the compound when Blessing clubbed him on the back of his head with the butt of his rifle. Jumping forward, Dimas grabbed his AK47 rifle before it fell to the ground. Checking to see if the weapon was loaded, Dimas turned towards Derek, 'It does not work; they don't trust their own men with ammunition,' he muttered in disgust as Blessing tied the man up, gagging him with canvas tape.

Using their night vision sights to scan the area, they fell in behind Dimas as he led them between two large, corrugated iron sheds. Almost at once, they were choking on the appalling stench of rotting flesh, 'What in God's name is it that smells so bad,' Derek whispered as he caught up with Dimas.

'The *derms* from all the lions they killed,' he said pointing to a patch of scrub behind one of the sheds. 'They use the exhaust from the truck to kill the lions in the small shed, so the skins are not damaged. Afterwards, the dead lions are dragged over to this big shed where they are skinned and deboned.'

'How do you know all this?' Derek asked.

'When they captured me at the farmhouse, Malema brought me here to help move the dead lions and the two tigers to this shed where the six skinners finished the job. Near my village in Angola, lions sometimes kill our cattle. But we did not hate them; so, for me to see them killed in this way is terrible. That is why this man Malema must die.'

'Your friend Blessing also wants to see Malema dead. But first, we must find all the men who work in this terrible place?'

'The one guarding me said they were all sent away when the Chinese man and the Boer left.'

Leaving Dimas to keep watch, Derek called Avi and Blessing together to decide what to do next. 'From what Dimas tells me, Malema, accompanied by at least three men, could still be holed up in the bungalow on the hill, planning an early morning departure.'

'Blessing, you've had more tactical experience than any of us, what would you suggest?'

'*Numzaan*, I've never been in favour of frontal attacks; I'd rather catch them by surprise when they try to leave in the morning.'

'Makes good sense to me,' Avi chipped in, 'there will be no medals for bravery on this one. Ask Dimas if he has any ideas on how they plan to leave the ranch.' Blessing called Dimas over and put that question to him.

'They have *Baas* Johann's little car; the Chinese man and the Boer took the big lorry.'

'That simplifies things,' Avi said, 'all we have to do is disable Johann's Datsun then deal with the occupants of the bungalow when they try to leave in the morning. Dimas, where is the Datsun now?'

'Maybe in the big shed behind the place where they kill the lions.'

'Is this where they gassed the lions?' Derek asked as he pulled open a door and stepped inside. 'Avi,' he called softly, 'do you have your Maglite?'

'Oh my God! It smells awful in there,' she said standing in the doorway as she handed him the torch.

Derek switched it on, shone it around the room then immediately turned it off, 'Don't come in here Avi, please stay outside. Tell Dimas and Blessing to get over here.'

'What is it?' she asked.

'You don't want to know; just get Dimas and Blessing in here.'

'What is it *Numzaan*?' Blessing asked as he and Dimas entered the room.

'The carcass of one of their lions,' Dimas speculated, 'perhaps they left one behind in their hurry.'

Derek switched on the torch and shone it on a tangled heap of bodies piled up in the furthest corner of the room, 'I think we've found the six skinners they let go yesterday.'

Dimas took the torch from Derek's hand and walked over to the dead bodies in the corner. 'They are handcuffed together and killed in the same way they killed the lions.' Then he was violently sick.

'God, how awful; those poor men,' Avi said as Derek put his arms around her, 'what other horrors are we going to find in this bloody place?'

'A terrible thought just crossed my mind; Blessing look in the other shed, see if you can find the Datsun.'

He was back in a few minutes; 'Nothing,' he said softly, 'the car is gone.'

'Which means our birds have flown! I'd venture you a million pounds to a pinch of shit, that house on the hill is empty. Watch this,' he said stepping out in the open and, shouldering his HK416, switched the selector from single rounds to automatic and fired two five-round bursts into the house.

As he expected, there was no reaction.

CHAPTER – 22 –

ALL IT TOOK WERE TWO phone calls to bring closure to the horror that was Grossendahl's Big Game Safari Ranch. Derek's first call was to Sylvia Kingston at the London Telegraph. 'Knowing how interested you are in stories centred around poaching and the exploitation of Africa's fast disappearing wildlife,' he said, 'I've got a juicy exclusive for you.'

'Darling, you know I'm interested. Who, what, when, where and why?'

'How soon can you get a reporter and a photographer from your Jo'burg office up to Potgietersrus, it's a small town about a three-hour drive north of Johannesburg.'

'According to my world clock,' Sylvia said. 'its two thirty in the morning your time; a bit early to be getting up even for you, isn't it?'

'I haven't been to bed yet.'

'That's quite an admission coming from you,' she said with a chuckle. 'But getting back to business, how do my people get in touch with you?'

'They don't. Tell them to go to the offices of the Potgietersrus Evening Star and ask for Johann Steyn; he'll fill them in and drive them out to the scene of the crime.'

'My people will be there by seven tomorrow morning at the latest, or they'll be looking for new jobs. You did mention an exclusive?'

'Guaranteed.'

'Good. What sort of slant are you looking for?'

'Pressure on the South African government through international wildlife conservation agencies; not doing enough to stop poaching and illegal wildlife trafficking etc.'

'Were I to come out myself, would you be around to make it well worth my while?'

'Unfortunately, not. I'm likely to be on the road myself.'

'Pity; another time maybe?'

'Maybe.'

Derek's next call was to Colonel Dlamini with the Directorate for Priority Crime Investigation on his private number in Johannesburg. *'Here God, Derek, it's nearly three in the morning. Why so blerrie early?'*

'Crime never sleeps Vusi; you of all people should know that!'

'You better have a good reason! Where are you now?'

'I'm calling you from Aapie Grossendahl's ranch not far from Potgietersrus. Do you know this place?'

'Only by reputation; what are you doing there?'

'Based on your lead, we've tracked down the kidnappers of the Middlebrooks and Dennis's girlfriend to this place.'

'How are they?'

'An unconfirmed source told us all three are dead and their bodies fed to lions.'

'Lions? Is this place a game reserve?'

'Grossendahl's ranch has nothing to do with the preservation of wildlife; quite the opposite in fact. All the lions in this place, including two tigers, have been gassed and butchered for their hides and bones for the Asian market. A dozen or so rhinos, also on the ranch, were shot for their horns.'

'And the perpetrators, where are they now?'

'Gone; flown the coop with the lion parts and rhino horns in a large, covered lorry sometime between six yesterday evening and midnight.'

'Any idea of their destination?'

'Our source believes the lorry is on its way to Jo'burg.'

'With traffic cameras, it should be easy enough for us to confirm. Oh! Before you go, I should ask who else knows about this place?'

'Johann Steyn, the editor of the Potgietersrus Evening Star and Sylvia Kingston; she's a reporter with the London Telegraph.'

'Here God! How did she find out?'

'I thought a bit of overseas pressure on the upper levels of government, including the State President himself, would help further your case against local and regional corruption. Was that wrong of me?'

Vusi laughed, a deep, hearty laugh, 'Derek you're a *blerrie skelm*! You knew damn well that would force my department's hand. If your little scheme goes to hell in a handbasket, you'd better have a job for me in your game reserve.'

———— ⟨⟨⟩⟩ ————

The South African Airways flight carrying Avi, Derek, Blessing and Dimas from OR Tambo to Skoonspruit landed late in the afternoon. 'Did you have a good holiday?' Etienne joked as he picked them up from the airport.

'Wonderful, glad to be back. How are things in Langulerni?'

'Busy; we're going high tech with input from your friend Rob Haydock.'

'So soon? He only just got here!'

'Truth is, we all think it's an excellent idea. Hopefully, it'll give us the upper hand in dealing with the growing sophistication of poacher incursions. By the way, a policeman from the Hawks called Riley's Camp just as I was leaving; he asked the boss to tell you he'd be flying in at six this evening and would like you to meet him at the airport.'

———— ⟨⟨⟩⟩ ————

Vusi Dlamini climbed into the passenger seat of Derek's Land Rover at Skoonspruit airport. 'No, don't start up, my plane is waiting to fly me back to Jo'burg as soon as we're done here. I'm only here because I don't want our conversation to take place over a possibly insecure phone line.'

'That doesn't sound good.'

'It isn't. Tell me, do you want the bad news or the really bad news first?'

'Let's start with the bad news first.'

'Okay; my people picked up the lorry registered to Grossendahl on traffic cameras as it headed south on the N1 from Potgietersrus to Johannesburg.'

'Well, I don't consider that bad news.'

'I haven't finished yet. A short while later, the vehicle was found burned out in a stretch of veld between Pretoria and Jo'burg. An eyewitness who came forward told our investigators that a white man torched the lorry shortly before he was seen getting into a white Ford Transit van. Also, my investigators were unable to find any sign of the cargo of lion skins, bones or rhino horns.'

'I'm not surprised. What about Malema and the Datsun car?'

'The car was discovered abandoned in an alleyway in Alexander Township. There was a black male body inside and another on the ground nearby; both were shot to death. And before you ask, Malema was not one of them. However, the two deceased males were well known to the police.'

'Sounds like a bit of housekeeping to me,' Derek commented, 'now, what's the very bad news you promised?'

'As I believe we both expected, my department has been pulled from the case with orders to hand everything over to a special unit under the direct control of the Department of State Security.'

'Shit! I assume this will leave us up the proverbial creek without a paddle?'

'Not entirely; a few of my people will continue to have their ears close to the ground but, when it comes to doing anything practical, our hands are tied.'

'I hope that's all the bad news,' Derek said. 'Now I must ask, did your investigators find anything when they searched the house on Grossendahl's ranch. It's just possible these people in their rush to leave, might have left behind some clue as to where they are going after Jo'burg?'

'We didn't have much time. By mid-morning, a unit from the DSS arrived by helicopter and ordered us off the ranch, but not before we scooped up most of the documents we found in the house. I've got them here in this briefcase for you and your people to sift through. It's going to be difficult for us to stay in touch by phone, so I've arranged with Steyn at the Evening Star to receive and send text messages on my behalf.'

'Sounds good to me.'

Vusi turned and shook Derek's hand, 'Okay, I'm off then; good luck my friend and good hunting.'

CHAPTER – 23 –

I T TOOK AVI, DEREK AND Rob the best part of the day to sort through the pile of papers jammed into the briefcase Vusi gave him. 'It's mostly receipts for the rental of a Ford Transit van, food, petrol and so on,' Rob said, 'nothing much to go on. Though this one is interesting, a receipt for fifty litres of petrol in Machava; isn't that in Mozambique?'

'Town just outside Maputo,' Derek replied. 'Now I'm only guessing, but the hotel and petrol receipts probably relate to the costs for the transport of rhino horn, lion skins and bones to somewhere in Mozambique. What I don't understand is how the hell they got any of these shipments through customs at the Komatipoort and Ressano Garcia border posts? Agents on both sides are usually on the ball.'

'Is there any other way they could have got into Mozambique?' Avi asked.

'Let me have a look at those receipts,' Derek said taking the handful from Rob. Quickly sorting through them, Derek gave a little chuckle, 'I'll tell you how they got into Mozambique; they went in through Swaziland. Look at this,' he said handing over three or four petrol receipts, 'Ermelo, Mbabane, Mbabane again, and here's one from Siteki. I wouldn't have thought there was even a petrol station anywhere near there.'

'Yes,' Rob countered, 'but they'd still have to go through a border crossing of some sort, wouldn't they?'

'Probably not; it's pretty wild country around there; lots of dirt tracks crossing and re-crossing the border dozens of times. A smuggler who knows his way around wouldn't have too much trouble getting across. It's almost too much to expect, but is there an address on any of those receipts?'

'On the surface, it looks as though they thought of that,' Avi said sifting through the paperwork, 'which is why most of these receipts and documents have no names or addresses on them. However,' she chortled, 'even the most meticulous bookkeeper slips up occasionally; I have one here that addresses a shipment to Schoveldt International Trading Company at 16 Avenida Jose Martinez, Cidade De Maputo, Mozambique.'

'Well, that gives us somewhere to start.'

'How about a receipt for a two-night stay in the Polana Hotel on Avenida Julius Nyerere, for a *Senhor* Sakchai Sakmokon; it's dated two weeks ago,' Rob said handing over a hotel receipt with a pleased expression.

'That's another good lead. I should get in touch with Vusi; he may know someone in the *Policia da Republica de Mocambique* or *PRM*, that's the local police service, who could give us some information on this Schoveldt business in Maputo?'

'Worth a try,' Avi agreed.

Vusi's reply, routed through Johann Steyn, arrived within the hour. 'Bad idea; local authorities unreliable. Suggest investigating in person. Good luck.'

'Do you think you might be able to kidnap this Sakmokon chappie,' Rob asked, 'or perhaps have him arrested by the local police and sent back here to face charges?'

Derek shook his head negatively. 'With all his contacts in government here, and most likely in Mozambique, he'd be out on the streets so fast our heads would spin.'

'So, what do you propose doing if you find him?'

'Couldn't say at the moment Rob,' Avi said quickly, 'we're on our way tomorrow to meet with Miriam in Jo'burg. She'll be the one to make that decision.'

As they walked back to their rondavel, Avi took Derek's arm, 'I had to jump in quickly back there, the fewer people who know what we may have to do the better.'

Avi and Derek left early the next morning by air for Nelspruit where, on his suggestion, they rented a white Ford Transit van like the van possibly being used by Grossendahl or Sakmokon. 'Might just help if some people assume we're connected in some way with the Schoveldt International Trading Company,' Derek said as they left Nelspruit on the N4 for the hour and thirty-minute drive to the Mozambique border crossing at Ressano Garcia. 'Should we be unfortunate enough that they decide to search our luggage, I trust you have all the paperwork for the two Beretta pistols?'

'Thanks to Miriam, I've everything they could want to see, including licenses and my certificates as an NRA licensed pistol instructor.'

'So, you've thought of everything,' he said reaching out and taking her hand, 'what about our accommodation in Maputo; with any luck, we'll be there in an hour and a half after we cross the border.'

'I've booked us into a sea view room in the Polana Hotel. Based on Sakmokon's choice, I figured it's probably the best hotel in Mozambique,' she replied placing his hand between her thighs and squeezing them tightly together. 'I'm sure you're going to like it.'

'You've not given me any reason to doubt that,' Derek replied with a grin, 'but first I suggest we check out the Schoveldt International Trading Company on Avenida Jose Martinez and get some idea of the scope of their operations in Maputo.'

Avenida Jose Martinez ran through one of the many light industrial areas that surrounded the city; a search for number 16 on the map in Avi's mobile phone brought them to a group of individual business units clustered around a large hardware store. Puzzled why the name Schoveldt Trading Company did not appear above any of the units, Derek left Avi in the van while he went to the hardware store to make inquiries. 'I'm sorry,' he said to a shop assistant, 'I don't speak Portuguese, is there anyone here who can speak English?'

'I can speak English,' an elderly mulatto man said emerging from a small office at the back of the store, 'how can I help you *Senhor*?'

'I'm trying to find out where the Schoveldt Trading Company has moved to; going by the signs outside, they are no longer at this address.'

'I'd like to find out where they've moved to as well. These people disappeared late one night, leaving behind a lot of unpaid debts.'

'Didn't pay their rent I assume?'

'Not only that; they also did not pay my son for all the work he did for them constructing wooden shipping crates.'

'These crates, any idea what they were for?'

'Goods they were sending overseas I assume. They did not say what the goods were, but they were quite specific about the various sizes of the crates my son had to build; some had to be four-foot square while others were nearly eight feet in length. Very secretive about it all too, I can tell you.'

'If I can get you the money these people owe you, can you think of anything else you could tell me about their business?'

'Come through to my office; we can talk there in private.' Politely declining an offer of coffee, Derek listened as the old man continued, 'As I told you outside, they hired my son to build eight sturdy wooden shipping crates all lined with heavy duty plastic. He had to provide them with dozens of large, super absorbent pads, rolls of bubble-wrap and bundles of straw. They packed all the crates late one night in their warehouse and had them ready the next morning for my son to secure them with steel banding. They even got him to stencil an overseas address on each one.'

Derek sat up sharply. 'You wouldn't still have that address, would you?'

'No, I'm sorry, I don't.'

'Is there any chance your son might remember it?'

'Unfortunately, my boy has a learning disability and doesn't speak much, but I'll ask him to come in here.' The son was a strapping lad, probably in his early twenties, but he shook his head negatively when the old man questioned him in Portuguese. 'I'm sorry,' the old man said, 'as you can see my son has many problems, reading being one of them.'

Derek rose to his feet, 'I'm very grateful for your help; if you gave me an invoice for the money these people owe you and your son, I would be happy to have it taken care of.' Suddenly, the young man brightened up and, chattering excitedly, ran out of the office.

'I apologise, I've no idea what got into him,' he said as his son reappeared carrying a mangled and torn cardboard stencil covered in black paint. 'Of course! I'd forgotten all about the address stencil they provided him with,' the old man chuckled, 'to read it, all we have to do is spread it out on the floor.'

'Nguyen Van Lamh, An Dinh Trading Company, Tran Hung Dao Street, Vung Tau City, Vietnam. Based on this address, I believe we've discovered the eventual destination for the lion skins, bones and rhino horn from Grossendahl's ranch,' Derek said as he showed Avi the photo he had taken on his mobile phone of the stencil.

'Any ideas on how the Schoveldt Trading Company planned to ship these crates to Vietnam?'

'I have some idea. The old man who owns the hardware store told me an old army lorry picked up the crates, presumably to deliver them to the docks. It's not much to go on, but let's worry about it after we've checked into our hotel.'

———⟨◇⟩———

The Polana Hotel, four storeys of elegant luxury, overlooked the beach and the rolling surf of the azure blue Indian Ocean. 'I must hand it to Sakmokon, there's nothing wrong with his taste for the finer things in life,' Avi commented as they stood on the balcony of their room admiring the view.

'A taste born of the suffering of others,' Derek reminded her, 'people like Kamlai who paid the price for talking to us.'

'Don't worry,' Avi said, 'I'll not hesitate for a second when it comes to ending his miserable life,' then changing the subject slightly she asked, 'any luck showing his picture to the receptionist on the desk?'

'She thought he looked familiar but suggested I show the picture to the head concierge when he starts work this evening. With a bit of luck, he might remember him.' Standing behind her, Derek wrapped his arms around her, 'Looks like a beautiful sunset and dinner's not for two hours, would you like to go for a walk along the beach or something?'

'Depends on what you mean by something,' she replied slowly rotating her bottom against his crotch, 'if what I'm feeling is that something, you have my undivided attention.'

'Now you've gone and done it,' he said, 'there's no way I can walk around with this bulge in my pants.'

'Wonderful, let's go through to the bedroom, I believe I know just how to take care of your problem.'

CHAPTER – 24 –

THE CONCIERGE HAD NO DIFFICULTY recalling *Senhor* Sakmokon. 'Terrible man, he did not like women. The last time he stayed with us he took a *prostituta* up to his room and beat her up. The front desk clerk, who saw the girl covered in blood running from the hotel, reported the incident to the night manager who asked *Senhor* Sakmokon to leave first thing in the morning. As a result, when he showed up yesterday, the manager refused to allow him to stay in this hotel.'

'How did Sakmokon take that?'

'He didn't like it and grew quite angry, especially when I further informed him that Herr Grossendahl, whom he apparently expected to meet here, had left the hotel the day before.'

'Grossendahl you say; this man was staying here?'

'He stayed with us for two days before he left on his flight.'

'Do you have any idea where he was flying to?' Derek asked handing the man a folded fifty-dollar bill.

'There's no need for that, sir. I'm only too pleased to be of assistance. At his request, I provided Herr Grossendahl with the address and directions to our closest travel agent. Unfortunately, the gentleman did not disclose his travel plans to me, so I am unable to answer your question.'

'Not to worry; you've been very helpful. However, I must ask whether you were able to recommend another hotel to *Senhor* Sakmokon?'

'Of course. I suggested the *senhor* try the Hotel Posada de Lorenzo on Avenida Friedrich Engels; it's only a short walk from here. Would you like me to inquire whether he's resident there?'

'That's very kind of you, but no thank you. Though, I would appreciate the name and address of the travel agent you recommended to Herr Grossendahl.'

'Not surprisingly, the girl in the travel agency would not discuss Herr Grossendahl's travel plans,' Derek said as he joined Avi at her table on the terrace watching the sunset. 'I'm afraid we're going to need your lock picking skills if we are to access the travel agency's files after hours.'

'All my skills are at your disposal,' Avi replied with a wink.

'I'll remind you of that later tonight.'

The lock on the alleyway side door of Eduardo's Travel Agency did not present much of a challenge to Avi's lock picking skills. 'If Eduardo had any idea just how easy it was for you to open his side door, I'd think he'd seriously consider bricking that door up!'

'Perhaps I should leave him a note to that effect,' Avi joked, 'in the meantime, we had better hope he doesn't decide to come back to work after dinner.'

Shading the beam from his Maglite, Derek began searching through the various filing cabinets looking for airline bookings, 'They have such a well organised filing system,' he said sarcastically, as he pulled out file after file shoved haphazardly into drawers. 'Sift through this lot,' he said passing the torch and a handful of folders to Avi, 'I'll take the rest of the drawer over to the window, there's just enough streetlight coming in for me to see what I'm doing.'

They were working on the third drawer when they both heard a key being inserted and turned in the lock on the side door, '*Merda*! I must have forgotten to lock it,' a male voice said softly, 'just as well we decided to come here instead of going to your place. No, don't turn on any lights; you never know who may be watching outside. Let's go through to my office; I've got a comfortable couch in there.'

A feminine voice urging Eduardo not to be too gentle preceded the sounds of a couple making uninhibited love on a creaky old couch. 'I've found it,' Avi whispered suppressing a giggle, 'I think we better get out of here while they're still otherwise engaged.' Tucking the file under her jacket, she followed Derek out through the side door closing it quietly behind them.

As they emerged from the alleyway next to Eduardo's Travel Agency, a large, matronly woman got out of a car parked on the street out front and, walking briskly down the alley, banged on the side door. 'Eduardo!' she shouted, 'I know you're in there with that bitch, open this door at once!' As a result of her pounding, the door sprang open of its own accord and, with a triumphant shout, the woman strode into the travel agency office.

'At this very moment, I'll wager you Eduardo wishes he was away on one of his tours to some remote part of the globe,' Derek said taking Avi's arm as they walked back to their hotel.

Finding a quiet table in the corner of the lounge, Avi spread out the contents of the file marked Grossendahl, Aapie. 'Hopefully, I grabbed everything relevant to his most recent bookings,' she said paging through some of the documents while Derek went over to the bar to order two whiskies. 'Two days ago,' Avi continued on his return, 'Grossendahl took a Linhas Aereas Mocambique flight to Johannesburg, where Eduardo's had booked him on a Lufthansa flight to Frankfurt. Following an overnight stay in that city, they had reserved a seat for him on a train going to Augsburg in southern Germany. Why the hell would he be going to Augsburg?' she wondered.

'Quite possibly he hopes to connect with Dieter Schoveldt's father, Barendt Schoveldt. It was the latter Schoveldt who orchestrated much of the terrorist activities that plagued Britain a year ago. Once Barendt's activities came to the notice of the authorities, they placed him on Scotland Yard's and MI5's most wanted lists. However, to the best of my knowledge, he has since managed to disappear off their radar screens. Personally, I'd venture good money he's hunkered down in a safe house somewhere in Europe.'

'Wasn't he one of the organisers behind the Chinese surface-to-air missile crises a few months back?'

'The same.'

'So, are you saying the new Deputy Director of MI5, with whom I understand you had a close relationship, has no idea where this Barendt Schoveldt may be currently hiding?'

'As far as I know, that's the case. But look,' Derek said anxious to change the course of the conversation, 'first things first. What about Sakmokon; why don't we take care of him now and worry about Grossendahl further down the road. Besides,' he continued throwing in his trump card, 'I'd like us to run it by Miriam first, get her take on what we should do next. Don't forget; she might not be too pleased when she finds out I've promised to reimburse the owner of the hardware store on Avenida Jose Martinez for his out of pocket expenses incurred by Schoveldt International.'

Finishing their drinks, they went up to their room where Avi took out a small leather makeup bag from the room safe. Unzipping the bag, she removed two Beretta .25 pistols, two three-inch-long sound suppressors, two eight-round magazines and a box of 50-grain copper jacketed ammunition. 'I checked each round over carefully before we left, they're good to go. Keep one in the breech, and do not load more than six rounds in each magazine.' Slipping her pistol into a small handbag, she stood and, smiling at him said softly, 'Let's go and get this over with.'

It took only ten minutes to walk from their hotel, down two flights of steps to the Avenida Friedrich Engels, then along the Marine Parade to the six storey Hotel Posada de Lorenzo. A recent addition to the Maputo hotel scene, the de Lorenzo prided itself on providing visitors with the very latest in modern hotel amenities including four high-speed lifts, two casinos and five restaurants offering a variety of cuisines ranging from Japanese sushi to American hamburgers.

None of these facilities, nor the variety of restaurants, were uppermost on their minds as they surveyed the dozen or so guests milling around the reception area inside the hotel entrance. 'I can't see anyplace where we can keep an eye on the reception area without eventually attracting attention,' Avi whispered in Derek's ear.

'If I may suggest,' he said squeezing her arm, 'there's a hotel phone near the lifts; why don't you call the reception desk and ask them to put you through to his room. When he answers, tell him there's a message for him from a Herr Grossendahl at the hotel reception desk. Hopefully, he will be curious enough to want to know why his partner ran out on him earlier.'

The telephone operator put Avi's call straight through to Sakmokon's room. When a male voice answered, she passed on the message and returned quickly to where Derek was sitting near the reception desk. 'I gave him the message and ended the call before he could ask any questions. We'll just have to wait and see if he takes the bait.'

'Don't look now,' Derek whispered a few minutes later, 'that's Sakchai Sakmokon getting out of the lift nearest to us.'

'Are you sure?'

'Positive; I'd recognise him anywhere.' They watched as Sakmokon walked quickly across the reception area to the front desk where he spoke briefly to one of the young women on duty. Smiling pleasantly, the woman shrugged her shoulders and shook her head negatively. Turning quickly, Sakmokon stared hard at the faces of everyone standing around the reception area. Derek tried to avoid his gaze, but he was too late. With a strangled cry, Sakmokon ran to one of the lifts and, with scarcely a second to spare, and to the surprise of the half dozen guests already in the lift, he leapt in just as the doors closed.

'Shit!' Derek cursed as he watched the buttons on the lift panel light up at the third floor, then the fourth floor, and finally the sixth floor. 'We've no way of knowing which of those three *blerrie* floors he got out on. 'I really fucked that up,' he cursed, 'we don't even know his bloody room number!'

'I doubt very much he's on his way to his room,' Avi said, 'after my call, he'll assume we already know his room number. No; if you ask me, I'd say he'd be most anxious to get as far away from us and this hotel as he possibly can. If I were I a betting woman, I'd say the odds are he's on his way to the parking lot as fast as he can run down at least three flights of back stairs.'

'Come on then!' Derek said, 'we'd better get a move on if we're going to get there first.'

—◆—

The parking lot for the Hotel Posada de Lorenzo was accessed through the garden entrance of the hotel and along a narrow road that wound its way through ornamental gardens and dense shrubbery. Running out of the front entrance and across the lawns, Avi and Derek eventually arrived at the parking lot. 'I hope to hell this is where he parked his car,' Avi said struggling to regain her breath.

'Perhaps we both need to spend a little more time on an exercise program if we're going to be doing this more often,' he joked hoping to take their minds off what they were about to do.

'Let's worry about that once we've taken care of this business,' she replied squeezing his hand for luck. Stepping into the shadows cast by a stand of dragon trees, she screwed the sound suppressor into the barrel of her Beretta and cocked the pistol. 'I suggest you do the same,' she said to Derek as he moved to a similar position across the road; 'be ready to shoot if he appears.'

Time seemed to stand still as they waited nervously for their quarry to appear from the direction of the hotel. 'Perhaps I was mistaken,' Avi thought to herself, 'maybe he did go to his room and, at this very moment, is phoning the lobby and asking the concierge to call him a taxi.' A sibilant sound from Derek across the road drew her attention to a shadowy figure making its way down the road towards them. As the figure drew closer, she recognised the jacket and trousers as the clothing Sakmokon was wearing when she saw him in the hotel reception area.

'Sakmokon, stay right where you are!' Derek ordered, 'or we will shoot.'

'Fuck you!' Sakmokon shouted as he attempted to draw a pistol from under his jacket. Two muffled shots, fired almost simultaneously, hit Sakmokon in the centre of his forehead, dropping him to the ground.

Derek ran forward and placed the barrel of his pistol behind the dying man's ear, 'This is for Kamlai!' he whispered as he fired another two shots. 'Help me drag him into the bushes' he said to Avi as she appeared at his side, 'with any luck they won't find him for a day or two.' Pocketing the pistol carried by Sakmokon, he started gathering a pile of fallen branches to cover the body while Avi quickly went through the dead man's pockets.

'I've got his wallet, passport, room number and even his key card; I suggest we took a quick look around his room; who knows what we might find.' They walked briskly through the front entrance of the hotel and rode one of the lifts to the forth floor. Using Sakmokon's hotel key card, they entered his room and, quietly closing the door behind them, turned on a bedside light and began a systematic search of the room.

'Look what I've got here,' Derek chortled as he pulled out a brief case from beneath the bed.

His smile of self-satisfaction disappeared in an instant as someone began hammering on the room door, '*Policia!* We know you're in there, come out with your hands up!'

CHAPTER – 25 –

'THIS IS BULLSHIT!' AVI YELLED striding up to the door, 'Fuck off you idiots before I call the real police!' Derek dared not breath until he heard the sounds of muffled laughter and two people running away down the corridor.

'*Jissus* Avi, you took a chance. How the hell did you it was a joke?'

'When you've stayed in as many hotels as I have that cater to football hooligans, you too would recognise their juvenile behaviour a mile off.'

'Well, I'll be a lot happier once we get out of here. Have you found anything else?'

'And how!' she said pulling out a Czech made Skorpion 9mm sub machine gun from under the bed. 'Add this to the Glock 17 he was about to pull on us and I'd say he was expecting trouble. Are we hoping to find anything else?'

'No; I think everything we could ever want to see we'll find in his briefcase.'

<hr>

Back at the Polana Hotel, Derek placed the Skorpion and the Glock pistol in the room safe then, opening the minibar, he poured two stiff whiskies before emptying the contents of Sakmokon's briefcase onto the bed. Sitting side by side, they each took a handful of documents and began sorting through them. 'Any ideas on what we're hoping to find?' Avi asked taking a sip of her whisky.

'Ideally, a Bill of Lading for the eight crates presumably picked up from Schoveldt's warehouse.'

'And I think I may have found something along those lines,' she said. 'It's an order made out by someone called Amin Shakil for the transport of goods from Schoveldt's on Avenida Jose Martinez to a warehouse in the port. While it doesn't list the goods, the date fits.'

'Is there a phone number for this Amin Shakil?'

'No, just an address; 51 Rua Timor, Malafafa. What do you think we should do?'

'Tonight, nothing. But I suggest we take a taxi to that address first thing tomorrow morning and talk to Mr Shakil.'

The first taxi driver refused even to consider it. 'Not safe place,' the driver of the second taxi complained, 'very bad peoples.' It took a promise of a fifty-dollar *bonsela* on top of his regular fare to convince him otherwise. Even Derek, once stationed in Mogadishu, had to agree Malafafa looked like a dodgy area. Shacks cobbled together out of sheets of rusting corrugated iron, plastic tarpaulins, old cars and cardboard, housed the residents of this overcrowded slum. Raw sewerage lay in pools in the ditches lining the garbage strewn narrow lanes, now home to dozens of beggars, assorted livestock and almost naked street urchins.

'Oh, my God! This is awful,' Avi said clutching Derek's arm, 'I'm not surprised some of the taxi drivers were reluctant to bring us here.'

He didn't reply as he struggled to find a street sign or house number. 'Are you sure this is Rua Timor?' he asked the driver for the third time.

'Oh yes, *Senhor*, this right place. Ah! Here is 51 Rua Timor!' the driver announced triumphantly, 'Now I find it, you give me big *bonsela*, yes?'

'Not now, only when you take us back to the Polana Hotel. You must wait here,' Derek said as he got out, warning Avi to stay in the taxi and keep the windows and doors locked. 'This shouldn't take too long.' Pushing open a rickety, wood and corrugated iron gate, he walked into a yard containing an old Bedford army lorry, its cargo area covered with a green tarpaulin, a dozen or so pigs, chickens and cats and a young boy who ran into one of the sheds presumably shouting for his father.

A middle aged, overweight man with a scraggly white beard emerged from the shed dressed in a grubby *jellabiya*, his broad smile revealing broken and blackened teeth. '*Effendi*, you are most welcome,' he said clasping his hands together in a gesture of prayer. Bowing obsequiously, he inquired, 'Would you like tea?'

'Very kind of you; but really, I am here on business; transport business,' Derek replied nodding towards the Bedford.

'Then *effendi*, you have come to the right place,' the man said extending his hand which he carefully wiped on his clothing, 'I am Amin Shakil, at your service. Please to take a seat,' he said gesturing to a row of rickety chairs arranged against a mudbrick wall. Clapping his hands together, he shouted to the young boy who stood watching shyly from the doorway of the shed, 'Afzal, *pese pese leta tatu chai* for our guest and his lady who sits in the taxi outside. Surely, sir, would she not be wishing to sit in the shade drinking tea while we conduct our business?'

'*Asante sana rifiki*,' Derek replied smiling to himself as he went out to the taxi and invited Avi to join him and Mr Shakil for tea.

'You speak Swahili?' Amin Shakil asked Derek as he returned with Avi.

'No; just a few simple phrases I picked up while in East Africa.'

'That is good; you are a man of Africa,' Shakil paused, 'I too am a man of Africa.'

'I'm glad to hear you say that my friend. As you will soon understand my inquiries today relate to this continent we both love and respect.'

'Ah! Here is our tea,' he said taking two mugs of tea off the tray carried by the young boy and handing them to Avi and Derek.

'My name is Derek Hamilton, and this lady is my friend, Avi Blum. We both work as game rangers in South Africa.'

'You are both most welcome in my house, how can I help you?'

'A few days ago, you delivered eight crates to the docks here in Maputo,' Derek said handing him the order docket they found in Sakmokon's briefcase.

'Ah yes! I remember those boxes were going to Vietnam. I made that delivery, but when I returned the next morning for my money, the owner of the building these people occupied told me they had left in the night without leaving a forwarding address.' Amin sat quietly sipping his tea, 'If you don't mind me asking *effendi*, what is your interest in those boxes?'

'We have reason to believe they contained the results of a widespread poaching ring operating in South Africa.'

'I did not know of this. Had I known, I swear I would not have taken the job.' Brightening he added, 'Perhaps the ship has not yet arrived in port? We could phone the port authority and ask if a Vietnamese ship has docked. I have their phone number here.'

'If you give me the number, I would be happy to do that,' Avi said taking out her mobile phone and, walking a short distance away, placed the call. Smiling, she returned with good news. 'The Motor Vessel Bac Ninh has been delayed with engine trouble and is not due to arrive in Maputo until sometime tomorrow morning.'

'Do you think it might be possible, Mr Shakil, for us to come up with a plan to retrieve those crates from the docks before the ship arrives?'

'Please allow me to make a few phone calls so I may answer your question more fully.' Two minutes later, he emerged from the shed, 'I have just spoken to the two young men who helped me deliver the boxes to the docks,' he said. 'As I do not have a forklift, their strong arms and backs will be required if we are to remove these boxes from the port warehouse. Also, and it shames me to have to say this, but we will need to pay *dash* to the watchman at the warehouse and the officials in charge of security in the port area.'

'All I need is for you to tell me how much *dash* we'll require for each official; I'll take care of the rest. When do you suggest we do this?'

'We must do it tonight; should the ship arrive early, they will want to begin loading their cargo right away. Let us meet this evening at ten on the corner of Albert Luthuli Boulevard and Avenida 25 de Septembro; I'll be driving my Bedford and will be accompanied by my two friends.'

———◆———

'Do you think we can trust him?' Avi asked as they emerged from their taxi back at the Polana Hotel.

'I don't believe we have any better options; if we don't stop those crates leaving for Vietnam, then Schoveldt International will have won this round and I'd rather that didn't happen.'

'Fair enough but, assuming my role as the devil's advocate, what do we do with the crates if we are successful?'

'I've been thinking about that. Wouldn't it be like icing on the cake if we could get these crates back to South Africa and hand them over to Vusi and his Hawks?'

'No two ways about that,' Avi laughed, 'if we were able to do that it would boost Vusi's standing with the government and it wouldn't hurt to have the Hawks beholden to us either.'

'Not to mention that it would piss off Schoveldt International's customers royally!'

CHAPTER − 26 −

THEIR PLAN TO RETRIEVE THE eight crates from the Maputo port area went off without a hitch; fueled in no small way by the substantial bribes Amin Shakil handed out to a variety of officials to make sure they would be looking the other way. 'Well, my friends, what do we do now?' Amin asked as they arrived back at his yard in Malafafa.

'I've been thinking about that all afternoon,' Derek replied. 'Mr Shakil, I would like to hire you and your Bedford to drive this cargo to the city of Xai Xai in Gaza Province where I will need to discuss this matter further with an old friend of mine. Would treble your usual mileage rate be acceptable?'

'Please call me Amin,' he said smiling, 'you drive a hard bargain Mr Hamilton; of course, I accept.'

'Naturally, you will have to make arrangements for your wife and son while you are away; if I can help…'

'No, Mr Hamilton, you misunderstand my situation. I am not married, and this young boy is merely a friend of mine,' he said winking and tapping the side of his nose. 'If it suits you and your lady, I suggest we leave before first light tomorrow morning. It's better we are not in Maputo should any of our officials get cold feet when the MV Bac Ninh arrives in port.'

The sun had not yet risen as Avi and Derek, driving their rented Transit Van, followed Amin's Bedford out of Maputo and onto the EN1 highway headed for Xai Xai. 'I need to get in touch with a man called Sandford Matsanga,' Derek replied to Avi's question, 'I'm hoping he can brief us on the current situation in a town called Massinger.'

'Why on earth would the situation in Massinger be of any interest to us; might I ask?'

'Massinger is but a short drive to the border separating Mozambique from the Kruger National Park. A little over a year ago, Sandford was behind the smuggling of boxes containing Chinese missiles and their launchers into the Kruger Park; that's how I got to meet him.'

'So, jumping ahead, I take it you're planning to ask for his help in getting our eight crates across the border and into the Kruger Park?'

'That's the general idea.'

'Fair enough; let's assume we're able to do that. Then what?'

'Well, we both know that rhinos are occasionally transported from *bomas* near Matetsi via a series of back roads into Languleni. So, it shouldn't be too difficult for Etienne or one of the other guys to meet us at some point and help us load the crates onto one of their lorries. Then, once we're safely in Languleni, we'll give Vusi a call to come and pick up the goods.'

'Sandford's outside in his workshop; he will be very pleased to see you, Mr Hamilton.'

'Thank you, Mrs Matsanga, how is Filipe?'

'Sir, he is doing well at the Eduardo Mondlane University in Maputo, many thanks to your generosity.'

'I'm pleased to hear that; however, don't forget Filipe earned every centavo himself. When you next see him, pass on my good wishes.'

Sandford was draining the oil from the sump of an old Chevrolet van when Avi and Derek walked into his workshop. His effusive greetings and the numerous cups of tea that followed made it a lot easier for Derek to ask for his help smuggling the cargo on their Bedford into the Kruger Park. While agreeing to help them, Sandford expressed his concern about the owner of the lorry, Amin Shakil. 'How reliable is this man; can you trust him not to betray you?'

'He's brought us this far; I've no reason not to trust him.'

'Your judgement of people has always been good my friend, let's just hope it doesn't let us down now.' Pausing to wipe his hands on a greasy cloth, Sandford continued, 'Eight wooden crates you say. Okay, assuming it will take two men to a crate, we will probably need another two willing helpers to help get each crate through the fence and into a safe hiding place while we wait for one of your ranger friends to arrive.'

'That's about the size of it; can we do this?'

'Let me call someone in Massinger who can give me some idea what things are like along the border.' Sandford was back in five minutes, 'As you may recall Derek, the roads in the interior are not the best. So, if we are to do this, we must leave first thing in the morning if we are to reach Massinger before dark. My friend has promised he will stay in touch with me on my mobile phone. Now this request is not negotiable,' he said smiling, 'my wife and I would be honoured if you would all stay the night with us.'

They had just finished a hastily prepared meal and were sitting around drinking a few beers on the *stoep* when Sandford's wife came in and whispered in his ear. '*Merda*,' Sandford cursed getting to his feet, 'you should all come and see this,' he said leading everyone to the kitchen where a small television was tuned to the evening news. The video that flickered across the screen showed Amin's old Bedford lorry covered with a green tarpaulin leaving the port area of Maputo.

'*Merda* is right,' Amin muttered, 'one of those bloody officials we bribed failed to turn off a surveillance camera. What did the news report say?'

'That the police are looking for this Bedford lorry in connection with a robbery in the port area,' Sandford replied, 'I think it's time you levelled with me; exactly what is going on?'

'You're quite right my friend; I should have been more upfront with you from the start,' Derek admitted before going on to recount everything that had happened following the raid on Grossendahl's ranch. 'Which brings us to where we are now. Please understand Sandford, I will not blame you if you feel this favour I'm asking is pushing our friendship a little too far.'

'And this from the man who did not hesitate to paddle down the Rio das Mortes to rescue me from the very people who employed that man Grossendahl. I would be offended,' Sandford continued with a smile, 'if you thought, even for a moment, that I wouldn't do everything I possibly could to help you. However, now that's settled, we've got some work to do. First, we must get the tarpaulin covering the back of this lorry painted white and attach fake business logos to both cab doors; that at least, will make us a little less conspicuous on the road.'

Leaving the Ford Transit van with Sandford's wife to return to the rental agency, the Bedford, driven by Amin and disguised by a freshly painted tarpaulin and fake door logos, rolled out of Xai Xai headed for Villa de Macia and the turnoff for Massinger. While stopped at a local trading store to pick up bottles of water, Sandford took Derek, Avi and Amin aside, 'It occurs to me our greatest danger on the road ahead may well be from Grossendahl's people and not the local police force. I think we should have a plan in place just in case we are stopped at a road block not set up by the police.'

'You raise a good point, my friend, let's put our heads together and see what we can come up with; Avi, Amin, any ideas?'

'Okay,' Avi began, 'between the four of us we've got two Beretta pistols with ten rounds apiece, a Glock with twelve rounds and a Skorpion with a single twenty-round magazine. Not bad, but a little light if we run into bad guys carrying real firepower.'

'I suggest we split our forces,' Derek said, 'one of us in the back of the lorry hidden under the tarp armed with the Skorpion, the rest of us in the cab up front with the driver carrying the Glock and the Berettas.'

'No gun for me please sir,' Amin said shaking his head, 'I don't like guns; better someone else takes it. I will be too busy driving anyway.'

'That settles it then,' Avi said, 'one-hour shifts in the back; I'll take first shift.'

CHAPTER – 27 –

AVI SAW THE CAR FOR the first-time, half way through her shift. She opened the small sliding window separating the back of the lorry from the cab and spoke to Derek. 'It might not be anything to be alarmed about,' she shouted to make herself heard over the noise of the engine, 'but this car's been behind us for the last twenty minutes. Despite having two perfectly safe opportunities to overtake us, the driver opted each time to eat our dust.'

'Amin, pull over to the side of the road; let's give them a chance to pass,' Derek suggested, 'if they don't take us up on our offer, then we may have reason to be worried.' Amin waited until they reached a flat stretch of road before driving off onto the grass verge. 'What's the car doing,' Derek turned and shouted to Avi through the rear window.

'Give it a minute for the dust to settle,' she shouted back from the peephole she had cut into the tarp covering the rear of their lorry. 'Oh shit! They've pulled over on the rise about half a mile back; they're just sitting there looking at us.'

'You said they; do you believe there's more than one person in the car?'

'That's the impression I got the first time I saw the car. Without binoculars, I really can't be sure.'

'Perhaps they prefer to stay well back of the dust and stones we are kicking up,' Sandford suggested.

'Can't argue with that,' Derek admitted, 'let's press on and see what they do next.'

'I'd be a lot happier if you'd join me here in the back,' Avi suggested. 'If you could climb through the rear window without us having to stop, we wouldn't tip them off that some of us are in the back under the tarp.'

'It will be a tight squeeze, but I think I can manage it.'

'Take the Glock,' Sandford suggested, 'between it and the Skorpion, you'll have more than enough firepower if this proves to be something other than just a car trying to stay well back of our dust cloud.' Derek managed to climb through the small window and, crouching between the crates, watched Avi as she kept an eye on the car through her peephole in the tarp.

'The dust cloud we kick up doesn't make it easy to keep them in sight,' she said to him. 'Every now and again, whenever we hit a stony stretch of road, the dust usually settles down. Only then am I able to figure out whether they're gaining on us or staying back just enough to keep us in sight.'

'Any idea what make of car it is?' he asked.

'Small; four passenger. Looks like a Nissan Micra or something like that. Not the ideal sort of car for a road like this; if there are two of them in the car, their kidneys would be taking quite a hammering.'

'If anything happens,' he asked, 'would you prefer the Glock or the Skorpion?'

'Glock any day,' she replied, 'never liked the Skorpion; bloody things are always jamming.'

'Not this one, I checked it over carefully and would stake my life on it.'

'That's exactly what you'll be doing if whoever is in that car isn't just out on a sightseeing drive.'

'We're coming up to the new bridge over the Mabalane River and the only two-mile stretch of tarred road between Villa de Macia and Massinger,' Sandford shouted to them through the cab window. 'Its the stretch where someone who knows this road might try to overtake us.'

'Thanks for the heads-up,' Derek replied as he crawled between the crates to Avi's position where he handed her the Glock. 'What's the car doing now?'

'I think it may have stopped, but I can't be sure because of the dust. 'No wait. There's another vehicle just coming onto the tarred section; it must have passed the Nissan. Looks like a Hummer and it's going like a bat out of hell.'

'Shit! I don't like the sound of that,' Derek said quickly crawling up to the rear window. 'We've got another vehicle coming up fast,' he yelled to

Amin, 'keep to the left side of the road, force him to overtake us on our right. Avi,' he yelled, 'what's he doing now?'

'Coming up on our right, he's...Oh fuck!' she swore as two shots rang out, 'they're shooting at our tires! Derek, you've got to stop them. Can you see them, they're coming up on our right side!'

Frantically, he clawed at the tarp loosening it just enough to get his head and the barrel of the Skorpion through the opening. As the Hummer drew up alongside the Bedford, a black man in the left front passenger seat leaned out of the window and aimed a pistol at their right front tire.

Furious, Derek pushed the change lever on the Skorpion to automatic and squeezed the trigger. Instead of the roaring discharge of its 20-round magazine, only a single shot rang out. The round, narrowly missing the man firing the pistol, hit the dashboard, spraying metal and plastic fragments around the interior of the Humvee. Panicked, the driver of the Hummer swerved violently to his right and drove head-on into the solid concrete bridge abutment. The force of the impact tore the engine from its mountings, flipped the large vehicle up into the air and sent it crashing down to land on its back in the dry bed of the Mabalane River thirty feet below.

Amin pulled the Bedford off the road just beyond the end of the bridge. Shaken, he remained in the cab while Sandford, Derek and Avi scrambled down the bank and ran towards the wreck of the Hummer. Its fuel tank, fractured by the violence of the crash, was leaking petrol into the badly damaged engine compartment where it started a small fire. 'The whole thing could explode at any minute,' Derek yelled, 'get well away from it!'

Backing off to a safe distance, they watched in horror as the driver, hanging upside down in his seatbelt, struggled to free himself as the growing fire threatened to engulf the vehicle. 'Bloody hell! I can't just stand here and watch him burn,' Derek shouted as he ran to the driver's side of the Hummer. The impact of the vehicle landing on its roof had buckled the driver's door making it impossible to open. Desperate to help the man, Derek kicked in the shattered side window, got down on his hands and knees and, crawling part way in, slashed at the seatbelt with his pocket knife. As the belt parted, he grabbed hold of the man's arms and had him almost halfway out through the window, when the petrol tank exploded.

The initial shockwave threw Derek ten feet away, saving him from certain death as the Hummer erupted in flames. Avi and Sandford rushed to his side and dragged him further away as ammunition began exploding in the burning vehicle. 'That was a brave, bloody stupid thing to do,' Avi yelled at him, 'that bastard was trying to kill us; why would you want to save his miserable life?'

'You're quite right. Had I managed to pull him to safety, I would then have shot him dead. The driver of that Hummer was our old enemy Phineas Malema and the other man, I suspect, his remaining partner who played a role in the murder of the six lion skinners at Grossendahl's ranch.'

PART THREE

CHAPTER − 28 −

'NO DOUBT ABOUT IT,' JACOB Riley said, 'I've got to hand it to you two; lifting the hides, bones and rhino horns and whatever else this Grossendahl and his cronies were shipping to Vietnam was a smart, if somewhat risky, move. I trust you looked after Sandford and that guy Amin Shakil who owned the old Bedford?'

'He certainly did!' Avi replied with a smile, 'Derek has no qualms when it comes to spending Miriam's money. I can assure you Sandford and Amin thought all their Christmases had come early.'

'Yes, money is all very well; but it must have occurred to you that whoever managed to find you on the road to Massinger, would have no trouble tracking down your friend Amin, not to mention Sandford and his family?'

'Of course, it occurred to us,' Avi jumped in, 'we managed to persuade Amin to abandon his old lorry and take a well-deserved rest with friends in Tanzania; while at the same time we convinced Sandford to arrange to meet up with his family in Swaziland. We spoke with him this morning, and all seems to be well.'

'By the way, how is Sandford? Do you think we might be able to persuade him to come and work for us?'

'I don't believe you would have too much trouble enticing him and his family to move permanently to this side of the border. Depending on what you have in mind for him, of course?'

'As you are aware, I've always considered our attempts to eradicate poaching to be almost entirely reactive with no serious attempts on our part to nip problems in the bud before they begin,' Jacob said. 'My idea is to come up with a more proactive plan; a plan which could include an intelligence network to detect and dissuade poachers long before they cross into the game reserve.'

'I couldn't agree more,' Derek said, 'and I believe Sandford would be just the man for the job. He's not a local and would not be beholden to anyone in the local population or the government. If you like, I'd be happy to give him a call and run the idea past him,'

'Good, go ahead and let me know what he thinks. By the way, have you been in touch with Vusi Dlamini yet?'

'Spoke to him the same day Etienne picked us up on the border. Vusi's planning on arriving here sometime tomorrow with his team; they're anxious to take delivery of this potential political firestorm. I only hope their charges against the corrupt officials who made this whole sorry business possible, hold up in court.'

'Dare I hope this could lead to significant improvements in government efforts to discourage poaching in our national parks,' Jacob said hopefully.

'Knowing some of the crooks in this government, I wouldn't count on it! However, on a more positive note, how's Rob doing?'

'Spending money at a rate even you couldn't better. In concert with Miriam, he's ordered an Israeli engineered surveillance balloon which will give us an almost round-the-clock ability to keep an eye on some of the longer stretches of fencing on our western border.'

'Sounds interesting! What can you tell us about it?'

'Well, from what I can recall, it's a truck mounted, helium-filled balloon carrying a payload of video and real-time infrared cameras as high as a thousand feet for up to three days at a time. I believe Rob plans to combine this with his current speciality of radio-controlled drones; I understand you've had some experience with them.'

'Hells bells! The only tool missing from his arsenal is a helicopter carrying six heavily armed game scouts ready to drop in on a bunch of unsuspecting poachers at a moment's notice,' Derek said with a laugh.

'Actually, I believe he has already discussed this requirement with Miriam and received a positive response!'

'So, all we will need are at least twenty-four heavily armed game scouts ready for action around the clock; tell me, where on earth are we going to find them?'

'Well, we aren't going find them as you put it; instead, we're going to have to train them ourselves. And I've passed that task onto Blessing and

Dimas; their time with 32 Battalion makes them ideal candidates for the job, and the sooner they get on with it, the better.'

'Have we had any problems with poachers lately?'

'Not since you left for Mozambique. However, Etienne left early this morning to pick up two rhino cows from Matetsi to add to our breeding program. As you know, I'm always a little nervous when we have rhinos housed in our holding pens.'

Seeing a Land Rover carrying half a dozen visitors arrive back from a morning game drive, Derek waited until the guests had entered the lodge before he wandered over to chat with the driver. '*Sawubona* Blessing.'

'*Hau Numzaan*, I am glad you are back safely. What news?'

'Good news my friend, that bastard Malema is dead.'

'How can you be sure? Did you kill him?'

'Didn't have to; I saw him burn to death in a car crash, right before my eyes.'

'You didn't try to save him?'

'I did, but the fire was too much.'

'Good; the gods did not want you messing with their plans for that man.'

'The boss tells me you and Dimas are going to train a new type of game guard ready to take on this new breed of poacher who is more likely to shoot back rather than surrender.'

'We need to do something *Numzaan* if we are not to lose this war to the *skelms*,' Blessing said as he drove off to refuel the Land Rover for the evening game drive.

About to return to their *rondavel*, Derek saw Avi approaching from the direction of the camp office. 'I've just received a text from Miriam,' she said as they walked to their *rondavel*, 'she wants to meet us in Pretoria in two days' time.'

'Another long drive,' Derek complained, 'just what we need.'

'Not this time, she's sending the same Gulfstream G550 that flew the Israeli Prime Minister and his entourage to Skoonspruit Airport to pick us up. We're moving up in the world. What do you think of that?'

'Right now, I'm looking forward more to making love to you and sleeping in late; then I am flying in a luxury jet.'

'My sentiments exactly!'

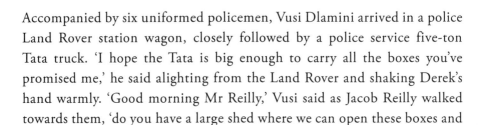

Accompanied by six uniformed policemen, Vusi Dlamini arrived in a police Land Rover station wagon, closely followed by a police service five-ton Tata truck. 'I hope the Tata is big enough to carry all the boxes you've promised me,' he said alighting from the Land Rover and shaking Derek's hand warmly. 'Good morning Mr Reilly,' Vusi said as Jacob Reilly walked towards them, 'do you have a large shed where we can open these boxes and see what we've got?'

'Of course, I'll get two of the drivers to take the vehicles out of the storage area, that should give you a large enough workspace. Providing you have no objections, I'd like to be present when you open these crates.'

Dlamini's six police officers carried the wooden boxes into the storage area and, armed with a variety of tools, began to pry open the lids. 'I'm particularly anxious to see what's in that long box,' Derek remarked to Vusi.

'Let's do that one first,' Vusi said pointing out the eight-foot-long crate to two of his officers. Within minutes they had the top off exposing tightly packed straw which they began removing a few handfuls at a time. 'What is it? What have we got?' Vusi asked.

'Tusks, sir; two huge tusks,' the officers replied lifting out two elephant tusks and laying them side by side on the straw beside the open crate.

'*Jirre God*,' Jacob Riley exclaimed, 'I recognise these tusks. They're from Gombandlovu, an old tusker who roamed the Punda Maria area for more years than I care to remember. When his name no longer appeared in game scout reports, the handful of us familiar with the old boy had always hoped he had drifted off into the Limpopo National Park in Mozambique, and not fallen prey to poachers. Colonel, I have no wish to see anymore, it would only break my heart. When you've completed your inventory, I would be grateful if you would all join me in our lounge, so we may raise a glass in farewell to all the magnificent creatures fallen victim to these unspeakable bastards.'

Two hours had gone by before Vusi Dlamini walked into the lounge, his sombre expression making it clear he did not bring good news. Gratefully accepting the stiff whisky Jacob thrust into his hand, he sat down at the round table and looked at the faces of the people anxiously awaiting his report. 'It's not good news I'm afraid,' he began. 'We have a total of nineteen rhino horns, ranging in size from a spectacular twenty-nine inches to a tiny two-inch nub hacked off a calf probably not much more than a few months old.'

Taking a long sip of his drink, he continued, 'There are twenty-three pairs of elephant tusks, the largest being the pair from the elephant Gombandlovu, identified by Mr Riley. The rest of the crates contained a number of elephant feet, probably for conversion into wastepaper baskets, the hides and bones from eighteen lions and two tigers. We also found fifteen zebra hides. The only good news, if I can call it that, relates to all the lion, tiger and zebra hides. They were improperly cured and had developed 'slip,' rendering them worthless.'

'Colonel,' Jacob asked, 'any idea where all the poaching took place?'

'I would think mostly in southern Africa; including Zimbabwe, Zambia and Botswana. We will be sharing this information with the relevant authorities in those countries once we determine whether they played any role in the commission of these crimes.'

'Colonel, you and your team are welcome to spend the night with us here in Riley's Camp,' Jacob said.

'You're most kind Mr Riley, but I must decline your invitation. My team and I intend to return to Johannesburg tonight as I will be holding a major press conference in Johannesburg tomorrow morning; if we are to succeed against the powers ranged against us, it is imperative we strike while the iron is still hot.'

As Vusi walked out of the lounge, he stopped to speak briefly to Derek and Avi, 'Todays success is the direct result of your bravery and efforts, thank you. Also,' he said slipping a folded sheet of paper into Derek's pocket, 'we found this amongst the and straw used as packing materials in some of the crates; I trust you will find it just as interesting as I did.'

CHAPTER – 29 –

THE GULFSTREAM G550 SWEPT IN low over Bon Accord Dam before touching down on the main runway at Wonderboom Airport. As it taxied up to the terminal, a limousine pulled out from behind a hanger and stopped at the bottom of the stairs rolled up by airport staff. As the cabin door opened, Miriam called up to them, 'It's good to see you two again, come on, get in; there's someone I want you to meet.'

'Milner Street, Waterkloof,' Miriam instructed the driver as the Cadillac XTS limousine left the airport.

'Nice wheels,' Avi commented as she sank back on the plush leather upholstery, 'almost as comfortable as the old Vauxhall left for us at OR Tambo when this whole business started.'

'Nothing is too good for my favourable team,' Miriam said ignoring the remark as she turned in her seat to face them.

'Waterkloof; that's a fairly upscale neighbourhood,' Derek said hoping to change the subject, 'this someone you want us to meet must be pretty important?'

'Yes, he is, and he's also my boss, so please, be on your best behaviour,' Miriam said as the car left the highway and entered the jacaranda-lined streets of Waterkloof before turning off on a gravelled driveway that led up to a palatial home built in the old Cape Dutch style.

'Very nice,' Avi said, 'does your boss live here?'

'You can ask him yourself, that's him coming down the steps.' A middle-aged man with grey hair, dressed in khaki slacks and a pale blue golf shirt, came up to the car and opened her door.

'You must be Avital Blum; I've heard only good things about you from your instructors, I'm Dov Harel,' he said shaking her hand. 'And you must be Derek Hamilton,' he said as Derek stepped out of the car, 'thank you both for agreeing to meet with me.'

'I didn't think we had much choice,' Derek said, 'its not advisable to turn down a request from Miriam Hyde-Eshar.'

'Which is why Miriam and I work so well together,' Dov Harel said as he ushered them through the front door and out onto a back patio overlooking a vast expanse of lawn and a sparkling blue swimming pool.

'Very nice place you've got here Mr Harel,' Derek said.

'Yes, it is; unfortunately, it's not mine,' he replied with a rueful smile. 'This place is mine for this week only then it's back to my small flat in Tel Aviv which, I can assure you, is nowhere near as grand as this. Please sit down,' he said waving them towards four patio chairs arranged around a glass-topped table, 'I've ordered coffee for everyone. Miriam, would you like to start?'

'Yes, thank you, sir. Mr Harel, as you may or may not know, is the Director of the Institute for Intelligence and Special Operations.'

'Is that Mossad?' Derek asked.

'We prefer to use the name Miriam gave you,' Dov said, 'there's too much media attention paid to the latter; which brings me to one of the reasons I asked Miriam to invite you both to Pretoria. On behalf of the Institute, I want to thank all three of you for bringing to a satisfactory close the investigation into the attempted assassinations of the Israeli and Palestinian prime ministers and the disruption of the Schoveldt International poaching operations in this country. My second reason for inviting you all to meet with me is to raise the regrettable fact that Schoveldt International is still very much in business, but no one, including my office, has the faintest idea where... Ah,' he said, 'here's our coffee.'

Once everyone had their coffee and the housekeeper had returned inside, Derek reopened the conversation. 'It's just possible Avi and I may have a lead as to where we should start looking.' Miriam and Dov stared expectantly at him. 'When Colonel Dlamini and his men opened the crates of horns, tusks and hides,' Derek explained, 'they came across an interesting item inadvertently forgotten amongst the straw used to cushion the more valuable objects.'

'And what did they find?'

'A front page from the weekly German newsmagazine, Der Spiegel, with the address of the subscriber, a Herr Karl Adler in Augsburg, clearly visible.'

'The relevance escapes me,' Dov Harel said.

'If I may,' Avi interrupted, 'when Derek and I looked into the sudden departure of Aapie Grossendahl from Maputo, we discovered his travel agent had booked him on a Lufthansa flight to Frankfurt with a rail connection on to Augsburg. While the name Karl Adler doesn't ring any alarm bells, we thought the connection to be too much of a coincidence.'

'A tenuous lead in my opinion,' Dov remarked, 'but, if it's all we've got, I suggest we follow it up right away. Miriam, if you would make all the necessary arrangements, I would like Avi and Derek to leave as soon as possible.'

'Of course, I'll see to it right away,' Miriam replied as she rose to her feet indicating the meeting was over.

'Sir,' Avi asked as she stood facing Dov Harel, 'there is one final matter I'd like to ask you about.'

'And that is?'

'A man called Abu-Jamal. When I made inquiries regarding his identity, I was ordered not to investigate him any further as it is believed he may be a close relative to the Palestinian prime minister.'

'In what way is this man Abu-Jamal involved in any of these matters?' Dov Harel asked.

'An informant of ours, later found murdered, described him as 'a very big boss' behind the kidnapping of Dennis Middlebrook's parents and his pregnant girlfriend, Julia. We believe this crime was carried out on Abu Jamal's orders to guarantee Middlebrook's participation in the assassination attempt on the two prime ministers. I understand this may be a sensitive matter for the government, but we would like to know whether this is an area we might investigate further?'

'You'll have to leave that with me,' Harel replied. 'Rest assured I will make the necessary inquiries and will get back to you with an answer as soon as possible.'

The same evening, Avi and Derek boarded Lufthansa Flight 573 at OR

Tambo Airport in preparation for their nine-hour flight to Frankfurt. Right on time, the giant Airbus A380-800 lifted off and flew into the darkening skies over northern Botswana. 'That's the Zambezi below us,' Derek said as he leaned over Avi and pointed through her window, 'I wouldn't be surprised if some of the elephant tusks found in that crate came from somewhere in the darkness below us.'

'Depressing thought, my love; but save that anger for when we find Grossendahl and his cronies. But, until that happy day arrives, let's enjoy the moment with a fine bottle of wine and good food, made even more enjoyable by the fact that Miriam and Dov are paying.'

The Airbus touched down shortly after five in the morning at Frankfurt am Main, Terminal One. However, it wasn't until two hours later, having cleared immigration and customs, that they finally boarded the InterCity Express train to Munich's Main Station. Alighting from the Express, they headed towards the main concourse of the station looking for the rows of luggage lockers where they were to pick up a bag containing various items of equipment they couldn't possibly have carried onboard their flight.

'We're looking for number 79,' Avi said as they walked down the rows, 'have you got the key?' Producing the key from his pocket, he opened locker 79, reached in and took out a black flight bag.

'Right,' he said, 'its back to the *Hauptbahnhof* to find a local train to Augsburg.' Settling down in their almost empty carriage, he handed the flight bag over to Avi, 'Take a look inside, let's see what goodies Mama Miriam has packed for us.'

Unzipping the bag, Avi looked inside and, after rummaging about for a moment, handed him two passports, 'We're British citizens,' she said, 'though I see Miriam has also included two Canadian passports just in case.'

'I'm quite happy to be a Brit for now; what I'm interested in is the hardware she's given us.'

Opening the bag again, Avi listed the weapons. 'Two Beretta .25 pistols and, an old favourite of mine, two Sig Sauer P226's with sound suppressors. I see she's also included suppressors for the Beretta's, sandwiched neatly between sizable wads of currency with denominations ranging from five to two hundred Euros. Though I've no doubt,' she continued, 'the debit card she gave you would enable us to purchase a small country in Europe.'

'If I were you,' he began, 'I'd start packing that all away, according to the last announcement over the PA, we'll be pulling into Augsburg in a few minutes.'

'What happens then?' Avi asked.

'According to a note enclosed with the British passports, we have a reservation at the Augsburg City Hotel on Holzbach Strasse, a short taxi ride from the station. But before we go there, I'd like to make some inquiries about renting bicycles.'

'Bicycles? Are we going on a cycling holiday?'

'I can't think of a better way of getting around the centre of the city; no traffic jams, parking problems and we can have nice cycle helmets to help us blend in with the local student population.'

'I suppose it could work,' Avi replied doubtfully, 'though I'd always imagined we would race around in a silver Porsche or a red Lamborghini.'

'I think you've been watching too many James Bond movies!'

The cycle path, which began at the Burgermeister Strasse bridge and followed the Wertach River, was the most direct route Derek could find on the map he picked up from the cycle rental shop. 'I'm not used to this,' Avi complained, 'its been years since I last rode a bicycle.'

'You'll get the hang of it quickly,' he said barely concealing a smile, 'it's a lot like riding a bicycle; once you've mastered it, you never forget!'

'*Voetsak* Derek! If I fall off, I'll never forgive you.'

'I wouldn't worry about that now; we're coming up to Ulmer Strasse, number 1769 should be amongst the row of two-storey townhouses opposite the park on our left. If we ride into the park, we can watch the townhouses from one of those benches.' While Avi leaned their bikes against the back of the bench, Derek walked over to a refreshments kiosk and bought two milkshakes, 'it would look a lot better,' he said handing her one, 'if we are sitting here enjoying ourselves rather than appearing to be keeping an eye on a particular house.'

'So far, we've not seen any activity around 1769; perhaps there's no one home,' Avi said as she dropped the two empty milkshake cups in a nearby waste bin. 'Let's take a ride around the back of the townhouses and see if there's a rear entrance leading off a service lane.'

Avi was right; a narrow service lane separated the row of townhouses from a stretch of tangled shrubbery clinging to the banks of a small stream funnelling storm water to the nearby Wertach River. 'Good bit of cover should we decide to come back later tonight to see if Herr Adler is at home. After a spot of dinner of course,' Derek added.

The chorus of frogs were startled into silence as Avi and Derek approached Ulmer Strasse 1769 through the overgrown shrubbery lining the service lane behind the row of townhouses. 'There's no sign of anyone inside the house from either the front or the back,' she said, 'and its way past eleven. If anyone was home, I'm sure we would have seen lights in at least some of the rooms. I think it's a chance worth taking.'

'Okay,' Derek replied, slipping the Sig Sauer under his belt in the small of his back, 'its dark enough to leave the bikes hidden in the long grass. Now everything depends on you being able to pick the lock on the back door.'

'Piece of cake,' Avi retorted, 'the impossible I can do right away, it's the miracles that take a few minutes longer.' True to her boast, she had the door open in seconds. Satisfied darkness had concealed their entry, Derek quietly closed the back door and switched on his Maglite, shading it with his hand so it wouldn't be visible to anyone watching from the street.

The house had a musty, unpleasant odour which they put down to it being unoccupied for some time, 'That's odd,' Avi whispered, 'there's hardly any furniture; it's almost as though no one lives here.'

They split up as they searched the ground floor. 'I can't find anything linking this place to this man Adler or Grossendahl for that matter; there aren't any papers in the drawers, no books on the shelves, nothing. I'll tell you what this place reminds me of,' he said whispering in her ear, 'a safe house, a bolthole for spies or people just like us! Let's see what we can find upstairs.'

'Bloody hell!' Avi exclaimed, 'the smell is a lot worse up here, you check this room while I search the next.'

Derek, who had a horrible idea what was causing the smell, cautiously opened the door to the room. In the shaded light from his torch, the figure of a man lying on the bed was unmistakable. Approaching the bed, he shone the light on the face of the man. Even with the features distorted in death and the teeth displayed in a rictus grin, Derek had no problem identifying the body of Aapie Grossendahl. The two bullet wounds in the centre of his forehead confirmed the cause of death.

'Derek,' Avi called urgently from the adjacent room, 'the police are here.'

'What?' he muttered softly as he rushed to the window and looked down at the blue and silver Mercedes car parked in front of the house, its flashing blue lights and the word *polizei* visible on the bonnet. 'Oh, Shit! We must have triggered a silent alarm,' he said grabbing Avi's arm, 'we've got to get out of here.' As they tiptoed down the stairs, they heard voices outside the front door and a scratching sound as someone tried a number of keys in the door lock. They had just closed the back door and were halfway over the wall when all the lights in the house came on.

'Do you think they saw us?' Avi asked breathlessly as they ran into the long grass to retrieve their bicycles.

'I don't think so; if they had, there'd be a lot of yelling and screaming. But there soon will be a lot of yelling and screaming once they get around to searching upstairs.'

'What do you mean?'

'I'll tell you about it later; but right now, we have to get as far away from here as we can. Like it or not, we'll have to push our way through all these bushes and wade through the stream, all the while hoping I'm right in assuming there's another cycle path on the other side.'

CHAPTER − 30 −

'ARE YOU SURE IT WAS Grossendahl?' Avi asked as they cycled back to their hotel.

'Despite the decomposition of the body, I'm as sure as anyone could be. It's my guess he's been dead for at least a week; taken out by two bullets to the head. From the position of the body on the bed and the absence of any signs of a struggle, I'd say he was shot while he was sleeping; probably by someone using a silenced pistol.'

'Sounds like a professional job, double tap and all that,' Avi said, 'so, what do we do now?'

'Right now, my first instinct is to leave town on the first available train.'

'And your second?'

'Tough it out and hope we didn't leave any clues behind, and that we do not appear on any surveillance cameras in the area.'

'We both wore latex gloves, and I was careful not to leave any clues when picking the lock on the back door. So, I'm in agreement with your second instinct; also, may I suggest we take the bull by the horns and revisit the scene of the crime first thing in the morning. Who knows, we could be lucky enough to see or hear something which might give us some idea what we should do next.'

❖

The park across from Ulmer Strasse 1769 was crowded by gawkers and the morbidly curious, held back by a barrier of red and white police tape. 'I expect they've already removed the body and the plainclothes people we see leaving the house are the tail end of their forensics team.'

'They don't look at all happy,' Avi said. 'unless the hit man or woman did a poor job and left Grossendahl's passport behind, the *polizei* wouldn't have a clue who he was.'

'Well, I'm afraid this was a bit of a waste of time,' Derek admitted, 'we're not going to learn anything sitting here in the park.'

'Why don't you go over to the refreshments kiosk and, taking your time, pick up five cups of coffee,' Avi suggested. 'I've just noticed three ladies I'd very much like to meet. I only hope my Arabic is still up to par!'

When he returned ten minutes later, Avi was sitting at one of the picnic tables in earnest conversation with the three ladies in question. He recognised they were speaking Arabic, though he had no idea what they were saying. Derek handed the coffees around, responding to the chorus of *shukran jazilan's* with a nod and a smile. After five minutes, one of the women looked at her watch and said something to her two companions. Almost at once, all three got to their feet and with a further chorus of *shukran jazilan's*, took their leave.

'I trust you're going to tell me what that was all about?' he said as they unlocked their bicycles and rode back towards their hotel.

'First, have you any idea where we can get hold of any photos of Barendt and Dieter Schoveldt?'

'The only possible source I can think of is MI5; they would have surveillance pictures of the old man, Barendt, but I'm not sure if they have any of Dieter Schoveldt. For my part, I've not met either of them. But why the interest?'

'The three women I was speaking to work as cleaning ladies in some of the townhouses in the same row as number 1769. In fact, they told me the woman who once worked for Herr Karl Adler, is employed nearby. I was thinking if...'

'We had a photo of either of the Schoveldt's,' he completed her sentence, 'she should be able to confirm whether Karl Adler and Barendt Schoveldt are one and the same person.'

'Exactly!'

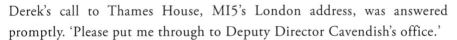

Derek's call to Thames House, MI5's London address, was answered promptly. 'Please put me through to Deputy Director Cavendish's office.'

'I'm sorry, sir, I cannot do that without knowing who you are and the purpose of your call.'

'Of course, you're quite right. My name is Derek Hamilton, and the purpose of my call is to acquaint the Deputy Director, Ms Cavendish, with information I am confident she will appreciate receiving.'

'Very well, sir, I will transfer your call to one of the Deputy Director's assistants; I'm sure he would be more than happy to help you.'

Derek was about to protest when the call went through, 'Simon Spenser,' was the abrupt answer.

'Good afternoon Simon, there's a good fellow, please put me through to Rachel Cavendish, it's rather urgent.'

'I couldn't possibly do that,' came the icy reply, 'without you explaining to me, in detail, what makes your call so important.'

'I'll tell you why it's important Simon. I've no idea how long you've worked for Rachel but, knowing her as I do, it would help you keep your job a lot longer if you did exactly as I asked.'

There was another click on the line as Derek's call went straight through. 'What the hell do you mean you don't know who he is?' he heard Rachel yelling in the background, 'who is this?' she demanded, picking up his call.

'*Jissus*, Rachel, the poor bugger is only trying to do his *blerrie* job; no need to be so *hardegat!*'

'Derek!' she shouted, 'it that you?'

'Guilty as charged. How are you, Rachel?'

'Its lovely to hear your voice again; *hoe gaan dit met jou?*'

'I see you've not forgotten your Afrikaans!'

'Of course not; I still think back to those days in Mozambique with fondness. But I'm sure you didn't call me to reminisce about times gone by.'

'Well in a way I have; did you or your people ever track down either of the Schoveldts, father or son?'

'Despite our best efforts, we never did. Don't tell me you've found them or something.'

'I wouldn't stake my life on it, but it's possible we may have found one of them.'

'By we, I take it to mean you and that Jewish girl, what's her name, Avital Blum?'

'Obviously, there's nothing wrong with your intelligence network, apart from the fact that you don't know where the Schoveldt's are.'

'My guess is they're in Augsburg?'

Okay, you've managed to put a trace on my phone; bully for you!'

'Derek, I don't want us to fall out again. Can't we just remain good friends?'

'I'd be happy with that.'

'Good, now how can I help you?'

'I need the most recent photos you have of Barendt and Dieter Schoveldt sent to my phone. Can you do that?'

'Barendt I can do, but we've nothing on Dieter; anything else?'

'Yes; while you're being nice to me I'd appreciate your opinion on the An Dinh Trading Company, apparently based in Vung Tau, Vietnam and operated by a Nguyen Van Lamh. And while you're at it, what can you tell me about a man known as Abu-Jamal, a rumoured close relation to the Palestinian prime minister.'

'Heavens! What an eclectic collection of *skelms*. You'll have to give me a day or two to consult with friends.'

'Not that I'm jealous or anything, but would the CIA man, Lawrence Faulkner be amongst these friends?'

'Let's stop while we're ahead shall we. A photo of the elder Schoveldt is on its way, and I'd appreciate you letting me know if you find him. Also, by way of a friendly warning, apart from his son Dieter, Barendt has two dangerous sidekicks, an Aapie Grossendahl and a Sakchai Sakmokon; you'll need to be very careful of them.'

'For once, we're ahead of MI5. Therefore, it gives me great pleasure to announce the unfortunate passing of Aapie and Sakchai, two gentlemen whom, I can assure you, will not be missed.'

⋐⬦⬦⭆

'Amira, she's the one to ask,' one of the cleaning ladies replied when Avi showed them the photo of Barendt Schoveldt.

'She's at work right now, number 1733, it's just a little way down the street; would you like me to come with you?'

'Thank you, but no. I wouldn't like Amira to think we're not concerned about protecting her privacy.' As it turned out, it was a wise move given the sexual abuse Amira had suffered at the hands of Karl Adler and his equally depraved son, Bruno.

'I was working as an English teacher in Aleppo when I had to flee for my life,' Amira told Avi who translated her story for Derek. 'I managed to get to Germany but, because I had a connection to one of the men who carried out a suicide attack in France, my claim for refugee status was refused, and I was ordered to be deported. Not wanting to be sent back to Syria, I went into hiding and, because I'm in this country illegally, these Adlers took advantage of my situation, knowing I could never complain to the authorities.'

'Ask her if either of these two men are still around?' Derek asked.

'Hold onto your horses,' Avi replied, 'I'm sure she's coming to that.'

Amira continued, and Avi translated, 'Then everything changed. A little over a week ago, another man arrived at the house. His arrival seemed to unnerve the Adlers who packed a few belongings and left at once. As soon as they got into their taxi, I grabbed my things and got out of the house as fast as I could. Luckily for me, one of my friends had to go to the hospital for a few weeks, so she arranged with her employer to take me on until her return.'

'Do you have any idea where these men went?' Avi asked.

'No, they never said anything to me.'

'This taxi that came for them do you recall the name of the company?' Avi asked.

'Uber is not a company; their drivers are all self-employed, but they are local people. I don't know the driver's name, but the women you spoke to at the park would know how to get hold of him.'

'Thank you, Amira, you've been a big help. Now I want to show you a picture on my phone; I need you to tell me if it's a picture of Karl Adler?'

The woman leaned forward and stared at the photo on Avi's phone. Choking back a sob, she cursed, '*Mughtasib*! Yes, that's him, Karl Adler. Bastard!'

'Thank you, Amira. Unfortunately, we could not find a picture of his son anywhere, but you've been a great help.'

Avi and Derek were almost out of the front gate of 1733 when Amira ran down the garden path towards them. '*Fraulein, fraulein*, talk to the people at the paper, they took pictures of everyone for the street montage.'

Amira's suggestion bore fruit. Two hours later, Derek and Avi emerged from the local newspaper office with a photo showing Barendt and Dieter Schoveldt posing side by side for a photographic montage featuring all the residents of Ulmer Strasse.

Their visit to the local Uber taxi driver's house was equally productive. 'I took the older man to an address in Hammerschmiede, then the younger man to the airport for his flight to Frankfurt,' the man told them.

'The younger man, did he say anything to you about where he would be staying in Frankfurt?' Derek asked, hoping this lead would pay out.

'Oh no! He wasn't staying in Frankfurt, he said he was flying on to Vietnam. That's all I can remember. But I do know the address of the house where I dropped the older man.'

'Can you give me that address?'

'Yes, of course, I have it in my book,' he said pulling a notebook from his pocket. 'Schill Strasse 67, it's on Izmir Platz next to the Lech river. It's easy to find, all you have to do is follow the cycle path along the river all the way to the Platz.'

This time, Derek's call to the Deputy Director of MI5, went through at once. 'Thank you for the photo. I've got to hand it to you and Avital, in no time flat you've managed to achieve what MI6 hasn't been able to do in over a year. Now, should you find these bastards before we do and are feeling a little squeamish about taking them out, feel free to call, and we'll send some people over who are untroubled by such niceties.'

'We appreciate your concern Rachel, but rest assured, squeamishness is not in our playbook. However, changing the subject; what you can tell me about the An Dinh Trading Company and Abu-Jamal, the supposed relative of the Palestinian prime minister?'

'I ran those two names past colleagues at MI6 and Lawrence Faulkner at the CIA. And by the way, Lawrence was very complimentary about your success in tracking down Barendt Schoveldt, so I don't think you should be so hard on him. Anyway, most of what I'm going to tell you came from Lawrence. Abu-Jamal, whose real name is Widad al-Mazigh, is a major fundraiser for a terrorist group closely allied with Hezbollah in Lebanon and Hamas in Gaza. al-Mazigh is high on the CIA's most wanted list, and he probably features on the Israeli list as well. Most recently, and this is probably how you first became aware of him, he was known to be behind the large-scale poaching of rhinos and elephants in Zimbabwe and South Africa, with most of the proceeds going to his favourite terrorist group.'

'Pretty well what we suspected; what did he have to say about the An Dinh Trading Company?' Derek asked.

'Well, in his words, the An Dinh Trading Company, run by Nguyen Van Lamh and his partners, is the sort of business any sensible person would want to avoid at all costs. He said he couldn't think of any criminal enterprise in which they are not actively involved, including the sale of rhino horn, ivory, lion bones, rare earth minerals and a wide range of addictive drugs. His advice is to steer well clear of them and leave it to the professionals.'

'Sound advice; the only problem is the so-called professionals are doing *fokkol* about it. Anyway, to end on a positive note, we managed to track down your old friend Barendt Schoveldt and his son, Dieter to a townhouse here in Augsburg. Then, about a week ago, their idyllic existence out of sight of the law, ended when Aapie Grossendahl showed up. His arrival, presumably unexpected, threw them into a bit of a panic, which they promptly dealt with by putting two bullets into Aapie's head and fleeing the coop. Dieter has since left for Vietnam and Barendt to a new hideout, located quite close by in the northern end of Augsburg.'

'Excellent work! How on earth did you find all that out?'

'Quite simple, we just spoke to the Uber taxi driver they used for their getaway.'

'Didn't it occur to either of you that, because it was all so easy, it could be a setup?'

'No, it didn't; you give these Schoveldt's too much credit.'

'Okay. Now do me a favour, see if your Uber taxi driver informant is still around. And when you've done that, please give me a call back; promise me you'll do that before you do anything else.'

'She's got a point you know,' Avi responded when he explained Rachel's concerns and her offer of help, 'in retrospect it did seem to be a little too easy. Still, there's no harm done if it turns out there's nothing to worry about, but on the other hand...'

'I agree, we've got nothing to lose; I'll call her right away.'

CHAPTER – 31 –

'I HATE TO ADMIT TO THIS,' Derek said when Rachel took his call, 'but our taxi driver does seem to have disappeared. He doesn't answer the door at his house, and his mobile phone is no longer receiving calls. I even called Uber, but it only prompted them to launch into a long lecture on how Uber taxi drivers were independent contractors responsible for their schedules.'

'Coupled with warnings I've just received from both MI6 and Lawrence at the CIA, I'd hold off rushing out to take care of Barendt until we can think this thing through,' she replied.

'What sort of warnings are we talking about?'

'Mostly chatter – by that, we mean lots of text messages flying back and forth between southern Germany, the Middle East and Southeast Asia.'

'It could be anything; can't they be more specific?'

'They're working on narrowing down the field,' Rachel warned, 'but these things can take time.'

'What worries us is that Barendt might suddenly get cold feet and take off again. If he does, we may never get another chance to take him out.'

'Okay, I know where you're coming from, but please let us help. Is this line secure?'

'Best that Mossad can come up with.'

'Good enough for me. MI6 has two special forces operatives on permanent standby in Munich; these men are highly trained and, if this is a setup, you'll at least have a fighting chance. Give me the go-ahead, and I can have them in Augsburg within an hour.'

───◆───

Izmir Platz, perched on the right bank of the Lech river, was in the heart of a residential area favoured by the Turkish *Gastarbeiter* community, primarily employed in Augsburg's service industry. Due to the devastating floods of a few years ago, the Platz had recently undergone repairs to the old, cracked and broken stone flagstones around the fountain, replacing them with modern tiles. To create a pedestrian-friendly environment, the Platz was encircled by a series of steel stanchions sunk deep into the ground and linked by a heavy chain to prevent vehicles from entering the area.

Schill Strasse 67, was a small, two-storey row house nestled along one side of the Platz facing the river. As neither Avi nor Derek had ever been there before, their knowledge of the Platz was derived solely from the map and street views available on their laptop computer. 'It looks okay to me,' Avi ventured, 'not the sort of place where a gang of murderous cutthroats might hide.'

A soft knock on their hotel room door announced the arrival of the two MI6 operatives, though neither looked anything like what Avi or Derek expected. 'We did some research on Izmir Platz before we left Munich,' the taller of the two men said, 'and decided that dressed as street sweepers wielding brooms, we would be less likely to draw the attention of anyone keeping watch on your target's address.'

'How do you suggest we do this?' Avi asked.

'We plan to arrive at the Platz at least half an hour ahead of you, giving anyone watching plenty of time to get used to the idea that we are nothing more than workers assigned to keep the Platz clean and tidy. We'll start work at the far end of the Platz and gradually work our way closer to the address in question, timing our arrival to coincide with your takedown of the fugitive. We will remain undercover unless we receive your signal.'

'How will we…?'

'You will each wear one of these signal devices on your wrist; all you have to do is press the button, and we'll respond in whatever manner seems appropriate,' the tall one said pausing to see if they had any further questions.

'Don't you want to know who we are and what this is all about?' Derek asked.

'If it's all the same to you, sir, we'd rather not know. If you haven't any further questions, my partner and I will make our way to Izmir Platz. Good luck to both of you.'

'And exactly how do you propose we go about doing this?' Avi asked Derek after the two men had left.

'I don't have any master plan up my sleeve other than going up to the door, pushing our way in and shooting the first person we encounter who looks like Barendt Schoveldt.'

———⊰⊱———

Parking and locking their bicycles to the railings at the pedestrian entrance to the Platz, they hung their cycle helmets on their backpacks and surreptitiously transferred their two silenced Berettas to the outside pockets on their lightweight jackets. 'A funny thing only just occurred to me,' Derek remarked, 'the taxi driver, who supposedly dropped Barendt off here, said all we need do was follow the cycle path along the river all the way here. Which leads me to wonder how the hell did he know we travelled around on bicycles?'

Alarmed by this revelation, Avi looked around the Platz but relaxed somewhat when she caught sight the two street sweepers; one was busy brushing leaves into a pan next to the fountain, while the other stood leaning on his broom a few doors down from Schill Strasse 67.

Avi and Derek, the two sweepers, and the half dozen or so customers relaxing on the patio of the coffee shop facing onto the Platz, looked up in alarm as a car, its engine racing and tires squealing, ploughed through the gardens along the river as it attempted to burst through the chains and stanchions surrounding the Platz. Prevented from driving onto the Platz, the car crashed its way along the outside of the protective barrier, causing the two sweepers to drop all pretence and pull out black, ugly looking automatic weapons from beneath their coats. Controlled five-round bursts of fire demolished the right side of the car, killing the driver and causing the car to swerve to its left and roll down the embankment to the edge of the river.

The car, packed with two hundred pounds of *TATP* exploded with an earth-shattering roar, creating a huge, churning ball of flame and a rapidly growing column of black smoke. The initial shockwave and secondary blast destroyed most of the upper floors of the townhouses facing the river, setting many of them ablaze. Car alarms from vehicles parked at the rear of the houses were set off by falling masonry as smoke and dust from the explosion, mingled with the acrid gasses from burning upholstery and plastics filled the area. Fortunately, for the handful of people gathered in the Platz, the sloping side of the embankment, deflected the force of the explosion upwards, saving their lives.

As debris from the upper floors of the houses fluttered to the ground about them, Avi and Derek were pulled from their shelter behind the fountain wall by the two street sweepers and hurried around to a back street and into a small van. 'Its preferable if we are not in this area when the first responders arrive; too many awkward questions,' one of the special forces operatives said turning around in his seat to face them.

'Well, and I think I speak for both of us,' Derek said squeezing Avi's hand, 'we owe our lives to your quick reaction, superior firepower and realistic expectations of what might happen.'

'Nah! I don't want to sound immodest, but when you've seen this sort of thing before, you get to develop a kind of sixth sense as to how these bastards are likely to react.'

'Here's to your sixth sense,' Avi said, 'it certainly saved our bacon.'

'Much of the real credit must go to our H&K G36c's. Fantastic weapon, a high degree of accuracy and firepower packed into nineteen lethal inches. Now let's deal with what's going to happen next; GHQ has instructed us to escort you to a safe house nearby, where you will stay for the time being. They deem it too risky to attempt to get both of you out of town as the people who want you dead will, most likely, be watching the airports and train stations.'

'The only person who wants us dead is Barendt Schoveldt,' Avi said, 'and, with a bit of luck, he will have died in that explosion.'

'I believe that was the intention of the people who organised the car bomb, though I very much doubt the unfortunate driver of the car was told anything about that part of the plan.'

'So, you're saying...' Derek jumped in, 'the car bomb, which someone detonated remotely, was intended for Barendt as well as ourselves?'

'That's Vauxhall Cross's interpretation of the chatter they picked up. Had these people not made the mistake of assuming the car could crash through the chain barrier around the Platz, their little plan would have succeeded.'

'And taken you and your partner out as well,' Avi observed.

'These things are always risky. Anyway,' he said pulling up outside a run-down cottage in a side street, 'this is the safe house. I'll park around the back so you two can make a quick dash for the rear door.'

Once inside, Avi asked the taller of the two about their belongings still at their hotel, 'Apart from needing a change of clothing, we have two Sig Sauer pistols, a set of fake Canadian passports and around fifty thousand in Euros in one of the bags. Not the sort of items one would expect to find in the ordinary traveller's luggage. Now,' she said, 'changing the subject slightly, what do we do in the meantime?'

'My orders are for both of you to sit tight while the higher-ups at MI6 assesses the situation; while they're doing that, my partner and I will make discreet inquiries about the health of your target, Barendt Schoveldt.'

Twenty-four hours had passed before the two special forces operatives returned to the safe house. 'You've got some good news for us I hope,' Derek said meeting them at the back door, 'we're getting a little stir-crazy cooped up in here.'

'First off, it appears Barendt Schoveldt was not at home during the attack; we know this because two men, conveniently for us, mugged him as got into his car at the rear of the townhouses at least three hours before the car bomb was detonated.'

'But how can we be sure it was our man?'

'In the very best tradition of helping themselves, this pair of foot pads relieved him of his wallet and mobile phone, both of which positively confirmed their victim's identity. It cost us five hundred Euros to purchase the mobile and wallet, which, I hope you don't mind, we took from your bags we picked up from the Augsburg City Hotel. Once you've had a chance to examine both items and are satisfied it was your man Schoveldt, we'll drive you to a nearby park where you can stretch your legs.'

'What have you got,' Avi asked Derek as he searched through the wallet, 'is it Barendt?'

'From this old South African picture ID – he's our man alright! There are no credit cards or any of the other items usually found in a man's wallet. No cash either, but given the circumstances of its recovery, it's not surprising. Anything on his mobile?'

'He made some calls to Vung Tau City, two to Beirut, one to Dubai and another to a number in Frankfurt. That's about it.'

'Any text messages?'

'Not a thing. We can guess the reason for the calls to Vietnam; Beirut is open to speculation; Dubai would've been the likely stopover for Dieter Schoveldt's flight from Frankfurt to Vietnam. But it's the phone call to Frankfurt I'm more interested in; he made this call four hours before the car bomb went off. Give me a minute while I call back that number.' Derek watched as Avi pressed the redial button on the mobile phone. 'Hello,' she said as someone answered, 'yes, thank you,' she continued in German, 'could you please give me your address,' she said as she grabbed a piece of paper and a pen. 'Go ahead, Hotel Karltonhof, Nidda Strasse, near the station you say? Yes, I know it, *ich danke dir.*' Switching off the mobile phone, she looked up a Derek, 'I'll bet you Barendt's checking into the Hotel Karltonhof as we speak.'

CHAPTER – 32 –

THE HOTEL KARLTONHOF ON NIDDA Strasse was a short, two blocks walk from the entrance to Frankfurt's main railway station where they were dropped off by the taller of the two special forces operatives. 'This is where we say *au revoir*; you're on your own from now on. Good luck nailing this bastard,' he said as he pulled out into the afternoon traffic. Walking briskly, Avi and Derek rounded the corner and turned into Nidda Strasse.

'Hotel Karltonhof, that's it across the street,' Avi said as they waited for the pedestrian walk sign to turn green. 'I will say one thing for Barendt, like Sakmokon, he has impeccable taste in accommodations,' she remarked as one of the two doormen, both wearing dark green and gold uniforms, greeted them as he held open the glass entrance doors. The oak panelled walls, low-key lighting and sumptuously carpeted and decorated reception area of the seven-storey Hotel Karltonhof can best be described as understated elegance. Potted palms and a tinkling fountain divided the reception area into several semi-private seating areas, all facing towards the marble and oak reception desk.

'Well, I hope his good taste encourages him to stay a little longer! I'm getting tired of chasing him around the world. Why don't you go ahead and check in while I make a few discreet enquiries.' Derek began by taking one of the doormen aside and showing him a photo of Barendt Schoveldt on his mobile phone. 'I've checked in here with a lady friend of mine and, between you and I, we're a little concerned her father may be staying at this hotel as well. Frankly, neither of us would like to bump into him accidentally. Perhaps you may have seen this gentleman recently?'

'I've been off on leave for the past few days, sir. May I suggest you ask

Helmet over there; he's been greeting guests at the door for most of the time I was away.' To Derek's disappointment, Helmet was no help either.

'He's calling himself Klaus Saukel. The young lady on the desk identified him right away when I showed her his picture,' Avi whispered in his ear, 'she told me he arrived yesterday and is checked into room 605 for a three-day stay.'

'What reason did you give for your question?'

'None; I thought I'd leave that to her imagination. Come on, I think we both deserve a drink, it's been quite a day, and we have a lot to discuss,' she said leading the way to the hotel bar-lounge, selecting a corner table as far away as possible from the noisy late afternoon clientele clustered around the bar.

'I don't blame you at all; they're a loud bunch, well on their way to getting pissed,' a tall, distinguished looking man in a dark suit, pale blue shirt and regimental tie remarked as he stopped at their table. 'I hope you don't mind if I join you,' he said pulling up a chair, 'this is a nice quiet spot to have our little chat. I'm Colonel Jeffrey Davidson,' he said handing a business card to Derek, 'I believe we have a mutual friend in London.'

'Judging by the Grenadier Guards tie, I'd say you're probably from MI6, which leaves me to wonder what piques your interest in Frankfurt?'

Leaning in close, Davidson said softly, 'We're aware you intend to terminate with extreme prejudice a guest staying at this hotel; a Herr Saukel I believe.' Derek and Avi did not reply. 'You see,' Davidson continued, 'Herr Saukel's continued well-being is of vital interest to some of our people; and for that reason, we would not want anything unfortunate to happen to him.' Standing up from their table, he said, 'Please consider yourselves warned.'

'Well, what do you think of that?' Avi remarked, 'I assume the mutual friend he refers to is your Rachel Cavendish at MI5, but I understood she was on our side?'

'That's the trouble with intelligence organisations; they have more sides than a rhombic cube. In other words, one hand never knows what the other is doing. So, whatever faction Colonel Davidson represents may not be singing from the same song book as our Deputy Director. I suggest we contact the only person who might know the answer, but, because we can't do that safely from this hotel, let's take a walk over to the railway station and see if we can find a working public telephone.'

'Derek,' Rachel said receiving his call, 'I was just about to call you; there's been a slight change of plan.'

'Would that change have anything to do with a Colonel Davidson, formally with the Grenadier Guards?'

'I see from your area number you're in Frankfurt; so, I have to assume the said Guardsman has been in touch?'

'Your assumption is correct. What the hell is this all about? Two days ago, with your help I might add, we were about to remove Barendt Schoveldt, or Herr Saukel if you prefer, from the realms of the living; now we're being told there's been a change of plan.'

'I assume you're calling from a secure phone in a safe place?'

'Frankfurt *Hauptbahnhof* to be precise. Even Colonel Davidson can't have bugged all the public phones in here.'

'Okay, this much I know,' Rachel continued, 'according to Lawrence over at the CIA, the Russians, and by that I take it he means the FSB, have developed a proprietary interest in our man. It appears he is in partnership with Widad al-Mazigh, who has managed to secure some huge arms deal with the kid running North Korea.'

'So why not take him out?'

'If you want my best guess, MI6 has him under surveillance and, for the time being, wishes to keep it that way. My recommendation to you and your girlfriend is to go back to South Africa; there isn't anything more for you to do there,' Rachel said as she ended the call.

'So, what do you think?' Avi asked.

'I think it's high time we had a chat to Miriam and see where she stands in all of this.'

It took two attempts before he got through to Miriam Hyde-Eshar's office at the Institute for Intelligence and Special Operations in Tel Aviv. 'Derek, I was wondering when you would call. Is everything alright your end?'

'Following the debacle in Augsburg, we managed to track our quarry to Frankfurt, but we've encountered an unexpected obstacle.' He went on to tell her about the meddling of MI6 in their plans and the apparent acquiescence of MI5 to their interference. 'Can you call me back in fifteen minutes, I want to run this by Dov Harel,' she said disconnecting the call.

'Well?' Avi said staring up at him, 'what do we do now?'

'We slip over to the Weinkelder Station Bar, order two whiskies and kill fifteen minutes before it's time to call her back.'

'We need to get Barendt Schoveldt out of there, alive if possible,' Miriam said answering his call.

'That's quite a tall order, Miriam. How do you suggest we go about doing that?'

'Dov and a hastily cobbled together team are brainstorming ideas as we speak. So far, we've managed to arrange for a vehicle to transport you and Avi and, if possible, Barendt Schoveldt to a small airfield where we can, at least, get the three of you safely out of the country. Of course, for all this to happen, you'll have to come up with a plan to get him out of the hotel from under the noses of the local British consular authorities. Incidentally, and we have this on good authority, they are flying in a special security team first thing tomorrow morning to arrange for his safe removal to Britain. Until this lot arrives, he will be under the protection of civilian security guards dispatched from the consulate.'

'In other words, if we're going to come up with a plan to counter their move, it's got to happen tonight.' Derek paused for a moment before continuing, 'There are probably a few things we are going to need; can I call you back once we've completed our own brainstorming?'

'Of course; and please remember, whatever ideas you come up with, try to avoid any violence and, whatever you do, make sure no harm befalls any MI6 agents or consular personnel.'

It took Avi ten minutes of pleading and cajoling, not to mention a gift of a hundred Euros, to persuade the night manager to relocate the guest originally booked into room 705, to another room in the hotel. 'It took some persuading, but he finally agreed. We can go ahead and move into room 705, directly above 605, Barendt Schoveldt's room,' she whispered to Derek as she handed him the card key.

'Didn't he want to know why you wanted that particular room?'

'I told him we had incredible sex in that room two years ago and I was looking forward to a repeat performance.'

Chuckling to himself, Derek arranged for a hotel porter to take the three large cardboard boxes which had just arrived, up to room 705. Tipping the porter generously as he left, Derek opened two of the boxes and began checking through the equipment Miriam had pulled together from her various contacts in the city.

Fifteen minutes into his inspection, there was a light tap on the door. 'Maid service,' Avi announced as she entered the room dressed in a maid's uniform and pushing one of the hotels' room service carts.

'Where did you get the uniform?' he asked.

'As in most hotels, the staff here have changing rooms in the basement where they keep extra uniforms and service carts. I simply found a maid's outfit that fitted and a spare linen cart. All I need now is the box of tricks, blond wig and the stage makeup Miriam promised, and my own mother wouldn't recognise me!'

The two consular security guards, ordered over to the hotel to keep an eye on Barendt Schoveldt until the MI6 team arrived, had stationed themselves in the corridor outside his room. They watched with growing interest as Avi emerged from the staff lift pushing her service cart. Ignoring them, she stopped outside 605 and, knocking authoritatively, called out, '*Zimmerdienst!*'

'I'm sorry miss, you can't go in there; no one is allowed to bother the gentleman inside.'

'What gives you the right to give orders to me. Germany is a free country; you Englishmen have no authority here. Karltonhof is a German hotel, in case you don't know.' At that fortuitous moment, the door opened, and Barendt Schoveldt looked out. '*Guten Abend, mein Herr*, these *Englander dummkopfs* won't allow me to tidy your room and turn down your covers,' Avi said leaning over her cart and watching with satisfaction as his gaze lingered over her breasts fetchingly displayed by a few strategic buttons left unfastened.

'*Ja, ja*, of course, you must be allowed to do your work in peace. *Wie in*

Fraulein,' he said inviting Avi to enter his room. Smiling sweetly at the two men from the consulate, she waited as Schoveldt opened the door to admit her and her service cart, before closing and locking the door behind her.

'Dirty old bugger,' one of the security guards muttered, 'did you see the way he looked at her tits?'

'Certainly did! I thought his eyes were going to pop out. How long do you believe we should give them?'

'I feel sorry for the poor old codger; he's probably for the nick when he gets to London. Let's give him half an hour; it'll probably take him that long just to get it up!'

Inviting Barendt to sit on the edge of his bed, Avi stood in front of him and slowly undid the rest of the buttons on her blouse. Stepping closer, she smiled invitingly at him. Needing no further encouragement, he reached out and, placing his hands on her hips, pulled her closer to him. While his attention was focussed on her breasts, Avi reached over to her cart and picked up a syringe loaded with ketamine from beneath a folded towel. Thrusting the needle into the carotid artery in his neck, she pushed the plunger home. Clamping her free hand over his mouth, she held him tightly to her body while she waited for him to lose consciousness.

Laying Barendt back down on the bed, she opened the large window and helped Derek, as he climbed down from the room above, to enter the room. 'I take it the ketamine worked?' he asked.

'Like a charm, he's out cold.'

'Good, give me a hand to get him into his harness.' Together, they wrestled Barendt into the mountain rescue harness and, carrying him to the window, clipped the carabiners on the rescue harness to those on Derek's harness. 'Just in case you're searched,' he said pocketing the used syringe and the two spares as he climbed back out onto the window ledge. Attaching his ascender to the climbing rope hanging down outside the window, he began the laborious climb back up to the room above. Struggling under their combined weight, he had paused for a short rest halfway up, when things began to go wrong.

First off, one of the struts on the climbing tripod he had set up in the room above give way with a loud crack. This was closely followed by

Barendt starting to regain consciousness. While he did his best to stifle Barendt's cries for help with his free hand, he braced for the sudden, jerk as his safety line stopped their rapid descent to the laneway six floors below. Congratulating himself on his foresight in attaching a safety rope to the pipes carrying the heating system in the room above, he fumbled in his pocket for the spare syringes of ketamine. Finding one, he pulled the cap off with his teeth and, jabbing the needle into Barendt's neck, pushed the plunger home.

'Jesus Derek, what happened?' Avi asked looking out of the window of 605.

'Nothing I can't fix,' he replied. 'Go on, get out of there before those consular guys begin to wonder why you're taking so long.' Seeing him continue his climb upwards, she closed the window and set about the second part of her plan. Smudging her lipstick, she refastened her blouse, making sure to leave one or two strategic buttons undone. Twisting her skirt to one side, she pushed her service cart to the door and, unlocking it, walked out of the room making sure the security guards saw her tuck a one hundred Euro note into her bra.

Looking at her blond hair, one of the security guards commented sarcastically, 'I can't believe you didn't get your hair messed up.'

'It wasn't my hair he was interested in,' she said tartly as she started to wheel her cart towards the service lift, 'for your information gentlemen, Herr Saukel wants me to come back in an hour.' As the lift doors opened, she pushed the cart in and pressed the button for the floor below. By the time the lift arrived on that floor, she had removed the wig and pulled on a black tracksuit she had hidden under the linen in her cart. Racing up the staff stairs to the top floor, she used her card key to enter 705 and, stepping over the twisted poles of the failed climbing tripod, rushed to the open window.

Peering out into the darkness, she could see Derek was in serious trouble. 'What can I do?' she asked as quietly as she could, afraid she might attract the attention of anyone who happened to be looking out of a window.

'There's a spare length of climbing rope in one of those boxes; see if you can attach it to one of the hot water heating pipes,' he said as quietly as he could. Avi rummaged about in the boxes and found a hank of rope that looked as though it would do the job. Attaching the rope to a heating pipe, she lowered it down to Derek. Feeling around in his pocket, he found a spare locking carabiner which he used to attach Barendt's rescue harness to the spare rope. He was about to free himself from the weight of the unconscious man when the window of the room below them opened. Freezing in position against the wall, he pulled Barendt close to him, clamping his free hand over his mouth, fearing the ketamine injection might suddenly wear off.

'There's no fucking way he could have got out through this window,' one of the consular security guards shouted to his partner as he peered out at the laneway below. 'It's at least a six-storey drop. If the old bugger had jumped, he'd be spread all over the pavement down there. No; my money is on that blonde bitch who supposedly came to turn down his bed and ended up fucking him. But don't ask me how she did it; we both checked, there was no one crouched under that service cart of hers. Look, you stay here; I'll go downstairs and see if I can find her.'

Afraid of making any sounds which might alert the other security guard as he searched around the room, Derek slowly let the spare rope take the full weight of Barendt's body. Relieved of that weight, he quickly resumed his climb to the window above. 'What happened, why did you suddenly stop?' Avi asked leaning out of the window. He waved her to silence, pointing to the now open window below. As she helped him climb through the window, she whispered in his ear, 'Do you think they saw you?'

'No, but *Jissus*, that was close; I was shit scared he would look up, I was dangling only a few feet above him. We haven't got much time, one of them is on his way downstairs to look for you; give me a hand to pull Barendt up in case one of them puts two and two together and comes up with four!'

Together they hauled Barendt's limp body up and over the window sill and laid him on the floor. Avi checked his pulse and breathing. 'He's out cold,' she said, 'did you give him a double injection?'

'No, just the one; I had to keep him quiet. What I can't understand is why the first dose you gave him wore off so quickly.'

'Ketamine is not an exact science; body weight, amongst other things, can throw it off. Anyway, we still have another syringe left just in case.' Straightening up, she looked at him, 'Well, what do we do now, bearing in mind the consular boys might decide to get the police involved?'

'Pack up the ropes,' he said opening the third box, 'while I get the wheelchair unpacked, and our friend here safely tucked in.' The stillness of the night was shattered by the sound of two gunshots, fired almost simultaneously. 'Shit!' Derek swore, 'those shots sounded like they came from 605; what the hell is going on down there? I'd better climb down and take a look!'

'Christ Derek! Don't you think we should be concentrating on getting ourselves and Barendt out of here; who cares if a consular security guard is guilty of an accidental discharge.'

'A double accidental discharge? I don't think so. I believe something a lot worse than that is happening downstairs; whatever's going on, it's bound to come back and bite us one way or another.'

Climbing over the window sill, he clipped his harness to the spare rope and began his cautious descent, all the while working his way over to the right side of the window of room 605. Jamming his fingers into narrow gaps between the stonework, he carefully edged his way closer to the window, feeling with his feet for a two-inch wide ledge he had noticed circling the building just below the sixth-floor windows.

As the sounds of the dwindling evening traffic rose from the streets below, the crisp crunch of pigeon droppings beneath his feet confirmed he had reached the ledge. Unclipping himself from the spare rope, he slowly felt his way along the ledge, hugging the stonework and doing his best not to think of the six-storey drop to the lane below. Locking the fingers of his right hand in a gap in the stonework, he leaned to his left and peered cautiously into the room.

A dark-skinned man stood in the centre of the room staring down at the body of one of the consular security guards lying on the carpet. Holding an automatic pistol loosely at his side, the gunman was in the midst of a conversation with someone on his mobile phone. On the other side of the room, a second man stood next to the bed searching through an open suitcase which, Derek assumed, belonged to Barendt Schoveldt. The frequent use of the words *na'am* and *la moshkelah* in the mobile phone conversation, confirmed the man on the phone was speaking Arabic. Unfortunately, even the gist of the conversation was beyond Derek's understanding of that language.

Suddenly the man searching through the suitcase looked up and caught a fleeting glimpse of Derek's face at the window. Pointing towards the open window, he yelled a warning to his companion prompted Derek to retrace his steps as fast as he could back along the ledge towards the dangling climbing rope, which now seemed to be miles away.

As Derek frantically tried to reattach his harness to the rope, the dark-skinned man leaned out of the window and, smiling, aimed his pistol directly at him. Bracing for the impact of a bullet, Derek watched in horror, then relief, as the gunman's head swelled to half its size again before bursting in a spray of blood and brains, his pistol falling to the laneway far below.

Avi kept her silenced Sig Sauer pointed at the window below as Derek frantically hauled himself up. 'Thank you!' he said climbing over the window sill of 705, 'I thought my number had come up.'

'I couldn't possibly have allowed that to happen,' she said helping him out of his harness. 'Come on, we've got to get Barendt out of here before anyone figures out what room we're in.' Working quickly, they bundled Barendt into the wheelchair and, draping a blanket around his shoulders, took the staff lift to the hotel service area on the ground floor. Exiting into the service lane, Avi and Derek took turns pushing their wheelchair bound captive out into Nidda Strasse and towards the main railway station.

CHAPTER – 33 –

THE STREETS AND SIDEWALKS WERE busy as the late evening theatre and restaurant crowds made their way to the trains and the taxis lined up in the taxi ranks around the station entrance. 'That man that just walked past us,' Derek whispered urgently to Avi, 'the one in the grey raincoat, I'm certain he's the other man I saw in room 605 rifling through Barendt's suitcase. If I can, I've got to find out who he is and where he's headed. Can I leave it to you to find Miriam's team and deliver our patient into their care?'

'Of course; just be careful.'

'I'll call you on your mobile phone as soon as I know something,' he said walking quickly away, being careful to keep at least half a dozen people between him and the man in the grey raincoat. He breathed a sigh of relief when his quarry ignored a busy taxi rank and continued past the main entrance to the railway station. Aware of the challenges he faced as the sole person tailing a subject who may be well versed in the art of spotting a tail, he frequently crossed to the opposite side of the street, changing his position regularly in case grey raincoat checked to see if he was followed. His caution paid off a few minutes later when his quarry, stopping to glance at the magazines in a newsvendor's kiosk, carefully looked over the crowd on the sidewalk behind him.

Derek continued after his target, occasionally crossing and re-crossing the street all the while praying he hadn't given himself away. His efforts appeared to pay off when the man in the grey raincoat suddenly turned off Nidda Strasse and headed down a narrow side street. Striding briskly through a small park, the man crossed another street and walked quickly up the steps of a rundown four-storey block of flats. Producing a key from his coat pocket, the man opened the front door and went inside.

Waiting until the man had gone, Derek walked up the steps and tried the front door. It was locked. 'Even if I got into the building, I've no idea which flat or floor he may have gone to,' he muttered to himself, 'if nothing else, at least I know where he may be living.' Retracing his route through the park, he stopped under a streetlight and entered the address of the block of flats onto his phone. On an impulse, he felt around in his pocket for the business card Colonel Davidson had given him when he tried to warn them off harming Barendt Schoveldt. Working quickly, he typed a short text message to Davidson describing what had happened and gave him the address of the partner of the man who shot the consular security guard. As he pressed send, a text came in from Avi, 'Package picked up; It's on its way. I'll be waiting for you in the Weinkelder Station Bar.'

Leaving the park, Derek was walking down the narrow side street that led back to Nidda Strasse, when two men, emerging from a darkened doorway, grabbed his arms and forced him into the front passenger seat of a large Mercedes car. 'Good evening Mr Hamilton, I see neither you nor your partner took my warning seriously,' a voice said from the gloom of the back seat.

'And a good evening to you too, Colonel Davidson,' Derek replied recognising the voice. 'A few moments ago, I sent you a text which should help you track down one of the members of an assassination team sent to bump off your Herr Saukel, or should I say Barendt Schoveldt, as we prefer to call him.'

'Yes, I just received it; a very nice gesture on your part. However, we've had this team under surveillance since they arrived in Germany. Right now, were waiting for the other partner to return home so we can arrest them both.'

'And I thought you were on top of things!' Derek replied. 'Colonel, had you read my text in its entirety, you would be aware that one of your consular security men guarding this Barendt Schoveldt was shot dead earlier this evening, probably by the very partner you were hoping to arrest!'

'Good God! Hamilton, are you sure of this?'

'Unfortunately, Colonel, I'm quite sure. Not that it's any consolation, but the partner in question is also dead.'

'Driver, I'd better get back to the Karltonhof right away,' Davidson said to the chauffeur as he started the car.

'If it's all the same to you, Colonel, I'd rather walk back.'

'I believe I'll join you, Derek,' another voice said from the dark shadows of the back seat. As Derek got out of the car, a rear door opened, and a tall, distinguished looking man joined him on the pavement. In the pool of light cast by a nearby street light, Derek noticed he was a little greyer around the temples, but still immaculately dressed in his signature grey suit, pale blue shirt and dark blue tie. 'Its been quite awhile since we last met,' the man said by way of a greeting.

'Not since we went our separate ways in the swamps of the Rio das Mortes in Mozambique,' Derek replied, 'when, if I remember correctly, you persuaded Rachel Cavendish to abandon me for the questionable privilege of becoming the Deputy Director of MI5.'

'I was hoping we could put all of that behind us,' Lawrence Faulkner said extending his hand.

Derek shook his hand. 'Assuming you're still with the CIA's London Station,' he said to Faulkner, 'may I ask why you're interested in this case?'

'The CIA is just as interested in this man Schoveldt as are our friends at MI6. I was wondering,' he said turning to face Derek, 'whether you have any idea where this man might be?'

'If everything has gone according to plan, I would say he was already on his way to Israel, a fate he richly deserves.'

The pair walked a few blocks along Nidda Strasse without speaking. As they neared the railway station, Faulkner said, 'This is as far as I go; can I offer you a lift anywhere?'

'Very kind of you, Lawrence. But I think I'll walk for a little while longer.'

'As you wish. Here is my private number in London,' he said handing a business card to Derek, 'please let your Israeli colleagues know that we are more than willing to work with them on the Schoveldt's, both father and son. Perhaps you can convince them that any such collaboration would be mutually beneficial.' With that, Faulkner shook hands with Derek once more and, waving his arm in the air, stepped into the back seat of a black Mercedes Maybach S 600 that quietly pulled into the curb alongside them.

As Derek turned to walk away, Faulkner lowered his window and called him back to the car. 'I almost forgot to give you this,' he said handing Derek a small photograph of an Arab man dressed in western style clothing. 'I do believe you're interested in finding this man. His name is Widad al-Mazigh; though he's sometimes known as Abu-Jamal. Our latest reports have him living openly in the town of Marjayoun in the southern end of the Bekaa Valley in Lebanon. As you are probably aware, he's a major player in the rhino poaching business in Africa.'

'Any suggestions where we should stay the rest of tonight?' Derek asked as he joined Avi at her small table in the corner of the Weinkelder Station Bar. 'Personally, I'm not particularly keen on returning to the Karltonhof.'

'Good,' she replied, 'while I was waiting for you, I asked that handsome young waiter over there, which hotel he would take his young lady to if he had an unlimited amount of money.'

'And his reply?'

'Quick as a flash he named the Steigenberger Hof on the Kaiserplatz. Apparently, this highly recommended hotel is but a short taxi ride from here.' Placing her hand on his arm, she said, 'I suggest you order two whiskies from the bar while I phone the hotel and make a reservation.'

'Unlimited amount of money?' he said smiling at her, 'Miriam will not be amused.'

'Miriam will not be staying with us tonight; it'll just be the two of us,' she winked.

The old-world luxury and elegance of their top floor suite met and, even surpassed their expectations, as did the magnificent night view over the city and the river Main. 'I'm surprised reception didn't bat an eye when we admitted we didn't have any luggage,' Avi remarked as they stood arm in arm admiring the view.

'I'm not in the least bit surprised; after all, Frankfurt is a broad-minded city. Anyway, before we can relax, I should give Miriam a call and pass on an interesting bit of information I was handed by the head of the CIA's London Station; something I'll share with you later over a drink or two.'

'I'll hold you to that; in the meantime, I'm off to the spa downstairs; I feel in need of some feminine pampering and relaxation. When you're done up here, come on down and find me.'

After bringing Miriam up to speed on the abduction of Barendt Schoveldt from his hotel room and, touching on his brief meeting with Lawrence Faulkner, she congratulated them on their successful mission. 'However, your meeting with Faulkner changes things. I would like to see both of you in my office in Tel Aviv by midday tomorrow at the latest. I'll book seats on the El Al flight leaving Frankfurt Main at eight tomorrow morning. Leave any weapons you have in your room; I'll have someone come by to pick them up while you're on your way to the airport.'

Thinking that Miriam could have been a little more effusive in her praises, he popped his mobile phone in the room safe and made his way downstairs to the spa in search of Avi. 'Ms Blum,' he said to the receptionist, 'dark hair, attractive woman. Came down fifteen minutes ago, looking for a bit of pampering and relaxation?'

She smiled up at him, 'You must be Derek. Your lady said you'd be down shortly. She's booked a steam room, number five; it's a few doors down the hallway. There's a change room on the left and a robe to put on after you've showered.' Derek showered, donned the fluffy white gown and, opening the door to number five, stepped into a warm, white mist of steam.

'For goodness sake, close and lock the door; you're letting out all my hot steam,' Avi protested.

'I can't even see you.'

'But I can see you,' she replied, 'keep walking to the sound of my voice.' He did as she instructed and, feeling her outstretched hand, felt his way to the bench where she was sitting.

'You're naked,' he said, 'what if someone else came in?'

'Unless it was the waiter from the Weinkelder, I'd tell them this steam room's taken. But you did lock the door, didn't you? And for goodness sake, you're not going to sit here wearing your robe, are you?'

'If I take it off, you know what it'll lead to, don't you?'

Sliding her hand up between his thighs, she gave a throaty laugh, 'I see what you mean.'

'I thought you came down for feminine pampering and relaxation?'

'I certainly did; if you feel along the bench, you'll find the massage oils the young lady on the desk gave me for my back rub.'

'*Bien sur, Madame,* that I can arrange,' he said faking a French accent as he selected three or four towels from a stack and laid them along the top of the bench, '*s'il vous plait Madame, Monsieur* Derek is ready!' Avi turned and, stretching out, lay face down on the towels with her head cradled in her arms. Derek poured a generous amount of the massage oil on his hands and rubbed it over her shoulders and back, slowly working his way down to her bottom and thighs. 'Perhaps *Madame* would care to lie on her back?'

'Only if *Monsieur* Derek can assure me he will take full advantage of my situation!' she replied as she turned onto her back.

Adding to the massage oil on his hands, he caressed her breasts and gently tweaked her hard nipples. 'You're very beautiful,' he whispered in her ear. Closing her eyes, Avi moaned appreciatively as he ran his hands slowly up and down her body, stopping just short of her dark, curly pubic hairs.

'You can go a lot lower you know,' she said opening her thighs a little wider, 'I'm feeling especially tense down there, but I do believe this is what I need,' she said reaching out and, taking hold of him, pulled him down on top of her. As he entered her, she locked her legs around him and, arching her back and thrusting up with her hips, drew him in deeper, kissing him and pushing her tongue into his mouth. Responding to the erotic pleasures of their lovemaking, Avi moaned and cried out, her body contracting and tightening around him as she neared her climax. It was more than he could resist, and he allowed himself the surging release he so badly needed.

They lay together for a long time, wreathed in the warm steam and the afterglow of their lovemaking until, with a soft knock on the door, the outside world intruded. 'Your time is up *Fraulein* Blum; we are closing shortly.'

Chapter – 34 –

Their El-Al Boeing 707-800 approached Israel from over the Mediterranean, crossing the coast near Ashdod before turning north to land at Tel Aviv's Ben Gurion Airport. 'I never realised how much I missed this troubled land until just now,' Avi said holding tightly onto Derek's arm as she wiped away a tear with her other hand. He responded by squeezing her hand and kissing her tenderly on her cheek.

Clearing immigration and customs, they walked out into the arrivals hall where they saw Miriam waiting for them. Embracing them, she led them to a car waiting outside. 'Straight to headquarters,' she instructed the driver as the car wound its way out of the airport before heading north to join the *Kvish HaHof* or coastal highway. 'Welcome back,' she said turning and looking at them, 'Dov Harel is most anxious to meet with you again.'

<hr />

Fifteen minutes later the car turned off the highway and, stopping briefly at a well-guarded checkpoint, entered a complex of tall office buildings. Their driver stopped at the top of a ramp at the base of one of the buildings and, entering a code number into a machine, waited for a steel mesh gate to slide open, before driving into an underground parkade. Miriam led the way to a high-speed lift which whisked them up to what they assumed to be the top floor, there being no buttons or floor numbers visible in the lift. The doors opened, and Miriam led them through a large office area crammed with desks with dozens of men and woman sitting in front of computers. In the far corner, Dov Harel stood up from behind an ordinary looking wooden desk. Shaking their hands warmly, he said, 'It's been a while since you two were last in Israel; even longer for you Derek. Welcome back both of you. Let's go and find a meeting room where we can talk without being disturbed.'

'I must say, sir,' Derek remarked, 'I expected your office to be a lot more, how can I put it…'

'Grander, more luxurious?'

'No offence meant, sir, but yes.'

'I'm sure Avital here will back me up when I tell you that here we concentrate more on getting the job done, and rather less worrying about appearances.' Opening a door, Dov peered in, 'It's empty, let go in here.' Once they were all seated around a table, he began. 'On the surface, it will seem as though nothing much has changed in Israel; but, for those of us responsible for the security of the state, things are a lot more troubling. The leaders of Hamas in Gaza appear to be psyching themselves up to fire another round of rockets into our country. Unfortunately, this time, they seem to have found the money to purchase markedly improved weapons from the crazies in North Korea.'

'Presumably,' Derek interjected, 'some of this money comes from the poaching of rhino and elephant?'

'Yes, it does. Orchestrated by the likes of the Schoveldts and shipped and sold by al-Mazigh to Nguyen Van Lamh and his An Dinh Trading Company in Vietnam.'

'So, the information I got from the CIA man about Widad al-Mazigh's whereabouts in Lebanon is correct?'

'To the best of our knowledge, it's still current.'

'If I may be so bold, sir, why haven't you done anything about it. I mean couldn't you just take him out with a drone strike?'

'And almost certainly start another war with Hezbollah? Right now, they've got their hands full in Syria, and we would like to keep it that way. So, if anything were to happen to al-Mazigh, it must look as though one of his many enemies in Iraq or the Lebanon decided to even the score.'

'You mean an assassination, shot dead by a person or persons unknown?' Avi asked.

'Given that he's laying low in a remote farmhouse near the village of Jebel Hasque and is usually surrounded by half a dozen heavily armed bodyguards,' Miriam said, 'we'd prefer if the job were carried out by a sniper.'

'Someone equipped with one of those long-range sniper rifles,' Derek suggested. 'The idea reminds me of the incredible long-range shots fired by a member of the British Household Cavalry in Afghanistan. If I recall correctly, he took out two Taliban machine gunners at a distance of over a mile and a half.'

'At that sort of range anyone around those men wouldn't have a clue where the shots came from,' Dov remarked, 'Miriam, would you look into the possibility of finding just such a marksman.'

'If I may, sir,' Derek interjected. 'I can understand Mossad's desire to put a stop to the funding al-Mazigh is funnelling to Hamas, but I ask you to also consider the pain and suffering we have felt in South Africa seeing our wonderful creatures slaughtered by poor African tribesmen coerced and bribed by a handful of unscrupulous whites and corrupt government officials. All of this in the name of the almighty dollar and to satisfy the misguided desires of a few Asian nations. Miriam, Avi and I have witnessed these atrocities at first hand and, with all due respect and, given our past efforts to assist your organisation, I believe we should be allowed the first crack at this man al-Mazigh.'

'I second that, sir,' Avi added, 'I can also attest to the fact that Derek is one of the finest rifle and pistol shots I have ever encountered.'

'Very well; I'll arrange for the two of you to spend a few days at Camp Filon, near Tiberius. While primarily a military base for one of our armoured brigades, Filon also houses one of our training schools for snipers. Colonel Yanni Aseret, who is in charge of the training program, will be the best person to judge your capabilities.'

The soldier on duty at the entrance to Camp Filon perused the passes issued by Dov Harel and, after conferring with someone on his phone, directed them to a parking area just inside the gate. 'Colonel Aseret is expecting you; go to the white building over on the right.'

As they entered the building, a surprisingly young man came up to them. 'You must be Hamilton and Blum? I'm Colonel Aseret, and this is Warrant Officer Bell,' he said introducing a soldier dressed in Israeli Defence Force fatigues, 'he'll take both of you out to our range where he will carry out a preliminary assessment of your abilities. Warrant, when you're done, please bring our guests back to my office.'

'Come this way,' Warrant Officer Bell said, leading them out to a vehicle park behind the building. 'Jump in,' he said pointing to a four-wheel drive Storm, 'its too far for us to walk.' Ten minutes later, after a hair-raising ride over a rough gravel road, he pulled up at a shooting range. 'I take it you're familiar with the Heckler and Koch G3A3 rifle?' he said handing Derek the weapon.

'Quite familiar,' Derek replied as he checked the rifle was unloaded and safe.

'Good, it's one of my favourite weapons for accurate shooting. I'm going to start you off at three hundred yards on a man-sized target. You have six rounds; fire one sighting shot, then with the rest, I want you to show me a tight group.'

Derek loaded the six rounds into the magazine, cocked the rifle and, setting the selector to single shots, knelt ready to fire. 'Surely you can't expect to get a good group at that range without lying prone?'

'Just you watch him,' Avi smiled at the Warrant Officer, 'I once saw him get a three-inch group at the same range standing.'

'Okay, this I've got to see,' Bell said, 'in your own time, carry on.'

Derek fired his sighting shot, then, peering through the spotting scope said to no one in particular, 'It shoots a little to the left,' before going on to fire the last five rounds in rapid succession.

'Fucking hell!' Bell muttered to himself as he used the spotting scope to check the target, 'come on, we're wasting our time out here; let's get back to the office.'

'In all my years Colonel, I've never seen shooting like it. At three hundred yards, he shot the tightest group I've ever seen at that range and, from a kneeling position! If anyone could pull this Lebanese job off, he'd be the man to do it.'

'Very well, Warrant, you've got three days to bring them up to speed on the Dragunov and the attendant toys that go with it.' Allocated quarters in the officer's section of the camp, Derek and Avi attended the first of many lectures and training sessions under the watchful eye of Warrant Officer Bell and his team of infantry weapons instructors.

'The SVD Dragunov is a Russian built sniper rifle currently in use by the Syrian army,' Bell began, 'it weighs in at a hefty eleven pounds and comes fitted with a bipod, sound suppressor and a rather good telescopic sight. Most importantly, we've acquired a few dozen rounds of the new Russian 7N14 match grade ammunition, which significantly increases the rifles accuracy to over one thousand yards. I will also include a ten-round magazine of armour piercing incendiary rounds just in case the need should arise.'

Pausing to take a sip from his glass of water, Bell continued, 'But in and of itself, this weapon isn't much use without its supporting aids. Over the next few days, you will familiarise yourselves with a pair of laser rangefinder binoculars, a 60-20x60x spotting scope, a thermal surveillance sight and, my favourite, an easy to use wind meter. This device will enable you to accurately calculate elevation and windage, critical to the success of your mission. And, while you are digesting all this new information, we will be providing you with up-to-date aerial surveillance photographs of the target, together with an update on the situation on the ground by a member of the security services.'

'Warrant,' Avi said, 'without being told as much, am I right in assuming the reason we are using Russian equipment is in the event of us being killed or captured, our mission cannot be traced back to Israel?'

Bell looked a little uncomfortable as he carefully crafted his reply. 'While that unfortunate rationale may seem plausible to some, my thoughts lean more to enabling you to abandon your Russian equipment following the success of your mission. Not much point in having to carry it all the way back is there?'

After a brief lunch in the cafeteria, Avi and Derek took their coffees outside to a picnic table on the grass. '*Jissus*, Avi, I'm beginning to wonder what we've got ourselves into. It's starting to dawn on me that if we're captured by the men guarding this al-Mazigh, the best thing we can hope for would be a mercifully quick death!'

'It's a little late to start worrying about that now,' she said, 'provided we do everything right, we might just be able to pull this off. Besides, wouldn't you like to be the one to put a bullet through this bastard's head?'

'Let's go back in, I'm anxious to look at their surveillance photos,' he said dropping their empty cups in a waste bin.

Warrant Officer Bell joined them as they stood looking at a series of high-resolution aerial photographs spread out on a table. Picking up a pointer, Bell drew their attention to a small village in the centre of one of the photographs. 'This is the village of Jebel Hasque and, a few miles north-west of here is the farmhouse where we believe al-Mazigh is living.'

'I'd feel a lot happier if we had someone on the ground who could positively confirm our man's presence in that house,' Derek said.

'We're working on that,' Bell replied, as an IDF sergeant joined them, 'but first I'd like to introduce you both to Master Sergeant Bar-Lev.'

'No need Warrant,' Avi said, 'we all met before at the Bahad Eight Training Camp outside Netanya.'

'Of course, now I remember you two; Sergeant Blum and the South African guy,' Bar-Lev replied. 'Please forgive me,' he said to Derek, 'I don't recall your name.'

'Hamilton, Derek Hamilton. Now that we all know who we are Sergeant, what can you tell us about the terrain around this farmhouse?'

'Glad you brought that up Derek,' Bell said injecting himself back into the conversation, 'Bar-Lev here is not only our surveillance expert, he will also be instructing you both in the art of camouflage and the use of our custom made ghillie suits.'

'What on earth is a ghillie suit?' Avi asked.

'A camouflage outfit used by a sniper to conceal his position. It usually consists of netting covered by strips of burlap and cloth coloured to resemble the vegetation common to a particular area. If I say so myself,' Bar-Lev continued, 'we make some of the best outfits available in this part of the world. Unless the people looking for you know exactly where you are, they're as likely to step on you as to see you.'

'So, you'd be able to supply us with ghillie suits which will blend in with the vegetation found around these areas of high ground?' Derek asked pointing to two raised features visible around the farmhouse.

'I don't see any problems there,' Bar-Lev replied.

'Now, all we have to do is work out how we are going to get close enough to the farmhouse without drawing anyone's attention?'

'A question that will have to wait until Mr Harel arrives for the briefing this evening,' Bell replied.

———◆———

Dov Harel arrived later that evening in a civilian-piloted AS350 Eurocopter. Landing near the main gate, he was quickly escorted to the briefing room where Colonel Aseret, Avi and Derek, Warrant Officer Bell and Master Sergeant Bar-Lev were waiting. Taking a seat at the head of the table, Dov thanked the Colonel and his team for their efforts in preparing Avi and Derek for the task ahead. 'Matters that I am not involved in,' Dov continued, 'have apparently come to a head. As a result, I've been instructed by the Prime Minister's office to implement, with the utmost urgency, the removal of this man al-Mazigh even to the point of employing a drone strike to achieve our objective. Something I would like to avoid if at all possible.'

'If it's any help,' Derek remarked, 'Avi and I are as anxious as you are to get on with the job. Right now, we're wondering how we're going to get close enough to the farmhouse to do the job?'

'Hence the purpose of our meeting tonight. Before I begin, I'm sure I need not remind everyone you are all signatories to the official secrets act; which means that any information disclosed here is not for discussion outside of this room.' Dov looked around the table before continuing. 'We have a man inside al-Mazigh's entourage who, for personal reasons, appears to have it in for his employer. According to our agent in Marjayoun, this man is willing, in exchange for the relocation of his family to Israel and a sizable sum of money, to keep us appraised of al-Mazigh's movements at all times.'

'Mr Harel,' Colonel Aseret interjected, 'and I think I'm speaking for everyone around this table, how sure are you that this man can be trusted?'

'No more, no less, than any other informant,' Dov replied, 'however, considering everything, he's the best option we've got so far.'

CHAPTER − 35 −

USING NIGHT VISION GOGGLES, WARRANT Officer Bell skillfully navigated the Storm all-terrain vehicle along a rough track through the rocky hills and valleys that formed the border between northern Israel and southern Lebanon. Finally, after frequent references to his handheld GPS unit, he pulled the small vehicle over to the side of the track and switched off the engine. 'This is about as close as I can take you. The border is five hundred yards to the west of us and, as far as we know, it's not patrolled with any degree of regularity. You've got your coordinates and GPS unit to guide you; be careful and take your time, you've got seven hours of darkness before you need to be in your lying up position. Derek, switch on your night vision goggles and confirm they're working; this Russian shit isn't as reliable as ours.'

'Good to go Warrant,' he confirmed, 'we'll be in touch once we're safely in position.'

'Good luck to both of you,' Bell said as he started his engine and drove off into the darkness. Adjusting their packs and hefting the two canvas bags containing the Dragunov and all its supporting equipment, Avi and Derek set off into the night.

A warm breeze rustled the grasses and small shrubs dotting the hillside as they wound their way down to the dry streambed that marked the lowest point on their ten-mile trek to their lying up position. Three hours into their journey, they stopped for a brief rest, dropping their packs and drinking sparingly from their water bottles. While Avi re-checked their position on the GPS, Derek whispered in her ear, 'How far do you think we've got to go?'

'By my reckoning, at least another two miles. If we can keep up this pace, we should be in position within two hours.'

Shaking out and donning their ghillie suits, they settled into their lying up position amidst the grasses on the otherwise featureless slope of the gently rising hill. 'The farmhouse should be somewhere in front of us, some nine hundred and fifty yards away,' he said as he re-checked their position on the GPS for what must be the fifth time. 'I must admit I'd feel a lot better if I could see a bloody light of some sort.'

'It's too early to expect anyone to be up and about,' Avi chided, 'let's get the rest of this gear stowed away and grab some sleep.' Scarcely an hour later, she woke him with a gentle prod in his ribs, 'Your wish has been granted,' she whispered, 'someone's up and about.' She handed him the spotting scope, 'A lantern's been set up next to the back door; it seems someone's getting a fire going under an outside boiler. I assume there's no electricity available in these parts, so it's a fire or propane gas only for the occupants of the farmhouse.'

'Now that we've got something to focus on, use the rangefinder and let's calculate the exact distance to the target.'

Avi rustled about setting up the device, 'It's a little more than we expected; eleven hundred and fifteen yards to be precise.'

'*Jissus*, that's a hundred and fifteen yards over the considered maximum accurate range for this rifle; I was hoping we would be a couple of hundred yards closer.'

'While checking through the night vision goggles,' Avi replied, 'I saw lots of small trees and rocky outcrops a hell of a lot closer to the farmhouse than we are right now.'

'And that's true. However, the reason Dov and I settled on this grassy stretch of nothing is precisely because there's nothing here; there are no trees, rocks or any other distinguishable features to draw and hold an observer's attention. I call it hiding in plain sight. While you set up your other toys, I'm going to call Dov to report we're in position and find out if his agent can confirm if our target is at home.'

Derek spent the next few minutes whispering into the satellite phone. 'Well,' Avi asked, 'what's the story?'

'According to Dov's agent, al-Mazigh spent last night in Marjayoun, but plans to return to the farmhouse sometime this afternoon. Apparently, there's a dinner meeting of sorts with a few Hezbollah big shots. Dov hinted that it would be a bonus if we could take out a few of them at the same time.'

'What a good idea! That would be like kicking half a dozen wasp's nests just to see what would happen.'

The warm midday sun, a welcome change from the freezing night, made it difficult for Avi, halfway into her watch, to stay awake. Her head, resting briefly on her folded arms, was jerked into high alert by the sound of a young boy whistling as he drove a flock of sheep up towards their position. Shaking Derek's arm, she whispered urgently, 'What the hell are we going to do if he spots us?' she asked, 'do we try to capture him or, God forbid, kill him?'

'Just keep calm and don't move. I think we're about to find out if Bar-Lev's ghillie suits are as good as he claims.' They lay watching as the now dispersed flock of sheep slowly grazed their way to where they lay, the shepherd passing within fifteen feet of them. Avi's heart skipped a beat when one of the sheep, stopping less than a foot away, stood staring directly into her eyes. She pursed her lips and blew gently into the animal's face. Startled, it jumped back but quickly resumed grazing a little further along. Relieved, they watched as the shepherd and his flock grazed their way up the gradual slope, before finally disappearing over the crest behind them.

'Now, what have we got here?' Derek said drawing Avi's attention to a small truck raising a cloud of dust as it bounced its way along the dirt road leading to the farmhouse. 'Keep an eye on them through the spotting scope; I want to know who they are and what they're doing here.'

'They're unloading four large propane cylinders and loading up what I assume are the empties; nothing much to worry about there.' About an hour before sunset, two men emerged from the farmhouse and began setting up a long trestle table and chairs on the grass verge outside the back door. 'I'd say they're getting ready for that dinner meeting.'

'*Jissus*, I hope al-Mazigh gets here soon,' Derek fretted, 'I was hoping to take this shot in daylight; God knows it's going to be difficult enough without having to worry about poor light. If we are correct in believing that table is being set up for this meeting, please give me the exact range and some idea of the current windage and elevation.'

'I put the range, centred on the middle of the table, at exactly eleven hundred and sixteen yards; eleven hundred and nineteen yards if you focus on the ornate chair they've set up at the far head of the table.' Switching instruments, she continued; 'Right now, the wind reads four mph, blowing from left to right, but it'll probably change as the sun sets. I'll recalculate your minutes of angle every two minutes from now on.'

'Hold that thought,' Derek said squeezing her arm as a black SUV roared up the dirt road, 'it looks like our guests have finally arrived.'

Squinting through the spotting scope, Avi carefully studied the faces of the three men who got out of the vehicle and stood around talking. 'Our man is not amongst them, and we are about to lose the light,' she complained as the sun began to dip below the horizon.

'How's the wind?' Derek asked.

'No change; still holding steady at four mph. Hang on, who the hell is this?' she asked as a man she had not seen before emerged from the farmhouse. 'Bloody hell! It's al-Mazigh, he's been here under our noses all along.'

'What's he doing? You must keep me posted.'

He's embracing the new arrivals, but it doesn't look like they're going to sit at the table. Fuck!' she cursed, 'they're all going inside the house.'

'Has the wing changed?' he asked urgently.

'No, it hasn't; but it's too late to take the shot, the bastards have all gone inside.' Quickly removing the magazine from the Dragunov, Derek replaced it with the magazine containing the armour piercing incendiary rounds from a pouch on his ghillie suit. Squinting in the rapidly fading light, he found his target, steadied his breathing and squeezed the trigger. Cycling the bolt, he again found his target and fired a second shot, and then a third. The resulting explosion lit up the whole area as the farmhouse erupted in a ball of fire, interspersed with dozens of secondary explosions.

'That'll teach them to store munitions in the house,' he said.

'My God!' Avi breathed, 'you were trying to hit the propane cylinders.'

'Trying?' he said laughing with relief, 'I thought my plan wasn't going to work; third shot lucky I suppose. I'd better get onto Dov and report our success and discuss his plans for our extraction.'

While Derek used their satellite phone to contact Camp Filon, Avi watched with growing unease as numerous vehicle headlights, intermingled with red flashing lights, appeared from the direction of Marjayoun. 'How the hell did they get here so soon?' she wondered out loud.

'Apparently, there was an attack on a police station just outside the town,' Derek said, 'the whole area is in a flap, we've got to get away from here as fast as we can. Dov's ordered us to leave everything where it is; he's given me the GPS coordinates of a location where he says someone will pick us up.'

'Leave even the rifle and all this gear?'

'Everything; he said to leave everything where it is and get away from here as fast as we can.'

Four hours later they arrived at the coordinates Dov had given to Derek. 'It's just a bend in a dirt track, there's nothing here,' Avi complained, 'how the hell will anyone find us out here?'

'Be patient,' he said taking her in his arms, 'at least we're not hunkered down on the hillside waiting for a line of Hezbollah's finest to sweep us up. I'm certain Dov won't let us down; in fact, unless my ears deceive me, I think I can hear a car.' They stood listening and then watching, as a pair of dim headlights appeared in the distance. 'Just in case it's not our ride, we'd better put some distance between us and this so-called road.'

As they crouched in the shelter of a few stunted trees, a small, light coloured Toyota car pulled up, and a woman wearing a hijab got out. She stood looking around anxiously until Avi and Derek emerged from the darkness. 'I was worried you might have got lost,' she said by way of a greeting, 'we must hurry, soldiers and police are out looking for you and the terrorists who attacked the police station. You must wear this,' she said handing Avi a hijab, 'and you must stuff this pillow under your shirt; you must look as though you're pregnant. I trust you did as you were instructed and left all your equipment behind?'

'Everything, except for this GPS,' Derek said handing the device to her.

The woman took it from him and threw into the darkness, 'Prepare yourselves, it's very likely we will be stopped and searched. The army and the police set up roadblocks everywhere. Leave all the talking to me.'

'Can you tell us where you are taking us?'

'I'm sorry, it is safer for everyone if you know nothing,' she said ushering them into the back seat of the Toyota. Getting behind the wheel, she started the engine and, turning the car around, drove back the way she had come.

Twenty minutes later, as they rounded a bend in the road, a string of lights and two soldiers waving red flares, signalled the car to stop. '*Kha'ra*,' she cursed, 'when I passed this way earlier there were no roadblocks. Quick,' she turned and handed a glass jar to Avi, 'open it and pour it on your belly and your legs; it's goat's blood, you must look as though you are having a miscarriage. Act like it!'

As a soldier approached the driver's window, the woman screamed something at him in Arabic and pointed to Avi in the back seat. The man, obviously discomfited, opened the rear door and shone his torch into the back seat at the same moment Avi let out a loud cry of anguish and pain. Panicked by her cries and the sight of the copious amount of blood on her stomach and legs, he gave a strangled cry, jumped back and waved them on.

'Very good,' their female driver said with a laugh, 'you almost scared me.' Managing to avoid any further roadblocks, they eventually reached the main road from the Syrian capital of Damascus to the port city of Beirut. 'I'm taking you both to the harbour where we have arranged for a fishing boat to take you out to sea to meet up with an Israeli navy Shaldag patrol boat which will take you to Haifa.

'Thank you for helping us; may we know your name?' Avi asked.

'Sorry, no names,' she said as she drove them onto the wharf where a fishing boat was waiting.

CHAPTER – 36 –

'NGUYEN VAN LAMH,' MIRIAM SAID wagging her finger as she, Dov Harel, Avi and Derek relaxed in the lounge of her Tel Aviv apartment. 'He's the kingpin behind almost all the illegal wildlife trafficking in Africa and south-east Asia, along with that man Dieter Schoveldt. At least, that's according to Barendt Schoveldt.'

'How is our old friend Barendt doing these days?' Derek asked smiling, 'happy to be in Israel?'

'I wouldn't go that far,' Miriam replied, 'but in all fairness to him, he's been most cooperative and has provided us with a great deal of valuable information on a variety of illegal activities, not to mention a few poaching enterprises still on the drawing board.'

'Getting back to this man Van Lamh,' Dov interrupted fixing his gaze on Miriam, 'what do you propose we do? And, before you answer that, please bear in mind our government's relationship with the Republic of Vietnam is on thin ice at the moment. We certainly can't afford risking another long-range shootout that could be traced back to us. Not to detract from your outstanding job in the Lebanon, of course,' he said smiling at Avi and Derek.

'As long as this man remains in business,' Miriam continued, 'poaching in Africa will not stop. His worldwide business empire is based on the sale of rhino horn, ivory, lion and tiger bones to markets around the world; wherever there's a demand and a profit to be made, you'll find Van Lamh there.'

'Surely by taking out major players such as Barendt Schoveldt and al-Mazigh, haven't we trimmed his sails somewhat?' Avi asked.

'I've no doubt that as we sit here discussing him, he's busy replacing each and every one of them with new operators,' Derek said, 'and, don't forget, there's still Dieter Schoveldt. As Shakespeare put it, 'We've only scorched the snake, not killed it."

'Quoting the Bard! Whatever next?' Dov laughed, 'but seriously, what can we do to stop him?'

'Travel to Vietnam and come up with a plan to close down his activities without unduly upsetting the authorities,' Miriam replied. 'Bear in mind,' she reminded Dov, 'we do have a card up our sleeve that we may be able to use to our advantage.'

'By that I take it you mean that Canadian fellow living in Saigon?'

'Yes, I do; and, by the way,' Miriam continued, 'Saigon is now called Ho Chi Minh City. More importantly, this Canadian, Andrew Cole, actually lives in Vung Tau where Nguyen Van Lamh has his business, the An Dinh Trading Company.'

'What's the story behind this man Andrew Cole?' Derek asked.

'He was born in Toronto to parents who emigrated from Germany to Canada following the end of the Second World War,' Miriam took up the story. 'Originally, the family name was Kola but, fearing their Jewish heritage might cause them problems; they changed their name to Cole. Then, in early 1965, after working for two years as a journalist in Toronto, Andrew went to Vietnam as a freelance reporter hoping to jumpstart his career.'

'When Saigon fell in April 1975, he elected to remain behind to cover the entry of the North Vietnamese Army into the city. The new government, believing he was a spy, sent him to a secret interrogation camp in the jungle near the Cambodian border. Following high-level appeals for clemency by our government, they released him a year later. After his release, Andrew elected to remain in Vietnam, eventually settling in Vung Tau.'

'I take it he's still living there?' Avi asked.

'Yes, he is,' Miriam replied, 'and we believe he has some personal connection with Nguyen Van Lamh.'

'How well do you know this man Cole and can we trust him?' Derek asked.

'Oh! We've been of some assistance to him in the past and, in return, he's helped us out on occasion,' Dov answered.

'And what does he do for a living? Is he still a journalist?'

'Heavens no; he runs a tourism business in Vung Tau. We understand he takes overseas visitors out diving on the reefs off a nearby island.'

'Exactly what action you decide to take is, of course, entirely up to yourselves; though I strongly suggest you run it by Andrew Cole first before making any decisions,' Miriam said when they met later at her office on the *Kvish HaHof* coastal highway. 'To avoid any direct connection with us, you'll return to Frankfurt where, travelling on Australian passports as Mr and Mrs Hamilton, you'll fly via Vietnam Airlines to Ho Chi Minh City. I've booked you into the Hotel L'Odeon for two nights, giving you enough time to get over your jetlag and get a feel for the country. When you're ready, take a taxi to the hydrofoil dock on the river; these high-speed boats leave on the hour, and it's the fastest and easiest way to get to Vung Tau.'

'How do we meet up with this Andrew Cole?' Derek asked.

'I've made reservations at the Pullman on Tri Sach Street in Vung Tau; it's an upscale hotel reasonably close to the Ngong Hai Dang area where Van Lamh has his principal residence. Once you arrive, I suggest you give Andrew a call. I can see you both have questions; keep them until you meet up with Andrew, I'm sure he'll be able to tell you everything you'll need to know.'

Their afternoon flight from Ben Gurion to Frankfurt was uneventful, but it did leave them with a three-hour wait for their Vietnam Airlines flight to Tan Son Nhat Airport, north of Ho Chi Minh City. 'How long is the flight?' Avi asked the attractive Vietnamese ticket agent at the Vietnam Airlines counter.

'It's about eleven hours, which means you'll arrive at your destination around midday, local time,' she replied. 'Have you booked your hotel?'

'Yes, it's already booked. We're staying at the Hotel L'Odeon, do you know it?'

'Good choice, the L'Odeon is an excellent hotel; I'm sure you'll like it. When you arrive at Tan Son Nhat Airport, take one of the taxis from outside the airport terminal, but do make sure it's a metered taxi. It shouldn't cost you any more than ten dollars. I hope you enjoy your flight!'

As their Vietnam Airlines Boeing 787-9 lifted off into the darkening sky, they watched the lights of Frankfurt drop away below, as a Vietnamese air hostess presented them with a glass of wine and the dinner menu. 'If all the girls look like her,' Derek whispered to Avi, 'I think I'll move to Vietnam.'

His remark earned him a sharp jab in the ribs, 'Keep talking like that mister,' she hissed, 'and you'll be in no condition to move anywhere!'

As the night sky lightened and breakfast was about to be served, he roused Avi, 'We should be landing in two hours. If I'm not mistaken, we've already flown over the Gulf of Thailand and are now crossing the coast of Vietnam, somewhere south of Vung Tau. If you're interested,' he said consulting a map he had taken out of the seat pocket in front of him, 'that's the Soai Rap River below us.' Noticing her distinct lack of enthusiasm, he asked, 'How are you feeling?'

'I've felt worse, but it's nothing a hot shower, great sex and a few hours' sleep wouldn't fix.'

'My thoughts exactly,' he replied. Clearing Immigration and customs, they walked out of the terminal and hailed a taxi to take them to the Hotel L'Odeon. Ten minutes into their ride, their jet lag caught up with them.

An hour later, their taxi driver had to wake them, 'Your hotel, *Madame, Monsieur*, the L'Odeon; we have arrived.'

Climbing out of the taxi, Avi remarked to Derek, 'Once we've fulfilled our need for hot showers, sex and a few hours' sleep, I'm sure we'll both see Vietnam in a better light.'

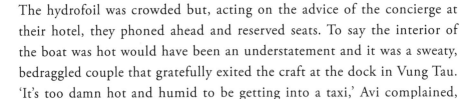

The hydrofoil was crowded but, acting on the advice of the concierge at their hotel, they phoned ahead and reserved seats. To say the interior of the boat was hot would have been an understatement and it was a sweaty, bedraggled couple that gratefully exited the craft at the dock in Vung Tau. 'It's too damn hot and humid to be getting into a taxi,' Avi complained, 'why don't we take one of those bicycle rickshaws and, hopefully, some cool air will wash over us?'

'Pullman Hotel on Tri Sach Street please,' Derek said to the diminutive Vietnamese man sitting astride his bicycle rickshaw, 'is it too far?'

'No, sir. I know it well; not far, not far.'

'I don't feel right asking this little guy to peddle us all around town,' Derek whispered to Avi.

'Then reflect your appreciation by the size of the tip you give him!'

Their room at the Pullman Hotel was on the top floor. It had a splendid view of Back Beach and the ocean and, over to the right, they could see the rising ground of the Ngong Hai Dang area where Miriam said their quarry, Nguyen Van Lamh, had his principal residence. Not wanting to waste any time, Derek phoned the number he had for Andrew Cole. 'You two got here a lot sooner than I had expected,' Cole said answering the call, 'I take it you've checked in at the Pullman?' Derek replied in the affirmative. 'Assuming you haven't had lunch, let's meet in half an hour in the Pullman Riviera restaurant. You'll find their seafood is terrific.' With that, Cole ended the call.

A tall, greying man wearing tropical whites and a neatly trimmed Van Dyke beard approached their table, 'You must be Avital and Derek Hamilton,' he said reaching out and shaking their hands. 'Welcome to Vung Tau, I'm Andrew Cole.' Smiling at them, he sat down at their table, 'If you don't mind me saying so, you're both a lot younger than I had expected, given the difficult task you've taken on.'

'I can assure you, Mr Cole, we're more than capable and please, call me Avi.'

'Forgive me, Avi, it was not my intention to question your joint capabilities; you both come too highly recommended by Miriam Hyde-Eshar for there to be any doubt there. My only concern is that you may not be fully aware of the nature of your adversary, Nguyen Van Lamh and his principal assistant, Dieter Schoveldt.'

'Schoveldt; is he here in Vung Tau?' Derek asked.

'He arrived about two weeks ago, and, as far as I know, he's living at the Ivory Palace.'

'Ivory Palace?' Avi asked, 'what on earth is that?'

'I'm sorry, I should explain. When Van Lamh arrived in Vung Tau, he purchased the old governors' residence built in the 1950's by a French colonial governor. Because it was common knowledge that Van Lamh was involved in the poaching of elephants in Africa and India, locals with a sense of humour nicknamed the residence the Ivory Palace.'

'What are our chances of getting close to either of these two gentlemen?' Derek asked.

'Not very good, I'm afraid. Neither Van Lamh nor Schoveldt venture out much in public and, apart from regularly visiting their favourite nightclub, they are either out of the country, on his private island or safely behind the walls of the heavily guarded Ivory Palace.'

'Could we get a look at either of them at this nightclub?'

'You certainly could. If you forgive me for saying so Avi, were you to dress up, you'd be bound to attract Van Lamh's attention. Despite his age, he still has an eye for attractive western women.'

'What about Schoveldt?'

'Oh, I'm afraid you're out of the running there. Your friend Derek here is more to his taste!'

Avi smiled, 'Then perhaps you might make arrangements for us to visit his favourite nightclub; though we will both need to upgrade our wardrobes if we're to make a favourable impression.'

'As far as the wardrobe department is concerned, I can steer you towards the best shops in town but, as far as his nightclub is concerned, all I can do is put you in a taxi with the address. If you haven't cottoned on already, I'm *persona-non-grata* as far as these people are concerned!'

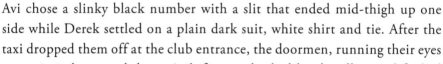

Avi chose a slinky black number with a slit that ended mid-thigh up one side while Derek settled on a plain dark suit, white shirt and tie. After the taxi dropped them off at the club entrance, the doormen, running their eyes appreciatively up and down Avi's figure, checked her handbag and frisked Derek for weapons. 'I must admit,' he remarked to her as they entered the club, 'its been quite some time since I was frisked so efficiently.'

'Could Van Lamh be afraid of something?' she smiled as a maître d' led them to a table on the side.

They had no sooner taken their seats when the maître d' returned, somewhat flustered, to their table, 'Please forgive me,' he apologised, 'you are invited to sit with the owner, Mr Van Lamh. Please be so kind as to follow me.' They stood and followed him to a large table set on a raised floor at the rear of the club.

A short, elderly Vietnamese man rose to his feet, 'It is my pleasure to welcome you to my club.'

'*Cam on ban* – thank you' Derek replied.

'No,' the man said with a smile, 'we only speak English here; it's the language of the world is it not? You have both come a long way from Australia; may I ask what brings you to my country?'

'I heard many good things about Vietnam from Australians who had visited in the past,' Derek replied as he pulled out a chair for Avi.

'You don't sound like an Australian to me,' a white man seated in the shadows at the far end of the table remarked, 'you sound more like a South African.'

'Please forgive me,' the elderly man said, 'let me introduce everyone. The ill-mannered gentleman at the far end of the table is Dieter Schoveldt. I, of course, am Nguyen Van Lamh, at your service beautiful lady and gentleman. Please welcome to my club.'

'You haven't introduced these young ladies,' Avi said indicating the young girls who sat on either side of the two men.

'Good friends, they are all good friends of ours.'

'Hookers, most likely,' Avi whispered to Derek as he sat next to her, 'did you see he had his hand up her skirt.'

'So, where in Australia are you supposed to be from?' Schoveldt asked.

'Oh, you probably wouldn't know it,' Derek replied.

'Try me.'

'Jabiru, in the Kakadu National Park in the Northern Territory. I work there as a wildlife biologist.' This reply seemed to take the wind out of his sails.

'So, how did a bloody South African become a wildlife biologist?'

'I thought it might be obvious to you. I trained in Pretoria, that's where I met my wife, Avi; from there we emigrated to Australia. If you don't mind me asking,' Derek said turning to face Van Lamh, 'how did you know we were from Australia? I don't believe we mentioned it to anyone.'

'You should be aware; I pay close attention to any foreigners who arrive in Vung Tau. Not because we fear them of course, but because we are pleased they have chosen to visit us, despite the great victory our forces had over them in the war of liberation. But I have forgotten my manners, what can I offer you to drink?'

CHAPTER − 37 −

O N THE TAXI RIDE BACK to their hotel, they discussed the evening. 'I'm not very keen on taking up Van Lamh's offer of a trip on his boat to this private island of his, wherever the hell it is,' Avi remarked.

'I agree; although I wouldn't mind accepting his invitation to attend the party at his house in Ngon Hai Dang,' Derek said, 'however, I'd like to run the idea by Andrew first.'

They met Andrew Cole for coffee at a small café near the beach. 'Based on what you told me over your mobile phone, I think you're both being a little over cautious; his invitation to visit Tan Hai Island is something you might wish to consider at a later date. Though, I do think it would be a good idea for both of you to attend the party at the Ivory Palace. If nothing else, you might come away with a better understanding of what makes Nguyen Van Lamh tick.'

Avi chose not to wear the revealing black dress with the thigh-high slit, instead settling for a businesslike black blouse, dark pink skirt and matching jacket she found in a boutique down the road from their hotel. Following her suggestion, Derek again wore his dark suit but, on this occasion, without the tie. As they walked out of the hotel entrance, a taxi driver standing on the sidewalk came up to them. 'Where to Mister?' he asked. Derek gave him the address. 'I don't know your accent,' the driver said as he opened the rear door of his taxi, 'where you from?'

'Australia,' Avi said, 'we live in Australia now.'

'Ah!' the driver replied as he pulled out into the traffic, 'Aussies; good blokes. Dinkie di, fair dinkum, Bondi beach.' He was quiet for a few moments. 'Van Lamh; not a good bloke, why you go there?'

'Because we must,' Derek heard himself tell the driver.

'Okay! I am Mr Minh, I keep an eye out for you,' he promised.

Nguyen Van Lamh's residence in the Ngon Hai Dang area covered five acres of prime real estate with spectacular views over the city; though none of this was apparent from the street because of the eight-foot-high stone wall that encircled the property. Mr Minh dropped them outside the ornate gates where one of the three security guards on duty accompanied them up to the foot of a flight of stairs leading up to a pair of elaborately carved entrance doors. Derek pressed the doorbell. While they stood waiting, he remarked to Avi, 'For a supposedly big party I don't see any other guests and, despite us being fashionably late, it appears we may be amongst the first to arrive.'

'Come in, we've been expecting you,' Dieter Schoveldt said greeting them from the entrance hall as a uniformed doorman held the doors open.

'I was afraid we might have arrived too early.'

'Not at all, you're right on time. Come on in; there are some people here who are most anxious to meet you.' He led the way down a long, carpeted hallway, 'As this is a private business meeting, Mrs Hamilton,' he said to Avi as he showed her into a small, sumptuously furnished salon, 'Mr Van Lamh would like you to join one of our female guests who has already arrived. You'll find plenty of champagne and snacks for your enjoyment while you wait for the other guests to join you.' Turning to Derek, he ordered brusquely, 'Come, Mr Australian South African, these are important people; we mustn't keep them waiting.'

'I'll be along just as soon as I find out what this is all about,' Derek said kissing Avi on her cheek. 'This better be good Schoveldt; I don't like being ordered about by the likes of you.'

Turning on his heel, Schoveldt led the way to a pair of double doors at the far end of the corridor. Pushing them open, he ushered Derek into a large panelled room. In the centre of the otherwise bare room, three men, none of whom Derek recognised, were sitting in three of the four ornate chairs arranged along the far side of a long, equally ornate table. Standing to one side of the table with his arms folded, was Nguyen Van Lamh. Derek smiled and nodded a greeting which, to his surprise, was not returned. Schoveldt produced a straight back wooden chair which he placed next to Derek. 'Sit down,' he ordered.

'From my perspective, this looks like a bloody kangaroo court,' Derek said out loud, 'could someone please tell me what the hell this is all about?' His request went unanswered as another man entered the room, approached the table and took his place in the vacant chair. The newcomer was Andrew Cole. Struggling to contain his growing unease, it dawned on Derek that he and Avi might have got themselves into a rather dangerous situation.

'This is the man who interfered with our operations in South Africa,' Van Lamh began, pointing directly at Derek. 'He stole a shipment of horns, ivory and bones from the docks in Maputo, costing us close to two million dollars. Then, together with the Israeli woman, he murdered Sakchai, one of our best operators and the son of our esteemed partner, Mr Sakmokon,' he said acknowledging one of the men sitting at the table.

'He and this Jew bitch are also responsible for the kidnapping of my father by the Israeli's who questioned and tortured him,' Schoveldt burst out angrily.

Van Lamh silenced him with an annoyed look. 'What is of concern to me right now, is the unexpected arrival of this man and this woman in Vung Tau. Because we have no way of knowing what information Barendt Schoveldt may have divulged to the Israeli Secret Service, I arranged for these two to be brought here this evening, so we might question them more closely. Dieter,' he said, 'please do what you can to convince Mr Hamilton of the seriousness of his situation.'

Derek sensed movement behind him at the same instant a vicious blow to the back of his head knocked him to the floor. When he regained consciousness, he found himself tied to the straight back wooden chair with straps and his hands handcuffed in front of him. The beating began right away. The four men sitting facing him watched impassively as Schoveldt set about his task with enthusiasm and relish. 'Please try not to kill him,' Van Lamh said to Schoveldt, 'at least not right away!' The thrashing continued with an efficiency that left Derek stunned and bleeding from numerous blows inflicted by a hard rubber truncheon to his head and face.

'Who do you work for?' Schoveldt demanded, 'it will make things easier for you and that bitch if you answer our questions.'

'Go fuck yourself; if anything should happen to either of us your father will pay the price!'

Schoveldt swung his truncheon at Derek's head with all the strength he could muster sending Derek and the chair he was tied to, crashing to the floor. Stunned, Derek could do nothing as his tormentor repeatedly stamped down hard on his neck, using the full weight of his body in an attempt to crush his windpipe.

'What, may I ask, is the purpose of this?' one of the men sitting at the table said to his fellow observers. 'I thought the idea was to elicit information from this man, not kill him right before our eyes.'

'This bastard handed my father over to the Israelis!' Dieter Schoveldt said repeating his complaint as he gasped for breath, 'he deserves to suffer!'

'I've had quite enough of this mindless brutality,' the other man at the table chimed in, 'Van Lamh, this is not getting us anywhere; if we're going to kill him, why don't we just get it over and done with.'

'I'd be careful with all this talk of killing,' Andrew Cole retorted as he got to his feet, 'especially where the Israeli woman is concerned. I have reason to believe she's a Mossad agent, and we don't want to bring those people down around our heads.'

'Gentlemen, you do me a disservice; I assure you, no harm will come to the Israeli woman, she's far too valuable to us as a negotiating tool,' Van Lamh said, 'as for this man, I couldn't care less!'

'What about the other woman you're holding; what did she do and what do you plan to do with her?' Cole asked.

'I believe she's a spy placed in our organisation by persons currently unknown to me. One of my staff members caught her making copies of documents relating to our importing business. If this proves to be the case, she will not find me lenient.'

'For my part,' Cole said walking towards the door, 'I'd rather watch this other woman being questioned; spy or no spy, I understand she's not a bad looker.' Following his observation, the three men rose from the table and followed him from the room.

'When you're finished with him,' Van Lamh said to Schoveldt as he turned to follow the others, 'take him outside and kill him, but do it quietly. I don't want the neighbours unduly alarmed.'

Despite the red mist of pain clouding his mind, Van Lamh's assurance that no harm would come to Avi gave Derek some peace of mind and the courage to endure whatever else his tormentor could dish out.

At last, exhausted from his exertions, Schoveldt removed the straps tying Derek to the chair and, pulling him to his feet, frogmarched him out into the corridor and through a side door that led outside. 'Come on, get moving,' Schoveldt snarled, 'it's my job now to send you to hell!' A light rain drifting in from the sea helped soothe the injuries to Derek's head and face as his tormentor stopped him at the top of a long flight of steps leading down to an overgrown garden, incongruously lit by smiling daisy-face solar lights. 'Hold it right here,' Schoveldt ordered as he removed a pistol from his jacket pocket and screwed on a long, cylindrical silencer, making sure Derek could see what he was doing.

'Would you mind taking these things off before you kill me?' Derek asked holding out his handcuffed wrists.

'Do you think I'm bloody stupid? Shut your fucking mouth and get on down there,' Schoveldt replied shoving him towards the steps. In a lot of pain and unsteady on his feet, Derek began cautiously making his way down, one step at a time. Halfway down, Schoveldt made a crucial mistake – he jabbed his gun into the small of Derek's back, 'Get going!' he ordered. Knowing the exact location of Schoveldt's gun hand, Derek spun around, grabbed his wrist and, pulling him off balance, caused the two of them to tumble headlong down the wet steps.

Landing on top of his intended victim, Schoveldt scrambled frantically to where he saw his gun disappear in the tangled mass of weeds. Desperate to stop him from reaching the pistol, Derek pulled up one of the smiling daisy-face light stakes from the garden and, using both hands, plunged it with all his strength into Schoveldt's back. Undeterred by the man's screams of pain, Derek stabbed him repeatedly in the neck and upper body with the sharpened stake. Covered in Schoveldt's blood, Derek clambered over his body, groping in the wet weeds for the gun. Finding it, he wrapped his fingers around the grip and, pushing the safety catch off, turned and fired two shots into Dieter Schoveldt's head as it lay bathed in the soft yellow glow of two smiling daisy-face solar lights.

The muted sounds of the shots attracted the attention of a security guard who appeared at the top of the steps, shining his torch around the garden. Realizing he would soon have company, Derek searched frantically through Schoveldt's pockets for the key to his handcuffs. Finding it and freeing his wrists, he scrambled down the steps, hoping the gate in the wall he could see in the gloom below was unlocked. It wasn't. 'Shit!' he swore as he pulled uselessly at the steel bars.

'Mister! Mister! It's me, Mr Minh!' a voice hissed at him from the darkness outside the wall. Peering out between the bars, Derek recognised the taxi driver who had brought them to the house earlier. 'It's locked,' Mr Minh said, 'you must go out that way, climb through rubbish bins.'

'I can't go yet,' Derek replied, 'I have to find the lady who came with me in your taxi. Shit! We're about to have company,' he said glancing in the direction of the three torches now playing around Schoveldt's body halfway down the steps. 'Change of plan, you'll have to drive me around to the front gate.'

'Mister, quick, you go through rubbish bins, I help you!' Derek felt his way along the wall following a foul smell until he encountered a huge rubbish bin. Clambering up the side of the bin, he let himself drop down into the darkness, disturbing a scurrying mass that ran over his feet and around his legs. Doing his best to ignore the rats, he felt his way along the side of the bin to where it fetched up against the outside wall. Stretching out his hands, he encountered a rubbish chute which he hoped would empty outside the wall. Climbing up, he slid down the chute face first. A pair of strong hands pulled him out and helped him to his feet on the roadway outside. 'Quick, we go this way,' Mr Minh said leading him along the pavement towards the steel gate in the wall, and his taxi parked further up the street.

'*Dung ban!*' one of the security guards yelled through the bars of the gate, shining his torch and pointing a pistol at them.

'He says we stop or he shoots!' Mr Minh whispered. Derek quickly drew Schoveldt's gun from his jacket pocket and fired at the black shape of the man behind the torch, prompting the other two security guards to take shelter in the bushes at the foot of the steps.

'Quickly!' Derek shouted to Mr Minh as they ran towards his taxi, 'we must go to the front gate; I've got to find the lady who came with me.'

'Can't go there Mister, too many policemans,' Mr Minh whispered as they got into his taxi.

'What do you mean?'

'After two big cars leave Ivory Palace, many policemans come.'

'I don't understand? Who left in the cars?'

'I park across street from front gate, wait for you to come then, not long two Chinese Hongqi cars, kind of car Mr Van Lamh like, leave quickly.'

'Could you see who was in the cars? Where did they go? Did you not follow them?'

'No. So sorry Mister, I not know you have troubles inside.'

'Of course, there was no way you could have known. If I asked you where they might have gone, what would you say?'

'Oh, I would say they go to Van Lamh boat in harbour, then go to Tan Hai.'

'Tan Hai; is this a place here in Vung Tau?'

'No mister, Tan Hai is island near Ham Luong River, two hour from Vung Tau. I take you to man who know Tan Hai. First, we go to doctor friend; your face not look okay.' Despite Derek's protests, Mr Minh drove into a poorly lit area of the city, stopping outside a Chinese herbal store. 'You come mister, he good doctor. Fix you up.' Derek followed him into the store, its shelves lined with small wooden boxes labelled with Chinese characters, glass jars containing roots, dried plants and unusual looking liquids, all contributing to the strange smell permeating the shop.

'Sort of place,' Derek thought to himself, 'where one would be able to buy a small amount of powdered rhino horn in a little paper envelope.' Later, with the worst of his cuts stitched and the rest of his injuries plastered with an ointment that he had to admit, relieved much of the pain, he followed his new-found friend back to his taxi. His benefactor now drove to an area of rundown wooden houses facing a water-front crowded with dozens of fishing boats and the occasional houseboat. Apparently, the man Mr Minh wanted him to meet lived on one of the more presentable houseboats linked to the dockside by a wooden gangplank. Mr Minh stopped at a locked gate at the head of one of the gangplanks, pressed a buzzer and spent the next few minutes speaking rapidly in Vietnamese to someone on the other end of the intercom.

'I tell Mr Duc how doctor look after you; he says please to come in, he always glad to meet Australian.'

CHAPTER − 38 −

THE DOOR OF THE HOUSEBOAT opened, and a man appeared, silhouetted against the light behind him. He was elderly, short in stature and wore a pleasant smile as he stepped out on the deck to greet them. 'Please come aboard Derek Hamilton, welcome to my humble home; it's always a pleasure to meet a visitor from overseas. I am Duc Tuan Trong, at your service. Please call me Duc and, with your permission, I will call you Derek. Come on inside, make yourself comfortable.' As Derek stepped into the interior of the houseboat, his eyes immediately went to the large number of black and white photographs decorating the walls of the small sitting room. 'Judging from your injuries,' Duc continued, 'I believe I would be correct in assuming you have been handled rather harshly?'

'You are quite right there. My harsh handling, as you so kindly put it, is part of the reason behind this late-night visit.'

'Before we get into that, let me get you a drink. If I guessed Scotch and water, would I be correct?'

'Absolutely; a whisky would be very much appreciated.'

'In the case of my good friend Mr Minh here,' Duc continued, 'I know he is partial to a Biere Larue, but I believe I'll join you in a Scotch.' While he bustled about getting their drinks, Derek took a few moments to look at the photographs on the walls.

'I see you served in the army during the Vietnam War. Captain Duc Tuan Trong, 51 Battalion, Rangers, Army of the Republic of Vietnam, it says on some the captions on these photos.'

Glancing over, Duc sighed, 'That was a long time ago. Yes', he continued, 'many years ago I joined the army and was fortunate enough to be selected for further training at the US Army Ranger School at Fort Benning in Georgia. That's where I learned to speak English. When I returned to Vietnam, I fully expected to serve my country until the war ended which, unfortunately for us, it did with our capitulation in April of 1975. On that fateful day, I was stationed with my platoon on Tan Hai Island when we received an order to lay down our arms,' he said handing Derek his drink, 'an order my fellow rangers and I chose not to obey until almost a week later. A decision, I'm sorry to say, we all had reason to regret over the next four years.'

'Mr Duc in re-education camp many years; terrible place for soldiers,' Mr Minh chipped in.

'I presume you had a good reason to make such a decision. What was so important about Tan Hai Island and where on earth is it?'

Duc smiled as he sipped his drink, 'Tan Hai Island; it's a little way down the coast not far from the mouth of the Ham Luong River. While small and insignificant, Tan Hai has a remarkable system of caves which both the Americans and the ARVN used in the latter years of the war for the storage of huge quantities of munitions, aerial bombs, mines and so on. During the last few months of my time on the island, the caves sheltered several dozen government officials and high-ranking military personnel who were all anxious to avoid capture by the North Vietnamese Army.'

'So, I take it your decision to fight on was to buy time for the escape or the evacuation of these people?'

'Precisely. As you can imagine, given the panic that ensued in the last few days of the war, it took quite some time for the CIA to make the necessary arrangements for their evacuation. And, before you ask, I was offered the opportunity to join these fortunate few but, as the offer did not apply to my men, I declined.'

'An action you should be proud of,' Derek added.

'My good friend, Mr Minh, has briefly explained your interest in Tan Hai Island; however, before we go any further into that, I would appreciate some background into the circumstances that brought you to my door so late at night.'

Not wishing to give away too much to a complete stranger, Derek realised he would have to satisfy Duc's curiosity regarding his presence in Vung Tau and the urgency in rescuing Avi from Tan Hai Island, if indeed that was where they took her. So, he began his story from the day they arrived at Tan Son Nhat Airport, with a summary on ivory and rhino poaching in South Africa.

'I appreciate you being honest with me Derek. I want you to know I too am deeply troubled by the unfortunate role my country finds itself playing in the destruction of that priceless heritage. It goes without saying, I am at your disposal.'

'Thank you for that. However, I must admit this situation is beyond my limited experience. Given what you know of this man and Tan Hai Island, do you think it is likely they could be holding my partner there?'

'Oh! I have no doubt that's where they would have taken her. You should understand Van Lamh's house, where you were so roughly handled, is used mostly for his business meetings, while his An Dinh Trading Company, located in the industrial area of this city, is nothing more than an elaborate front. Tan Hai Island is, without doubt, his main base of operations.'

'So, what can you tell me about this island?'

Refreshing their drinks, Duc continued, 'Some ten years ago; Van Lamh bought Tan Hai Island, all one hundred and fifty acres of it, from the local government. In no time at all, he had several buildings constructed on top of a high cliff that overlooked a small harbour, abandoned at the end of the Vietnam War. By the end of the third year, he had improved the harbour and its facilities to the point it could handle cargo vessels of up to three thousand tons. Van Lamh and his organization also made good use of the extensive tunnel system carved out of the caves at the base of the cliff to store goods of questionable legality.'

'And all of this under the watchful eyes of the authorities?' Derek asked, 'how on earth could he get away with it?'

'Friends in high places and the lavish distribution of bribes would be my best guess,' Duc answered as he finished his drink. 'Now,' he said, 'let's think about getting your partner out of Van Lamh's clutches. Do you have access to firearms?'

'All I have is a Chinese made Type 54 pistol fitted with a silencer; I kept it as a souvenir of my visit to his house.'

'Any good?'

'It's a .38 calibre weapon with an eight-round magazine, of which I've already used four rounds; though I did manage to get a full spare magazine from the previous owner.'

'Unfortunately, it's not much to go with,' Duc said. 'I should warn you Van Lamh maintains a sizable security force on the island to discourage unwelcome visitors; therefore, our need to avoid detection at all costs. Fortunately, I do have a few camouflage outfits and a working set of night vision binoculars.' Duc was silent for a few moments, 'In your line of work, have you ever used a crossbow?'

'Strangely enough, I have. In the early days in South Africa, we used a type of crossbow to dart big game for relocation or veterinary purposes. Of course, with the advent of the more powerful compressed air dart guns, the usage of crossbows declined. Why do you ask?'

'During the war, we often used these silent weapons to take out sentries around Viet Cong hideouts. Instead of the usual arrows, we fired heavy bolts which, if placed accurately, efficiently took care any unsuspecting guards without making too much noise.'

'At what sort of range?' Derek asked.

'As close as possible, but certainly no further than fifteen or twenty feet. Because my eyes are not what they once were, I would have to leave that sort of thing up to you.'

'I'd need to practise a few times.'

'Plenty of time for that tomorrow. It's too late for us to leave now; if we are to land undetected on the island, we have to arrive when it's completely dark.'

'Actually, I was hoping we could leave tonight. I'm sure you can understand I am anxious to make sure my partner is safe.'

'Of course, I can appreciate your concern. However, Van Lamh and his friends would have only arrived on the island a few hours ago, and are probably still debating amongst themselves exactly what they are going to do with your partner. If, as you say, that man Cole warned them of her possible connection to the Israeli Secret Service, I believe they would take that into serious consideration. I'm sure they're all aware that Mossad's long reach includes Vietnam. Hopefully, this will give them pause for reflection; time we must put to good use in the morning.'

As the sun rose over the harbour, Derek was out on the small deck at the rear of the houseboat practising with the crossbow when Duc emerged from a doorway. From his demeanour, Derek immediately sensed something was amiss. 'I'm very sorry,' Duc began, 'a few moments ago, I checked the website of our local newspaper to see if there was any mention of the police presence at Van Lamh's house last night.'

'And?'

'Apparently, security staff at the house called the police late last night when they discovered the body of a young woman, apparently beaten to death, in one of the meeting rooms.'

'There was a young woman waiting in one of the salons when Avi and I arrived at the house. Later, I heard Van Lamh telling the four men in the room where I was held that she had been caught making copies of sensitive documents. I'm sorry to say this, but I can only hope she was the young woman murdered, and not my partner Avi.'

'If that's the case, then this isn't good news for me,' Duc said. Seeing the puzzled expression on Derek's face, he explained, 'I persuaded a young journalist lady I knew to infiltrate Van Lamh's organisation to gather information on his criminal activities. She was the one who told me of your contact with Cole, your visit to Van Lamh's nightclub and, finally, his invitation to a party at the Ivory Palace. It was on her advice that I arranged for Mr Minh to chauffeur you around that night.'

'Duc, I'm truly sorry about your young lady; Van Lamh has a lot to answer for,' Derek replied. 'But I trust you'll understand why I hope Avi is not the woman found murdered at the Ivory Palace.'

Later that day, Derek joined Duc Tuan Trong in the lounge of the houseboat. Offered a whisky, Derek declined. 'I'd better keep a clear head for what I have to do next.'

'And what, may I ask, is that my friend?'

'I have to contact some people in Israel and explain what has happened. To do that, I must ask you to allow me to use your phone.'

'Of course, you are most welcome,' Duc replied handing his satellite phone to Derek. 'For privacy, I suggest you make your calls from the deck outside.'

Derek's call to Miriam Hyde-Eshar and Dov Harel at the Directorate of the Institute for Intelligence and Special Operations in Tel Aviv lasted for over fifteen minutes. Concluding the call, he joined Duc in the lounge. 'Well,' Duc said, 'I gather from your expression your call did not go as well as you had hoped?'

'You could say that again. My report on Avi's kidnapping by Nguyen Van Lamh shocked them to the core; that, combined with the news of Andrew Cole's defection to the enemy, provided the final straw that broke the proverbial camel's back. As a result, I've been ordered not to take any further action and, instead, to lie low until a friendly cargo ship can be rerouted to Vung Tau to get me out of Vietnam.'

'Priding myself as an astute judge of character, would I not be correct in assuming you have little or no intention of following those orders?'

Smiling, Derek confirmed Duc's conclusion. 'You know me better than I realised. I'd be most grateful if you would agree to continue with the plan to take me to Tan Hai Island.'

'Of course. However, bearing in mind that I probably know more about that island than any man alive, I believe I should accompany you, if only to ensure you do not get into any further trouble.'

CHAPTER – 39 –

THE SUN WAS ABOUT TO set as Duc's seventeen-foot fishing launch with Mr Minh at the helm, burbled its way out of the small harbour and into the open waters of the Vinh Ganh Rai and the South China Sea. Two miles out, Mr Minh steered south following the coast towards the mouth of the Ham Luong River.

Two hours into their voyage, a huge black mass of rock rising over a hundred feet out of the dark sea, appeared off their port bow. 'That's Tan Hai Island over there,' Duc said to Derek. 'We're approaching from its leeward side where the waves are a lot calmer, and there's a small cove with a sandy bottom where we can come ashore without being seen. Once we've landed, Mr Minh will take the launch over to the small fishing village of Lao Dat on the mainland. You can see its lights over there,' he said waving in the direction of a few scattered pinpricks of light visible along the dark shoreline off their starboard quarter.

'How will we let him know when we're ready to be picked up,' Derek asked, 'do we signal him with torches?'

'No; much too risky. We're better off calling him on my satellite phone, especially since Mr Minh, who has a sixth sense about these things, tells me a dense fog will soon be drifting in from the sea.' As soon as they entered the small cove, Duc jumped off the prow of the launch into two feet of water, 'Already,' he said laughing, 'I feel as though I'm a young man embarking on a great adventure!'

Derek followed him into the water and up the beach as Mr Minh backed the launch out into deeper water then, holding the tiller hard to starboard, he motored out into the darkness. 'Okay, where do we go now?' Derek asked.

'There used to be a trail somewhere around here that led up to Van

Lamh's house and the buildings on top of the cliff; wait here while I scout around,' Duc said. With that, he switched on his night vision binoculars and walked into the dark jungle that lay just beyond the beach. He was back in five minutes. 'I've found it; it's a little overgrown, but still usable. Here, keep hold of this,' he said pressing a short length of rope into Derek's hand, 'it'll prevent us getting separated in the dark.' Leaving the beach, they entered a pitch-black world of tangled vines, dense vegetation and strange rustling sounds in the undergrowth around them. 'It's only rats,' Duc said, 'nothing to be alarmed about, the whole island is infested with them.' After a hundred yards of battling their way up a steep incline, Duc suddenly stopped, 'Excellent! Now I know exactly where we are. We've reached the base of the rocky outcrop where our old escape tunnel came out. If, by any chance, we're unable to get to the house and buildings across the open ground above, we're going to have to come back here and search around for the entrance of that tunnel.'

With Duc leading the way, they continued up the steepening incline, before finally emerging into a wide, mostly treeless, grassy area. 'We should be able to see the lights of Van Lamh's house and the surrounding buildings from here,' Duc said. Struggling to see anything in the darkness, Derek stared in the direction indicated, but it was only when they moved closer that he could make out the lights from the house. Moments later, a dense patch of fog wafting up from the sea below hid them from view.

They had only moved a few feet further up the trail when Derek spotted the red glow of a cigarette through the fog some ten yards ahead of them. Tugging on the rope, he came up behind Duc and, whispering in his ear, warned him that someone was watching the trail leading to the house. Accepting the night vision binoculars from Duc, Derek quietly cocked and loaded the crossbow. Satisfied the weapon was ready, he circled around and stealthily approached the unsuspecting smoker from behind.

The man was sitting with his back against a small tree with his legs stretched out in front of him as he enjoyed his cigarette. Carelessly, his M16 rifle stood just out of reach, propped up against another tree a few feet away. Realizing the success of their mission, and quite possibly their lives, depended on avoiding detection, Derek resolved to eliminate the careless sentry.

The crossbow bolt struck the man in his right temple, emitting a sound scarcely louder than a hammer blow against a block of wood. The victim slumped forward, shivering in his death throes as he slowly collapsed onto his side. Checking the body for vital signs, Derek satisfied himself that the man was dead. 'Surely his mother must have warned him that cigarette smoking was bad for his health,' he remarked as he returned to Duc's side.

'We've got to hide the body somewhere,' Duc said ignoring Derek's macabre attempt at humour, 'there's always the chance someone might come out to relieve him from his watch.' Using the night vision binoculars, Duc looked around, 'If I remember correctly, we're not far from the edge of a cliff with a drop of some fifty feet to the sea and the rocks below. If we push him over the edge, they might think he got lost in the fog and fell over in the dark.'

Retrieving the bolt from the man's head, Derek helped Duc drag the body to the cliff edge and push it over. Returning to the tree where the man had been sitting, Derek picked up his M16 rifle as they continued their cautious approach to the house. 'I don't like the look of that fence,' he remarked to Duc as he peered through the night vision binoculars, 'it must be all of eight-foot-high, and I can see rolls of razor wire strung along the top. If I were a betting man, I'd give you evens it's either electrified or alarmed or both.'

'I wouldn't take you up on that bet,' Duc replied. 'With no other options open to us, I suggest we go back and search for the entrance of that escape tunnel.'

Unwilling to take the risk that someone keeping watch might spot their torch lights, it took them almost an hour of stumbling around in the dark to find the overgrown and partially blocked exit of the old escape tunnel. 'Careful where you put your hands,' Duc warned, 'in addition to the rats, places like this attract snakes such as the pit viper.'

'Oh! Thanks a lot, that's all I need to hear.'

'Our soldiers called them two-step snakes; once one bites you, you walk two steps, and then you die! Come on; they never go far into the tunnels; they prefer waiting for their prey around the entrances,' he chuckled. Clearing debris from the opening, Duc got down on his hands and knees and crawled into the small tunnel. Reluctantly, Derek followed, expecting to be bitten by a deadly snake at any moment. 'You can stand up now,' Duc said switching on his torch and shining it around, 'this part of the cave system has probably not been used since the war ended in 1975.'

'Compared to other caves I've seen, this one looks man-made.'

'And that's because most of this cave system was enlarged to allow access for handcarts, and, in some places, even jeeps.'

'The Americans did all of this during the Vietnam War?'

'No; what you see around you began as early as 1946 when the French Far East Expeditionary Corp enlarged these caves to store various types of munitions. Their efforts continued up until their eventual defeat at Dien Bien Phu in '54. After that, work on increasing the size and the scope of the tunnels continued under the Americans, and finally the South Vietnamese Army until the fall of Saigon.'

'I assume the North Vietnamese Army eventually removed all the munitions stored in these tunnels following the fall of Saigon?'

'For their sake, I hope they did. I say that because, during the time I was on Tan Hai, we had a serious problem with the hundreds of tons of old aerial bombs that were leaking napalm into some of the tunnels where the Americans had also stored a huge number of mines.'

'Anti-shipping mines?' Derek asked.

'Yes; you may be too young to recall Nixon's orders to close Haiphong Harbour with air-dropped mines. Well, one bright sunny morning a small freighter arrived off Tan Hai and unloaded five hundred, 2000lb Mark 55 mines, which they stored in one of the tunnels. They were still there when my platoon was removed from the island.'

Their progress along the tunnel came to an abrupt halt when they encountered a cinder brick wall blocking the tunnel. 'There's a small gap in the brickwork down at the bottom,' Duc said shining the beam from his torch along the base of the wall, 'I'll crawl through and see if it's clear on the other side.' Derek watched as Duc and the light from his torch disappeared through the narrow opening. He was back in a moment, 'Come on through,' Duc said peering back through the opening, 'it appears we've reached some of the old munitions storage areas. If they haven't walled off all the connecting tunnels, we should be able to get close to the storage areas added on later by Van Lamh.' Passing the M16 rifle through to Duc, Derek got down on his stomach and crawled through the opening.

'What's that odd smell?' Derek asked as they walked past a partially bricked off side tunnel, 'if I didn't know any better, I'd say it was a mix of laundry detergent and petrol.'

'Now you know what napalm smells like,' Duc replied shining his torch on the apparently dry, white coloured ooze that had flowed out through cracks in the base of the wall. 'Obviously, for some unfathomable reason, they never got around to removing and disposing of the old aerial bombs and anti-shipping mines stored in these tunnels. Watch out where you walk and, before you ask, I haven't a clue whether this stuff is still volatile or not; though I suspect it probably is.'

'So, from what you're telling me, this whole island is nothing more than a gigantic bomb waiting to go off!'

'As my platoon sergeant at Fort Benning used to say, *That's it in a nutshell!*'

Carefully avoiding the patches of napalm that had congealed and dried on the floor of the tunnel, Derek asked, 'I see all the tunnels on our left are completely blocked off by cinder brick walls; any idea what lies beyond them?'

'Van Lamh's new storage areas I expect.'

'Surely,' Derek observed, 'wouldn't he have been more than a little concerned about the huge amount of unexploded munitions stored behind a relatively flimsy cinder brick wall?'

'You'd have to ask him that question yourself.'

———⊰◈⊱———

Changing the subject, Derek said to Duc, 'Turning to our immediate problem; wouldn't you agree that in order to completely brick up all the tunnels leading into his new storage area, his builders would have needed an access door of some kind to complete the job fully?'

'Makes sense to me,' Duc replied, 'let's move on to the end of this tunnel and see what we can find.'

A steel door set in the corner of the last cinder brick wall stood out in the light of their torches. 'If I'm not mistaken, that's the access door we're looking for,' Derek said. However, no matter how hard they pulled on the handles, the door would not budge.

'Must be jammed or rusted shut; our problem now is getting it open without making too much noise,' Duc said rummaging around in a pile of old building materials left behind by the builders of the wall. 'What about this,' he said holding up an old bent screwdriver. 'If we can jam this in between the door and the frame, we should be able to pry open a gap wide enough to use this steel lintel bar to buckle the frame and pop the lock.'

'Well worth a try,' Derek said as he struggled to force the lintel bar into the narrow gap created by the screwdriver. With both of them pulling on the lintel bar, the door frame began to bend outwards then, with a noise that sounded as loud as a pistol shot, the bolt of the lock popped out of the frame, and the door creaked open.

The storage area, bathed in the yellowish, orange glow from row after row of overhead sodium-vapour lights, was far larger than Derek had expected. But, apart from a huge number of open wooden packing crates, it appeared to be mostly empty. '*Jissus*! I fully expected to see this area packed with elephant tusks, rhino horns and God knows what else!'

'Look out through there,' Duc said pointing towards a open loading bay door that led out onto a fog-shrouded dock area, 'I think there's a ship tied up to the dock; it wouldn't surprise me if they've only recently finished unpacking and reloading everything on board. I believe your unexpected arrival in Vung Tau has put them into a state of panic.'

'Somehow, I've got to take a closer look at that ship. If nothing else, I must get its name and country of origin,' Derek said as he stared at the fog blanketing the dock.

'By all means, but be careful. Just because we can't see anyone around,' Duc warned, 'it doesn't mean there aren't any guards on duty. If you take advantage of the fog and, providing you keep to the shadows along the far wall, you should be able to get close enough to read the name on the ship's stern. Meanwhile, I'll scout around for some way for us to get up to the house and buildings above.'

Cradling the M16, Derek edged his way along the wall to a point where, despite the fog rolling in, he managed to read the name on the stern. 'It's the Bac Ninh' he said rejoining Duc, 'registered in Vung Tau! It's the same bloody ship Sakmokon contracted in Maputo to pick up the crates from

Schoveldt's ranch.' He went on to tell Duc about the role they believed the Bac Ninh played in shipping poached ivory and rhino horns to Vietnam. 'What I'd like to know is where this ship is headed once it leaves here.'

'Most likely a destination in China. Somewhere a little off the beaten track; ideally a port where official scrutiny is lax or non-existent,' Duc replied. Changing the subject, Duc continued, 'I've found out how Van Lamh and his friends get up to his house from here; they have installed a cargo lift at the back of the warehouse, but it requires a key to operate it. Of course, even if we managed to get hold of a key, I don't imagine our arrival upstairs at two in the morning would go unnoticed.'

'I agree. Their security is tight; I counted three guards on the dock and at least one I could see onboard the ship. You know this island better than anyone, is there anything else you can suggest?' Derek asked.

'How are you with heights?'

'I believe I can manage. Depends on what you have in mind though!'

'Around the start of the French Indo-china war, the local governor of Vung Tau had a small lighthouse constructed on top of the cliff above us. Access to this lighthouse was either up the same path we took when we landed on the island, or via an iron ladder bolted to the cliff face. It's the ladder on the cliff face that I'm thinking of,' Duc said. 'Normally, anyone attempting to climb this ladder would be seen the guards on the dock but, thanks to the fog, it should be quite feasible. Regretfully, I do not believe I am physically capable of making the climb myself.'

'This is my fight, my friend; you've already done far more than I have any right to ask of you,' Derek replied handing the M16 rifle over to Duc. 'Keep this with you in case you encounter any of the opposition.' As Duc started to protest, Derek stopped him adding, 'Nonsense, I couldn't possibly climb the ladder carrying it and, besides, I still have my pistol and the crossbow. However, I would appreciate it if you would delay your departure on your launch until just before dawn.'

'So, am I right in assuming you have some plan in mind?' Duc asked taking the weapon.

'Of course, I have!' Derek replied. 'I'll rescue Avi and, if I can find them, kill the four men who watched me being beaten up. Having accomplished that, Avi and I will take Van Lamh hostage and force him to use his lift to get us back down here. Finally, we'll take the tunnels to the beach where we will meet up with you before dawn.'

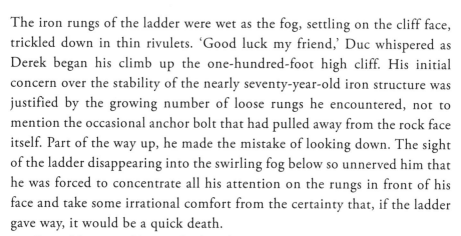

The iron rungs of the ladder were wet as the fog, settling on the cliff face, trickled down in thin rivulets. 'Good luck my friend,' Duc whispered as Derek began his climb up the one-hundred-foot high cliff. His initial concern over the stability of the nearly seventy-year-old iron structure was justified by the growing number of loose rungs he encountered, not to mention the occasional anchor bolt that had pulled away from the rock face itself. Part of the way up, he made the mistake of looking down. The sight of the ladder disappearing into the swirling fog below so unnerved him that he was forced to concentrate all his attention on the rungs in front of his face and take some irrational comfort from the certainty that, if the ladder gave way, it would be a quick death.

Scrambling quickly up the last few rungs, he crouched down on the cliff top listening intently for any indication that someone on watch might have seen or heard him. 'No matter what happens up here,' he promised himself, 'there's no bloody way I'm going back down that ladder!

CHAPTER – 40 –

A LIGHT BREEZE BLOWING IN FROM the sea created gaps in the fog, allowing Derek his first glimpse of Van Lamh's cliff-top lair. The buildings were laid out in a semicircular shape with a two-storey building in the centre, and four, single-storey buildings arranged along either side. Pulling the night vision binoculars from the pouch on his camouflage jacket, he carefully scanned the buildings fully expecting to see someone keeping watch. But, apart from one or two lights burning in some of the windows on the lower floor of the two-storey building, there was no sign of anyone around.

After waiting a good five minutes, Derek began to cautiously make his way towards the two-storey building in the centre, intending to look in through the windows where he could see a lights burning inside. He was crouched below the level of the nearest window when a door in one of the smaller buildings on his right suddenly opened, spilling a pool of light out on the ground. Scarcely daring to breathe, Derek froze in place as a man, emerging from the doorway, walked a few paces before stopping and lighting a cigarette. Drawing on his cigarette, the smoker strolled on towards the edge of the cliff, where he stood gazing at the fog swirling below. Finally, having finished his cigarette, the man flicked the butt off the cliff and, turning, walked back towards the open door. As the light from the room fell on his face, Derek recognised him at once. It was Andrew Cole.

As Cole stepped inside and turned to close the door, Derek jumped up and stuck the barrel of his pistol in Cole's face. 'One sound and you're a dead man,' he hissed as he pushed him back into the room, kicking the door closed behind them. 'Are you alone?'

'Yes; this is my room,' Cole stammered looking at Derek, his eyes wide with fear. 'Christ! I thought you were dead.'

'I'm sure you did. Unfortunately for you, your friend Schoveldt cocked up my execution. So, here I am very much alive and looking for the slightest excuse to put a bullet in your brain.'

'Someone would hear the shot and come running,' Cole said hopefully.

'Two problems for you, Andrew. This gun has a silencer and, even if someone did come running, it would still be your brains decorating the wall behind you.'

'I did what I could to stop Schoveldt from beating you to death and, don't forget, I was the one who talked the men around the table out of harming your wife or your girlfriend; whichever she is,' Cole pleaded.

'If you want to live a little longer, you'll tell me where she is right now.'

'Ah! I thought as much; you haven't a clue where she is. If you did, you wouldn't be standing here right now making idle threats.'

'It all boils down to just how fond you are of walking. The thing is, Andrew, you have ten seconds to answer my question before I put my first bullet into your kneecap. I believe the Irish Republican Army found people a lot more amenable to answering questions after just one bullet.'

'She's locked up on the ground floor of the main building next door,' he blurted out, 'but I warn you, Van Lamh has a guard posted outside her door at all times.'

'Which brings me to my next question. Where is he now and how many men does he have up here?'

'He lives in an apartment on the top floor of the main building next door and, as far as I know, close to half a dozen guards are stationed on the floor below.'

'And the lift?'

'That's in the main building as well.' Smiling a wolfish grin, Cole said, 'For your sake, I hope you've brought a sizable force with you; though I'm beginning to think you might be trying to wing this one your own.' Moving quickly, Derek struck Cole on the side of his head with the butt of the pistol, knocking him unconscious. Tearing up one of the bed sheets into strips, he bound and gagged him and left him lying on the floor next to the bed. Removing the crossbow from the pouch on his camouflage jacket, he tensioned the weapon and loaded one of the bolts.

The guard on duty in the main building, looked up in surprise from the book he was reading as Derek appeared through the doorway. Unfortunately, he ignored Derek's gestures to raise his hands and not make a sound; instead, he jumped to his feet and reached for the pistol on his belt. Reacting immediately, Derek raised and fired the crossbow, burying the bolt in the man's forehead.

Adding the guard's pistol to his pouch, Derek searched the dead man's pockets for the keys to the room he was guarding. Opening the door, he cautiously entered the room. Light shining in through the open doorway revealed a figure lying, apparently asleep, under a blanket on a narrow bunk. Reaching out, Derek gently pulled back the blanket. Startled, Avital Blum sat up and threw off the rest of the covers, 'What the fuck do you want now?' she shouted. She was still wearing the dark pink jacket, skirt and black blouse she had on when they arrived at Van Lamh's house in Vung Tau; though her outfit was now quite dirty and one of the sleeves on the jacket was torn.

'I came to ask if you wanted to get out of here,' Derek replied lifting her in his arms and holding her close.

'Oh, my God! Derek! It's you?'

'Yes, it's me; are you ready to go now?'

'Let me get my shoes on first,' she said pausing to gather her thoughts. 'One of my heels has broken off; it makes it difficult to walk. Anyway,' she continued, 'how the hell are we going to get out of here; we're right on top of a bloody cliff, just in case you haven't noticed! The only way up or down is in the lift and fuck face upstairs isn't about to help us.'

'I believe you're right on that score; which is why I was hoping you'd have some idea on how to operate the lift.'

'I wouldn't have a clue; they pulled a hood over my head whenever they took me out of this room for questioning. But, I'm pretty sure the lift doesn't always stop at this level; as far as I know, it usually goes straight up to his apartment upstairs. Also, I have an idea you need a key to operate it.'

'Wait here,' he said, 'I know someone who might be able to help us. Keep this handy until I get back,' he said handing her the guard's pistol.

'Don't worry,' she laughed, 'I'm not about to go anywhere.' Derek was back in two minutes prodding Andrew Cole into the room with his hands still tied behind his back and Derek's pistol pressed firmly against the back of his head.

'Jesus!' Cole said staring at the guard lying dead in a pool of blood with the crossbow bolt jutting out of his forehead. 'Schoveldt was right; you are Mossad assassins sent to kill us!'

'And if you don't want to join your friend there, you'll need to show us how to use the lift to get down to the ground.'

'If I help you, I'm a dead man!'

'If you don't help us, I guarantee you'll be a dead man a lot sooner. But, I tell you what, in exchange for your help, I'll get you off this island alive and onto the mainland; after that, you're on your own.'

'Bull shit! Even if we did manage to get down to the ground alive, we'd never make out it past the security guards.'

'Once we take Van Lamh hostage, the heat on us will disappear.'

'Come on! Do you honestly believe Van Lamh is the power behind this business? Think again; he's just a figurehead. The real power lies with General Ho and his two partners. They were the three men sitting around that table in Vung Tau happily watching Schoveldt do his best to beat the living daylights out of you.'

'I've never heard of this General Ho; who the hell is he?'

'Only the top man who runs this entire enterprise; easily the largest and most successful poaching and illegal mining operation in Africa south of the Sahara. Hell! The general and his partners own half the politicians in Vung Tau, this fucking island and the cargo ship Bac Ninh, which right now is tied up at the dock below with over a hundred tons of ivory, rhino horn, lion bones and a thousand forty-four-gallon steel drums filled with rare earth minerals in its hold. Apart from the numerous people they have working for them in at least ten African countries, they also have dozens of security guards on this island who will make damn sure you and this girlfriend of yours will never get away from here alive.'

'If all of this is true, where will I find this General Ho and his partners now?'

'Already safely onboard the Bac Ninh, getting ready to ship the results of two years of poaching and illegal mining to a leading triad syndicate operating in a remote harbour somewhere on the Chinese mainland.'

'Be that as it may,' Derek said, unwilling to let Cole see his surprise and concern, 'my offer still stands; either you help us get down to the ground, or I will kill you now. What's it going to be?' he said jabbing the barrel of his pistol hard against Cole's neck.

'Okay, okay, take it easy!' Cole pleaded. 'Every night Van Lamh locks the lift on the same level as his apartment upstairs, but I swear I've no idea where he keeps the key.'

'In that case, we'll just have to ask him. Now, how do we get up to his apartment?' Seemingly resigned to his fate, Cole led them towards a narrow staircase which, he said, accessed the floor above. As they reached the narrow landing at the top of the stairs, Cole broke away from Derek's grip and, leaping forward, burst open the door, triggering a shrill alarm bell. Pushing Cole into the room ahead of him, Derek promptly shot the guard on duty as he reached for a machine pistol lying on the table beside him. 'Quickly now, which room is Van Lamh's?' Derek demanded, shoving his gun in Cole's face, 'answer me truthfully you lying bastard, or you'll die right now!'

Cole never got the chance to respond to that question. A door in the far wall opened and Nguyen Van Lamh, firing a Mac 10 machine pistol, rushed into the room. Cole, who was in the direct line of fire, took at least ten 9mm rounds in his chest and head before the violent recoil tipped the barrel of Van Lamh's Mac 10 upwards, firing the remaining twenty rounds into the wall above their heads. Three shots from Avi's pistol, struck Van Lamh twice in the neck and once in his forehead, killing him instantly. 'You murdering bastard!' Avi cursed her victim, 'that's for that poor girl you had killed; I'm only sorry you didn't suffer the way she did.'

'I take it you refer to the girl Van Lamh had murdered at his house?'

'Yes. It was horrible; I'll tell you about it sometime.'

Derek went over to the lift and tried to open the door. 'Cole was right; the bloody thing needs a key. Check his pockets,' he said pointing at Van Lamh, 'he may have it on him.' Reacting to the voices of security guards yelling orders on the floor below, Derek quickly closed and locked the door at the top of the stairs. 'That's not going to hold them for very long,' he said, 'while I search his room, see if you can find a spare magazine for his Mac 10.'

The pounding on the door at the top of the stairs began almost immediately. 'I think they've got hold of a sledgehammer,' Avi shouted to

Derek, 'it won't be long before they break the door down. Any luck with that key?'

'Nothing that even looks like a key,' he replied as the heavy blows began to splinter the wooden door jamb. Avi fired two shots into the wall next to the door, temporarily putting a stop to the attack on the door.

'Bloody wall must be bulletproof; you'd better hurry up and find that key and soon,' she said checking Van Lamh's pockets once more.

'I expect they'll be through at any minute,' he warned as the hammering on the door intensified, 'while I've no idea how many of them there are, let's make damn sure every shot counts.' As they checked the magazines on their weapons, a thought suddenly occurred to Derek, 'His neck,' he shouted, 'did you check around his neck?' Crouching on the floor beside Van Lamh's body, Avi inserted her fingers into the bloody mess of shattered vertebra, arteries, muscles and veins, feeling around for a chain or cord that might have held a key.

'Anything?'

'Yes! I have it!' she shouted, wiping the blood off a key on her jacket before handing it to him, 'try it, I'll watch the door.'

Taking the key, he rushed over to the lift door, lifted a metal flap and tried to insert the key. 'It doesn't fit! Maybe there's another key? Quick as you can!'

Fumbling in her haste, Avi again pushed her fingers deep into Van Lamh's shattered neck, desperately groping around for another key. 'I can't feel anything,' she sobbed in desperation. At that instant, the stairway door gave way to the hammering and collapsed into the room. With a shout of triumph, the man wielding the sledgehammer leapt across the shattered door and into the room.

Derek shot him in the head, giving the other security guards close behind, pause for thought. 'Look for a second chain or another cord around his neck,' he shouted to her.

Feeling around the base of Van Lamh's neck, Avi's fingers brushed across a thin metal chain. 'I've got it!' She shouted as she pulled it from the gore. Snapping the chain, she ran over to the elevator door, lifted the metal flap and, inserting and turning the key, caused the lift door to slide open. 'Let's get out of here,' she yelled as Derek fired another shot through the open doorway, buying just enough time for the lift doors to close behind them.

CHAPTER – 41 –

'I THOUGHT YOU WERE NEVER COMING,' Duc said as the lift doors slid open. 'Hurry, I can't hold them off for much longer. Once they realise I'm running short of ammunition, they'll pluck up the courage to rush us.' He ushered them along a corridor which led towards the storage area, the steel door and the tunnels beyond, now their only possible avenue of escape from the island.

'How many of them are there?' Derek asked as Duc paused to see if the way across the storage area was clear.

'Too many; when the alarm bells went off, I watched at least half a dozen security guards leave the ship and join the others guarding the dock. Believing you were about to make your exit, I fired a few rounds in their direction, forcing them to take cover. We've been trading shots now for the last ten minutes.' Looking at Avi, Duc smiled and held out his hand, 'You must be the beautiful young lady Derek was most anxious to rescue. Please call me Duc.'

'And you must call me Avi. I can't tell you how much I appreciate all you and Derek have done to get me out of here.'

'I'm also pleased to tell you,' Derek added, 'Avi put a bullet into Van Lamh's head shortly before she found the key to get the lift going so we could get down here.'

'Well done Avi; though I would have given anything to have done the job myself. However, before we begin celebrating his death and your narrow escape, I've still got to get the two of you across the storage area, through that steel door and into the relative safety of the tunnels. While I can't see the opposition right now, I'm reasonably sure they've taken cover somewhere outside the loading bay door. Right, there's no point putting it off any longer. So, if you're ready, let's get on with it.' They nodded in agreement. 'I'll go first,' Duc said, 'once I get to the door, I'll keep their heads down while you two run across.'

Derek readied the Mac 10, 'Okay, I'll cover you; go when you're ready!' Holding the M16 rifle across his chest, Duc ran towards the steel door. A shouted alarm from outside the loading bay door produced two poorly aimed shots which buried themselves in the wall, too late to stop Duc from reaching the door and ducking inside. 'They're on alert now, but it's possible they may still believe Duc is on his own. When I say go, run like hell for the door, I'll do my best to keep their heads down.'

'Wish me luck,' Avi said kissing him as she kicked off her shoes, hiked up her skirt and turned to run.

Derek fired a long burst towards the loading bay entrance as Avi sprinted towards the steel door, zigzagging to present less of a target. Only yards short of the door, she cried out in pain and dropped to the ground. Despite the heavy fire now coming from the loading bay area, Duc dashed out and dragged her inside. Ignoring the gunfire, he reappeared in the doorway with an M79 grenade launcher and, aiming at a point just beyond the loading bay; he fired off a grenade. The resulting explosion stunned the gunmen almost as much as it surprised Derek.

Taking advantage of their temporary confusion, Derek dashed towards the steel door, jumped through and immediately went to Avi's side. 'How is she? Is she badly hurt?' he asked in a panic as Duc examined her.

'Looks like a through and through bullet wound to the inside of her upper right thigh. There's no severe bleeding so I assume the shot missed any vital arteries, and because Avi ran with her skirt pulled up, the bullet did not carry any clothing material into the wound. I'm about to apply a battle dressing, but as the wound is in a rather delicate position, I'd rather you took over while I keep an eye on our friends outside.'

'Come on you two, this is no time to be coy; I'll let you know if I think the touching is inappropriate,' Avi said through gritted teeth, 'bloody hell it hurts!'

'Fortunately, I've got a few of the fentanyl 'lollipops;' they're the latest painkillers used by the US Marines, along with a few extra battle dressings. Derek, you had better take them; Avi will need to have her dressing changed a couple of times before you reach Vung Tau.'

'But we're all going back together aren't we?' Derek asked.

'Not this time. I've got a few scores to settle before I can ever think of leaving Tan Hai.'

'Duc, I can assure you Van Lamh is dead,' Derek said, 'I saw Avi put three bullets into him. The blood you see on her hands comes from thrusting her fingers into his neck looking for that bloody lift key. I give you my word he's dead.'

'It's not Van Lamh who concerns me. Did you see anyone else while you were up on top?'

'Only that man Cole, and he was accidentally shot dead by Van Lamh himself.'

'No one else? What about the other men who were at the Ivory Palace where Mr Minh picked you up?'

'Of course! I'd almost forgotten what Cole told me about them. According to him, they are already on board the Bac Ninh, which he said is leaving for China in the morning.'

'Did he mention any names?'

'I recall him mentioning a General Ho. Any idea who he is?'

'He's the son of a bitch who took over this island when my platoon eventually surrendered. He was the one who made sure we all suffered in the so-called 're-education' camps and, to punish me further, he had my wife, Anh, imprisoned in Dinh Mai, where she died of cholera.'

'I'm sorry Duc, I had no idea.'

'Now you know why I must stay. I've got to make sure Ho and his partners never leave this island alive.'

'But you're only one man against dozens; let me get Mr Minh to pick up Avi, and I'll come back and help you.'

'Thank you, Derek, you're a true friend, but please understand this is a mission I must accomplish on my own. Now I insist, take my satellite phone, when you get out into the jungle, call Mr Minh, he will get you both to Vung Tau and will arrange for a doctor for Avi's leg. Leave me the M16 and the Mac10 just in case the other M79 grenades I found are duds. The two of you should go now,' Duc said shaking Derek's hand and kissing Avi on her cheek, 'make sure you're well away from the island before sunrise. Good luck to you both,' he said turning to face the loading bay door.

Mr Minh arrived as a pale pink hue brushed the horizon in the east. 'Duc is not coming back with us,' Derek told Mr Minh as he helped carry Avi to the launch, 'he says he has unfinished business on Tan Hai.'

'Okay, I understand,' Mr Minh replied sadly. 'Come, we not have much time; we go quickly,' he said as he started up the motor and backed the launch out of the cove before steering towards the still dark coastline and the distant harbour at Vung Tau.

⤙◈⤚

Fifteen minutes into their voyage, a deep, rumbling roar drew their attention towards Tan Hai Island as orange and red fissures burst wide open along its dark cliffs and rocky headlands. Unable to look away, they watched with a mix of fascination and fear as a cataclysmic explosion blasted millions of tons of rock high into the air, ripping the island apart. 'Tsunami will come, we must go!' Mr Minh yelled as the thunderclap of sound echoed around them.

'You're right, here it comes!' Derek warned as the pale light of dawn revealed an enormous wave racing across the sea towards them. 'Head straight towards it,' he shouted to Mr Minh, 'we've got to get up and over the wave before it reaches shallow water and crests.' Steering towards the oncoming wall of water, Mr Minh gunned the motor as the launch rose up the forward slope of the wave, its propeller racing as it crested the peak and careened down the rear slope, burying its bow in the trough of the next wave. Hugging each other with relief, Avi and Derek watched as the bow of their launch slowly emerged from the dark waters and Mr Minh resumed his course for Vung Tau.

GLOSSARY:
SOUTH AFRICAN WORDS

Aieee: Expression of surprise

Au fait: Familiar

Au naturel: Nude

Au revoir: Goodbye

Baas: Boss

Baba: Father

Bakkie: Open back truck

Blerrie: Bloody

Boma: Enclosure

Bonsela: Gratuity

Dagga: Marijuana

Dash: Bribe

Derms: Entrails

Donga: Gully

Drankwinkel: Liquor store

Dummkopf: Fool (German)

Effendi: Lord or master

eGoli: Johannesburg

Fokker: Fucker

Fokkol: Fuck all

Fotoagentskap: Photo agency

Fraulein: Miss (German)

Guten Abend: Good Evening

Hardegat: Hardarse

Hauptbahnhof: Main station

Here God: Lord God

Ich danke dir: I thank you (German)

Induna: Chief or boss

Inhlwathi: Python

Ja: Yes

Jellabiya: Arab garment

Jirre: Jesus!

Kaffir: Derog. Term for a black African

Kha'ra: Shit

Kia: Hut

Klaar: Finished

La moshkelah: No problem

Meneer: Mr (Afrikaans)

Merda: Shit (Portuguese)

Mevrou: Mrs (Afrikaans)

Mhhumbi: Rhino

Mughtasib: Rapist

Ngiyabongo: Thank you

Na'am: Yes

Numzaan: Boss

Os Terriveis: The Terrible Ones (Portuguese)

Panga: Machete

Piccanin kia: Small hut

Polizei: Police

Ratel: Honey badger

Rhiyani: Helicopter

Rondavel: Circular thatched hut

SAPS: South African Police Service

Sawubona: I see you (Zulu greeting)

Senhor: Mister (Portuguese)

Shukran jazilan; Thanks a lot (Arabic)

Skelm: Crook

Spoor: Tracks

Stoep: Porch

Tackies: Running shoes

TATP: Triacetone triperoxide (A volatile cocktail of acetone and hydrogen peroxide.)

Tjopper: Slang – helicopter

Troepe: Troops

Veldskoens: Desert boots

Vliegtuig: Aeroplane

Vloek: Swear or curse

Voetsak: Bugger off

Wie in: Come in

Yebo: Yes

Zimmerdienst: Room service (German)

OTHER BOOKS BY TONY MAXWELL

Searching for the Queen's Cowboys
Travels in South Africa filming a documentary on Strathcona's
Horse, a Canadian regiment that fought in the Anglo-Boer War.

Pacific War Ghosts
A lavishly illustrated book detailing the author's experiences travelling
the World War II battlefields of the South Pacific photographing wrecked
aircraft, tanks and guns left behind by that momentous conflict.

The Young Lions
Action, adventure and erotic entanglements play out against
the sweeping background of the discovery of gold in South
Africa and the outbreak of the Anglo-Boer War.

The Brave Men
In this sequel to 'The Young Lions,' the action, adventure and erotic
entanglements continue against the backdrop of a South Africa
recovering from the tragedy of the Anglo-Boer War, while the world
teeters on the brink of an even greater disaster, the looming Great War.

A Forest of Spears
Derek Hamilton, working as a close protection officer in Somalia,
falls in love with Rachel Cavendish, a British Intelligence Officer.
Kidnapped and held for ransom by the Somali terrorist group al-
Shaman, Derek is finally freed only to discover Rachel has been recalled
to London to deal with a new terror threat. The two do not meet
again 'til they join forces in a life or death struggle hunting down the
terrorists behind a frightening threat to airlines around the world.

Printed in Great Britain
by Amazon